Annie Groves lives in the North-West of England and has done so all of her life. She is also the author of *Ellie Pride*, *Connie's Courage* and *Hettie of Hope Street*, a series of novels for which she drew upon her own family's history, picked up from listening to her grandmother's stories when she was a child. Her most recent novels are *Goodnight Sweetheart*, *Some Sunny Day*, *The Grafton Girls* and *As Time Goes By*, which are based on recollections from members of her family who come from the city of Liverpool.

Her website, www.anniegroves.co.uk, has more details, or visit www.AuthorTracker.co.uk for exclusive updates on Annie Groves.

Annie Groves also writes under the name Penny Jordan and is an international bestselling author of over 170 novels with sales of over 84,000,000 copies.

By the same author

ANNIE GROVES

Across the Mersey

HARPER

This novel is entirely a work of fiction.
The names, characters and incidents portrayed in it are the work of
the author's imagination. Any resemblance to actual persons, living
or dead, events or localities is entirely coincidental.

Harper
An imprint of HarperCollins*Publishers*
77–85 Fulham Palace Road,
Hammersmith, London W6 8JB

www.harpercollins.co.uk

This paperback edition 2008
1

First published in Great Britain by HarperCollins 2008

Copyright © Annie Groves 2008

Annie Groves asserts the moral right to
be identified as the author of this work

A catalogue record for this book is
available from the British Library

ISBN 978-0-00-785795-1

Set in Sabon by Palimpsest Book Production Limited,
Grangemouth, Stirlingshire
Printed and bound in Great Britain by
Clays Ltd, St Ives plc

All rights reserved. No part of this publication may be
reproduced, stored in a retrieval system, or transmitted,
in any form or by any means, electronic, mechanical,
photocopying, recording or otherwise, without the prior
permission of the publishers.

This book is sold subject to the condition that it shall not,
by way of trade or otherwise, be lent, re-sold, hired out or
otherwise circulated without the publisher's prior consent
in any form of binding or cover other than that in which it
is published and without a similar condition including this
condition being imposed on the subsequent purchaser.

Mixed Sources
Product group from well-managed
forests and other controlled sources
www.fsc.org Cert no. SW-COC-1806
© 1996 Forest Stewardship Council

FSC

FSC is a non-profit international organisation established to promote the
responsible management of the world's forests. Products carrying the FSC
label are independently certified to assure consumers that they come
from forests that are managed to meet the social, economic and
ecological needs of present and future generations.

Find out more about HarperCollins and the environment at
www.harpercollins.co.uk/green

For all those whose hearts are in Liverpool,
no matter where their lives may have taken them

I would like to thank the following for their invaluable help:

Teresa Chris, my agent.

Susan Opie, my editor at HarperCollins.

Yvonne Holland, whose expertise enables me 'not to have nightmares' about getting things wrong.

Everyone at HarperCollins who contributed to the publication of this book.

My friends in the RNA, who as always have been so generous with their time and help on matters 'writerly'.

Tony, who as always has done wonders researching the facts I needed.

ONE

Saturday 19 August 1939, Wavertree, Liverpool

'Come on, you four. Hurry up, otherwise we're going to miss the ferry and then we'll be late. And don't forget your gas masks,' Jean Campion called up the stairs to her son and daughter.

She exhaled a small sigh of relief mixed with irritation when she heard her daughter Grace calling back down, 'Just finishing putting the ribbons in the twins' plaits, Mum.' This was followed by the thumping of her son, Luke's, size tens on the landing.

'Stop worrying, love,' her husband chided her mildly. 'We've got a good hour yet before we need to be there, although why that sister of yours can't bring her family over here to Wavertree to celebrate your birthdays for once I don't know.'

'Vi's always liked putting on a bit of a show,' Jean reminded her husband with a small smile.

'Doing a bit of a show-off, more like,' Sam grumbled. 'Doesn't she realise that folks have got better things to do, with the country on the brink of war?'

Jean put down her handbag and went over to him, putting her hand on his arm.

Sam worked for the Liverpool Salvage Corps, a unit of skilled tradesmen originally set up by the city's insurance companies. The Salvage Corps specialised in recovering goods from, and minimising the losses at, commercial premises damaged by fire and 'other perils'.

The Salvage Corps worked closely with Liverpool's Fire Brigade, and there had been many evenings over this last year when Sam had had to attend meetings and exercises to help prepare the Salvage Corps for the important role it would have to play if war was declared. As well as working for the Salvage Corps, both Sam and his son, Luke, like so many others determined to do their bit, had signed up for part-time Air-Raid Precautions duties with their local ARP post, and the year had been busy with preparations for a possible war with a shower of information leaflets from the Government covering everything from the evacuation of children from cities, to the sandbagging of vulnerable build-ings; the making of blackout coverings to ensure that no buildings showed lights that could be used by night-time enemy bombers seeking a target; the building of air-raid shelters and a dozen more precautions.

War! The threat of it lay across the whole country like a dark shadow that everyone had been hoping would go away. Now they could hope no longer, Sam said. Not with the Munich crisis and everything.

Every garden seemed to have cultivated an air-raid shelter, and for those who didn't have the space to build one, there were the public shelters. Everyone had got used to the sight of ARP wardens; ARP warden posts, the Territorial Army Reservists doing their drills, and every housewife had fretted and complained about fitting blackout-fabric-covered frames to their windows at night.

'Come on, Sam,' Jean coaxed her husband. 'I know how you feel about our Vi, and I know that the ferries and that will be busy, what with it being such a nice day and the kiddies still being out of school, but we've always gone over to her on our birthday.'

'Aye, we have, but that doesn't make it right,' he agreed, giving her the same smile that had caught at her heart all those years ago when she had first fallen in love with him. 'You're a softie, lass, and you allus have bin,' he told her affectionately.

Ignoring her husband's comments about her twin – after twenty-three years of marriage it would be a fine thing indeed if she didn't know that he didn't much care for her sister's husband or the way in which they lived – she straightened his tie, which was new, like his worsted suit. She had bought it in the half-price sale at Blackler's Department Store, along with a new suit for Luke. Forty-five shillings apiece they'd cost, not that she'd told Sam she'd spent that much, but she'd had a bit put by and the suits had been too good a bargain to miss, even though Sam had grumbled that it was daft buying him a suit when he only ever wore one for church and his last one, bought five years ago, still fitted him. She stood back to check that Sam's tie was just right, her head on one side.

There was one thing for sure, she admitted proudly, whilst her twin sister might have the posh house 'over the water', as the local saying went, on the other side of the River Mersey in Wallasey, where the well-to-do folk lived, and a husband who by all accounts was making more money that he knew what to do with, her Sam still was and always had been the better man of the two, and not just because even now, at forty-seven, he still stood six foot tall and had a good head of thick dark hair on him. Vivienne's Edwin might have the money and his own business, and all the fine new friends he was making now that he had put himself up for the council, but her Sam had the nicer nature. He was a good husband and a good father too, even if the elder two had started complaining that he was more strict that he needed to be and that other youngsters their age were allowed more freedom.

Jean knew perfectly well that by 'other people', Luke, who was coming up for twenty, and Grace, who was just nineteen, were referring to their cousins.

There was no getting away from the fact that whilst she and Vivienne were twins, and as alike as two peas in a pod on the outside, twenty-three years of marriage to two such very different men meant that they were now very different on the inside.

Family was still family, though, which was why she had bullied and cajoled hers into a state of freshly scrubbed neatness and their best clothes, ready to make the journey across the Mersey, from their pin-neat three-storey terraced house on Ash Grove in Wavertree to the much larger house on Kingsway in Wallasey Village, where her sister and her family lived. The Borough of Wallasey might include New Brighton and Seacombe, but as Jean's sister was fond of saying, so far as she was concerned, it was Wallasey Village that those in the 'know' recognised as the 'best' address in the borough.

At last they were ready to leave, the back and the front doors were locked and they were free to set off down towards Picton Road to catch the bus that would take them to the Pier Head and the landing stage for the ferry terminal at Seacombe, from where they could catch another bus inland to Wallasey Village itself.

'Ta, thanks, love.'

Jean shared a proud parental look with Sam, as Luke gave up his seat on the *Royal Iris*, one of the two ferries that sailed every quarter of an hour between Liverpool and Seacombe, to a harassed-looking young woman holding a young child and both their gas masks.

Jean was proud of all her children, but there was no getting away from the fact that your first always had a special place in your heart, she acknowledged.

Whilst Luke took after his dad, and had inherited his height along with his thick dark hair and bright blue eyes, Grace took after *her* side of the family, and had inherited the same petite, shapely figure, rose-gold curls and dark blue eyes as Jean's younger sister. The twins, though, Louise and Sarah, with brown hair, hazel eyes and freckled noses, were herself and Vi all over again.

It was a perfect August day with warm sunshine, and so it was no wonder that the ferry boats ploughing their way across the Mersey to the sandy beaches of New Brighton had their full complement of two thousand passengers apiece, Jean acknowledged.

Their mother had always joked that her twin daughters had chosen to make their appearance on the hottest day of the year. Mam had been dead for nearly ten years now, worn out by looking after a husband who had never recovered properly from being in the trenches, and the birth of a third child when she had been in her late forties. She and Vi had been in their teens when their sister, Francine, had been born. Francine was closer in age to their children than she was to them.

The ferry was approaching the Seacombe landing stage. As always the thought of seeing her twin was filling Jean with a mixture of pleasure and discomfort. Pleasure at the thought of being with the sister she had been so close to as they grew up, and discomfort at the thought of being with the person that sister had become.

'Lou, just look at you,' she complained to the younger of her twins as Sam gathered his family together. To one side of him Luke mimicked his father's proud stance and protective eye for the girls' welfare as they queued to get off, all of them holding on to the gas masks the Government had issued, and which they were supposed to carry at all times.

'Where's your hair ribbon?' Jean asked Louise. The twins were devils for losing their hair ribbons, no matter how tightly she tied them on.

'It's in my pocket.'

'What's it doing there? It should be on the end of your plait.'

'Sasha pulled it off.'

'No I didn't,' her twin defended herself immediately, giving Louise a swift nudge in the ribs.

'Grace didn't fasten it properly,' Louise amended her story, both the twins giggling as they exchanged conspiratorial looks over this patent fib.

'I don't know!' Jean shook her head with maternal disapproval. 'No one looking at you would ever think you were grown-up girls of fourteen. The minute we get off here, I'm going to have to redo that plait of yours.'

Luke looked so handsome in his new suit, navy blue just like his dad's. Sam might have shaken his head, but she'd reminded him that Luke was young man now – old enough to be called up to do his six months' army service in a month's time when he reached his twentieth birthday. He'd been apprenticed to an electrician friend of Sam's since he'd left school and as soon as he was out of his apprenticeship Sam was going to put him forward for a job with the Salvage Corps. That couldn't happen soon enough for Jean. Working in the Salvage Corps was a reserved occupation, and so he wouldn't be sent off to fight.

Not that the men in the Salvage Corps didn't face danger. In the last year alone, three men Sam worked with had lost their lives in the course of their work.

The ferry finally docked, allowing the passengers to stream off. Everywhere Jean looked she could see happy families determined to enjoy themselves, the girls and the women in their best summer frocks and the men in their suits, whilst the children were equipped for the beach with their buckets and spades.

'Do you remember when we used to bring our four here for the beach?' she asked Sam nostalgically.

'How could I forget? They took that much sand back with them, you'd have thought they were building a second Liverpool bar,' he laughed, referring to the sand bar beyond the docks.

'Do you remember that time you put Luke up on that donkey and it ran off with him?'

'Scared me to death, but he managed to stick on like a regular little trooper,' Sam agreed.

'And then when the twins buried their doll and couldn't find it?'

'I remember when that sister of yours turned up with her two and little Jack, and he wandered off. She didn't half give him a pasting when she found him.'

A sudden sadness clouded Jean's eyes, causing Sam to touch her arm and mutter awkwardly, 'Sorry, love, I wasn't thinking.'

Jean nodded and made herself smile. Best not to think of that other little one, baby Terry, who had come too soon and lived for such a short space of time, nor of how poorly she had been. He would have been nine now if he had lived, the same age, give or take a couple of months as Vi's Jack.

Jean started to frown. She couldn't help feeling guilty about Jack sometimes. Vi had claimed that she wanted another child, but Edwin certainly hadn't, and Jean didn't think they would have had him at all if she hadn't been carrying her poor little Terry. Vi had always had that competitive streak in her that meant that whatever she, Jean, as the eldest, did, Vi always had to try to outdo her.

'Come on, you lot, hop on and look smart about it,' Sam said. He waited until they were all on the bus and sitting down before getting on himself and telling the conductor, 'Six to Kingsway.'

'Turn round so that I can redo that plait,' Jean instructed Louise, ignoring the protests she made when she replaited her hair quickly and tightly, while warning the twins, 'Now remember, you two. If your auntie Vi offers you a second piece of cake you're to say "No, thank you". I don't want her

9

thinking that they don't know their manners,' she told Sam, answering the unspoken question in the look he was giving her.

'Huh, chance'd be a fine thing. Mean as they come, your Vi is. Besides, she isn't the cook you are, love, so I doubt they'd want a second piece.'

'Go on with you. It will probably be shop bought and fancy,' Jean told him, but his compliment had touched her, and it was no good her pretending that she wasn't pleased to have him praising her home cooking and not Vi's fancy shop-bought cake, because she was.

'More money than sense, the both of them,' Sam told her. 'Look at the way Edwin's gone and bought that young idiot Charlie his own car.'

'It's for his job, on account of him putting Charlie in charge of the office.'

'Aye. It makes as much sense as giving him a fancy title for doing what amounts to nowt, if I know young Charlie.'

Jean looked anxiously at her husband. She knew that it hurt Sam that he couldn't give their own children the same luxuries their cousins enjoyed, even though he tended to disapprove of Edwin's business practices and the way he treated those who worked for him. Edwin owned a small business that fitted pipe work in Merchant Navy vessels, and the current threat of war had brought an increase in the amount of work Edwin was being asked to do and consequently an increase in the money he was making. But no increase in the wages he was paying his men, as Sam had remarked to Jean.

The next stop would be theirs. Jean could feel the familiar fluttering in her tummy. She did so hope that Vi wasn't going to be in one of her 'difficult' moods.

Vi, or Vivienne, as she now insisted on being called, stood in her bay window of her bedroom, craning her neck so that she could see as far down Kingsway as possible through her net curtains. Brand new, her nets were, and how she was expected to keep them looking like that if she was going to have to have those nasty blackout frames put up every night she didn't know. You'd think that living here in Wallasey there'd be no need for that kind of thing, not like down in Liverpool with its docks, or Wavertree where Jean lived. Edwin had been furious when he'd had to have his beautiful lawn dug up so that they could get their air-raid shelter put in and she didn't blame him. Luckily they'd been able to put it out of sight of the house at the bottom of the garden behind the apple trees.

Jean and her family should be here soon. She lifted her hand and patted her newly permed hair. Jean might be the elder by ten minutes but she, Vi, felt far superior. She looked down at her new dress. Silk not cotton, and a birthday present from Edwin. Edwin was doing very well for himself with his business and she'd done very well for herself in marrying him, as Edwin himself liked to remind her. Vi's mouth thinned slightly.

Jean would never have been able to manage a

husband like Edwin. Where were they? She had told Jean half-past two. Perhaps she ought to have insisted that Edwin and Charlie should drive down to the ferry terminal to pick them up, but Edwin was in one of his moods, complaining that Charlie was spending far too much time enjoying himself and not enough doing what his father paid him to do, which was to sweet-talk their customers, and she hadn't wanted to provoke any further ill-tempered outbursts. She just hoped that Bella would remember that she had promised to help her with the tea and not linger at the tennis club. A fond maternal smile replaced Vi's frown at the thought of her daughter, Isabelle. Privately she had always felt sorry for her twin having three daughters who were all so inferior in every way to her own Bella. Grace looked far too much like their younger sister, Francine, for Vi's liking, and they all knew where those kind of looks had got her! Singing on a stage for her living was most certainly not what she wanted for *her* daughter. And as for Jean's twins, well, they were fair enough but she doubted that they were going to grow up anything like as attractive as Bella, with her large blue eyes and her soft blonde hair, and most of all her sweetly dutiful manner. Vi's chest swelled with maternal pride and triumph. Everyone who met Bella remarked on the sweetness of her nature and her modesty. It was no wonder that she was so popular.

She could see a familiar group of people walking down the road. Yes, it was definitely them, and her sister was wearing the same frock she had worn for their birthday tea last year. It was just as well they had only moved here to Kingsway this spring. She certainly didn't want her new neighbours talking behind her back about the fact that her sister was coming to visit her wearing a year-old frock. You'd have thought that Jean would have had a little more thought for her new position, Vi thought crossly as she stepped back from the window and hurried downstairs.

Her husband and son were both in the front room. Edwin was reading his newspaper whilst Charlie was standing in front of the fireplace, looking bored.

'I don't know why you had to invite them here, Vi. You know what a busy time this is for me, with the business expanding and my duties with the ARP.'

'I suppose you'd have preferred us to go to them, would you?' she challenged him, continuing without waiting for him to answer, 'I couldn't believe it when Jean actually suggested that she should do the tea this year.'

'Where's Jack?' Charlie asked, ignoring his mother's comment.

'I've just seen him outside, although he should be upstairs doing his homework.' Vi's mouth thinned again.

'Here's Bella,' Charlie announced, as a car drew up outside.

'Looks like Alan Parker has brought her home.'

Alan Parker was the only son of a fellow local councillor, with whom Edwin had become friendly.

Councillor Parker was a very influential and well-to-do man, and although neither of them had said anything, Vi was well aware that she and Edwin were thinking that Alan Parker would make a very good husband for their daughter.

'I hope she's remembered about the tea and doesn't invite Alan in.'

'Looks like you can stop worrying, Ma,' Charlie told her, as they watched Bella take her leave of her escort and then walk towards the house, her tennis skirt showing off the slender length of her tanned legs, her blonde hair caught back in a bandeau, and an immaculate white cardigan draped just so around her shoulders, her gas mask in the pretty matching white carrying case Vi had bought her earlier in the summer.

'I'll go and let her in. Charlie, run upstairs, will you, and tell Jack to come down?'

'You're late. Your auntie Jean will be here any minute,' Vi warned her daughter as she opened the front door to let her in.

'Sorry, Mummy. I would have walked home but Alan insisted on driving me and then we were later leaving than we'd planned because he wanted to get tickets for the big Tennis Club dance next weekend.'

'He's invited you to go with him as his partner?'

'Yes. I'm glad Auntie Jean's going to be here because I asked him to get four so that I could invite Grace to come along as well. I thought it would be a bit of a treat for her. She could stay here overnight so that she doesn't have to worry about getting home.'

'Grace? Well, that's very thoughtful of you, darling, but I wonder if it was wise.'

'She was saying the last time I saw her that she hardly goes out at all, only to that St John Ambulance group she's joined.' Bella pulled a face and shuddered. 'I know she's always wanted to be a nurse but I'd hate having to do anything like that. It makes me feel faint if I cut my finger. It's bad enough having to roll all those bandages for the WVS. But at least I'm doing my bit.'

'Of course you are, darling.'

'Anyway, Alan's parents have got Alan's cousin staying with them. He's in the RAF but he's on leave at the moment and, of course, Alan feels he has to include him in things, so I thought that Grace could partner him.'

'Well, yes, darling, but Grace is a shop girl, remember, for all that she's your cousin, and I wouldn't want her to feel uncomfortable or embarrass you mixing with your friends at the Tennis Club.'

'Oh, there's no need to worry about that, Mummy.'

Vi was about to warn her daughter that, on the contrary, there was every need to worry if she was to make the right kind of impression with Alan's parents, but before she could do so the doorbell rang.

Jean looked quickly and a bit anxiously at her brood. It was a hot day and both her husband and her son were beginning to look uncomfortable in

15

their suits. Sam was even tugging impatiently at his collar.

'Sam,' she hissed warningly, but it was too late, the door was opening and Vi was standing there, her attention immediately focusing on Sam's attempts to loosen his collar.

'Jean. At last.' Why was it that Vi so frequently managed to sound bossy and disapproving, Jean wondered ruefully.

'We had to wait for a bus because the first one was full with it being such a nice day,' she explained as she and Vi exchanged brief hugs.

'Oh dear, yes. I tend to forget how unreliable public transport can be now that I've got both Edwin and Charlie to drive me wherever I need to go. Really I can't think how we went on when we only had the one car, especially now that Bella has joined the Tennis Club and is so much in demand. Come on in, anyway. I thought we'd have tea outside, seeing as it's such a lovely day.'

'So that the twins don't spill tea on her carpet again is more like it,' Luke grinned, muttering his aside to Grace as they followed their parents into the house.

'That wasn't their fault,' Grace whispered back. 'It was actually Jack who spilled the tea but they took the blame for him.'

'Poor little tyke. It's hard to believe sometimes that Mum and Auntie Vi are twins, isn't it?'

'Very hard,' Grace agreed feelingly.

'We'll go straight through into the garden, I think.'

Jean exchanged looks with Sam as they all trooped through her sister's kitchen and out into the garden. They hadn't, Jean noted, been invited to walk through the sitting room at the back of the house and out into the garden via the French windows that Vi had showed off to her so proudly when they had first moved into the house earlier in the year. But, of course, Vi hadn't had her new carpets put down then.

The garden, its lawns shorn as short as possible and its flowerbeds weed free and rigidly immaculate, was empty, a white cloth flapping gently on the card table set up for the birthday 'tea' and six deck chairs drawn up in a straight line.

'Where is everyone?' asked Jean.

'Oh, well, with you being late, Edwin said that he might as well catch up on a bit of work. He's been ever so busy just lately, what with the business and then all his ARP duties and the council. He'll be out in a minute, I dare say. Bella's just run upstairs to change out of her tennis things, and Charlie's with his father.'

'And Jack?' Jean asked.

Vi tensed. 'He should be in his room doing his homework. His last report said that he spends far too much time daydreaming. Edwin's completely out of patience with him, but I saw he'd sneaked outside into the garden earlier.'

Her voice suggested that Jack could expect to be punished for his transgression and Jean winced inwardly but knew better than to say anything.

'Do make yourselves comfortable whilst I go

and put the kettle on,' Vi continued. 'Bella will be down in a minute, I expect, Grace. Bella has got a lovely surprise for you. She's such a wonderful daughter, Jean. She got me flowers for my birthday and a bottle of scent. Edwin bought me my new frock, of course.'

'It's lovely,' Jean offered dutifully.

'Pure silk,' Vi told her proudly, adding, 'Oh, here are Edwin and Charles.'

Vi's husband and son were casually dressed in cavalry twill trousers and smart sports shirts, and looked cool and fresh.

'Yes, do take your tie off if you wish, Sam,' Vi offered, causing Jean's face to burn a little at the recognition that her sister was patronising her family. That Sam knew it too was evident from the tight look of anger she could see hardening his mouth.

'I'll come with you and give you a hand with the tea, Vi,' Jean began, only to be told firmly, 'I'd prefer it if you called me Vivienne from now on, Jean. Mrs Lawson, who's in charge of our local WVS group, was saying to me only the other week, when she asked me to be her deputy, what an elegant name Vivienne is and what a shame it is to shorten it.'

Luke and Grace exchanged mirthful looks before turning away to hide their amusement.

'Got your papers yet, Luke?' Charlie asked, coming over to join them as the two sisters headed for the kitchen.

'No, but I'm expecting to get them any time,' Luke answered. 'What about you?'

Charlie gave him a knowing grin and a wink, tapping the side of his nose meaningfully. 'No fear of me being called up. I've made a smart move and joined the TA. A chap I know told me that once you're in you're exempt from having to do your six months, and that means that I get to stay at home and attend TA sessions a couple of times a week, whilst other chaps who aren't as on the ball end up being send hundreds of miles away to some godforsaken army training camp. You should think about doing it yourself, Luke. Dad reckons that there's no chance of us going to war, no matter what the papers might say. He reckons Hitler will back down. Mind you, we're not complaining about all the doommongers, not when we're doing very nicely thank you out of it. We've got that much work on we've had to take on extra men. Course, that means that things are a bit of a doddle for me at the moment.' He gave Luke and Grace another wink. 'There's not many pretty girls that say no to a spin in a brand-new car on a nice sunny day.'

'I wouldn't have thought that your father would approve of that,' Luke told him.

'No, I dare say he wouldn't – if he knew.'

In the kitchen Jean dutifully admired the new linoleum floor Vi was pointing out to her.

'It's all very nice, Vi – I mean Vivienne – but I don't know how I'd feel about not having an outhouse to do me washing in.'

'Oh well, as to that, Edwin insists that we send everything to the laundry. He can't abide having

19

wet washing hanging all over the place. He's even talked about getting someone in to do the heavy cleaning, especially now that I'm getting so involved with the WI and the WVS. Mrs Lawson has good as said that she wants me to be her second in command.'

'I don't know,' Jean marvelled, shaking her head. 'Remember how our nan used to carrying her washing down to the wash house?'

Vi's face changed colour and she looked over her shoulder before pushing the door to and saying quickly, 'I'm surprised at you bringing something like that up, Jean. It was a long time ago and it's best forgotten.'

'Well, I'm surprised at you, our Vi. Anyone would think you were ashamed of Nan now that you've moved to Wallasey. A hard worker she was, and proud as well, even if she and Granddad were poor.'

'Your Luke will be getting his papers soon,' Vi announced, changing the subject as the kettle came to the boil.

Jean's face creased with maternal concern. 'That's right. Sam's got a place waiting for him in the Salvage Corps and once he's in it he'll be in a reserved occupation but he isn't out of his apprenticeship yet.'

'Well, I can understand that you'd want to keep him safe,' Vi agreed, 'but for myself I can't help feeling that it's a young man's duty to serve his country. My Charlie joined the TA the minute he could.' She gave her twin a lofty look. 'Of course, we fully support him,' she added untruthfully, conveniently forgetting how furious Edwin had been when he heard what Charlie had done, and how he'd said that Charlie should have waited until he had a few words in the right ears before jumping the gun like he had.

'As busy as he is, Edwin's still volunteered to oversee our local ARP unit and of course now that he's on the local council he'll be expected to take on a more managerial role. I dare say he'll be put in charge of something or other – not that he believes for one minute that there's going to be a war.'

'Sam thinks there will.'

Vi gave her twin a superior smile. 'Well, I rather think that my Edwin is in more of a position to know what's going on than your Sam, Jean. After all, he's got important men from the War Office and the navy coming down to see him all the time, on account of the work that's needed to be done refitting so many Merchant Navy ships.'

'But surely that means that there's more likely to be a war than not be one?' Jean argued valiantly.

'It might look that way but, take it from me, the Government is just taking precautionary measures, that's all. Now I think we've got everything. Will you bring the milk and the hot-water jug for me?'

Outside in the garden Sam and Edwin were standing together looking awkward whilst Luke and Charlie were laughing at something and the twins, Jean was glad to see, were playing with

Jack, who had obviously been allowed to escape from his homework.

'I had a letter from Francine yesterday wishing us both a happy birthday,' she told Vi. 'She's still in America singing with Gracie Fields. She said that she misses Liverpool but I don't expect she'll be coming back now with all this talk of war.'

'Well, I certainly hope that she doesn't. I haven't forgotten all the trouble she caused, and now that Edwin's moving up in the world, the last thing he needs is a sister-in-law who's on the stage parading herself all over the place.'

'Vi,' Jean objected, 'that's not very nice. And not very fair either. Our Francine's done really well for herself.'

'Yes, and we all know how,' Vi retorted darkly. 'Edwin refuses to so much as have her name mentioned, and no wonder. America's the best place for her. I don't want her coming back and showing us all up, especially not now, with Isabella joining the Tennis Club and mixing with such a smart set. Did I tell you about the young man she's seeing? His father is on the council, and his mother comes from a very well-to-do family. He's taking Bella to the big Tennis Club dance next weekend. Bella is so generous. She wants your Grace to make up a foursome with her and Alan and Alan's cousin. Of course, I told her that poor Grace would probably feel a bit out of her depth, what with all the other young people at the Tennis Club either working for their parents or, like Bella, working in an office, but no, she's determined that Grace should be included. She'll have to spend the night here, of course, and I dare say that Bella will have a dress she can borrow.'

There was no chance for Jean to make any response because they were now within earshot of the men, but she could feel her heart burning with indignation on her daughter's behalf.

As she put the milk jug and the hot water down on the table next to the cups and saucers already laid out with military neatness, Jean tried not to feel envious of her twin's pretty Royal Albert china, with its roses and its gold edging, nor to compare it with her own far more practical and robust cups and saucers, oddments, in the main, bought from the market. Every time she saw Vi's tea set she felt envious, and then cross with herself for being so silly. What did a few cups and saucers matter, after all?

'More cake, Sam?'

'No, thanks, Vi. I've never bin keen on shop bought, not with my Jean being such a good cook.'

A small smile twitched at the corners of Jean's mouth as she listened to her husband and saw her twin bridle slightly.

Jack was a bit too pale and quiet for her liking, Jean decided, watching her nephew as he sat on the grass and drank his lemonade. In looks he resembled her own twins and was therefore physically more like Vi than either of her other two children, but that similarity didn't seem to endear him to her.

Suddenly, despite the smartness of her twin's home and garden, Jean found that she was longing for the familiar comfort of her own much smaller and shabbier home.

'It's been lovely, Vi, but I think we'd better make a move. With it being such a nice day there are bound to be long queues for the ferry,' she announced, causing Sam to look at her in both surprise and relief. 'I'll give you a hand washing the tea things first, though,' she offered, ignoring Sam's twinkling smile.

'There's no need for that. Bella will help me with them.'

They were both on their feet, equally aware of their eagerness to have the ritual sharing of their birthday over and done with.

There were already long queues waiting for the ferries back to Liverpool, but Jean didn't mind. It gave her the opportunity to chat over the afternoon with Sam as they stood in line.

'Vi was telling me that Edwin would like to have Jack evacuated if it does come to war. Poor little boy. Vi should never have had him really, and I blame myself that she did.'

Sam put his hand over hers. 'You've nowt to blame yourself for, love. It is a shame that the poor little lad isn't better thought of, but there's nowt you could have done. You know what your Vi's like. She's never liked thinking that she's being outdone.'

'Especially not by me,' Jean agreed ruefully. 'She

was determined to have Jack from the moment she knew I was pregnant.'

'Aye.' They shared a mutually understanding look that was tinged with pain and sadness.

'It might have been different if our little Terry had lived,' Jean said quietly. 'He and Jack could have been good friends.'

'Like our Luke and Grace are with your Vi's Charlie and Isabelle, you mean?' Sam asked her drily. 'I could hear Charlie boasting to Luke about that ruddy car of his and how he spends his time driving about in it, showing off.'

'Edwin won't tolerate that. Vi told me herself that the only reason Edwin has given Charlie a car of his own is because he needs him in the business.'

'You mean because he wants to keep him out of the army if it does come to war,' Sam corrected her. 'Mind, I can't blame him. I don't mind admitting that I'm relieved that Sid's got a place waiting for our Luke with the Salvage Corps. What's that look for?'

'A lot of parents will have to see their sons go off to fight if it does come to war, Sam. Do you think that it will?'

'Edwin reckons not, but I can't agree with him. One thing's for sure: if it does then we'll bloody well have to win,' he told her bluntly.

Jean shivered and moved closer to him. 'The twins will be leaving school next summer. Maybe there'll be some jobs going at Lewis's that would suit them.'

'I can't see them two bowing and scraping to the posh women that our Grace has to serve,' Sam chuckled.

Jean smiled as well. Grace worked in the À La Mode Gown Salon of the big store as a junior salesgirl and she often entertained her family over tea with tales of the well-to-do women who went there to buy their clothes.

'Mum, did Auntie Vi say anything to you about this dance at the Tennis Club that Bella wants me to go to?' Grace leaned over to ask, her face bright with excitement.

'She did, love. I wasn't sure that you'd want to go.'

'Of course I do. Bella was telling me all about it. It sounds lovely. She says she's going to ask Auntie Vi to buy her a new dress. She's seen the one she wants. It's pale blue silk embroidered with white marguerites.'

Some of the brightness faded from her face, and Jean knew exactly what she was thinking. Her heart ached for her daughter, who was never likely to own anything as expensive as a silk frock, never mind have a new one every time she felt like it.

'Well, I dare say we can make up a new sash for your polished cotton, love. Suits you a treat, it does, and you've got the advantage over Bella, you being that bit taller and having such a lovely neat waist.'

The little boy in front of them in the queue dropped his ice-cream cornet and started to cry bitterly, whilst his mother, who looked harassed and was clutching both their gas masks, tried to calm him. His noisy tears brought an end to any private conversation. Luke disappeared, only to reappear five minutes later carrying three cornets, one of which he gave to the delighted child and the other two to the twins.

'You're just as soft as your dad,' Jean mock-scolded him, after the child's mother had thanked him profusely for his generosity, and explained, 'I thought I'd give him a bit of a treat, like, with a day at the seaside, what with me being told that he'd have to be evacuated if there's a war, and his dad already away in the army, but it's bin a long day for him and he's got himself a bit overtired.'

'It's only an ice cream, and the poor little chap had only had a couple of licks of it,' Luke answered his mother now, before turning to his father. 'Dad, Charlie was saying that he's joined the TA because he reckons that it means he won't have to go away to do his six months' training. He was showing me his uniform.' There was a note of envy in his voice. 'I reckon that if I were to join them—'

'You'll do no such thing,' Sam stopped him sharply. 'The TA lot will be the first in if it does come to war.'

'Charlie reckons they'll be posted to home duties.'

'Aye, well, he would reckon that, him and that father of his being the clever sods they are.'

'Sam,' Jean objected, 'language!'

'Sorry, love, but it gets my goat, it really does, the way that ruddy Edwin reckons to be such a

know-it-all. I'm your father, Luke, and it's me you
listen to. We've been through all of this already.
If there's to be a war then you can do your bit
just as well here at home with the Salvage Corps,
aye, and you'll have a decent job wi' it if there
isn't a war. There's no sense in rushing off joining
summat like the TA.'

Jean listened anxiously. This wasn't the first time
that father and son had clashed over the issue of
Luke joining up for active service should there be
a war. Like any mother she desperately wanted to
keep her son safe.

The *Royal Daffodil* was pulling away from the
dock full of passengers and with any luck they
would be on the next ferry to leave.

Jean hoped so. It had been a long day, and now
she was tired and ready for her own home, and a
nice cup of tea and a slice of bread and butter.

TWO

Tuesday 22 August

Grace hummed happily under her breath as she and the other girls working in Lewis's exclusive À La Mode Gown Salon got their department ready for the store to open, the Tuesday after the family's visit to Wallasey.

The gowns were kept in the long row of floor-to-ceiling cupboards that filled one wall of that area of the store. The entrance to the Gown Salon was framed by silk curtains, and the carpet was thicker and a different pattern from that on the rest of the floor. All the girls working in the Gown Salon were expected to dress appropriately and were allowed to buy at a special discount the white silk blouses they all wore with their plain black skirts.

On very special occasions and for very special would-be purchasers the curtains framing the entrance could be closed. Three velvet upholstered and extremely uncomfortable chaise-longues were provided for customers, in addition to two large cheval mirrors.

It wasn't unheard of for naughty schoolchildren with nothing better to do to try to peep round the curtaining to watch customers parading in front of the mirrors in the gowns they were trying on, although the head of the salon, Mrs James, was very swift to ensure that they were given stern warnings and shooed away.

On one never-to-be-forgotten occasion, Grace had actually found her own twin sisters concealed behind the curtains, their presence given away by their familiar giggles as they tried to demonstrate to one another the 'walk' of a particularly demanding client who had been trying on gowns. Luckily Grace had spotted them before anyone else, and even more luckily she'd ensured that the lollipops they had been sucking did not end up stuck to the heavy curtains.

Just thinking about that incident now made her smile and shake her head.

'You're in a good mood this morning,' Susan Locke, another salesgirl, commented as she came hurrying in, looking over her shoulder to check that she couldn't be overheard before she added, 'Thank heavens Ma James isn't here yet to dock me wages for being late.'

'She said on Friday that she'd have to see a dentist. She's been having really bad toothache,' Grace told her.

'That explains why she was in such a bad mood all day Saturday, when you was having your day off, you lucky thing.' Susan pulled a face. 'I hate having Monday for me day off like I had this week. Listen, do you fancy coming out for a bite of dinner wi' me today?'

'I'd love to but I can't. I've got to go down to haberdashery and see if I can find a bit of something to make a sash to freshen up me polished-cotton frock, only I've been invited by my cousin to the Tennis Club dance in Wallasey at the weekend.'

'You can't wear a cotton frock to a posh tennis club dance,' Susan told her knowledgeably. 'I've served some of them wot's come in here looking for frocks for that kind of thing and they allus go for summat fancy and silk. In fact, I know exactly what you should wear. That green silk you was modelling for that chap wot came in the other week. Suited you a treat, it did, and he certainly thought so as well.' She gave Grace a meaningful look. 'If you ask me, that tale he gave about wanting to see it on you on account of him wanting to buy it for his sweetheart and you looking like you was the same size as her was all so much malarkey. We used to get one chap coming in here that regular with that kind of tale, you could set your watch by him. Allus came in when the new stock arrived, he did, and wanted to have us try on them frocks what had the lowest necklines. Ma James used to have him out of the salon as quick as a flash if she was here when he came in. He had me trying on this red crepe one Christmas. Came up to me and patted me on the backside, he did, when no one was looking.

31

Aye, and peered down me front as well. Dirty bugger.'

Grace laughed.

'Listen, I meant what I said earlier about you borrowing that green silk frock,' Susan told Grace in a hushed voice later in the morning when they were in the small room at the back of the salon where the girls had their tea breaks and ironed the gowns. 'You wouldn't be the first to do it by a long chalk. Borrowed one meself the Christmas before last, I did, when the chap I was seeing then wanted to take me to his office do. There was one girl even borrowed her wedding frock and no one the wiser.'

'I couldn't do that,' Grace protested, firmly refusing to be tempted by the memory of how perfectly the green silk had fitted her and how wonderful she had felt in it.

Her parents would have been horrified and shocked by Susan's suggestion, deeming it dishonest.

'Why not? It's not like it's stealing or anything,' insisted Susan. 'You just take it wi' you when you leave on Saturday after work and bring it back on Monday. Perk of the job, if you was to ask me, but if you don't mind going to a posh do looking daft in a cotton frock and having all them other girls there laughing at you then that's your funeral, isn't it, especially wi' all them frocks just hanging there doin' nowt. That green silk could have been made for you, Grace. Fitted you like a glove, it did, and there's not many would have the waist for it, nor the colouring. Mind you, I have to say that I'm surprised that cousin of yours would invite you to a posh do like that, from what I know of her.'

'What do you mean by that?' Grace demanded uncertainly.

'Well, when she's bin in here wi' her mother she's been all hoity-toity and keen to let us know how much better than us she is, hasn't she? I must say I was surprised when you first introduced her as your cousin, you being such a decent ordinary sort and her being so full of herself.'

Susan's comment made Grace feel too uncomfortable to respond. It was true that there had been times, especially since they had grown up, when Bella had made her feel that she considered Grace's side of the family to be inferior to her own, but Grace had always dismissed this as Bella simply not understanding how hurtful she was being and not really meaning any harm. In fact, it was because of this attitude on the part of her cousin that she had been so pleased when Bella had invited her to the dance. Family meant a lot to Grace and she wanted to get on with her cousins and be close to them.

It was St John Ambulance tonight and, as always, the thought of going to her first-aid class delighted her. As a little girl Grace had dreamed of becoming a nurse but the training to become a proper nurse, at a teaching hospital like Liverpool's Mill Road or the Royal, rather than merely working at one of the infirmaries that took on girls to care for the long-term ill, was costly and lengthy, with the uniform costing twenty-one pounds up front and a probationer nurse's wages only eighteen shillings a week for the first year. It would also have meant her having to live in at a nurses' home, so she wouldn't have been able to help out at home with her wages or an extra pair of hands, and so she had felt it her duty to take the job at Lewis's, for which a kind neighbour whose cousin worked there had put her forward.

It was gone six o'clock before her work was finally over for the day and she was free to leave. The warmth of the still sunny August evening made her feel that she would rather walk home than sit on a bus, even though that would take her a good half-hour.

Their house was the end one of a terrace, which meant that there was a side passage that led to the gardens at the rear of the houses, and as Grace opened the gate into their own garden she heard her mother calling out from the kitchen.

'Is that you, Grace, love?'

'Yes, Mum.' Grace went to join her.

'Just look at these cups,' her mother told her, gesturing towards the solid-looking plain pottery cups she was drying. 'I know it's daft but I felt that envious of Vi's lovely china when we were there. Proper bone china it is too, and so pretty. It reminded me of a little doll's tea set we used to play with when we were kiddies. It belonged to our nan's sister, our great-aunt Florence. She kept in it a corner cupboard in her front parlour and she'd let us play with it when we went to visit her. I can't tell you how badly I wanted that tea set, Grace.'

Jean laughed. 'Of course, Vi wanted it as well and there were some fair words said between us as to who should have it. In the end it went to Great-aunt Florence's own granddaughter. Of course, now Vi can afford to have proper china of her own.'

Grace frowned as her mother gave another small sigh. Personally she had thought her auntie Vi's china nothing to get excited about but she could see that her mother felt differently.

'I can't see Dad and Luke being happy with them fiddly little handles,' she pointed out.

Jean laughed again. 'No. And that's exactly what I told myself as well. I'm just being daft, like I said. Even if I had the money I wouldn't go wasting it on summat that would only end up broken.

'Run down to the allotment, will you, love,' she told Grace, changing the conversation, 'and tell your dad to bring up another lettuce, and some tomatoes? I want to use up the rest of this beef and we might as well have it cold with it being such a warm evening.'

The allotments weren't very far away and, as Grace had expected, when she got there she found her father deep in conversation with several of the other men, all of them looking serious enough for her to hesitate about interrupting. But on the other hand Mum wouldn't be too pleased either if they didn't get back soon, and with the lettuce and tomatoes she had asked for.

Whilst she stood there undecided her father looked up and saw her. Saying something to the other men, he came over to her.

'Mum sent me down to tell you that she wants a lettuce and some toms for tea, Dad. Is everything all right?' she asked him as she walked with him towards his plot. 'Only it looked like you were all talking about something serious.'

Grace knew she was lucky to be part of a family in which her parents encouraged their children to talk to them rather than one that observed the traditional 'children should be seen and not heard and speak only when they were spoken to' rule. Since all the talk of war had started, her mother and father had included her and Luke in their discussions about what was going on. But even so, there was something in her father's expression now that made Grace wonder if she had perhaps overstepped the mark.

'I'm sorry if I shouldn't have asked,' she began, only to see her father shake his head and put his arm around her shoulders in a rare gesture of fatherly affection.

'It's all right, lass, you've done nowt wrong. It's just that there's bin a bit of news that's teken folk a bit aback, and we were just discussing it.'

'What kind of news?' Grace asked, assuming he was going to tell her about yet another new instruction from the Government.

'Seemingly Russia has announced that it's entering a non-aggression pact with Germany, and we all know what that means,' he told her heavily.

For a minute Grace was too shocked to say anything. Her throat had gone dry and her heart was pounding.

'That means war, doesn't it?' she managed to ask eventually.

Her father nodded sombrely. 'It looks pretty much like it. Now, do you think your mum will want a few radishes as well?'

Grace recognised that her father did not want to continue to discuss the shocking news.

War! Was it her imagination or as they walked back home together was there really a brassy tinge to the evening sky and a brooding sulphurous prescience of what was to come?

'My brother reckons that we'll be at war before the month's out, and he says that his unit have been put on standby alert ready,' Lucy, one of the other first aiders, was telling everyone importantly when Grace arrived at the St John Ambulance Brigade station at the local church hall for their regular Tuesday evening meeting. Originally when Grace had joined the St John Ambulance Brigade, like all the other young cadet members, her 'responsibilities' had included running errands and doing other jobs for local elderly people, and generally making herself useful. Grace still called to see Miss Higgins, a spinster in her late seventies who lived in the next street, knowing that as well as liking having someone to run her errands, the elderly lady enjoyed the opportunity to talk about her youth and to gossip about her neighbours.

Now, as a fully qualified first aider, Grace got to wear a navy-blue drill overall and an armband printed with the words 'First Aid', in addition to being issued with a steel helmet, but tonight it was so warm that she had removed the helmet whilst she and the girl partnering her prepared their 'patient' for her ambulance journey to hospital, having been on hand when she was 'rescued from a bombing incident'.

A splint secured the patient's leg, and several bandages had been applied to her torso. Moving the deliberately unhelpfully inert body of their patient in the heat of the enclosed space of the church hall had left Grace's face flushed and damp, and now she sat back a little anxiously on her heels, awaiting the inspection of her work by one of the senior nurses from Mill Road Hospital, who had volunteered to come to teach the volunteers all the basics of first aiding.

Sister Harris's approving 'very nice Campion' had Grace's face glowing for a far more satisfactory reason than the heat of the church hall.

'I hate this bit,' her partner groaned when, their work inspected and passed, they set to carefully removing and rewinding the bandages. 'Do you think it's true, like Lucy says, that it's going to be war now, Grace?' she asked worriedly.

'I hope not, Alice,' was all Grace could say, but she couldn't help dwelling on the concern she had seen in her parents' eyes over tea and her father's keenness to listen to the BBC news, and the heaviness she had heard in her father's voice earlier when he had told her about the developments in Russia.

'If there is then I don't know about you but I'm going to make sure I do my bit. I've got a cousin who's thinking of joining the WRNS and I'm considering going along with her. They've got the best uniform of the lot, she reckons, and she should know, her dad being in the navy. You've got a brother, haven't you? What service is he going for?'

'Luke's going into the Salvage Corps, like our dad,' Grace told her automatically and then flushed. There was something in the other girl's expression that made her feel defensive and protective on her brother's behalf, although Alice hadn't come out and said anything.

'It's every bit as dangerous as joining up,' she felt obliged to say.

'I dare say it is,' the other girl agreed but she didn't meet Grace's gaze, and Grace noticed how, as soon as their patient was back up on her feet and the bandages and splint had been returned to their correct places, Alice didn't linger to chat, going instead to join some of the other girls.

'Campion, I'd like a word.'

Grace looked apprehensively at Sister Harris. Was she too going to quiz her about her Luke's plans?

However, when Sister Harris had drawn her into a quiet corner of the hall what she did have to say was so surprising that it drove all thoughts of Alice's comments out of Grace's head.

'You'll have heard the news about Russia, no

doubt,' Sister Harris began, barely waiting for Grace to nod before continuing. 'No one wants war but since it looks like we're going to have it, it makes sense to be prepared. Captain Allen tells me that you work in Lewis's?'

'Yes, Sister.' Captain Allen was the retired army captain in charge of their St John Ambulance Brigade unit.

'Have you ever thought of enrolling to train as a full-time nurse?'

Hearing Sister Harris saying those words, and so matter-of-factly, was such a shock that Grace couldn't speak. But then she managed to overcome her feelings to say as calmly as she could, 'I did think I'd like to do nursing when I was growing up but . . .' She hesitated, unwilling to say to someone who plainly had come from a family that had been able to afford her training that she hadn't wanted to burden her parents with that kind of cost.

'Well, maybe now is the time to think of it again,' Sister Harris told her firmly, without waiting for a full explanation. 'You're an excellent first aider, quick to learn and good at doing what you should when you have learned. The nursing profession needs girls like you, Campion, especially now. I happen to know that the Government is very keen to get new nurses trained up, and in fact we have been asked to put forward the names of young women who we think might be suitable candidates for such training.'

Was Sister Harris actually saying that she felt

she was good enough for her to recommend? Grace could hardly believe it. Her chest felt tight as her heart swelled with pride and delight.

'So I'll put forward your name, shall I? It will mean a lot of hard work but I'm sure we all want to do our duty and give what assistance we can to the Government.'

'Well, I . . .' Now Grace could feel her heart lurching sickening downwards as her excitement came up hard against the reality of her situation. She could see that Sister Harris was looking irritated and impatient. Flustered and embarrassed she burst out, 'I'd love to, really I would, Sister, but it's my family.'

'You mean that your parents wouldn't give their permission?' Sister was frowning now. 'I find that very hard to believe under the present circumstances, Campion – not to say positively unpatriotic.'

Horrified, Grace blurted, 'Oh, no, I mean . . . well, the truth is, Sister, that . . .' Her voice dropped and she looked over her shoulder, checking she wouldn't be overheard. 'Mum and Dad have four of us at home, and my sisters are still at school, so . . .' Grace bit her lip, floundering, not wanting to say that it was out of the question for her to expect her parents to go without her financial contribution to the household, never mind find the money required to buy the uniform and the books she would need before entering the Probationary Training School, but to her relief Sister Harris immediately realised what she was trying to say and the sternness faded from her expression.

'Ah, I see, Campion. Well, my dear, it's there for you to think about and I would be delighted to recommend you. If you should see a way to undertaking the training the cost would be around twenty pounds for your uniform and your books, you'd be paid eighteen shillings a week during your first year, and of course you'd be living in.' She patted Grace on the arm. 'My advice to you is to have a word with your parents and tell them what I've told you. It would be a pity if the nursing service were to lose the opportunity to acquire a girl like you.'

Her praise left Grace feeling slightly dizzy.

Ten minutes later, when Grace stepped out of the church hall, she was surprised to see Luke waiting for her.

'I thought you were going to an ARP meeting tonight with Dad,' she said.

'I was – I did – but I thought I'd come this way and walk back with you.'

Smiling at him, Grace tucked her arm through his. They were close in age and close emotionally as well, and she sensed immediately that he had something on his mind but she also knew him well enough to wait to let him tell her in his own time what it was. It was no mere impulse that had brought him round this way to walk home with her.

'There were a lot of them that was there tonight saying that their lads had had letters and that, telling them to report to their units . . .'

Grace gave a small shiver. She didn't need Luke

to explain to her what that meant – not after what her father had told her earlier. The whole country must surely know now that although no official declaration of war had been made, things were moving towards that with increasing speed.

They were walking only slowly and Luke was dragging his feet a bit, scowling and scuffing the side of his shoe in a way that she knew would have drawn a rebuke from their mother. Something was definitely wrong.

'They were painting out the name of Edge Hill Station when I cycled past it earlier on me way home from work. Mr Smethwick that's in charge of the ARP unit said that the Government has given orders that anything that might identify a place to the Germans had to be got rid of.'

Abruptly Grace stopped walking. 'It's going to happen, isn't it?' she asked in a hushed voice. 'We *are* going to be at war with the Germans.' She gave a little shiver, then told him sadly, 'There were some kiddies in Lewis's at dinnertime, brought in by their teacher. They'd been to choose gas masks for themselves, ready to be evacuated. I heard the teacher saying that the school had thought if they were getting them from Lewis's it would be a bit of a treat and it wouldn't scare them so much. Thank goodness the twins are old enough not to have to go. I reckon it would break Mum's heart if they did.'

'I can't say anything at home but I fair hate listening to other chaps talking about how they'll do their bit for the country, Grace, whilst thanks to Dad all I'm going to be doing is skulking here at home like a ruddy coward.'

'Luke, that's not true,' she protested, genuinely shocked. 'Of course you'll be doing your bit. And, anyway, as for Charlie, he said himself that the only reason he's joined the TA is because it means he can stay at home and show off to pretty girls in his car.'

Luke squeezed her arm and then told her with elder brother directness, 'If I was you I'd think twice about going to that Tennis Club dance with Bella, Grace.'

'I can't not go now,' she protested. 'Not when I've said that I will. Besides, I think it will be fun.'

'Well, all I can say is that you'll need to watch out. If you ask me Bella's up to something. She might act like she's all sugar and spice but you and me know what she's really like. Remember how she always managed to get you blamed for things she'd done when we were kids?'

Reluctantly Grace nodded. 'But that was years ago,' she told him, 'and I dare say she only did it because Auntie Vi can get so cross.'

'A leopard doesn't change its spots,' Luke insisted.

Grace looked up at her elder brother, her heart filling with pride. Luke might tease her sometimes and pretend that having three younger sisters was a nuisance but Grace knew how protective of them all he was.

'You're the best brother in the world, do you know that?' she told him, hugging his arm.

'You won't be saying that when everyone's calling me a coward for not joining up. If Dad has his way I won't even get to do my six months' training. He'll have me straight in the Salvage Corps and on reserved occupation duties,' Luke told her angrily.

'That's because he wants to keep you safe. Dad lost his older brother in the last war,' Grace reminded him.

'But that should be my decision, Grace, not Dad's,' said Luke fiercely. 'And, anyway, it will be a different war this time. Everyone says so.'

They had drawn level with a lorry being unloaded opposite a small school. Grace glanced semi-curiously at the activity and then froze before turning to look beseechingly at Luke, hoping he would tell her that she had mistaken what she had just seen, but instead he told her grimly, 'They're unloading cardboard coffins. They were telling us at the ARP class tonight that the Government has given orders that emergency mortuaries are to be set up and stocked with them, just in case.'

'Here's that cousin of yours.'

Susan's whisper, accompanied by a sharp nudge in the ribs, had Grace straightening from picking up a stray thread from the carpet and turning to see Bella coming towards her. She was wearing a pretty pale blue linen summer dress and jacket, and a neat little hat trimmed with white flower petals.

'Oh, there you are, Grace, good,' Bella announced,

immediately sitting down on one of the chaises, and then crossing one slim leg over the other. 'Oh, no, just look at that dirty smudge on my sandals.' She bent down and kicked off her sandal. 'Take it somewhere and clean it off for me, will you, Grace? I'm meeting Alan in ten minutes and I don't want him seeing me looking all grubby.'

Grace was just about to pick up the sandal when Susan said in a loud voice, whilst grimacing warningly at her, 'Grace, don't forget that the manageress said you were to go and pack up that frock for Mrs Lynsey ready for tonight's post, will you?'

Grace, who knew perfectly well that she had no such task and that Susan had made it up because she did not approve of her cousin expecting her to clean her shoes, hesitated.

Bella said irritably, 'Hurry up, do, Grace. I haven't got all day.'

'We don't clean shoes here, love,' Susan informed her, obviously unable to hold back her irritation any longer. 'You want to tek them sandals down to the shoe department if they need cleaning, although if you was to ask me a bit of spit on your hanky would do the job just as well.'

In different circumstances the look of outrage on Bella's face would have made Grace laugh aloud, but Bella had a spiteful side to her and Grace felt alarmed on Susan's behalf when she saw the narrow-eyed glare Bella was giving her friend.

'It doesn't show, Bella, and I don't think for one minute that Alan will notice it, not when he's got you to look at,' Grace flattered her.

Bella preened and tossed her head. 'I'm sure you're right, Grace, but of course one wants to look one's best. Actually, that's why I'm here. I just wanted to have a word with you about Saturday night.'

'If it's been cancelled because of what's happening—' Grace began, trying not to sound disappointed.

'Cancelled? Of course it hasn't! It's the big dance of the season. How could it possibly be cancelled? No, what I've come in for is to tell you that I want you to make sure that you keep this cousin of Alan's occupied so that me and Alan get a bit of time to ourselves. Alan's told me that there's something very important that he wants to tell me.' Bella looked smug and triumphant. 'I'm sure I don't need to tell you what that's likely to be.'

She looked down at her left hand meaningfully, and then jumped up from her seat exclaiming, 'Oh, is that the time? Alan will wonder where on earth I am. It's lucky that my boss was called away after lunch otherwise I might not have been able to sneak out when Alan rang to say he wanted to see me. I only just had time to ring Mummy and tell her that I'll be bringing Alan home to tea with me. Now remember, Grace, I don't want you showing me up, so for heaven's sake wear something decent. Oh, yes, and Mummy said to tell you that it makes much more sense for you to go home instead of staying overnight.'

As soon as Bella had left the salon, Susan told Grace firmly, 'You've got to borrow that green dress, and put that ruddy madam of a cousin of yours in her place. Snotty piece.'

'Susan . . .' Grace protested weakly.

'Well, she is and you know it. If I was you I'd refuse to go to her ruddy Tennis Club dance.'

Grace sighed. The truth was that now, after seeing Bella, her initial excitement had quite gone and she was wishing that she could get out of going, whilst knowing that she could not. If she tried, then Auntie Vi would get on to her own mother and that just wouldn't be fair.

'Who's this Alan she was going on about, then?' Susan asked.

'His name is Alan Parker,' Grace explained. 'He's the son of a councillor that Uncle Edwin has got friendly with.'

'A councillor, eh? There's posh then.' Susan pulled an unkind face. 'Your Bella is obviously expectin' to get a proposal and a ring out of him come Saturday, and I reckon that she won't be too fussy about how she gets them.'

'A lot of couples are getting engaged on account of what's happening with Germany,' Grace pointed out, trying not to show how uncomfortable Susan's assessment of her cousin was making her feel.

Susan was the closest to her age amongst those working in the Gown Salon. Grace liked her and had welcomed Susan's overtures of friendship when she had first come to work there. She had quickly discovered that Susan was intensely loyal to those she cared about, but she was also extremely forth-right and could be blunt to the point of unkindness.

'Mebbe so,' Susan allowed. 'But I reckon that if that cousin of yours gets engaged it will be because it suits her and not because her chap is going off to war. She's that kind. And if you can't see that then that's because you're too soft-natured for your own good.'

'I know what you're saying,' Grace admitted. 'But there is another side to Bella. Look how kind she's been, inviting me to this dance.'

'Kind? Huh, not her. She'll have some reason for doing it that suits her, you wait and see,' Susan prophesied darkly. 'Anyway, after the way she's just bin looking down her nose at us, I reckon there's all the more reason for you to borrow that green silk frock. Show her a thing of two, that would. It's obvious she reckons she's the bee's knees. Well, put you in that frock and it won't be the only thing around wot's green, I can tell you that. She'll be choking on her jealousy.'

'Susan!' Grace felt bound to protest.

'It's the truth. Twice as pretty as her, you are, or at least you could be. Only you can't see it.'

Bella smiled smugly as she surveyed her own reflection in the mirror of Lewis's powder room. She had just finished reapplying her new 'Paris Pink' lipstick, her skin was creamily flawless, thanks to a fluff of Yardley face powder, and she had dabbed plenty of Ma Griffe scent on her wrists and her handkerchief before leaving home.

No one seeing both her and Grace in the Gown Salon five minutes ago would ever have guessed that they were cousins. Grace looked so drab and plain in her white blouse and black skirt, and with her hair tied back and only the merest hint of lipstick. Bella knew her cousin would be the perfect foil for her own beauty on Saturday night. There was nothing like a plain friend to make a girl look even better and so encourage her chap to recognise how lucky he was. Bella looked down at her left hand, her smile widening. She could see Alan's ring on her finger already. In fact she had as good as picked it out from the rings on display in the window of Wallasey's most exclusive jewellers. Not one but three bright shiny diamonds of a satisfyingly impressive size.

Mrs Alan Parker!

'Mr and Mrs Edwin Firth request the pleasure of your company at the Marriage of their Daughter Miss Isabella Firth with Mr Alan Parker.'

Bella exhaled happily. Alan was everything she wanted in a husband. His father was an important and very well-to-do local businessman; his mother was the chairwoman of all the most important Wallasey women's committees. They had no daughter of their own so naturally, she, their daughter-in-law, would be adored and spoiled. Alan's parents would buy them a smart detached house not far from their own, and she would live the life of a new young wife whose husband had the time and the money to indulge her every whim.

She was so glad now that she had held back last year when the son of the most well-to-do man where they had lived before moving to Kingsway had started dropping hints that he wanted to propose to her. David had been all very well in his way, but his family's position could not compare with that of Alan's.

Not that it had all been plain sailing exactly. There had been the small matter of the girl Alan had already been seeing when they had first met – an 'accidentally on purpose' bumping into him as she left the tennis court – but Bella had soon seen off Trixie Mayhew, who had gone all pale-faced and quiet when Bella had taken her to one side to confide in her that she felt Trixie ought to know that Alan had told her how attracted he was to her but that he felt he couldn't ask her out because he was already seeing Trixie. Naturally Bella had known that Trixie was the kind of girl who wouldn't want to stand in the way of the man she loved's longing for someone else. And of course when Alan had turned to her for comfort when Trixie had told him that she didn't want to see him any more, and had refused to say why, Bella had been more than ready to give him that comfort.

Bella knew that it would shock girls like Trixie and her cousin Grace to learn how determined she was to make sure that Alan proposed to her. But that, of course, was why girls like them ended up with the husbands they did, whilst girls like her got the pick of the crop. And now if she had judged the situation correctly, and she was sure that she had, Alan had taken the hints she had been dropping and *was* about to propose. And not before time! She had been beginning to get a bit impatient. After all, they had spent the whole summer as a couple, and she had made it clear what she wanted and expected, losing no opportunity to make him aware of how fortunate he was to have a girl like her and what a perfect wife she would be.

Now her goal was in sight. Surely the reason Alan had telephoned her at work so unexpectedly to ask her to meet him could mean only one thing? He wanted her to choose her ring before Saturday so that he could 'surprise' her with it at the dance. She had pretended to appear casual on the phone, suggesting that he meet her outside Lewis's instead of letting him pick her up from her office. After all, she didn't want him thinking that she was desperate!

Daintily Bella sauntered out into the street. She was late, of course, but not so late that Alan would have grown irritated, and so it caught her off guard not to find Alan waiting for her as they had arranged.

Her smile changed abruptly to a small tight frown. She looked briefly down Ranelagh Street. It was unthinkable that Alan should have stood her up or gone off in a huff. She was a girl who was worth waiting for, and she had been at pains to make sure that Alan knew that, just as she had been at pains to make sure that he realised how many other young men wished they were in his shoes.

Alan was the kind of man who needed to know

that his peers envied him, and Bella had been more than willing to assist him in this vanity.

The sound of a car horn followed by Alan calling out her name caught her attention, her eyes widening slightly as she saw him waving to her from the driving seat of a brand-new cream MG Roadster, its hood down.

'I say, Bella, hurry up, will you?' he called out impatiently. 'I've already driven past here twice.'

The drivers of the other cars in the street were all turning to look and, by no means averse to this attention, Bella made a pretty show of looking bashful, whilst at the same time ensuring that everyone was aware of how elegant and smartly turned out she was as she hurried towards the car.

'Goodness, Alan, fancy calling out to me like that in the street. Everyone was looking at me,' she told him as she got into the car and closed the door.

'What do you think of her?' he demanded excitedly, ignoring her comment.

What Bella thought was that she was irritated and put out to discover that his reason for wanting to meet her was because he wanted to show off his new car, and not because he wanted to take her to choose an engagement ring, but she was far too wise to say so. Men needed to be indulged at times, and this was definitely one of those. And besides, being sweet and nice now, and encouraging his obvious good mood, would pay off later when she pressed home the point that it would be both convenient and expected of them to announce their engagement on Saturday.

'A real beauty, isn't she?' he enthused, oblivious to what Bella was thinking. 'Dad gave me the keys this morning. Said he'd been going to keep her as a surprise for my birthday, but he'd decided I might as well enjoy her now whilst the weather's so good. She's got the sweetest-sounding engine you've ever heard.'

'A new car for your birthday – your father is very generous, Alan.'

'The old man can afford it,' he told her with a careless shrug, a gesture that made him look exactly like his father. Both the Parker men were of average height and solidly built with light brown hair, pale blue eyes and ruddy complexions.

The draught from the motion of the car was already tugging at her hat. Bella frowned and looked pointedly at Alan, waiting for him to comment on how pretty she looked before she was obliged to remove it. When he didn't, she turned stiffly away from him to remove her hatpins and place her hat on her knee.

'I've had a word with Grace. Just to remind her about the dance on Saturday, and that she's partnering your cousin.'

'Seb? Oh yes. He's such a dull fellow. He actually went off to spend the afternoon in the library. Lord knows why. It's a bit of a bore having him hanging around all the time, but the old man is pretty keen on making a bit of a fuss of him, seeing as his father has done so well for himself. Of course, he isn't my first cousin or anything. It's his step-mother who's Dad's cousin but Dad reckons the connection is worth hanging on to.'

Bella shook her head. She wasn't particularly interested in Seb Atkins, who looked at her some-times in a way that she didn't like one little bit. Men were supposed to admire and adore her, not look at her as though she bored and irritated them.

'I dare say there won't be many more Tennis Club dances if it does come to war,' Alan told her.

'All the more reason for us to make the most of this one then, with a special celebration of our own,' Bella told him softly, putting her hand over his as he reached for the gear shift.

'Thought we'd take this pretty little baby for a bit of a spin, go try out her paces,' Alan told her, annoyingly ignoring the opportunity she had just given him to suggest that they take advantage of the dance to announce their engagement.

'A spin? I've already told my mother that you'll be coming home with me for tea,' Bella protested, not liking this change to her carefully arranged plan, which had involved discussing their engage-ment in front of her parents as though it were already a fact.

Bella had learned as a child that the best way to get round her father's ever-ready veto of anything that involved him spending any money was to simply behave as though the issue had already been discussed and agreed. She had never ever asked, 'Please may I have ballet lessons?' but had stated instead, 'When I start my ballet lessons . . .' It was a trick she had borrowed from her mother and it worked.

Since so far Alan had been oblivious to her hints about their getting engaged, she had changed her tactics and begun to talk about their engagement as though it were an accepted fact and the question not so much 'if' as 'when'.

As a soon-to-be-engaged couple it was natural and wise that they both spent time with one another's family. Irritatingly, Alan's parents had not yet extended their invitations beyond casual visits to their home to a proper formal tea party, as Bella felt they should have done, a mistake for which they would pay once she was married to Alan. However, her own parents, especially her mother, were much more up to the mark, and Mummy had been briefed that Bella was expecting Alan to 'have something special to ask me very soon'.

'Your mother won't mind if we change our minds,' Alan told her carelessly, adding, 'Trixie would have jumped at the chance to come with me.'

'Trixie?' Bella questioned sharply. 'When did you see her?'

'She'd called round to see my mother. Something about her own mother and the WVS.'

Bella thought she had successfully seen off the other girl weeks ago, so Alan's casual comment about seeing her was not something she wanted to hear, especially not when the place where he had seen her was his own home. It was unthinkable that Alan's parents could possibly prefer Trixie as a daughter-in-law to her. And certainly impossible that Alan should think of her as his wife!

'Yes, you're right, I'm sure that Mummy will understand,' Bella allowed graciously, before adding in a mock-little-girl voice, 'Of course, I shall expect to be properly rewarded for sharing you with your new car when I thought I was going to have you all to myself.'

The words might be little-girl lisped and sugar sweet but the look she was giving him was pure Salome and she could see from his smile that he recognised that.

'I'm so glad that you won't have to go and be part of this horrid war – if it does happen,' she told him, changing the subject.

'My father's made sure that there's no way I'll be called up if it does,' Alan boasted. 'With him being a Master Builder and me working for him, we're both in reserved occupations, and besides, Dad has plenty of contacts, thanks to him being on the council, and plenty of work coming in as well, what with people wanting shelters put up and walls and that reinforced just in case. I can't for the life of me understand chaps like Seb who go and volunteer when they don't need to.'

Bella nodded her head and tried not to look as bored as she felt. The means by which the money was earned to pay for her new dresses and everything else her family enjoyed was not something that interested her, and once she and Alan were married she intended to make sure that he understood that.

A couple of hours later they were deep in the Cheshire countryside, and Bella was beginning to feel increasingly bored with Alan's monologue about the attributes of his new car.

'I want to talk about us, not your car,' she protested, pouting. 'You haven't told me how nice I look or said you love me, not once since you picked me up.'

'Of course I love you,' Alan told her carelessly, suddenly braking and pulling the car off the main road and on to a rutted cart track that had plainly not been used in a long time. Several yards down it, he stopped the car beneath the branches of a full-leafed oak tree.

'Alan,' Bella protested as she realised that they were enveloped in dense greenery and hidden from sight.

'Come on,' he told her, as he reached over and put his arm around her. 'Don't act all coy on me now, Bella, not when you've been throwing out such tempting hints. You're far too pretty for a chap to be able to resist, and you know it,' he added, bending his head to kiss her.

'Say you love me first,' Bella pouted, holding him off.

'Of course I love you.'

Satisfied, Bella allowed him to kiss her, mentally imagining how she would show off her ring at work.

But when Alan started to fondle her breasts and then to unbutton the front of her dress, she tensed and tried to push him away. He was breathing hard, a glazed expression in his eyes, his face flushed. She had never realised before *quite* how much he looked like his father.

'No,' she told him, but he ignored her, pushing down her brassiere to squeeze and press her naked breast whilst he kissed her so roughly that her mouth hurt.

This, though, was the price she must pay to be Alan's wife; the price every woman paid to get the husband she wanted, Bella told herself. Men who were as popular as Alan was needed a bit of an inducement to help them to recognise which girl they should choose.

Not that she intended to let Alan go 'too far'. Her mother had warned her about the dangers of that when she had told her the story of her own two sisters and how one of them had ended up married to a man with no money and no prospects, whilst the other had not married at all.

A well-to-do husband was the goal every woman needed to achieve if she wanted a comfortable life, and it was in part so that she could have the chance to do that that her mother had nagged her father into moving to a better part of Wallasey, Bella knew. So if getting that husband meant pretending she was enjoying Alan's intimacies when she wasn't, then that was exactly what she would do.

Alan's hand was on her thigh now, and edging towards the hem of her skirt. Bella trapped it where it was, preventing him from moving it, but he pulled away and then touched her again, this time catching her off guard as he pressed his hand into the V between the top of her legs. Shock and revulsion jolted through her. His hand felt heavy and hot and unpleasantly damp, even through her clothes, and she shuddered to imagine what it would feel like if he was actually touching her flesh.

Thinking about being engaged to Alan and showing off her ring produced the most deliciously exciting tingling feeling right through her body but enduring his physical touch made her freeze.

'Come on,' she could hear him demanding thickly. 'Come on, Bella . . . Let me.'

'Don't be silly. You know that I can't until we're properly engaged.'

To Bella's relief he released her immediately. Even better, he shifted back to his own half of the car instead of leaning all over her.

'Engaged?'

'Yes. You know, Alan, I do think that we really ought to go public soon. My parents keep dropping hints and I know that my father is expecting a visit from you. After all, you've said how much you love me, and you know that I love you. Of course we must get engaged.'

Determinedly Bella stressed the word 'must', straightening her clothes at the same time to underline her meaning.

Alan's face was still flushed, and there was an unfamiliar and very stubborn look in his eyes. Bella gave a small gasp as, without a word, Alan started to reverse the car back out on to the main road. Things weren't going the way she had expected and planned at all. Bella quickly dismissed her unease. What was there to feel uneasy about, after all? Alan must want to marry her. How could he not do when, as her mother was always telling her, she was so very pretty.

Even so, Alan was behaving very selfishly and she had a good mind to tell him so, but she was also aware of how often her own mother allowed her father to get away with the same kind of selfish behaviour, and then made him pay for it later. There could be no question, of course, about Alan not proposing to her and that was all that really mattered. There would be plenty of time for him to learn the error of his ways once she had his ring on her finger, Bella decided determinedly.

THREE

'Here you are, you two,' Grace smiled, handing the twins a bag of broken biscuits she had bought on her way home. 'It's them iced gems you like and some other iced fancies.'

'Now don't you go eating those before you've had your teas,' Jean warned them.

Grace pulled a face and said, 'Sorry, Mum, I should have waited and given them to them later.'

'It's all right, love,' Jean assured her eldest daughter, as the twins opened the back door and hurried out into the garden. 'It was a kind thought to treat them. You're a good girl, Grace.'

At her mother's praise Grace's eyes stung with tears. She went over to her and hugged her tightly.

'Everyone's talking about what might happen if it does come to war, Mum. One of the women from Foundation Garments was crying her eyes out in the cloakroom today, 'cos she was having to get her kiddies ready to be evacuated.'

Jean looked through the kitchen window at

the twins sitting on the double swing Sam had built for them when they were younger. Lou's arm was round Sasha's waist, and their heads were together as they examined the contents of the biscuit bag.

'Me and your dad have talked about what we should do for the best for the twins, and your dad reckons that we'll be safe enough up here, seeing as we're a fair distance from the docks and that. It's like I told him, I couldn't let them go off on their own, not for anything I couldn't, even though they reckon that they as will be taking the kiddies in will look after them like they was their own. And I'm not minded to leave your dad and you and Luke neither.'

'Bella said that Auntie Vi said that Jack was to be evacuated.'

'Well, that's their business, I suppose,'

Grace could tell from her mother's expression that she didn't approve but she also knew that her mother would not want to criticise her sister openly.

Jean glanced back through the window. The twins were engrossed in whatever it was they were saying to one another. Had she and Vi ever been that close? She supposed they must have been. She hoped when her two grew up they didn't grow apart like she and Vi had done.

She looked round her small kitchen. Vi would turn her nose up at it, but Jean loved her neat small house and all the memories it held. Everything in her home had a special place in her heart, and an equally precious memory attached to it.

One of the first things Sam had done when they had first moved in was put a lovely new gas geyser on the wall next to the sink so that she could have hot water whenever she needed it. There'd already been one in the bathroom over the bath, although now they'd got a nice new electric immersion heater in its own cupboard, put in for them by one of Sam's pals in the Salvage Corps.

Only last year they'd repainted the kitchen in a pretty bright yellow, and Sam had put down new linoleum, a piece he'd got cheap when they were doing a salvage job at a warehouse – a lovely pattern it had on it too, and there'd been enough left over to do the bathroom as well.

She'd managed to get the end of a roll of fabric to make new curtains: yellow with a big red straw-berry pattern on it.

She'd been desperate for a proper dining-room table and some chairs once the twins were out of their high chairs, and she'd been thrilled to bits when Sam had taken her to a second-hand shop to show her the oak table he'd seen there, espe-cially when the shop owner had shown her the two leaves that pulled out to double its size. A set of chairs being sold off as salvage had joined the table in the back room, and then a sideboard. She and Sam had reupholstered the chairs them-selves.

Vi's house might be full of expensive things, but

hers was full of love, Jean told herself stoutly, and she'd sooner have that any day of the week.

'Set the table for me, will you, Grace? Your dad and our Luke will be in soon. I've got a nice bit of ham, the last bit on the bone so Mr Gregory let me have it a bit cheaper. There's enough for tomorrow's sandwiches.'

'I'll just run upstairs and get changed, Mum, and then I'll come and give you a hand,' Grace told her.

She'd been debating whether or not to say anything to her mother about what Sister Harris had said to her. She desperately wanted her parents to know how Sister Harris had complimented her but at the same time she didn't want them thinking she was upset because she couldn't go nursing.

Back downstairs, she started to set the table for their evening meal. The radio was on and when Gracie Fields starting singing, Jean sighed. She had been washing a lettuce but now she stopped, turning off the cold tap and turning to Grace.

'I wonder how your Auntie Francine is getting on in America.'

'Didn't she say anything in the card she sent for your birthday?' Grace asked.

'Only that she's working hard and that there's a lot of sunshine. But then she's never been one to say very much, unless it's to make a bit of a joke of things. Oh, that's your dad and Luke back, and they'll be wanting their teas. Go and call the twins in for us, will you, love?'

'Teatime, you two. And you'd better make sure you eat it otherwise you'll get me into trouble,' Grace warned her siblings, 'and then I won't bring you any more biscuits.'

'Aww, Grace.' Sasha pulled a face whilst Lou giggled and demanded, 'Look at this, Grace,' and then licked one of the iced gems and stuck it on her face. 'If I go to school like this do you think Miss Richards will send me home sick?'

'More like she'll keep you behind and have you writing out lines,' Grace warned her, grimacing when Louise removed the biscuit and sucked the icing off before eating the biscuit base.

'Come on, and don't forget to wash your hands.'

'What's this about you telling folk we're on the breadline?'

Jean frowned at the grim note in Sam's voice. It was rare for him to get angry with his children, especially Grace, who had always been such an eager-to-please girl, but Jean could see that he was angry now.

Grace put down her knife and fork, her stomach tensing. 'I never said that, Dad.'

Ignoring her, Sam continued, 'Captain Allen came to see me today. He said as how Sister Harris had told him she'd recommended that you should train as a nurse but that you'd said that your dad was too poor to pay for your training.'

Jean looked anxiously from her husband's face to her daughter's.

Grace flushed and bit her lip, tears welling in

her eyes. 'I'm sorry, Dad; I didn't mean to do anything wrong, but—'

'Well, you can go back and tell her that I've said you'd no business talking to her about our private family business.'

'I'm sure Grace didn't mean any harm, Sam,' Jean tried to intercede.

'Mebbe not, but she's caused plenty.'

Pushing back her chair, Grace stood up, demanding shakily, 'Well, what was I supposed to say? You've always told us we've got to tell the truth and with Sister Harris saying that she was going to put me forward for training . . .'

Unable to finish her sentence, Grace turned and ran out of the room and up the stairs in tears.

Everyone round the table had gone silent.

Sam pushed away his plate. 'I'm going to the allotment.'

'All right, you two, no leaving this table until you've finished your teas,' Jean told the twins, smiling gratefully at Luke as he continued to eat.

She had to wait until Luke had gone out to his ARP meeting and the twins were back outside in the garden before she could go up to Grace.

'I'm sorry, Mum,' Grace apologised tearfully, 'but I was that taken by surprise when Sister Harris said about me training as a nurse.'

'I understand, love, and so I'm sure does your dad really, but men have their pride, you know, especially your dad.'

'I was going to tell you about it before tea . . . I wish that I had now,' Grace admitted.

'Well, then, in future you'll know better, won't you? Now dry your eyes and come downstairs and do the washing up for me, will you? I've got to go out.'

Grace tried not to look surprised. Her mother never went out in the evening unless it was to pop round to see a neighbour.

Jean stood watching Sam for a few seconds. He had his back to her, bending over his spade as he turned over the soil, his movements sure and steady.

On the raspberry canes at the far end of the neat allotment the fruit was beginning to ripen. In front of the raspberries, cloches covered a neat line of cucumbers. In the small greenhouse were the tomatoes that were Sam's pride and joy, and alongside the greenhouse the immaculately tended beds filled with lettuce, radish and the like.

Nearly half the allotment was given over to Sam's potatoes, and the green tufts of the carrots marked the place where the summer crop finished and the autumn veggies began.

Sam had taken on a second allotment with three other men on which they were planning to keep chickens under the small orchard of fruit trees they had planted there.

The evening air was full of the scent of the nightstock that had seeded itself in the small bed next to his rose-covered tool shed where Sam germinated the flowers that Jean loved.

Jean opened the gate to the allotments and walked down the neat path that divided Sam's. He must have heard her coming because he stopped work and turned round, shading his eyes from the evening sun.

'I've brought you a ham sandwich,' she told him. 'You can't go working like that without something to give you a bit of energy.'

She sat down on the wooden bench he had built years ago when he had first got the allotment and she had been carrying Grace. She'd come down here many a sunny afternoon and evening then, bringing Luke in his pushchair so that she could sit and talk to Sam as he worked.

His brusque, 'How's Grace?' eased relief into Jean's anxiety. She knew him so well and she could guess how he was feeling right now. Sam loved his children and she knew that Grace's tears would have upset him, no matter how angry he was feeling.

'She's upset, just like you are. She got caught on the hop when Sister Harris said she wanted to put her up for proper nursing training. You know how she's always wanted to be a nurse.' She bent down to pull out a piece of chickweed that must have escape Sam's normally keen eye for weeds, before admitting, 'I blame meself really, Sam. I'm the one that's always told her that money doesn't grow on trees, and with the four of them to feed you can't be expected to pay for expensive treats. She's been a good girl, you know that, always bringing home little treats, as well as giving me a fair bit of her wages. Mind you, like I've told her, it was wrong of her going saying what she did without talking it over with us first.'

'Wrong? Aye, it were that all right. I do me best, Jean. It's bad enough having ruddy Edwin and that sister of yours looking down their noses at us, without me own daughter . . .'

Sam turned back to his digging.

So that was it! Jean had known that something more than Grace's admission that she didn't think her family could afford to pay for her training had got him all wrought-up.

It was hard for a proud decent man like her Sam, who had grafted all his life, to see men like Edwin smirking and sneering, just because they'd done better for themselves.

'Well, as to that, I wouldn't swap my life for our Vi's – not for anything, I wouldn't. I reckon you're in the right of it, love, when you say that Edwin hasn't come by his money as honestly as he might have done.'

Sam stopped digging and turned to look at her. 'It gets my goat, it really does, having to listen to him boasting about what he's done and what they've got,' he admitted reluctantly. 'It makes me feel like I've let you and our kids down, Jean. I saw the look on our Luke's face when young Charlie was talking about that car of his.' He gave a bitter laugh. 'All our Luke's got is a bike.'

'Sam Campion, I'm ashamed of you,' Jean scolded

him. 'Luke's never given that car of Charlie's a second thought, I know that for a fact. It's that Charlie's joined the TA he minds. We've brought our four up to know better than that. Come and sit down here with me, love,' she told him, patting the seat next to her and then reaching for his hand.

'I'll tell you straight that I couldn't live like our Vi does – not for a minute, I couldn't. I was only telling meself when we came back after visiting them how glad I was to get home. And I'll tell you something else. I'm the one who's got the better husband, and it isn't just me that thinks so. Our Francine's always said that. You're a good man, Sam Campion, and I've never for a minute regretted saying yes when you asked me to marry you. A decent honest hard-working husband who loves his family.'

Sam squeezed her hand and then wiped his free hand across his eyes.

Jean gave him a minute to get himself back under control before continuing calmly, 'I've bin thinking. I've got a bit put by out of the house-keeping you give me; especially with you giving me a bit more since you had that rise just after Christmas. I reckon we can afford for our Grace to do her training. She was only doing her best love, not wanting this Sister Harris to go making plans and then her having to say she couldn't do it. She's thoughtful like that, is Grace. She's always wanted to be a nurse – you know that – but she's settled herself down at Lewis's and made the best of it. I've been ever so proud of the way she's set to to do her bit for the war effort and I know you are too. It's a real compliment to her and to us that she's been recommended for proper training, but bless her, she's never so much as said or boasted about it.'

A couple of sparrows were fighting over a worm Sam's digging had unearthed.

'Well, you're right about that, love,' Sam admitted, 'but I felt that ashamed when Captain Allen came in and said in front of everyone how it were a crying shame that she couldn't do her training on account of me not being able to afford to pay for it.'

Jean's heart swelled with wifely indignation.

'If you ask me it's that captain who should be feeling ashamed, speaking out in public like that without him knowing the full story, about how our Grace had got it wrong and had not wanted to put her dad to any extra expense, not knowing that he'd already got something put aside just in case. Of course, not all parents are like us and try to bring up their children to respect money and to understand that it doesn't grow on trees, and I shall say as much too when I see Elsie Norris tomorrow up at the shops.'

'That old gossip?'

Ignoring him, Jean continued determinedly, 'In fact if I was you, Sam, I'd say the same to a couple of them as you work with, and them that's in the ARP with you as well. No need to say too much, mind. Just a bit of a casual mention.'

Sam shook his head, but he was smiling as well.

'I can see you've got it all worked out. I've allus said that you've got a clever head on your shoulders, Jean.'

'Well, I was clever enough to marry you,' she agreed, 'but any woman would want to do her best for her family. That's only natural. Grace is ever so upset, love,' she added quietly. 'Cried her eyes out, she has. She thinks the world of you, you know that.'

'Perhaps I was a bit hard on her, but she should have said summat to us first instead of going and doing what she did.'

Jean knew when to let things rest. Sam had his sticking points and what man had ever liked admitting he was wrong?

'She's learned her lesson, love, and, like I said, she didn't mean any harm. You know what I think?'

Sam was looking at her with a twinkle in his eyes now. 'No, but I reckon you're about to tell me.'

'I reckon it would be a very good thing indeed if you went along with Grace to the next meeting and had a word with this Sister Harris yourself. Explained to her, like, that Grace had got it wrong, and told her how proud you are to have Grace being offered such a chance.'

The last rays of sunshine were warming the greenhouse roof.

'That way you'd be able to ask her a few questions as well, and find out exactly what's going to be involved. Grace said something about her having to live in, and if that's the case then we'll have a spare room to let out.'

Sam was grinning now. 'You think of everything,' he told her admiringly.

'Well,' Jean told him practically, 'it would be daft to have a room standing empty when it could be being used. I've said as much to Grace and told her as well that if she'd come to us first, we could have discussed everything properly and without all this upset.'

It would help to soothe Sam's sore pride if he thought that she held Grace more to blame than him. Poor Sam. Jean could well understand how having to listen to Edwin's boasting had upset him.

Luke aimed a morose kick at the pebble in the middle of the pavement. It was just so ruddy unfair. Why couldn't he make his dad understand how he felt? All the lads he knew, the ones he'd gone through Scouts and then the Boys' Brigade Band with, were in uniform now, all grinning broadly as they talked excitedly about doing their bit, whilst everyone clustered round them, especially the girls, especially Pam Harrison. Luke's scowl deepened. He stuffed his hands in his pockets and slouched along the road.

He'd seen the looks they were giving him, looks that said he hadn't got the guts to join up. Even ruddy Charlie was in uniform, although from what he said, he'd no intention of doing any fighting.

'Fool's game, that is, mate,' he'd told Luke cheerfully.

There was no point in talking to his mum either. Normally he could rely on her to intercede for him with his dad, but everyone knew how mums were about this war. He'd already heard more tales than he wanted to remember from those who had joined up, talking about their mothers' tears and protests.

'Like I told me mam,' Pete Riley, one of the other apprentices, had boasted only yesterday, after announcing he was joining the RAF, 'I'm a man now, leastways that's what the Government says. Mind you, I'm not saying there aren't some advantages . . .' He had grinned and winked before continuing, 'That little redhead I've been running around after for the last six months is all over me like a rash now. Course, if me mam knew that she'd be making even more of a fuss.'

It was all very well for his father to talk about the importance of him getting into the Salvage Corps and saying that even if there was a war it wouldn't last for ever, and he didn't want to be in the same position as them what had come back from the last time with no job to go to.

'You'll be doing your bit, don't you worry about that, son,' he had told Luke. But to Luke the thought of working on dull salvage operations when all his friends were going to be heroes in smart uniforms, was one that only made him feel more desperate to join them.

He was beginning to suspect that even his boss thought he was a coward. There, he'd said it, the word that no one was saying but that he knew everyone was thinking. He could see it in their eyes when they refused to look at him properly and the way conversation stopped whenever he walked in on the lads he had grown up with.

'You want me to what?'

Bella looked at her brother. They were sitting in his car outside their parents' house, Charlie having brought Bella back from the Tennis Club.

'You heard me, Charlie.'

He shook his head. 'If you want to try and force Alan's hand then you go ahead, but don't involve me in it.'

Bella looked at her brother with irritation. Did he really think that she'd have bothered involving him if she didn't have to?

She had been furious when Alan had refused to come in with her after bringing her home, and even more furious when he had told her casually that he couldn't stay because his parents were entertaining Trixie's mother and father and that he was expected to be there.

She had every right to expect him to marry her, and somehow she'd find a way of making sure that he did.

It hadn't taken her long to come up with a plan, but in order for it to work she needed Charlie's help and now he was being difficult. Well, she had the answer to that.

'Of course I've got to involve you in it; other-wise it isn't going to work, is it? How can you make a big fuss about Alan having to do the decent thing by me 'cos you've caught him out doing what he shouldn't with me, if you aren't involved?'

'I still say it won't work.'

A familiar stubborn look had tensed Charlie's face and an equally familiar truculent note had entered his voice, but Bella was determined to get her own way.

'Yes it will,' she overruled him. 'Look, all you have to do is come outside and find us, like I've just told you. And don't forget, make sure you bring someone with you, like Mr Baxter.'

Charlie forgot about being stubborn, and twisted uncomfortably in his seat instead. 'He's the President of the Tennis Club,' he protested.

'I know that. And he's a neighbour of Alan's parents, as well,' said Bella smugly, before returning to her plan. 'I'll be there crying, telling Alan to stop, and you can make a big fuss,' she informed her brother. 'Then I'll say that Alan and I are engaged, and that he forgot himself a bit in the excitement of me saying yes.'

'I'm not doing it.' Charlie was determined and adamant but he was no match for Bella.

'Yes, you are, Charlie,' she told him sweetly, 'because if you don't then I'll tell Dad about that little bit of business you've been doing without him knowing anything about it, and you pocketing the money.'

'How do you know about that?' Charlie cursed as he saw the look of triumph on her face.

Bella had always been a sly cat, and never more so than when she wanted something. He pitied Alan Parker if he did end up married to her. Bella had got him well and truly trapped now and no mistake. He'd have to go along with her stupid plan because if he didn't he knew she would make good her threat.

Sisters! He'd just as soon not have had one.

FOUR

'Phew, I was beginning to think we were never going to get finished,' Grace sighed in relief as she and Susan hurried down the staff staircase of Lewis's and out into the early evening sunshine.

A last-minute message from Bella had meant that instead of getting changed at her Auntie Vi's, Grace had had to change into her cotton frock in the cloakroom at Lewis's, whilst Susan eyed her critically and gave her advice on her hair and makeup.

'Are you sure I'm not wearing too much lipstick,' she asked her uncertainly, 'only—'

'Of course you aren't. You wait until some chap starts trying to kiss you, you'll be glad you've put a bit extra on then,' Susan assured her without explaining the logic of her statement.

'Real mean of that cousin of yours, it was, to say you had to go ready-dressed, especially when she'd said first off you was to change at her place. I wouldn't stand for it meself.'

'I am beginning to wish that I hadn't said I'd

go,' Grace admitted. All she could really think of at the moment was the excitement of knowing that she was going to train to be a proper nurse.

'Well, you are going,' Susan told her, 'and what's more you're going to put that cousin of yours well and truly in her place when she sees you in this.'

Grace's eyes rounded in disbelief when Susan rummaged in the large bag she was carrying and produced a paper bag, which she opened to show Grace the green silk dress that was inside it.

'Here, go on, take it,' she commanded, pushing the bag towards Grace.

'Oh, no, I couldn't, Susan.'

'Of course you can, and you'd ruddy well better an' all after all the trouble I've bin to to get it for you. You'll look a real treat in it and no mistake. I just wish I could be there to see the face on that snotty cousin of yours when she sees you in it.'

Susan had really taken a dislike to Bella, Grace acknowledged.

'You can get changed into it in the ladies in Lyons. I'll come with you and give you a hand.'

'No, Susan, I can't, honestly.'

'Come on,' Susan ignored her protests as she took hold of Grace's hand and virtually dragged her along the road and into Lyons.

Half an hour later Grace was staring at her reflection in the mirror, feeling horribly guilty and ungrateful, whilst Susan puffed out her cheeks and demanded, 'Now aren't you pleased I got it for you?'

Susan was so pleased with herself, and Grace

knew that she had wanted to be kind. It seemed mean not to thank her.

'It is a lovely dress,' she agreed. 'But taking it from the Gown Salon—'

'Oh, give over, do. Like I told you, everyone does it, even Mrs James, I reckon.'

'She never!' Grace protested, diverted.

'Come on, you'd better get a move on, otherwise you're going to be late.'

With her own dress packed away along with her work clothes, Grace hugged Susan and then picked up her now quite heavy bag.

It was good job that her stole and her evening bag were both white and didn't clash with the silk gown, she decided, feeling very self-conscious as she waved goodbye to Susan and set off for the ferry terminal.

'Just you remember what we agreed,' Bella told Charlie as she came downstairs, giving him a warning look before opening the lounge door and stepping inside.

'What do you think, Mummy?' she asked, doing a small pirouette in the new ice-blue gown she had persuaded her mother to buy her for the dance, whilst Charlie grimaced.

'You look beautiful, darling. What time is Alan picking you up? I thought that Daddy and I would ask him in for a drink before you go. We really ought to have his parents round for a bit of supper soon.'

'He should be here soon, but he'll have that

wretched cousin of his with him, don't forget.'
Bella pulled a face. 'Seb and Grace will have to
go to the Club with Charlie. There won't be room
in Alan's car.'

'There won't be room in mine either,' Charlie
protested, but neither his mother nor his sister was
listening to him.

'There's the doorbell now,' Vi announced.

'There's no car outside, though. I expect it will
only be Grace,' Bella said carelessly. 'You'd better
go and let her in, Charlie.'

If Grace hadn't already been feeling self-
conscious and guilty because of the attention her
frock had attracted during her journey to her
aunt's, the look on Charlie's face when he opened
the door to her would have certainly made her feel
both those things.

'I say . . .' he told her, giving a long appreciative whistle. 'Bags I the first dance with you, cos.'

'Charlie, hurry up and close the door. I don't
want you standing there when Alan arrives. It looks
awfully common.'

'Hark at her ladyship,' Charlie grinned, cocking
his head in the direction of the lounge door. 'Gawd
knows what she's going to be like once she gets
Alan's ring on her finger.'

'Come on, we'd better do as she says.'

Grace always felt a bit uncomfortable around
her aunt and uncle, and now she really was wishing
she hadn't agreed to come, what with the dress
and everything. She'd been tempted to change out
of it at the landing stage, but there'd been a queue

for the ladies and another one at the other end, so she'd pushed her guilt to one side and got on the bus instead.

Now, though, as she stepped into the lounge and its two occupants went completely silent as they stared at her, Grace wished that she had managed to get changed.

'Where did you get that dress from?' Bella demanded without bothering to welcome her.

'A friend lent it to me,' Grace told her. She knew that her face had gone red. Bella was giving her a narrow-eyed look whilst her mother was looking very cross indeed.

'Well, I must say I'm surprised that anyone would want to lend out such an expensive-looking gown,' said Vi.

'Yes, so am I,' Bella agreed.

'I'm not sure that wearing it was a wise decision, though, Grace dear,' her aunt announced patronisingly. 'You don't look very comfortable in it. That's always the trouble when a girl tries too hard and steps out of her own class. It always shows.'

'Alan's here, Mummy. Just remember,' Bella hissed at Grace as her mother went into the hall, 'it's Seb you'll be partnering, so that me and Alan can have a bit of time to ourselves, so don't start hanging around me all night. Charlie's going to drive you and Seb there, aren't you, Charlie?'

Without waiting for her brother to reply, Bella turned to check her reflection in the mirror above the new tiled fireplace, whilst her mother went to answer the door.

Grace couldn't help noticing the speed with which Bella's cross expression and demanding voice changed the moment her mother called out, 'Bella darling, Alan's here.' Almost miraculously a smile replaced her earlier frown, her voice as soft and sweet as fresh cream as she jerked her head warningly to Grace, mouthing, 'Come on' before hurrying into the hallway.

To Grace's surprise Alan Parker, instead of being the swooningly handsome matinée idol type she had imagined, was a rather ordinary-looking young man of around medium height and build, with a pugnacious expression, slightly protruding pale blue eyes, and brown hair.

'Seb, do come inside properly and be introduced to my cousin,' Bella instructed the young man who was half hidden by the open front door. 'I should warn you that Grace isn't actually a member of the Tennis Club. She works in Lewis's,' Bella added disparagingly. 'I've told her that she's not to disgrace you, though.'

Grace could feel her face starting to burn with misery and humiliation, which was made even worse when her partner for the evening stepped into the hallway. Alan Parker's cousin was everything that Bella's boyfriend was not. He was tall, broad-shouldered and very good-looking, the uniform he was wearing making him look distinguished and smart, despite the fact that his leg was in plaster and he was having to use crutches. His hair was thick and dark and nicely barbered.

'I can see that your cousin is teasing us both,'

he told Grace, offering her both his hand and the kindest smile she had ever seen. It was so warm and understanding that she could feel her earlier misery melting away. 'And I'm going to be escorting the prettiest girl at the dance.'

Bella flashed them an angry look. 'You wouldn't say that if you could see her in her Lewis's uniform,' she tittered angrily. 'I really don't know how you can work there, Grace, especially with that horrid common girl who works in the Gown Salon with you.'

'Come on, Bella, otherwise we're going to be late,' Alan interrupted her irritably, thrusting a box containing a corsage of flowers towards her.

'Oh, how lovely. Look, Mummy, my favourite flower. Alan darling, you are so thoughtful.'

'Bet she ordered it herself and told him what she wanted,' Charlie muttered irrepressibly in Grace's ear as they all watched whilst Bella begged Alan with prettily sweet insistence to pin the corsage on for her.

'Thank you, darling,' she told him once he had finished, raising herself up on her tiptoes to kiss his cheek and then pouting when he rubbed his skin, protesting that she was covering him in lipstick.

'Seb, Charlie is taking you and Grace in his car. Grace can sit in the back so you'll have plenty of room for your crutches. Alan, come on, darling. I dare say that everyone will be waiting for us to arrive.' She gave a tinkling little laugh. 'It's so embarrassing, but everyone seems to take their lead from me and Alan. I suppose it's flattering really.'

'And entirely natural,' Grace heard her auntie Vi saying firmly.

'I'm really sorry that you've been forced to travel with us, instead of with your cousin,' Grace apologised to Seb.

'I'm not,' he told her cheerfully. 'In actual fact, Alan isn't my cousin. Our relationship is rather more tenuous than that. It's very good of his parents to put me up, though, whilst I wait for the medics to pronounce me fit for service. With any luck I should be off their hands by this time next week and back with my unit.'

They had reached Charlie's car, and Seb opened the door and told her cheerfully, 'There's no need for you to risk creasing your outfit clambering into the back. I'll sit there.'

'Oh, no, you mustn't,' Grace protested, but it was too late. Seb was already settling himself in the back of the car.

'This is going to be such a wonderful evening,' Bella told Alan, hanging on to his arm possessively as they walked from his car to the Tennis Club entrance. Through the open double doors it was possible to see into the square hallway, which was decorated with bunting in the Tennis Club colours and cleverly cut-out paper streamers of tennis racquets and balls. On a table underneath the central light stood an impressive floral arrangement provided by those mothers who were on the roster for the church flowers, the flowers in shades of red, white and blue, but Bella wasn't particularly interested in the effort the Social Committee had made to strike a cheery yet patriotic note in the décor for the dance. After all, she had far more important things on her mind than a few paper streamers and some flowers.

She breathed a deep sigh, keeping a firm hold on Alan as they went inside, whispering softly to him, 'When we're married and our children are growing up I shall tell them about tonight and how special it was.'

'Now look here, Bella—' Alan began grimly.

But Bella pretended not to be aware of what he was saying, exclaiming instead, 'Goodness, look over there at Trixie, queuing to get in. What an awful fright she looks, doesn't she? Poor girl. I really must give her a few tips about how to make the best of herself. Not that she's got much to make the best of, mind you. Did you tell your parents that mine want them to come over to supper tomorrow? Daddy is getting awfully father-like about young men who take liberties, and the fact that you haven't spoken to him yet,' she told Alan archly, 'but there's no need for you to worry. He's a pussycat really. Wasn't I clever inviting my cousin along for Seb, so that we could be on our own?'

'What exactly happened to your leg, or is it something you'd rather not talk about?' Grace asked Seb with genuine interest, as they walked towards the Tennis Club together.

Although he had made light of it she was pretty sure that Seb had been uncomfortable in the back of the car, which was why she was deliberately walking slowly, letting others overtake them to join what was now a small queue waiting to get into the Club. Charlie, too impatient to wait for them, had gone ahead, and had already disappeared inside the building, following Bella and Alan, who had gone inside before the queue had formed.

'On the contrary, I'd adore talking about it, especially to pretty girls,' Seb grinned. 'Or at least I would if the truth wasn't so very dull. I broke it on a training exercise,' he told Grace, bending down to whisper in her ear, 'but normally I tell people that I was engaged on a highly secret mission that I'm sworn not to talk about.'

Grace giggled. She was enjoying herself more with every minute she spent in Seb's company. She felt as comfortable with him as though she had known him all her life but at the same time something about the way he looked at her and the sound of his voice gave her a deliciously fizzy sensation inside her stomach that made her feel giddy and heady with excitement and happiness.

'What kind of break was it? I'm going to be training as a nurse soon, you see,' she explained when he gave her a quizzical look, 'so . . .'

'So naturally you find my leg utterly fascinating,' he agreed so straight-faced that it took Grace a handful of seconds to realise he was teasing her again and she burst out laughing.

'You're a dreadful tease,' she chided him, mock severely, 'and from now on I shan't take a single word that you say seriously.'

'Not even if I were to tell you that you are the most enchanting girl I have ever met?'

Grace stared at him, the colour coming and going in her face, her eyes wide with shyness and confusion. She wasn't used to men like Seb and she certainly wasn't used to them flirting with her.

Her parents were very careful and watchful, and normally the only boys with whom she had any social contact were those she had known since childhood. Seb wasn't just a boy, though, was he, she acknowledged. He was all grown up and a man. Her heart gave a flurry of fast beats.

Grace might not be very experienced but she had a good deal of common sense, so once her heart had returned to its normal beat she responded firmly, '*Especially* not if you were to tell me that. Is it the military hospital you have to go to about your leg?'

She wasn't aware of the rueful look Seb gave her as he looked down at the top of her head.

When he had been informed by Bella that her cousin would be his date for the evening, he had assumed she would be a young woman very much in Bella's own mould and had resigned himself to an evening of boredom, fending off the unwanted overcoy approaches of the kind of girl he most disliked.

Grace, though, was the complete antithesis of her manipulative little baggage of a cousin, and

Seb recognised that she had no idea just how enchanting she was or how very sweet he found her. Which was just as well, and the way it must stay. It would be all too easy to enjoy the sympathy of a girl as sweet as this one, and they had all been warned about the dangers of doing that.

In fact, there were an awful lot of things he and the young men who had been recruited with him had been warned against saying and doing, Seb reflected as he drew Grace gently to one side and reached into his pocket, saying ruefully, 'What an idiot I am. I nearly forgot this,' as he produced a delicate cream-flowered corsage. 'Shall I pin it on for you?'

Grace struggled between the warnings her mother had given her about not allowing young men to adopt overfamiliar behaviour towards her because of what it might ultimately lead to, and her own confusing sweet thrill of pleasure at the thought of accepting Seb's offer, before saying recklessly, 'Yes, please, if you wouldn't mind.'

Seb, who thought she had the sweetest and most expressive face he had ever seen, guessed what she had been thinking, especially when she had turned her head to look towards the cloakroom. When they had been told during their training that they needed to make the most of whatever opportunities came their way to facilitate their mission, he doubted that putting that training to use in this sort of fashion was what the RAF had had in mind, he acknowledged, as he stepped forward, his body screening Grace from everyone else in the entrance to the Tennis Club.

As he leaned forward to pin the corsage on the front of her frock he heard her catch her breath and felt her tremble slightly. His own hands trembled a bit themselves. She was just so irresistibly sweet, and it would have been the most natural thing in the world to take her in his arms and drop a light kiss on that pretty little nose of hers. But of course he must do no such thing. One of the requirements of his acceptance for his training had been that he should not be married or thinking of getting married. As they had all been warned, the chances of them surviving a war, given the secret nature of their work, were very slim indeed.

Bella and Alan had already found a table when Grace and Seb joined them.

Charlie had been to the bar and he winked at Alan as the waitress brought over their drinks, telling him, 'Got you a double G and T, seeing as Bella reckons you need a bit of Dutch courage to come up to the mark.'

Bella gave her brother an angry look. She could do without that kind of comment, thank you very much.

'Trixie's just come in.' Alan finished his drink, and started to stand up. 'She's on her own, so I'll go and tell her to come and join us.'

Immediately Bella made a grab for his jacket, hissing furiously, 'You'll do no such thing. What will people think? You're with me. Let her go and find her own partner. Anyway,' she told him, 'I want to dance.'

'Well, I want another drink. It's your turn to get the drinks in, Seb. I'll have another double.'

'What would you like to drink, Grace?' Seb asked her, smiling.

'Oh, a lemonade please.'

'A lemonade,' Bella mimicked unkindly. 'What a baby you are, Grace. I'll have a G and T, Seb.'

Grace tried not to look as shocked as she felt. Neither of her parents ever drank spirits, her mother only having the occasional port and lemon or a sherry at Christmas-time and her father sticking to beer.

'You really don't look at all comfortable in that dress, Grace,' Bella told. 'It doesn't suit you at all.'

'Stop being such a cat,' Charlie told his sister, unexpectedly coming to Grace's rescue. 'You're just jealous because Grace's dress looks better than yours.'

Grace could have sunk through the floor when she saw the look of fury on Bella's face, especially when Charlie's comment made Alan look more closely at her, and announce in a slightly slurred voice, 'Charlie's right, Bella.'

Grace didn't like her cousin's boyfriend, and even though she felt that Bella was behaving very badly, she still felt sorry for her.

'So you're going to train as a nurse, then?'

Grace nodded.

They had just finished eating their buffet meal, and she and Seb were alone at the table, Charlie having gone to join some friends at the bar whilst Bella and Alan were dancing.

'I didn't think that I'd be able to, not even when Sister Harris said that she wanted to put me forward, not with the twins still being at school and our Luke only an apprentice, but then Mum said she'd got a bit put by and Dad said that the country would be needing more nurses if there was to be a war,' Grace told him, her tongue slightly loosened by the shandy Charlie had insisted she have to drink.

Seb deduced from Grace's artless confidence that her parents were not in as comfortable circumstances as her cousins' family were. He had seen how both her cousins, but especially Bella, looked down on her, although in his opinion she was worth ten of the other girl.

Seb had no particular liking for the Parkers, but he had been grateful to them for putting him up whilst he was attending the local military hospital and waiting to be pronounced fit for duty.

He knew that both Alan's parents, but especially his mother, wanted Alan to drop Bella and go back to his previous girlfriend, Trixie, and it was equally obvious to him that Bella wasn't going to give Alan up without a fight.

'I'm sorry I can't ask you to dance,' he apologised to Grace. He was indeed sorry, for he would have loved the opportunity to hold her close. She really was the most adorable girl. It was perhaps just as well that he would be going back to join his unit soon.

* * *

Bella was in a foul mood. So far Alan had determinedly ignored every attempt she had made to bring the conversation round to the subject of their engagement. To make matters worse, now, whilst he was dancing with her, instead of holding her close as she was trying to get him to do, he was actually looking at Trixie. And there was Grace, whom she had only invited to come tonight out of pity, looking as though she was having the time of her life.

'What are you doing?' Bella demanded as Alan released her the second the music stopped, turning away from her.

'I'm going to go and ask Trixie to dance,' he answered her truculently.

Charlie had been plying him with double G and Ts all evening and now, as well as being slightly unsteady on his feet, his face was flushed and his behaviour belligerent. Bella could see her chance to achieve her goal slipping away from her. She looked round for Charlie. He was standing at the bar. She sent him a significant look, which he acknowledged by lifting his glass.

'Why don't you ask her later?' Bella suggested, forcing her lips into what she hoped was a sweet smile, before adding coaxingly, 'It's so hot in here. Why don't we go outside? We haven't been alone together all evening.' She moved closer to him, her voice softly suggestive.

Alan hesitated, still looking at Trixie, who, to Bella's relief, was now getting up to dance with someone.

'I suppose so,' Alan agreed unenthusiastically.

'Me and Alan are just slipping outside for a bit of fresh air,' Bella informed Grace almost aggressively, for once forgetting to use the 'posh' voice she normally favoured, and sounding far more like the Bella Grace remembered from when they had been much younger. Bella was holding on to Alan's arm, determined to make sure that he didn't escape from her.

'Oh, Bella, do you think you should?' Grace whispered. 'Only Alan seems to have had a lot to drink.'

'Like I just said, I need some fresh air,' Bella insisted, glaring at her. Was Grace stupid or what? Couldn't she take a hint? Didn't her cousin understand that she wanted to be alone with Alan?

'I'll come with you, if you like.'

Bella was furious. Grace was a stupid interfering prissy nobody. Her mother had been right to tell her not to invite her. Grace was already turning towards the exit and Bella seized her chance. Another few seconds and Alan would cotton on to what she had said and he'd be off to stand at the bar and watch his precious Trixie. Well, Bella wasn't having that! Grace needed to be stopped. Deliberately Bella brought her heel down on the hem of Grace's silk gown and kept it there so that when Grace tried to walk towards the door, one of the seams in the delicate panelling of the skirt ripped under the strain.

Grace gazed down at the tear in the back of her dress in shocked disbelief. Bella was shrugging and saying petulantly that it was her own fault for borrowing a dress that was too long for her and that she wasn't going to be blamed for the damage to it.

'Come on,' she commanded Alan firmly, ignoring Grace's distress. 'Let's go outside.'

Grace's eyes filled with tears. Where the seam had given way along one of the pretty bias-cut inserts in the skirt the fabric was torn and frayed in a way that she could see immediately was beyond mending.

Seb watched sympathetically. He was pretty sure that Bella had damaged Grace's frock deliberately.

'It may not be as bad as it looks,' he tried to comfort her as he tactfully led her back to their table out of sight of the curious glances she was attracting. 'I believe the Singer sewing machine can work wonders.'

Grace shook her head, beyond comfort. 'It can't be mended; the silk is too frayed. It isn't my dress.' Fresh tears welled in her eyes at the enormity of her predicament.

Discreetly Seb passed her a clean white handkerchief. 'I'm sure your friend will understand.'

Grace shook her head and gave a small sob, and burst out, 'I should never have worn it. Oh, I so wish that I had not. I knew it was wrong, and it serves me right that this has happened.'

Seb frowned. She was clearly very distressed, so much so that his protective instincts were automatically aroused.

'Your friend may be upset, but—'

'You don't understand. I've done a really dreadful thing.' Grace stopped him. 'It doesn't belong to a friend; it belongs to Lewis's Gown Salon, where I work.'

Seb's frown deepened. He wasn't sure just what the rules might be about borrowing clothes from the shop where one worked, but he suspected that it wasn't something that was normally allowed. Grace hadn't struck him as the kind of girl who would deliberately flout the 'law', but he could understand that a young woman who was looked down on by her better-off cousin could have been tempted to 'borrow' a rather grander frock than she might actually possess, even if he also felt rather disappointed to discover that Grace had given in to that kind of temptation.

Seb didn't allow any of what he was feeling to show, though, as he murmured something sympathetic and reassuring.

'I should never have listened to Susan,' Grace told him miserably. 'I knew it was wrong. But she'd gone to so much trouble and . . . and I didn't want to hurt her feelings by refusing. It serves me right for doing it,' she told him bravely, her face pale but set now that she had stopped crying.

'Perhaps the Shop will be able to have it repaired?' Seb suggested.

Grace shook her head. 'No, it can't be mended. I shall have to pay for it. We are allowed to buy things at staff discount so . . .' she gave a small gulp, 'they might let me pay for it weekly out of my wages, although it will take me for ever.'

'But I thought you were about to start training as a nurse,' Seb pointed out.

Grace swallowed and lifted her head proudly. 'I was, but I shan't be doing that now. Not with this frock to pay for, and . . . and I *want* to pay for it. What I did was very wrong. I knew that all along and, to be honest, I'd have much rather worn my own cotton dress. This is lovely but it isn't mine and it isn't me. I feel so very ashamed of myself. My parents will be shocked, I know.'

Poor child, she was paying a heavy price for her moment of natural vanity, Seb thought compassionately, his earlier assessment of her character reasserting itself as he listened to her quietly determined voice. She had guts, though, he thought with admiration.

Her whole future was ruined, Grace acknowledged, and all for the sake of being silly and for wearing a frock that she had no right to be wearing. She deserved to be punished.

What on earth was she going to say to her parents after the sacrifice they were prepared to make so that she could do her nurse's training. Grace had never felt more miserable and in despair.

Bella looked anxiously toward the Tennis Club. Where was Charlie? She had been out here with Alan in the thankfully still warm darkness of the small tree-shadowed garden that separated the Tennis Club building from the courts – a favourite place for Tennis Club 'courting couples', although tonight thankfully they had it to themselves – for what felt like for ever. She hated the revolting way he was slobbering all over her, and now the smell of his gin-laden breath was making her feel sick. He pawed at her breast, almost breaking one of the fragile shoulder straps of her dress. As it threatened to snap so too did Bella's temper. Where was Charlie?

'Aww, come on, Trixie,' Alan protested.

Trixie! He had called her Trixie. Furiously Bella tried to push him away, her determination to force him to marry her forgotten in the heat of her outrage, but he was refusing to let go of her.

'I'm not Trixie,' she told him

He gave her an ugly look. 'No, you aren't, more's the pity. If it wasn't for you she'd be with me and—'

'Here, I say, what the devil do you think you're doing, Parker? Let go of my sister.'

For once in her life Bella didn't have to manu-facture her reaction. She'd been so furious with Alan that she'd forgotten all about Charlie, who was now approaching them with Mr Baxter, the President of the Tennis Club, in tow. Mr Baxter had a very stern expression indeed on his face.

Henry Baxter was in his fifties, a bachelor, and the Chief Clerk to the local council. He had rather a soft spot for Bella, being completely taken in by the flatteringly admiring manner she adopted towards him.

Bella immediately played up to the situation, sobbing some crocodile tears on Charlie's shoulder whilst Henry Baxter took a firm grip on Alan's arm and refused to let him go.

'Please don't be cross with Alan, Charlie,' she begged her brother dramatically. 'It's my fault. We've been talking about getting engaged for so long that when Alan suggested that we come outside, I thought it was because he wanted to surprise me with an engagement ring.'

Bella could hear Alan's enraged denial, but Charlie stepped in smartly, announcing, 'Well, if you're engaged . . . although I have to say that this isn't the kind of behaviour a chap expects from his brother-in-law-to-be, Parker, and I dare say my father will have some pretty sharp words to say to you. It looks to me as though you've terrified the life out of poor Bella.'

'I feel so ashamed,' Bella wept. 'What will people think? Oh, Mr Baxter . . .'

'There, there, my dear,' Henry Baxter comforted Bella. 'Don't know what you thought you were about, Parker, bringing Miss Firth out here instead of formally announcing your engagement inside, like any decent well-brought-up young man would.'

Alan swore. 'I'm not getting engaged to her,' he began, hiccuping, and then turned away to be sick on the grass, before adding, 'and no one can make me.'

''Fraid you've no choice now, old chap,' Charlie told Alan. 'I dare say my father will have a thing or two to say about the way you've behaved towards my sister, and it won't stop there, not now. Not the done thing at all to trifle with the affections of an innocent girl, especially when there's about to be a war on.'

'I shall be speaking to your parents about your

behaviour tonight, Parker,' Henry Baxter told Alan sternly. 'We do not tolerate this sort of thing here at the Tennis Club.'

'Oh, Alan,' Bella gave her new fiancé a reproachful look, 'I'm so disappointed. I thought tonight was going to be so special and romantic, and now you've gone and spoiled it all. Still, at least we're engaged.

'Do you think we *should* make an announcement, Mr Baxter?' Bella appealed to the President. 'Only I'd hate people to think badly of Alan. I'm sure he didn't mean to . . . to . . . well, I know he would have made things official tonight if he'd had time to get me a ring as we'd planned.'

'An excellent idea, my dear. Parker, you are a very fortunate young man to have such a loyal and beautiful fiancée – far more so than you deserve. But your father will still be hearing from me,' Baxter added grimly.

'Bitch. Bitch.' Alan swore at Bella the minute the President was out of sight. 'As for me marrying you . . . you can go to hell . . .'

'Here, I'm not letting you get away with insulting my sister like that,' Charlie warned Alan, 'and if you've taken more liberties with her than you should then—'

Bella started to cry loudly. 'I didn't want to let him, Charlie,' she sobbed, 'but I couldn't stop him, and he promised me he wanted to marry me.'

There, let Alan try and get out of that, Bella thought triumphantly as she sobbed on her brother's shoulder.

* * *

101

Grace was feeling increasingly uncomfortable. Bella and Alan had been missing for ages, and now Charlie had disappeared as well. She could see the speculative looks their now almost empty table was attracting.

'Oh, here's Bella now!' she exclaimed in relief as she finally saw her cousin coming back into the room, followed by Charlie and Alan. Charlie had his arm round Alan's shoulders whilst Alan himself looked dishevelled and was staggering slightly.

Ignoring Grace and Seb, Charlie urged Alan on to the dance floor, taking hold of both Alan's hand and Bella's as he held them up in the air and shouted, 'Congratulate the lucky man, everyone. Alan here has just got himself engaged to my sister.'

From right cross the floor Bella could see the white shocked look on Trixie's face as Charlie made his announcement. She had won, Bella acknowledged gleefully. Alan was hers. He had to marry her now.

'Sorry I can't give you a lift back, old chap, but there's this girl, you see. I'm sure you understand,' Charlie told Seb drunkenly as everyone started to file out of the Club at the end of the evening.

'What about your cousin? Surely you don't expect her to make her own way back to your parents' house?' Seb challenged Charlie.

'Oh, Grace ain't staying with us. No, she's going home. You'll be able to catch the last bus down to the ferry if you're quick, Grace.'

Seb was astounded and disgusted by Charlie's

lack of concern for Grace's safety, but at the same time he acknowledged that he hadn't been looking forward to being driven by Charlie after witnessing just how much he had had to drink.

Grace was glad that the evening was at an end. She felt so ashamed of herself, and wasn't surprised that Seb had gone so quiet after the announcement of Bella and Alan's engagement.

They were outside now. For some reason Grace didn't entirely understand, her aunt and uncle had arrived shortly after the announcement of Bella's engagement and had taken the newly engaged couple off with them whilst she had been changing into her own clothes ready for her journey home.

Charlie too had now deserted her, and she and Seb were alone. She turned to him.

'Thank you so much for a lovely evening. I've really enjoyed it. I do hope that your leg will soon be fully mended . . . oh.'

She looked uncertainly at Seb as he tucked her arm through his own and said firmly, 'Now where do we catch this bus for the ferry?'

'Oh, no. You needn't come with me. It will be out of your way and it's late,' she protested, but Seb wasn't listening.

They were just in time for the bus, having run the last few yards to arrive out of breath and laughing.

'You are so kind,' Bella told Seb as she stepped on to it, her eyes widening as he followed her. Was he going to travel all the way to the ferry with her? The thought gave her a warm glow deep inside.

A glow that grew even warmer when she discovered that Seb wasn't just planning to see her safely to the ferry, he was going to escort her all the way home.

'Oh, no, you mustn't . . .' she protested.

'Indeed I must,' he corrected her. 'I would never forgive myself if I allowed you to travel home on your own, and somehow I can't imagine that your parents would be very happy about that either.'

Grace bit her lip, knowing that he was quite right.

'You're quite safe with me; I give you my word on that,' Seb assured her.

'Oh, yes, I know that,' Grace agreed so innocently and immediately that Seb discovered that quite shockingly he was very tempted to show her that far from being the safe brotherly type she obviously saw him as, he was very much a man. But of course there was no way he was going to risk taking her in his arms, no matter how much he might feel tempted to do so.

Bella lay in bed, gloating over her triumph. She had no idea just what her father had said to Alan's father when he had telephone Alan's parents and asked them to come round. She had not been privy to that discussion, and even though she had tried to listen to the raised voices from her bedroom she had only been able to make out the odd word.

Not that it mattered what had been said, as her mother had told her when she had come upstairs to her immediately after the door had closed behind

Alan and his parents. She was now engaged to Alan, and would very soon be Mrs Alan Parker. The sooner the better, in fact, it had been decided.

'I hope Alan's father is going to buy us a decent house, Mummy.'

'Of course he will, darling. Especially under the circumstances. Your father was very firm about that.'

Bella's smile turned to a scowl. She still hadn't got her engagement ring, though, and she meant to have one, the biggest one she could get out of Alan and his horrid parents. She had seen the tight-faced look Alan's mother had given as she looked up towards Bella's bedroom window as they left. Well, she would soon learn that she, Bella, was going to be the one who said what Alan could and could not do, and who he could and could not see, not her.

FIVE

'Grace, what's wrong, love?'

Jean lifted her hands from the soapy washing-up water, where she had been washing the cutlery, whilst Grace did the drying. It was a task they always shared, and one Jean looked forward to because it was one of the few occasions during her busy week when she and her elder daughter had time on their own to chat properly.

She'd been looking forward to hearing all about the Tennis Club dance and had expected Grace to be in the happiest of moods now that she knew she could do her nurse's training but instead her normally sunny-natured daughter was quiet and withdrawn, and had barely said a word.

'Nothing's wrong, Mum,' Grace fibbed uncomfortably. She had hardly slept, and when she had she had ended up dreaming about the silk dress, waking up with a start, her heart pounding. Why had she been so stupid and . . . and dishonest? As well as her dread about telling the salon manager, she also felt bitterly ashamed of herself.

'Nothing's wrong? Then why have you been drying that plate for the last five minutes is what I'd like to know. Come on, love, you can tell me.' Jean hesitated. It wasn't in her nature to criticise others, nor to talk about them behind their backs, but when it came to her children her maternal instincts came first, and she wasn't having her Grace made unhappy by something that her sister or one of her family might have said to her.

'If summat was said or done last night to upset you . . . ?'

Her mother's sympathy was too much for Grace to bear. She put down the plate she had been drying, her face crumpling.

'Oh, Mum, I've done the most dreadful thing. I'm that ashamed of meself. I don't know what came over me. Ruined me whole life, I have. You and me dad will never forgive me.'

Jean's heart turned over and then lurched painfully into her ribs. Grace was normally a sensible girl who knew what was what and right from wrong. She'd made sure of that. Accidents happened when young people fell in love, but Jean didn't want any of her children saddled with an unexpected baby on the way before they'd said their vows in church. What she'd never expected, though, was that her Grace would turn out to be the sort that let a lad she wasn't as good as engaged to, at the least, persuade her into doing what she shouldn't.

Sam would be heartbroken. He thought the

world of his children and was that proud of them, even if he didn't always let them know that. It would be the drink, of course – that and the excitement of mingling with Bella's posh friends. Jean's heart swelled with maternal indignation as she thought of her daughter being plied with drinks and then taken advantage of by some young chap.

Torn between venting her shocked despair and wanting to comfort her daughter, there were a hundred things she wanted to say, but in the end the only thing she could say was, 'Oh, Grace.'

'I'm so sorry, Mum.' Grace was crying in earnest now. 'I knew I shouldn't have done it but Susan had gone to so much trouble, even though I'd told her that I couldn't do it and that it was wrong, even though she said that everyone borrows clothes from the salon on the quiet, even the manageress. I didn't want to hurt her feelings. She's been a good friend to me, but I knew the minute I put it on that I shouldn't have done.'

Jean listened to Grace's hiccuped muddled words and felt as though a weight had been rolled off her heart. Her daughter hadn't gone and done what she shouldn't with some lad. But then hard on the heels of her initial relief came the shock of realising just what Grace had done.

'You went to the dance wearing a dress from the salon that you'd no right to be wearing?'

Miserably, Grace nodded her head. She could hear the scandalised disbelief in her mother's voice.

'Grace, that's stealing.'

'It didn't seem wrong the way Susan talked about it. She said that everyone did it.'

Jean was angry now, her anger fired as much by relief that she didn't have to worry about Grace getting herself into the kind of trouble no mother wanted her daughter to be in, as by her dismay at what she had done.

'Never mind what someone else said. If this Susan told you to lie down in the road in front of a bus would you do it? Me and your dad have brought you up to know what's right from what's wrong.'

'I know that, Mum. But . . . well, Susan was that determined I was going to wear it. She said that no one would know and that she would put the dress back for me on Monday morning but it got torn when Bella stood on it and now . . . I'll have to tell the manageress what's happened and ask her if I can buy it with me staff discount.'

Jean was horrified at what Grace had done. It ran counter to everything she and Sam had taught their children, and she knew that Sam would be even more disappointed in Grace than she was herself.

'Well, I can't help you out paying for it, Grace, and I wouldn't do neither. What you've done is very wrong.'

'Yes, Mum.'

'How much will it cost?'

'Seven guineas,' Grace told her in a small voice.

'Seven guineas!' Jean went over to the table and sat down on one of the chairs.

'I thought I'd ask if I could have two shillings taken out of me wages every week until I've paid for it.'

'But you won't be having any wages. Not with you doing your nurse's training.'

Grace's eyes welled with fresh tears. 'I can't do that now, Mum, not with this frock to be paid for. It serves me right, I know that, and I've only myself to blame.'

Jean looked at her daughter's downbent head. She knew how much doing her nurse's training meant to her and her heart ached for her. But Grace was quite right, the dress – and her 'crime' both had to be paid for. Even so . . .

'Oh, love.'

Her mother's soft words and warm hug brought fresh tears to Grace's eyes.

'I wish I could help you but—'

'I wouldn't expect you to do that, Mum, even if you had the money.' Grace stepped back from Jean and lifted her head determinedly. 'I've made me bed and now I've got to lie in it. There's no one to blame for this but meself.'

Jean said nothing. Privately she could think of at least two people who probably shared as much of the blame as Grace although they would get away with it scot-free. One was this Susan she worked with, and the other was her own sister for making Grace feel she wasn't good enough to meet Bella's posh friends wearing her own clothes.

'Even if I could pay for the dress, Mum, I'd

probably still not be able to go ahead with me nursing. The hospital will want a reference from Lewis's. I can keep on with me St John Ambulance work, though. Alan's cousin was ever such a nice chap. Came with me all the way from Wallasey, even though I'd said there wasn't any need,' Grace told her, putting on a deliberately cheerful voice.

Jean frowned. 'I thought your cousin Charlie was going to bring you home.'

She had been in bed but awake, waiting for the sound of Grace's key in the lock last night, and it had never occurred to her to ask how her daughter had got home, since she had assumed that Charlie had made sure she was safely delivered.

'So did I, but I'm glad Charlie didn't really because he'd had ever such a lot to drink. Auntie Vi and Uncle Edwin came for Bella and Alan.'

She would have something to say about the way she'd treated Grace, the next time she saw her twin, Jean decided. Fancy leaving her to make her own way home. She would never have done anything like that if their positions had been reversed. But that was it, wasn't it? In Vi's eyes Jean and her family were second class and un-important, just as Sam had told her.

'Give us the dress then, so that I can get it back on the rail before Mrs James gets in.'

Grace shook her head. She had met up with Susan as arranged a couple of streets away from Lewis's.

'It got torn at the dance,' she told Susan. 'I've decided that I'm going to own up to having borrowed it to Mrs James and ask her if I can buy it with me staff discount.'

Susan looked horrified. 'You can't do that. She'll never let you, and we'll both be out of a job.'

'I've got to do it, Susan, but don't worry I won't say anything about you. My getting it torn wasn't your fault.'

'Give it here,' Susan demanded, grabbing the bag from Grace before she could stop her. 'You'll be done for if you own up to having borrowed it. I'll put it back just like I said and—'

'But it's torn and—'

'Well then, we'll just have to pretend that a customer did it, won't we? Look, Grace, Mrs James will never believe that you took it into your head to borrow it on your own. She thinks a lot of you, she does. I reckon she'll be questioning the lot of us before you can say, "Here's your cards" and there's not one of the girls working in the salon who's going to want that. No, the best thing for everyone is if I put the frock back and we say nothing. With a bit of luck it could be weeks, maybe months, before anyone comes in and tries it on, especially if I put it right at the back of the wardrobe.'

Grace shook her head 'Susan, I can't do that. It's dishonest and—'

'Well, you won't be doing it, will you? It's me wot took it and me wot will get into trouble, you know, not just you. Anyway, you won't be able to say anything to Mrs James today. It's her day off – remember? Come on, we'd better get on our way otherwise we'll be late.'

Grace had had the most dreadful morning, jumping with nerves every time anyone came anywhere near the salon and now Rosemary, who was in charge in the manageress's absence, had sent her to the small back sewing room 'for a rest' because she looked so poorly.

Susan had urged her to have a cigarette to calm her nerves, but smoking it had made her feel even sicker, and so she had stubbed it out. She wasn't a big smoker at the best of times.

The door to the sewing room burst open and Susan came in, her face flushed with excitement and her eyes sparkling.

'You'll never guess what's happened. A chap has just come in and bought that ruddy dress.'

'Bought it? A man? But how? What about the tear . . . ?'

'Asked to see Mrs James, he did, at first. Then when I told him that she wasn't in, he said he'd come about a dress. Described the green silk to a T, he did an' all. You should have seen his face when I told him that it was hanging up in the closet. "The frock is still available for purchase?" he asked me, ever so posh, like. "Of course it is," I said back.'

'Susan . . .'

'Offered to go and get it for him to have a look at too, I did. Of course I didn't show him the bit wot got torn.'

'Susan . . .'

'Told me to wrap it up for him and he paid cash. Ever so good-looking, he was. Pity he'd got his leg in a plaster mind . . . Here, what are you doing?' she demanded indignantly when Grace sprang from her chair and ran to the door.

Seb. It just had to be him, Grace felt sure, but where had he gone? Was he still in Lewis's or had he left? She ran all the way down the dark cold staff stairway, and out into the street. Lewis's main entrance was on Ranelegh Street so she ran round the corner of the building, heading for those doors to ask the uniformed doorman breathlessly if he had seen a man leaving with his leg in plaster and carrying a Gown Salon box.

'His leg in plaster, you say?' The doorman was a veteran from the Great War and a bit hard of hearing. 'We'll be seeing plenty of them before too long, and worse an' all, if you was to ask me.'

Grace tried not to feel impatient. She looked up and down the busy street and then across the road, shading her eyes from the sun, and then felt her heart turn over as she saw Seb walking into a café further down Ranelegh Street.

Thanking the doorman, she ran across the road, dodging the traffic, just managing to catch up with him as he opened the café door.

The moment he heard her calling his name he turned towards her.

'I was in the sewing room. Susan came in and told me what you'd done. Well, at least she told me what had happened and I knew it must be you and so . . . oh, Seb . . . 'Her voice broke and she started to tremble.

'Come on, let's go and have a cup of tea, or will that get you into trouble?'

'No. Mrs James is off today. She's the manageress and she's a bit of a tartar. Rosemary is in charge and she won't mind if I take my dinner hour.'

Five minutes later they were seated at a small table amongst the other shoppers, drinking the tea Seb had had to pour for them both because Grace's hands had been shaking too much.

He had insisted on ordering her some welsh rarebit as well, saying that she looked as though she needed something to eat.

'You shouldn't have done it,' she told him. 'I don't deserve it. What I did was wrong and I should be punished for it.'

'It was wrong,' Seb agreed, 'but you weren't entirely to blame.' Privately he felt that most of the blame lay with Grace's snobbish aunt and uncle and her dreadful cousin. 'I'd planned to have a word with your manageress and offer to cover the cost of the dress, thinking that you would have handed it over to her before I could get to speak with her.'

'I would have done if she'd been in,' Grace admitted. 'Susan grabbed it off me before I could stop her and said she was going to put it back. I told her she mustn't but she said if I owned up it would get her the sack as well as me. I couldn't believe it when she came rushing into the sewing room and said that someone had bought it. It made me feel sick with guilt to think that she'd let someone buy it, knowing what had happened to it, but then she said about the man who had bought it having his leg in plaster and I just knew that it must be you.' Her eyes were shining with gratitude and relief.

'You still shouldn't have done it, though. I don't deserve so much kindness. I'll pay you back of course, but . . .'

'You will pay me back, Grace,' Seb agreed, suddenly becoming serious, 'but not with a few shillings a week that you can't really spare. A lot of men like me are going to need a lot of young women like you before this war is over. Doing your nurse's training is far more important than paying me back. This country needs girls like you.'

'Oh, Seb.'

'Now I want you to promise me that you won't go and make a silly martyr of yourself by confessing to something that no one else needs to know about now. And I want you to promise me too that you'll work hard to become the best nurse you can be.'

'I promise,' Grace told him fervently.

'Good. Now eat your lunch before it goes cold.'

Obediently Grace did as he had told her although she wasn't really hungry. However, whereas before she had been too miserable and upset to eat, now she was too excited and overjoyed.

116

She gazed at Seb with something close to hero worship. How lucky she was to have met such a wonderful person. She would never forget him. Never. And she would do as he had told her and work as hard as she could at her training.

They parted on the pavement outside the café, turning in opposite directions. Grace was halfway across the road when she changed her mind and turned back, running down the street after Seb. He stopped and turned round when he heard her.

She was running so fast she almost collided with him. He put out his arm to steady her. Grace looked up at him. She was slightly out of breath and her heart was pounding, and not just because she had been running, she knew.

She put her hands on his upper arms and raised herself up on her tiptoes to kiss him on the cheek. He was the first man she had kissed, apart from her father and her brother, and she was careful not to look at his mouth.

'Thank you,' she told him emotionally. 'I shall never forget what you've done for me. Never.'

Seb looked down into her face. She was so very lovely. He thrust the dress box towards her and told her gruffly, 'You'd better take this. It isn't any use to me.'

And then as she took it from him, to Grace's surprise, he bent his head and kissed her fiercely on the mouth.

The whole world seemed to go still and silent. Grace trembled, and lifted her free hand towards his face, but Seb had already released her and was stepping back from her, and walking away from her.

Grace watched him until he had disappeared into the crowd. Her eyes were smarting and yet she felt happy – elated, in fact – as though she wanted to sing and dance and tell the whole world what a wonderful special person he was. Grace heard the bang of the daily One o'clock Gun from the docks as she hurried back to work, and as she registered its familiar sound she knew that it marked a place in her life that she would never forget, dividing what had been from what was to come.

From now on she was never going to forget how lucky she had been, and how much she owed to Seb's kindness. Never ever again was she going to make the mistake of doing something she knew to be wrong. And what was more, she was going to be the best nurse she could possibly be, she told herself fervently.

Half-past six and Grace was normally home by now. Jean had been keeping an anxious eye out for her daughter ever since it had turned six o'clock, which she knew was daft because Grace didn't even finish work until six. She hadn't said anything as yet to Sam about what Grace had done. He had been so proud about the fact that she was to train as a nurse after his initial anger, and Jean knew how hurt and disappointed he would be. She would have to tell him soon, though. She gave a small sigh as she reached for the iron. Both Sam and

Luke were late in for their tea tonight as well, and she had been so on edge that she'd almost been glad of having the washing to iron. She tensed as she heard Grace's footsteps outside the back door, knowing how upset her eldest daughter would be at having to give up her hopes of training as a nurse, but when the back door opened and Grace came in, far from looking upset she was glowing with happiness and excitement.

'Mum, you'll ever guess what's happened.'

'You'd better tell me then, hadn't you, love?' Jean suggested. 'And pretty sharpish before your dad gets in because I haven't said anything to him yet about what's happened.' Jean frowned as she saw the dress box Grace was carrying, and her frown deepened as Grace started to explain disjointedly and excitedly all about a certain Seb Atkins, who had saved her from disgrace and despair by buying the frock she had damaged.

The more Grace enthused about her rescuer the more Jean felt inclined to mistrust him. It was typical of Grace that she always thought the best of other people, but Jean knew what Sam would have to say about a young man who bought his daughter an expensive frock – if she were to tell him, of course.

'Wasn't that a wonderful thing of him to do, Mum?' Grace was demanding.

'I don't know about wonderful, Grace. In my day a young man certainly didn't buy a girl a frock, not if she was a decent girl, that is, and he respected her,' she added warningly.

Grace flushed and gave her a reproachful look. 'He isn't that sort at all, Mum,'

'Well, it's plain you don't want to think so, love, but you've only met him the once and here he is buying—'

'He didn't buy it for me, Mum. He bought it because he wants me to train as a nurse,' Grace told her. 'That's what he said to me, and he made me promise that I would. Oh, and I shall, and I want to be the very best nurse there is, Mum.' Grace clasped her hands together, the look of shining dedication in her eyes making Jean's heart miss a small beat at the sight of so much vulnerability.

'He said that if there is war then men like him will need girls like me, girls who are trained nurses . . . and then he gave me the dress and . . . oh, Mum, I can't believe it. I was so sure that I'd gone and spoiled everything. But now . . .'

Jean watched her worriedly. What Grace had done was very wrong and yet, as her mother, she couldn't help but feel relieved that she was not going to be denied her chance to do what she so desperately wanted to do, even if she also knew that Sam would not approve, and would think that Grace should endure her deserved punishment. He had such strong moral values, did her Sam, and she respected him for that, but a mother was still a mother, and now that Grace had let slip that this Seb was about to rejoin his unit and hadn't made any attempt to suggest they meet up again, she was beginning to feel a bit less worried.

'Well, let this be a lesson to you, Grace,' she

told her daughter sternly. 'You've been very lucky to have things work out as they have, but think on in future, and don't go letting yourself be persuaded into doing what you know isn't right. We've brought you up to know better than that and, like I said, your dad would be that disappointed if he knew what you've done.' Jean paused. The last thing she wanted to do was to encourage any of their children to think they should keep secrets from their father but she knew Sam, and if he were to be told the full tale she suspected he would insist on Grace owning up to what she had done, even if it meant she lost her opportunity to do her training.

'Your dad's got a lot on his mind at the moment, what with being in the ARP as well as having to do his own work, so there's no need to give him any more to worry about by telling him any of this. It would only upset him and he's that proud of you.'

Jean reached for her overall and sprinkled it with water before unrolling it and starting to iron it. The colours were beginning to fade but there was plenty of wear left in it yet.

'Yes, Mum,' Grace agreed meekly.

'Now you'd better take that box upstairs and get it out of the way. We can have a look at the frock later and see if there's anything that can be done with it.'

Grace gave a small shudder, and looked conscience-stricken. 'I could never wear it again, Mum, not after what I did.'

'Maybe you can't, but some other girl might be glad of the opportunity to wear it,' Jean told her firmly.

'The service is to be at eleven o'clock three weeks on Saturday, after the banns have been read, and the wedding breakfast will be at the Splendide Hotel.' Vi took a sip of her tea, and then dabbed delicately at the corners of her mouth with a snowy white starched napkin. Really, one would have thought that Alan's mother would have made a bit more of an effort with her appearance. Vi would have been ashamed to go out wearing such a dull-looking tweed skirt, not a Jaegar by the looks of it, and what looked like a hand-knitted twinset. The colours didn't even match. The skirt was brown and the twinset navy blue. She looked down at her own teal-blue jersey afternoon frock with its lace cuffs, and felt happily superior to Bella's mother-in-law-to-be.

'The vicar said he'd never known so many couples come to him wanting to be married just in case it comes to war,' she informed her. 'He's actually had to turn some people away but he said that of course he could make room for us, seeing as my Edwin is a councillor, and of course your own husband as well, Mrs Parker. Now, I'm seeing the printer tomorrow about the invitations and the order of service. We're having Evans's to do the catering.' Vi gave Alan's mother an arch look as she mentioned the name of Wallasey's most expensive catering firm. 'Mr Firth insists. He won't have anything less than the best, I'm afraid.' Vi patted the pearls she was wearing complacently.

The two women were sitting in Vi's smart new front room, and so far Alan's mother hadn't spoken a single word.

Well, of course Vi could understand that. After all, she must be feeling that ashamed of herself after the way her son had behaved toward Bella, frightening her like that. But as she'd said to Bella on Sunday morning when she'd taken her up a cup of tea, young men could get carried away with their passionate feelings, especially when they were as in love as Alan obviously was with her.

Naturally too she had tried delicately to find out exactly how far things had gone but Bella had been so terribly upset that she hadn't pursued the matter. Fortunately she had managed to ascertain that whatever had happened had only happened for the 'first time' so that even if the unthinkable were to result, no one could possibly raise their eyebrows at a honeymoon baby arriving a couple of weeks or so early.

'Bella wants to have her cousin Grace as one of her bridesmaids, of course, and, bless her, she's said that she'd like to ask Trixie to be the other, just to show there's no hard feelings. She's such a thoughtful girl like that. I know already that you're going to love her as though she were your own daughter. It's such a special bond, I always think, between a mother and a daughter. Such a shame you only have a son, but then, you'll have my Bella now.

'I'm afraid that Edwin is still a teeny bit cross with dear Alan for the way he upset Bella. He's such a protective father, but like I've said to him, we knew what was in the wind and that it was only a matter of time before Alan called to ask formally for Bella's hand.'

Vi saw the murderous look Alan's mother was giving her but chose to ignore it. After all, if anyone should be giving murderous looks to anyone it should be her. It was their darling Bella whom they had found in hysterics at the Tennis Club after Charlie had telephoned them and insisted they needed to be there. As she'd told Alan's mother when they had driven round to see his parents, the minute he had realised what that happened Edwin had been all for forbidding Alan to see Bella again but, like any mother, she had wanted to see common sense prevail.

Of course, as she had also told Alan's parents, thanks to the quick thinking of the Tennis Club President no real harm had been done and everyone knew that Alan and Bella were now engaged, but in view of the circumstances they naturally felt that the sooner the wedding took place the better.

Vi's mouth hardened as she remembered how Mrs Parker had tried to suggest they call out a doctor to examine Bella to confirm whether or not Alan had a duty to marry her. She had soon put a stop to that.

All in all she was very pleased with the way things had worked out, especially once she had realised just how close to the Parkers Trixie's family were.

'Of course, the young couple are going to need somewhere to live, and with your Alan working for his father I dare say you'll want him close to you. There's a detached house up for sale five down from you,' Vi informed the other woman.

'Mr Parker doesn't like rushing into things,' Alan's mother told her coldly. 'He says no good ever comes of it. There's no reason why Alan shouldn't stay where he is.'

'Well, personally I think that a young couple should have their own roof over their heads.'

'It wouldn't be their own roof, though, would it, Mrs Firth, not with Alan's father having to pay for it?' Alan's mother put down her tea cup and stood up. 'I really must go. I've got a committee meeting this evening.'

'Bella will be sorry that she missed you, but what with Alan coming round and insisting that he wanted to take her out to buy her her ring . . . Of course, it's only natural that he wants to make it up to her for the way he behaved on Saturday. Bella was shocked at how much he'd had to drink.'

'Drinks bought for him by your son, I believe,' Alan's mother told Vi in an arctic voice.

'Charlie is just so very generous. Too generous really, sometimes.'

Mrs Parker looked pointedly at her watch.

'Such a shame you have to go when we haven't finished discussing all the arrangements yet. I'm taking Bella to choose a wedding gown next week, and then there's the bridesmaids' frocks. I've telephoned Trixie's mother to tell her that Bella wants Trixie to be her bridesmaid. It's a pity she's such a plain girl. Not a patch on Bella, of course.'

'Mr Parker and I are very fond of Trixie.'

'Well, yes, I'm sure you must be, but of course you'll love Bella – everyone does. She's going to make such a wonderful mother.' Vi sighed sentimentally, but her eyes were cold as she watched the anger burn in Alan's mother's eyes.

She had known the minute they had driven round there on Saturday night that Mrs Parker was one of those mothers who thought their sons could do no wrong and who was prepared to defend and protect him no matter what. Well, she had soon made sure that Edwin let them know exactly what Alan had been up to with their Bella and how distraught she was. Far too distraught to come into the house. She had told Mrs Parker very bluntly that had her Charlie behaved like Alan then she would have insisted he do the right thing by the poor girl involved – not that Charlie would ever behave so badly.

Even then, knowing the whole situation, Vi suspected that the Parkers would have wriggled out of admitting that Alan had no option other than to marry Bella, if it hadn't been for the fact that their engagement had already been announced in front of the President of the Tennis Club.

Vi couldn't believe that Mrs Parker actually thought that that Trixie, with her horsy face and moony expression, would be a better wife for her son than her own Bella. Stupid woman. And mean too, suggesting that Bella move in with them.

The sight of Sam beaming from ear to ear when he came in from work was enough to make Jean feel less guilty about not telling him what had happened. He had such a lot on his mind at the moment that it wouldn't be fair to add another burden to the ones he was already carrying.

'You look pleased with yourself,' she told him. 'You're a bit later than I was expecting, though. The others have already had theirs, and I've got to go out to my WVS meeting tonight, so you'd better get washed up and sat down at the table.'

'Sorry, love,' Sam apologised, rolling up his shirt-sleeves over the sink and turning on the tap. 'Fred Wilson collared me when I was on me way home, He's our Group Warden.'

Jean nodded as she removed the cottage pie she'd plated up earlier for him from the oven. By the time Sam had washed his hands and was sitting down, Jean had put his dinner in front of him and had the kettle on.

'Aye, Fred had a bit of good news he wanted to tell me,' Sam continued. 'Seems that the Government has decided that it's going to pay us a bit of summat for being in the ARP, even though it's only part time. It's not much, mind,' he warned, but Jean could see how pleased he was. Luke will be getting it as well, and I reckon it won't do any harm to carry on as we have been doing and put it to one side for the future. Where are the kids?'

'Luke's out at band practice,' said Jean. 'Grace has gone to find out what she needs to do to get started with her nursing training, and the twins have gone off to the park with that friend of theirs. They'll be back at school next week so they might as well enjoy what's left of their holidays. I had a message earlier saying that they wanted volunteers down at the school to help get the kiddies evacuated, so I've said I'll go and give a hand. Poor little mites, and their mothers as well.'

'It's for their own good, Jean. If it does come to war then the Government wants them to be safe.' He put down his knife and fork and looked at her. 'I've bin thinking meself, about the twins and you.'

'You're not the only one. I've bin thinking about it too, but, like I've already said, Sam, I'm staying put and so are the twins. I'd never have a minute's peace, worrying about you, if I didn't, and I'd never have any peace if the twins weren't here with us.'

'Well, I can't say that I wouldn't prefer to have you here because I would, but the Germans are going to be out to get Liverpool, lass – we all know that, what with the docks and everything – and I'd feel a lot easier in me mind, know that you and the girls are safe.'

'We'll be as safe here as anywhere,' Jean said to him firmly. 'We've got that shelter in the garden, and besides, how can you be expected to help fight a war if you aren't getting a decent meal to eat and clean clothes to wear? No, Sam, my mind's made up. We're staying.' She paused. 'I do hope that our Vi doesn't really mean to send Jack away. I'd have him here rather than let her do that, but of course there'd be a ruckus if I offered.'

They exchanged looks, and then Sam cleared his throat.

'Aye, poor lad. But he's their lad, love, and it's not up to us to interfere.'

'But, Sam . . .'

'I know, love but there's nothing we can do. You know that.'

Jean straightened her shoulders and poured them each a cup of tea.

'Do you reckon then that it's going to be war?' she asked.

Sam pushed back his chair and stood up, going over to her. Jean stood up as well, her anxiety shadowing her eyes as he put his arm around her and she laid her head on his shoulder.

'Yes, and there's no point in me pretending that there isn't,' he told her gruffly. 'You've got far too much sense to be teken in by summat like that.'

For a few seconds they simply stood there in silence, Sam's arm around Jean, and her head resting on his shoulder. Sam could feel her tears seeping through the fabric of his shirt. There was a huge lump in his throat. Jean so rarely cried.

'At least we'll have our Luke here with us, not like some families who've got to watch their lads going off to fight,' Sam tried to comfort her.

'I'm worried about him, Sam,' she responded.

'Something's bothering him. Has he said anything to you?'

'No, not a word. What do you reckon's up with him then?'

'I don't know,' Jean admitted.

SIX

Sunday 3 September

The sound of the twins' muffled giggles had Jean looking along the pew and giving them a warning shake of her head. Dust danced in the long bars of sunlight striking through the high windows and onto the stone floor. She hoped the vicar's sermon wasn't going to go on for too long this morning. She'd got a nice piece of beef in the oven and she didn't want it spoiling, and besides, she needed to sort out what she and the twins were going to wear for Bella's wedding. A turn-up for the books, that had been and no mistake. And Vi could say what she liked about them getting married fast because there might be a war; it still wouldn't stop folk putting one and one together and getting three, as the saying went.

From the pew she could see where the Boy Scouts were standing. Jack had told her all about the badges he'd got when she'd seen him at Vi's. It didn't seem two minutes ago since their Luke had been marching off proudly in his own Scout's uniform, his hair slicked down straight.

She'd telephoned Vi yesterday from the telephone box at the end of the road, after the postman had brought the wedding invitation, and she'd been a bit taken aback when Vi had told her that Jack had been evacuated already.

'His headmaster said we should, since they'll be closing his school down if there is a war.'

Jean bent her head and said an extra special prayer for her young nephew, and then another one for all those other children who had been sent away from their homes, and for their mothers as well.

In the pew in front of them old Mrs Knowles from round the corner had fallen asleep, her hat coming down over one eye, its feather trembling in time with her snores, which was no doubt the cause of the twins' mirth, Jean recognised ruefully.

Dutifully Grace tried to concentrate on the vicar's sermon, but the warm beams of sunshine striking through the Sunday morning torpor of the worshippers, combined with the excitement that was fizzing away inside her, was too much of a temptation, drawing her thoughts outside the church to more exciting things. This time, next week she'd have started her training. She was to report to the nurses' home next Saturday morning and, like her mother had said, they were going to have to get their skates on if they were going to get in time everything on the list she'd been given.

Lewis's had been ever so good to her as well,

giving her a day's leave without docking any of her pay. Oh, she just couldn't wait, although of course she was going to miss home and her family. She just hoped though that she'd be able to be Bella's bridesmaid. A real surprise that had been, to all of them.

'Perhaps the young man that was so kind to you will be at the wedding,' her mother had suggested.

Grace knew that she had coloured up and she knew too that her mother had noticed, but she was determined to be realistic about Seb and his kindness to her, and so she had said determinedly, 'Well, he could be, Mum, although he told me that he isn't really related to Alan at all. And . . . well, I got the impression he wasn't very keen on him, and if he's already back with the RAF, he may not be able to be there.'

'Well, never mind,' her mother had responded. 'I'd have liked to thank him for his kindness to you, though.'

'How many breaths do you think it will be before her hat falls off?' Louise whispered to her twin.

'Ten,' Sasha responded.

'I bet you it's fifteen. And if I win you've got to kiss Tom Lucas.'

'I'm not kissing him. You kiss him.'

'Sally says that he sticks his tongue right down your throat.'

'Why would he want to do that?'

'It's what they do in France, she says.'

'Mum's watching us . . .'

The sudden realisation that the vicar had stopped speaking virtually in mid-sentence caused not only Jean but virtually the whole congregation to look first towards the pulpit and then back towards the now open door, where the verger and two of the sidesmen were in earnest conversation. The verger broke away and started to hurry down the aisle, his robes billowing with the speed of his progress. He reached the pulpit, saying something to the vicar, who had leaned down to listen.

Several seconds passed. Mrs Knowles woke up abruptly in mid-snore and straightened her hat. The vicar stepped down from the pulpit to stand in front of the congregation.

'It is my sad duty to inform you that we are now at war with Germany.'

Immediately Grace looked towards her parents. Her mother's face had lost its colour and her father's mouth had gone stern. The twins were standing close together, their arms round each other.

Luke stood apart from his family, a grim, almost bitter, expression shadowing his face as he watched some of the other young men gravitate towards one another and begin a low-voiced conversation. Why couldn't his father understand how it made him feel, knowing that he was going to be safe here in Liverpool whilst his friends went off to fight? The service summarily finished, the congregation was moving swiftly towards the open doors. Half a dozen young men in various service uniforms, who had been attending church with their families, were very much the centre of attention, receiving approving smiles and words of encouragement as older men went up to them to clap them on the shoulder or pat them on the back.

Luke could feel the backs of his eyes burning drily with shame and anger.

'Oh, Sam, do you think it's really true?' Jean asked anxiously as they all left the church.

'I reckon so. We'll know more when we get home and listen to the wireless. Luke, we'd better check in with the ARP post this afternoon,' he told his son, 'and I'll have a word with Andy Roberts to see if he's heard anything.'

Andy Roberts was the most senior of the Salvage Corps men and acted as an unofficial co-ordinator and 'foreman' for the group.

'Does that mean now that Hitler's going to march into Liverpool?' Lou asked anxiously.

'Don't be daft,' her twin responded dismissively. 'He can't march across the Channel, can he?'

'No, but he can ruddy well bomb it,' Arthur Edwards, one of their neighbours, told them, having overheard the twins' conversation. Arthur was a widower, and Jean normally made up a bit of a plated dinner for him on a Sunday. 'There's going to be some tears shed before tonight's over,' he added dourly. 'There's hardly a house in the street that's not sending one of its men off to fight. I'm surprised that you ain't in uniform yet, young Luke. Alf Simpson's two lads have both joined up this last month and the Bristows from number sixteen's son's in the Merchant Navy.

'Luke's going to be working in the Salvage Corps with me,' Sam told their neighbour sharply.

'Oh, Mum . . .' Grace's voice broke as she went into her mother's arms, and they hugged each other.

They were less than halfway home when they heard a booming noise, similar to that made by the One o' clock Gun down on the docks, followed by another. Before the echoes of the second had died away Sam was shepherding his family towards the nearest public shelter, which happened to be in the grounds of a school. New and purpose-built with brick walls and a concrete slab roof, the shelter might be ugly, but right now it was a very welcome sight indeed.

Joining in with the shrill wail of the air-raid sirens, small children snatched up by their parents had started crying. Jean kept the twins in front of her, telling them to hold on to one another, conscious of the press of people seeking safety, but everyone was doing their best to keep calm, even if there were some very set and frightened faces.

Inside, the shelter was very similar to the one at the bottom of the road, which they had all been down to have a look at once it had been erected earlier in the year, although much larger. Bunk beds lined the walls; there were buckets filled with sand as emergency fire extinguishers, and a dedicated ARP post right by the door for those who would be in charge of getting everyone in and keeping a check on everything. Electric cables supporting solitary light bulbs dangled from the ceiling here and there, the bulbs giving off pools of light. Without any windows there was no chance of that light giving away their location to Hitler's Luftwaffe. There was even a door marked 'WC', which was more than they had in their shelter, Jean thought enviously.

As Sam guided his family to one of the bunk beds so that they could all sit down he commented admiringly on how well equipped the shelter was.

'We'll be all right in here, love. They've got a supply of stoves stacked up over there, and their own water supply,' he told Jean, before going back to join the other ARP men outside, helping to make sure everything proceeded as it should. Jean watched him leave with some anxiety – for his safety, not their own.

'Blimey, that Hitler don't believe in wasting much time, does he?' an old lady puffed as she sat down on the bed next to the Campions'. The twins were packed in tightly between Jean and Grace, and a group of men a few yards away were joking that the ARP warden hadn't thought to stock up with a few crates of beer.

'Shame on you, Harry Meadows,' a woman, whom Jean guessed must be his wife, objected sharply. 'Talking about drinking beer on a Sunday, and when we've only just come out of church. You should be praying to the Good Lord to save us, not thinking about beer.'

Lou shivered and moved closer to Jean. Jean put her arm around her, and hugged her tightly, hoping that Lou wouldn't be able to feel how fast her own heart was beating and guess how very afraid she was.

You could almost feel the effort everyone was making not to be afraid, or at least not to let their fear show. But it was there, Jean could see it in the eyes of other mothers and in the way they kept their children close to them. People were talking in low voices, quickly, anxious not to miss any sounds from outside.

Jean looked towards the shelter entrance. The door was still open; she could just about see Sam standing with the other ARP men. She wished desperately that he was with them, but he had his duty to do. Grace was holding Sasha as closely as Jean was holding Lou, and she felt a surge of pride for her eldest daughter.

'It's cold in here, Mum,' Lou complained.

It *was* cold, and damp as well, Jean suspected, but far more important than the discomfort, and the fact that the beef would be ruined, was that they were safe.

Lou was pulling a face. 'Pooh,' she objected, wrinkling her nose. 'It's horrid in here, really smelly.'

Jean nudged her daughter and gave her a warning look, even though she was forced to acknowledge that Lou's criticism was well deserved.

The beef would be ruined now. What a waste.

Sam was coming towards them, and Jean waited

anxiously as he stepped carefully over outstretched legs.

'It's all right,' he told her. 'False alarm. Captain Cocks, from the Fort Perch Rock Battery ordered a couple of rounds to be put across the bows of a vessel trying to enter the closed Rock Channel approach to the Mersey. I dunno about scaring them off – he's certainly put the fear of God up all of Liverpool. Not that the powers that be will be too put out, mind. I dare say it's given them a chance to see if the civil defence measures are working as they should.'

As they all stepped out into the sunshine, Grace was thinking that the next time she heard an air-raid siren she could well be in her nurse's uniform and on duty waiting for the injured to be brought in for treatment. It felt funny to be both so frightened and yet at the same time so determined to rise to the challenge of what war could bring.

'I think I'd better stay on here to lend a hand, if you don't mind love,' Sam told Jean, as she gathered her family together.

It was only natural that he should want a chance to talk things through with the other men who had been clustered together by the exit to the shelter as they left, Jean acknowledged as they made their way home.

She felt tired and miserable, and her head had started to ache, but most of all she was thinking about Jack, and how he must be feeling.

'Poor little lad,' she said under her breath.

'What's that, Mum?' Grace asked.

'I was just thinking about Jack,' Jean told her. 'Your Auntie Vi's had him evacuated.'

'Of course, Edwin suspected all along that this was going to happen, and that it would be war. He's got very close contacts with the Ministry, you know – not that he'd ever breathe a word out of turn. They have absolute trust in his discretion. To be honest, that's why we gave in when Alan begged us to allow Bella to marry him. They're so very much in love, and with it being war, well, one never knows what might happen . . .'

'But I thought that Alan Parker worked for his father and doesn't have to join up,' the neighbour Vi was talking to queried.

It was early in the evening, and naturally everyone wanted to talk about the morning's announcement that they were now at war.

Vi had only come out to deadhead the last of her roses, but her trug was at her feet without anything in it, and she was determined to ignore her neighbour's telltale glance towards her own front door when she had such an excellent opportunity to reinforce the fact that it was Edwin's perspicacity in recognising that war was about to be declared that was responsible for Bella's swift marriage, and nothing else.

'Well, yes, of course, but one never knows what may happen . . .'

Really, Vi thought, humming happily to herself ten minutes later as she returned to the house, things could hardly have fallen better. She now had the perfect explanation for anyone who chose to ask questions about the hurried nature of Bella's marriage.

Edwin was in the lounge, listening to the wireless and drinking a G and T – his second of the evening, not that Vi was counting, of course. Edwin with his bald head and his neat moustache had grown somewhat portly over the years, and had developed a decided air of importance. Unlike Jean's Sam, he was not a tall man, and unlike him too, he was now wearing spectacles.

'Of course, I had my suspicions that this was going to happen,' he told Vi, puffing out his cheeks, both of them ignoring the fact that it was only a couple of weeks since he had been saying that there wouldn't be a war at all, in private as well as in public. 'Just as well I had the foresight to expand the business, because we'll certainly be getting more work. Charlie will have to pull his socks up a bit, mind. I don't want to see work we could have had going to someone else because he's not doing his job properly.'

'Well, that's a fine thing to say, and about your own son too. I'm surprised at you, Edwin, I really am,' Vi retaliated. 'Poor Charlie's doing his best. It was gone eight o'clock three evenings last week before he came in for his meal.'

'He needs to spend more time working and less time at that ruddy Tennis Club,' Edwin told her.

'Edwin! Language!' Vi reproved him. 'Jean's going to be getting herself in a state. She was all for telling me I'd done the wrong thing when I said that we'd had Jack evacuated, but she'll be wishing she'd had the sense to do the same with her twins now, I shouldn't wonder.'

Edwin gave a bored grunt.

'Edwin, I really do think you should speak to Alan's father, you know. Poor Bella's terrified that that dreadful mother of Alan's is going to try to make them live with them after they're married. It's like I was saying to my WVS group, it doesn't look very good when a prominent Wallasey Village businessman and a local councillor acts as though he can't afford to set his newly married son up in a house of his own. I'd be ashamed if that was us and our Charlie.'

Edwin gave another grunt.

'If you were to ask me then I'd have to say that I'm a bit worried that Mrs Parker is one of those mothers who have to have her son tied to their apron strings. I've already told Bella that she'll have to watch out for that. She will be Alan's wife, after all. You know, I was thinking, if you were to mention to Mr Parker when you see him tomorrow at the council meeting that you're prepared to give the young ones a cheque to pay for the new furniture they'll need for that house that's up for sale near the Parkers, then that just might make him realise—'

'Give it a rest, will you, Vi? If the Parkers won't buy them a house then there's nothing I can do about it. Get me another drink, will you?'

Vi got up and took the glass he was holding

out to her. She knew when not to cross her husband, but at least she had planted the right seed in his mind. Bella had sobbed her heart out after they'd got back from church this morning after Alan had told her that he thought they should move in with his parents instead of setting up their own home.

Well, she'd see about that, Vi assured herself. She wasn't going to have her Bella getting less than her due. If push came to shove then she'd see to it that Edwin bought them a house, and she'd make sure that everyone knew who'd had to pay for it.

She was very disappointed in the Parkers. Very disappointed.

'Hey, Charlie, I've been looking for you everywhere. Where the hell have you been? You were supposed to pick me up over half an hour ago.'

Charlie grinned, ignoring the harassed and irritated expression on the face of his friend, as Brian got into the passenger seat of Charlie's car. It was true that Charlie had promised to pick him up outside his house, prior to them both attending a regular Territorial Army meeting, and it was equally true that Charlie was very late. Not that Charlie himself cared.

'Sorry, Brian, but I had a bit of important business to attend to,' he told him, winking meaningfully. 'A certain pretty girl had heard that war had been declared and she wanted to say a proper goodbye to me. I tell you, mate, this TA uniform is worth its weight in gold for the effect it has on the girls.'

'Oh, yes? Well, you won't be feeling so pleased with yourself when you hear what I've got to tell you. We're in deep shit.'

'Ruddy hell, what for?' Charlie scratched irritably at his neck where the rough fabric of his TA battledress had chafed his skin. Girl pleasing or not, he would be glad to get out of it and into his civvies. To tell the truth, the last thing he felt like doing now was going down to the local drill hall where his unit of the Territorial Army volunteers was based. For one thing, he suspected that his father would want to give him a lecture about the effects of the war on the business and the importance of him keeping his nose to the grindstone, and Charlie knew from experience that the best time to endure one of Pa's lectures was on a Sunday evening after the old man had had a couple or three G and Ts rather than a Monday morning when his temper and his stomach were still soured by them.

'Didn't you hear that message they gave out on Friday over the wireless, saying that all army personnel have to report a.s.a.p. to their drill hall?'

'No, I can't say that I did,' Charlie told him, shrugging dismissively. 'We're only in the TA, for heaven's sake. It's not like we're in the real army, is it?'

'Hasn't Luke come back with you?' Jean asked Sam when her husband walked into the kitchen.

They'd all been glued to the wireless since they'd got back, even the twins.

Old Mr Edwards had come round to tell them that the *Liverpool Echo* had brought out a Sunday edition and that he'd got them a copy.

It had made Jean's heart bump against her ribs to see the bold headlines announcing the commencement of war instead of the normal front-page advertisements.

'No. I thought he left with you and the girls.'

Jean looked at the clock on the wall. It was gone six o'clock. Luke wasn't the sort to ignore family meal times without warning her in advance. Her heart started to beat too fast and too heavily.

'He'll be with the other lads, talking about what's happened, I expect,' Sam told her.

Jean nodded, but deep down inside she felt something was wrong. Not that she'd say so to Sam. He'd just laugh at her and say she was being a fussing mother hen.

'You'll be hungry,' she told him. 'You missed your dinner, after all. I'll make you a sandwich.'

'Ta, love.' Sam sat down and picked up the paper, quickly becoming engrossed in it, whilst Jean filled the kettle and set about cutting bread. The wireless was on and she could hear the sound of the twins' voices from their bedroom upstairs.

The kitchen door opened and Grace came in, holding a piece of paper.

'Mum, look at this list. I just hope we're going to be able to get everything it says I have to have.'

She sat down at the table, frowning over the

list, and then got up again when she saw that the kettle was boiling.

That was typical of Grace, Jean thought gratefully. She never needed to be asked, and she was always quick to help.

Sam had eaten his sandwiches and she and Grace had done the washing up. It was gone seven now and Luke still wasn't back, and Jean couldn't help continually glancing at the clock.

It was nearly eight when Luke finally came in.

'There you are. I'll put the kettle on,' Jean told him, not wanting to let on how worried and uneasy she had felt. He was back now, after all.

'I've joined up. I've got to report for training tomorrow morning.'

The cup Jean had been holding slipped through her fingers onto the linoleum. She looked at the broken pieces of pottery and then at her son, afraid to move or speak in case she made what he had just said real, when she knew that it surely couldn't be real. Luke didn't need to join up. He was going to work in the Salvage Corps with Sam.

Sam! She looked at her husband. He was getting to his feet, his face burning a dark angry red, his fists clenched at his sides.

'You've done what?'

'You heard me, Dad. I've joined up. It's no use you looking at me like that. I had to.'

'You had to do no such bloody thing. I'd got you a place in the Salvage Corps. All you had to do was wait another couple of weeks.'

'It's all right for you to say that, you don't know what it's like,' Luke objected fiercely.

'It's because I do ruddy well know what it's like. I watched more than one man cough himself to death from the gas in the trenches. You're the one that knows nothing about what war's like, Luke.'

'Not war, no. I do know what it's like to be called a coward. That might not bother you, Dad, but it bothers me.'

Sam's face changed colour from red to white. Jean had never seen him look at anyone the way he was looking at Luke now. Instinctively she moved over to him, begging, 'Sam . . .'

'You don't need to protect me, Mum,' Luke told her, his young face hardening too. 'I'm a man now, not a kid.'

'A man? You're a fool, that's what you are,' Sam told him. 'I'd thought you'd got more about you than to listen to a lot of daft lads doing a bit of name-calling. I thought you'd got a bit of sense, but you haven't. You're a ruddy fool, Luke.'

'I might be a fool but at least I can hold my head up now.'

Again that unfamiliar look crossed Sam's face. He shook his head as though trying to shake it away, like a man coming up for air from deep water.

'Aye, for as long as you can keep it on your shoulders.'

'Sam!' Now it was Jean's turn to feel her face drain of colour and her heart start to thump uncomfortably fast.

'What do you want me to say? That I think he's done the right thing? Well, I don't.'

Beneath Sam's bitterness Jean could sense his pain, but she could also tell that Luke couldn't see that. His face was bleak with misery and anger.

They'd both raised their voices and were facing one another like enemies, these two who were so alike and whom she loved so very much. It was almost more than she could bear.

She looked at Grace. 'Go upstairs and sit with the twins, will you, love? They'll be wondering what's going on.'

As soon as the door had closed behind Grace, Jean tried to intervene.

'Luke's only done what he thinks is right, Sam.' She put her hand on Sam's arm but he shook it off. She had never seen him so angry, Jean admitted, her heart sinking. For all that Sam had an easygoing nature, he had a streak of stubbornness in him when it came to what he believed to be right. In Sam's eyes, by defying him and enlisting, Luke had shown that he didn't value or respect his father's advice, and Jean knew that Sam would find that very hard to take.

'Well, you've made your bed now, and you'll just have to lie in it,' Sam told Luke. 'I hope you're proud of yourself, because I'm certainly not. Like I've said, you're a ruddy fool, and after all I've said to you, all I've done to try to get you into the Corps.'

'The Salvage Corps. That's all that matters to

you, isn't it? You never even asked me what I wanted to do, or even if I wanted to be apprenticed as an electrician. No, all you could think about was what you wanted. Well, now I've done what I want. I'm not a kid, Dad, I'm a man, and if you don't like that then too bad.'

This was war, Jean recognised: this horrible cruel merciless tearing apart of family ties and loyalties. This senseless destruction and pain.

Luke was opening the back door, whilst Sam ignored him.

Alarm filled Jean. 'Luke, what are you doing? Where are you going?'

'I'm not staying here. Not now. I've got a couple of mates I can stay with. We joined up together.'

'Luke,' Jean protested. 'Sam, stop him . . .'

'Like he just told you, he's a man now, so let him go and be one.'

Couldn't Sam see the sheen of tears in Luke's eyes? Didn't he realise what he was doing or what was happening? Luke, their son, was about to go and fight a war. They may never see him again. How could Sam let that happen with so many cruel words still lying between them?

For the first time in the whole of their time together Jean found that she felt not love for her husband but something that felt much more like bitterness and anger.

She ran out after Luke, ignoring Sam's command to 'Let him go', catching up with him at the gate and grabbing hold of his arm, her tears rolling down her face.

'I'm sorry, Mum, but I had to do it,' he told her gruffly.

And then he was gone, walking away from her as straight-backed as though he was already in uniform and marching.

She was shaking from head to foot when she walked back into the now empty kitchen. She could hear the girls coming downstairs. They came into the kitchen, Grace shepherding the twins in front of her. For once they were quiet, holding on to one another, their eyes round and stark with confusion and pain.

'We heard Luke leave,' Grace told her mother.

Jean couldn't trust herself to speak.

'Where's Dad?' Grace asked.

'I don't know.' Nor did Jean feel as though she cared, she recognised. Anger and pain welled up inside her. How could Sam have let Luke leave like that?

'Dad's gone down to the shelter,' Lou announced.

'He goes there sometimes to think about things,' Sasha supplied. 'That's what he told us, wasn't it, Lou?'

Jean stared at the twins. Were they right? She hadn't known that Sam did that. How had they known? Not that she really cared. Right now all her pain and all her love were for Luke, her first-born. Who but a mother could ever know what it felt like when that new life was placed in your arms for the first time and that well of almost unbearable emotion took hold of you; that need to protect that life from all harm? That love, that feeling, never went away.

Charlie was drunk. In fact he was very drunk indeed. It took him several minutes to climb out of his car. He staggered towards the front door, leaning against it whilst he searched for his key.

When, before he found it, his father opened the door for him he half fell into the hall. He could see his mother standing behind his father. They were both in their nightclothes, and his mother had rag curlers in her hair.

His father's face was red with temper. 'Where the hell have you been?' he demanded.

'The bloody bastards have called up the TA. Given us all Part One and Part Two orders,' Charlie told them. 'Bastards . . . bastards . . .' His voice slurred over the words as he collapsed onto the floor, and then dragged himself up to lean against the wall, swaying slightly. 'You've got to help me, Dad. You've got to get me out . . . I only joined because they said they'd never call up the TA Reserves . . .'

'You're a bloody fool, you know that, don't you? I warned you that you were taking a risk, but you wouldn't listen, and now look at the mess you've got yourself into. None of this would have happened if you'd listened to me and kept quiet.'

'Yes, well, I didn't, did I? But you can sort it out, can't you?'

When her husband made no reply, Vi put her hand on his arm, saying sharply, 'Edwin, you've got to do something; speak to someone. The Ministry.'

His face grew even redder as he shook her off. 'I told you not to go getting yourself into the TA in the first place,' he reminded Charlie again. 'If you'd left well alone I could have wangled it that you'd be on the reserved occupation list, but it's too bloody late for that now.'

Charlie's stomach heaved and he was violently sick on the hall floor and his father's slippers.

SEVEN

Grace could hardly believe that it was finally happening and that she was about to begin her nursing training, but overlying her excitement as she walked towards the hospital's nurses' home where she had been told to present herself, was her anxiety for her brother, and her awareness of her mother's anguish.

Luke was in an army camp somewhere now, undergoing his training. There was an unfamiliar and very strained atmosphere at home, and as excited as she was at the thought of beginning her own training, Grace also felt guilty for leaving her mother when she was so very upset.

And yet at the same time as she shared her mother's anxiety, Grace could also understand how Luke felt and why he had joined up.

In the battered leather suitcase she was carrying, and which she and Jean had bargained for in a pawnbroker's dusty shop, were all the items on the list she had been given when she had received the letter informing her that she had been accepted for her training: three pairs of black stockings, one pair of flat black serviceable shoes, a selection of safety pins and studs, a packet of white Kirbigrips, two plain silver tiepins, one pocket watch with a second hand, one pair of regulation nurse's scissors, money for textbooks, six exercise books, pens and pencils and two drawstring laundry bags clearly marked with her name. Although the cost of her uniform and the textbooks would exceed her first year's earnings, her board and food, and her laundry would be provided free of charge.

Since Sister Harris had recommended her there had been no need for her to attend an interview, and it had also been Sister Harris who had measured her for her probationary uniform and sent those measurements to the hospital.

The letter she had received had told her the date on which she was to report to the nurses' home for her probationary training; that she would find her uniform waiting for her in her room; that she was to change into it and then wait in the probationary nurses' sitting room for further instructions; that she must not under any circumstances whatsoever leave the hospital wearing her uniform.

Had she done the right thing? Did she really have what it took to become a nurse? Ought she to have stayed where she was at Lewis's? What if the other girls didn't like her? What if . . . Grace's eager footsteps halted, but it was too late for second thoughts and doubts now. The nurses' home was right in front of her and the nurses' home sister, thin, grey-haired and sharp-eyed, was watching her.

Behind her stood two other sisters with lists in their hands.

Nervously Grace approached them.

'Name?' one of them barked.

'Er . . . Grace . . . Grace Campion.'

The sister was frowning for so long over her list that Grace began to wonder if it was all a mistake and she wasn't going to be allowed to train after all, but then to her relief she nodded her head and handed Grace a key with a number on it.

Now what was she supposed to do? Uncertainly she looked at the sister, but she didn't look back, turning instead to the girl who was now standing behind Grace. Another girl who had had her name ticked off by the other sister was making her way into the home, so Grace followed her.

Several girls were already inside and Grace joined them as they walked along corridors and up and down flights of stairs looking for their rooms.

The smell of carbolic lingering on the air was somehow in keeping with the green-painted walls, and shiny clean linoleum.

Grace found her room up two flights of stairs and halfway along a corridor. Her arm aching from the weight of her suitcase, she unlocked the door and went inside. Her room was small and very basic. The paint on the walls was peeling, especially around the small sink in the corner. A small dark brown wardrobe stood against one wall, along with a dressing table-cum-desk and a chair.

The iron-framed bed was covered with a green bedspread that looked thin and worn. The room felt cold and Grace shivered, suddenly overwhelmed with homesickness and a longing for her own pretty attic bedroom.

Her uniform was lying on the bed, the dresses short-sleeved, with a separate uncomfortable-looking set of collars and cuffs. The dresses were patched and darned and had obviously been passed on many times before they had come to her. Next to them was a long navy woollen cloak with a dark purple lining and purple straps that crossed at the front and fastened at the back. Grace looked for her cap, her heart sinking when she saw the two oblongs of white cloth the size of a nappy starched as stiff as a board. How on earth was she supposed to transform those into a nurse's cap?

Mindful of the list of rules she had been sent with her acceptance letter, Grace had already removed the pale pink nail polish she normally wore before leaving home, along with her pretty silver chain and locket. Student nurses were not allowed to wear any makeup or jewellery. No pictures or posters were to be hung on the walls, and slippers were not to be kept on the floor.

Quickly Grace unpacked her case and put everything away, then changed into her uniform, her fingers clumsy with nervousness.

She checked her appearance in the mirror, worrying that the hem of the dress might not be the regulation twelve inches above the floor. The fabric of her uniform dress felt uncomfortable and scratchy, and she wasn't sure which pockets she was supposed to put everything into. Her thick black stockings looked drab and her shoes felt heavy and clumsy. Grace checked her letter again. Once she had changed into her uniform she was to make her way down to the student nurses' sitting room for a 'welcome tea'.

Feeling awkward and uncertain, Grace hesitated just inside the open door to the student nurses' sitting room, which was already busy with other girls dressed in their uniforms. The tables were each set for six, with individual plates containing two sandwiches and a slice of Victoria sandwich.

A cheerful-looking girl with ginger hair and freckles came up to her and smiled. 'If you're looking for a table there's a spare seat on ours,' she offered.

Gratefully Grace followed her over to one of the tables where four other girls were already seated.

'Now we've got a full table I suppose we'd better introduce ourselves,' the ginger-haired girl suggested. 'I'm Hannah Philips.'

'Grace Campion,' Grace followed her, listening carefully as the other girls gave their names: Iris Robinson, small and pretty with dark hair and huge dark eyes. Jennifer Halliwell, who spoke with what she explained to them was a Yorkshire accent, adding that her family were originally from Leeds. Doreen Sefton, who said that if the war went on for long enough she wanted to join the army as a nurse, once she had done her training, and finally the prettiest of them all, in Grace's opinion, Lillian

Green, who had blonde curls and huge blue eyes, and who was so slim and delicate she looked as though she might blow away in the lightest wind, and who giggled and explained that she had decided to train as a nurse after she had met a gorgeous-looking doctor at a friend's party.

After they had eaten their sandwiches and cake, and drunk as much tea as they wanted, Home Sister stood up and gave them a talk about what was expected of them and the high standards set and demanded by the teaching hospitals. She emphasised how fortunate they were to be given the opportunity to train at such a prestigious hospital.

Their lessons, they learned, started at eight o'clock in the morning and did not finish until six o'clock at night. At the end of their three-month training they would sit an exam and if they passed it then and only then would they be allowed on to the wards, as that lowest of nursing ranks, the probationer.

Once they'd been dismissed, everyone made their way back to their rooms.

'You'll find that the six of us will tend to stick together now,' Hannah told Grace knowledgeably, when they were the only two of the original six who had still not reached their rooms. 'So it's a pity we've got Green as one of our number. That sort always causes trouble. You mark my words.'

Grace didn't know what to say. Hannah had already told them over tea that her elder sister and her cousin were both qualified nurses, and she certainly seemed to know the ropes better than anyone else.

'I don't mind a bit of a lark around but when it comes to chasing after doctors, saying that you've only taken up nursing so that you can do that . . .' she gave a disapproving shake of her head.

Alone in her own small room, Grace undressed, hanging up her uniform carefully, and then once she was washed and in her night things she sat down to write to her family.

Her head was buzzing with all that had happened. There was so much she wanted to write that she hardly knew where to start. She felt both uncertain and excited, half of her wishing that right now she was at home in her mother's kitchen, with its familiar sights and smells, and most of all her mother in one of her floral pinafores bustling about looking after them all, and the other half of her sharply aware that she had taken the first step from being a girl at home to being an independent young woman. She stifled an exhausted yawn. She didn't want to write anything that would alarm her mother, like how hard the work was going to be, or how nervous she had felt listening to Home Sister's stern warnings about the penalties for not making the grade or breaking one of the very many rules. It had been such an extraordinary day – a day that would live in her memory for ever. There were things like meeting the other girls in her set that she would always share with them; things that were apart from the life she had known at home.

And yet these were also things she wanted to share with her family.

It would take her ages to write down everything she wanted to say, Grace admitted, stifling another yawn, and some of it would have to wait until she had her first time off.

In the end she simply wrote that the day had gone reasonably well and that she was well and happy, but that she missed them all.

'Oh, darling!'

Vi dabbed at her eyes with the lace-edged handkerchief she had removed from her handbag, whilst Bella ignored her mother's emotions, pursing her lips and studying her reflection in the mirror.

They had arrived at the exclusive modiste's on Bold Street just over an hour ago, having had to make an appointment, as Madame Blanche only 'received' one bride at a time.

Her 'salon' was on the first floor, its décor very pink and supposedly 'French'. Everything that could be was swagged in pink silk, even the changing cubicles, and the chaise-longue and chairs on which mothers waited, handkerchief in hand, for that moment when their daughter appeared from behind the mirror screens, magically transformed by Madame and her staff into 'the bride'.

Initially Madame had been inclined to be slightly off hand. She was busy. Everyone wanted to get married because of the war. She had even – although very discreetly – added a bit extra to the prices of her gowns because of the high demand.

But then she recognised what an excellent advertisement for her gowns Bella would be, especially when she had measured her waist and found it to be a mere twenty-two inches, and she had thawed slightly.

'And the bridesmaids – will they be dressed by us?' she asked Vi once Vi had got over the emotion of seeing Bella looking everything that a bride should be.

It was Bella who answered her, saying carelessly, 'Oh, no. I'm having only two bridesmaids, after all, and we've already got them something.'

Madame incline her head. She wouldn't have expected a bride as pretty as this to insist on her having her bridesmaids dressed to their disadvantage and her advantage, but quite plainly in Madame's opinion that was what she intended. So far as the bride herself went, though, Madame doubted she'd seen a better one the whole year.

Bella preencd and posed in her gown, the most expensive one they had been shown, and she had known immediately that she wanted it. Plain heavy satin trimmed with thick lace, and designed to show off a small waist, it might have been made for her. The only alteration necessary, as Madame had said, was a fraction reduction of the waist because hers was so tiny. That would show Alan's mother and stop those cold angry looks she kept on giving her. It might have suited Bella to have both sets of parents believe that Alan had 'forgotten' himself, in order to expedite their marriage, but it certainly did not suit her ambitions for her

161

future to be talked about behind her back by the Tennis Club set as someone who had 'had to get married'.

She certainly wasn't going to have either Grace or Trixie wearing an expensive dress either. Why should she? If Grace had had any consideration at all she'd have waited until after the wedding to go and start training to be a nurse. It was ridiculous, her doing something like that anyway, trying to show off and get herself involved in nursing because of this wretched war. And as for Trixie . . . well, the only reason Bella had wanted to have her as her bridesmaid was to show Trixie and Mrs Parker that she was the one who was marrying Alan. Trixie wasn't even one of her friends, and she wasn't going to become one either. Why should she want to make a friend of a plain dull girl like Trixie? Of course, she was another one involving herself in this wretched war fuss, as well.

Vi tried not to look too appalled when Madame informed her of the cost of Bella's dress. Edwin wouldn't be pleased. She tried to suggest that Bella have a less expensive wedding gown but the truth was that her heart wasn't really in it. From the moment she had seen her darling standing there in it, looking a true vision of beauty and modesty, her heart had swelled with so much maternal pride that she had agreed with Bella that it was impossible for her to wear anything else.

Edwin was constantly preaching economy, with regard to the wedding, especially since she had insisted to him that they could not let poor Bella move in with her in-laws and that if the Parkers didn't do something for the young couple to enable them to have their own house then they must. But at the same time as he was saying he wasn't made of money he was also boasting about how much money he was going to make because of the war.

'We've just got the flowers and the cake to sort out now, darling,' Vi told Bella as they left Madame's salon.

'And the house,' Bella reminded her sharply. 'Don't forget about that, Mummy. I can't possibly move in with Alan's parents.'

'Of course not, Bella, and no one's suggesting that you should. It's just that your father thinks that maybe you should consider something a bit smaller to start off with.'

Bella pouted. She had set her heart on a four-bedroomed detached house in the same road as Alan's parents, but with a larger garden. The kind of house, as she had pointed out determinedly to her father, that people would expect her and Alan to have.

'Aye, well, let Alan's father put his hand in his pocket and pay for it then,' her father had responded sharply, but Bella knew how to get round him.

'I don't think Mr Parker's business is going to do as well out of the war as yours is, Daddy. I've heard him say so,' she had told him, slipping her arm through his as she added, 'In fact, Alan has as good as said that his father is just a little bit jealous of you because you're so successful, and

I don't suppose they're going to like it very much if you buy us a house.'

She would get the house she wanted, Bella knew – one way or another.

'It's such a pity that this wretched war has come now,' Vi sighed now, as they made their way home. They would have to cross the Mersey using the ferry, and then get the bus, but with such a satisfactory day behind them, and so much to talk about, neither of them minded. 'I'm afraid that we shan't be having as many guests as we would have done, because of it. Your auntie Jean's written to say that Luke probably won't be able to come, and it's the same for Charlie,' Vi added, as they found seats on the bus that would take them down to the Pier Head and the ferry, ready to make the crossing to Wallasey.

Bella pulled a face. 'I'm not bothered if Auntie Jean doesn't come. It's a pity we haven't got some really smart relatives, Mummy. That would show the Parkers.'

Vi could only agree with her. Her twin sister wearing her one good coat with her husband dressed in a half-price Blackler's suit was hardly going to impress the likes of the Parkers. Mrs Parker was the type who would know immediately what everyone was wearing had cost and judge them accordingly, Vi decided, conveniently forgetting that that was exactly what she would do herself.

'It's just so selfish of Charlie to have gone and got himself called up for the TA just when I'm getting married,' Bella complained. 'I was relying on him and Luke to be groomsmen and now they probably won't be there.'

'Well, darling, I'm sure Charlie's equally unhappy about what's happened himself. He never intended to get involved in this, as you know, and Daddy is still very cross with him.'

Of course, it was typical of her sister Jean's family that Luke had volunteered for the army and was now undergoing his initial training and that Grace was training as a nurse, Vi reflected ungraciously. She just hoped her twin didn't live to regret it. She'd heard that nursing had a dreadful coarsening effect on a young girl and was little better than being a skivvy.

Vi was every bit as put out about the fact that the war had stolen some of their shared mother-and-bride glory as Bella, even though she had initially been the first to recognise what an excellent excuse it had provided for the speed with which Bella was getting married. It was bad enough that Mrs Parker was refusing to be as publicly enthusiastic and grateful for the fact that she was getting such a prize as a daughter-in-law as she ought to have been, without this talk of the war to detract from Bella's big day.

The Parkers had even had the gall to suggest that the wedding should be kept low key because of the war, but Vi had put her foot down on that idea.

'Oh, no, Mrs Parker, I don't think so,' had been her saccharine response. 'I'm sure that everyone will be grateful to have something to cheer them up a bit. Really, Edwin feels that it's our duty to carry on as though the war hasn't been announced.'

'But with so many families having seen their young men go off into the services, and Mr Parker being on the council, eyebrows might be raised.'

Vi had been delighted to be able to point out smugly, 'Well, with our own son already in uniform, and my Edwin so involved with the Ministry, I doubt that any eyebrows will be raised in *our* direction, Mrs Parker.'

Not, of course, that that she wanted to fall out with Bella's mother-in-law-to-be, but she had seen the way Mrs Parker's cronies had looked at *her* that first WVS meeting after the engagement had been announced.

'I expect you'll be seeing Alan tonight, will you, Bella? After all, you haven't seen him all week.'

'I can't, Mummy. There's so much to do still for the wedding. I thought you and I and Daddy might go and have another look at the house tonight. I'd really like to get that front room re-papered before we move in, and you said you thought it needed a new stove for the kitchen, if Daddy does buy it for us. I do hope that he will, Mummy. I couldn't bear to have to live with Alan's parents.'

Of course she would really have rather gone out to see a film with Alan, or at least she would have done if he wasn't being so beastly and unkind to her. And, anyway, it was for his sake really that she was being a good fiancée and organising things for their new home, not that her father had actually said yet that the would buy it for them, but Bella knew that he would.

Grace was exhausted. The first day of their training had passed in a blur of information and her own anxious fear that she wouldn't remember any of what she had been told, or worse, that she would do something so dreadful that she would receive one of the ignominious warnings from Sister Tutor that several of the other girls in her set had had during the course of the day.

Watching and listening whilst Sister Tutor and Home Sister had shown them the correct procedure for making up a hospital bed had told Grace just how much she had to learn. Who could have imagined that such a simple procedure could sound so complicated whilst looking so easy. The sheets must be pulled tight and not have a single wrinkle because that could cause a patient to develop bed sores. They must not be shaken vigorously because that could spread dust and infection.

Their day had started with fifteen minutes of morning prayers led by the principal sister tutor, after which they all had to don their starched aprons and follow the pinned-up rota of cleaning chores, which included the lavatories and the floors, overseen by the stern eye of the sister tutors. Everything had, they were told very firmly indeed, to be spotlessly clean, and everything had to be done in a strictly regimented and fixed fashion, and woe betide anyone who did not adhere to that routine.

Their first day's true lessons had been of the chalk-and-talk variety, although at first few of them had even been able to take their eyes off the life-size male torso, bereft of limbs and, of course, private parts, positioned close to the blackboard. This torso showed the male anatomy from head to groin in what they had all agreed later was truly gruesome detail.

And then there had been Mrs Jones, the dummy on which they would have to practise various procedures. Mrs Jones lived in the Practical Room, which also contained hospital beds, stainless-steel trolleys, rubber tubes, face-mask jars and shining instrument cupboards filled with frightening-looking equipment, sterilisers and bandaging, and shudder-inducing Skelly the skeleton, so that they could memorise each part of the body.

'Phew, thank goodness there aren't any more lessons today,' Iris sighed in relief as the girls all made their way towards their dining room for their meal.

'That's nothing, you just wait,' Hannah warned them, whilst Lillian pouted and complained, 'I thought it was going to be a lot more fun than this. I didn't come here to be a char.'

'What about you, Grace?' Hannah asked. 'What did you think of today?'

'I don't know yet. There seems so much to learn, and knowing we've got to get it right because people's lives will depend on us is such a big respon-sibility. I want to do it, but I'm not sure I can.'

The day had left her feeling overwhelmed and

yet at the same time inspired. She couldn't wait to write home about it. The twins, in particular, would love hearing about Skelly.

When Sam came in for his tea, Jean watched him carefully whilst trying to make sure that he didn't realise she was doing so.

Sam hadn't said a single word about Luke since their son had left, and at first she had been so upset by what had happened that she hadn't felt inclined to talk about it herself. But it wasn't in Jean's nature to blame or punish those she loved, and as the days went by she became increasingly concerned about Sam.

Where he had been so upright and proud when he walked, now he seemed to stoop, his head bent as though he wanted to avoid looking at anyone. He looked older and diminished somehow. He also seemed to have withdrawn into himself, rarely speaking, his expression bleak. It hurt her to see him like this every bit as much as it had hurt her to see Luke walk away, but Luke was her son, her child, and like any mother she felt protective of him, whilst Sam was her husband and it was towards him that she looked for *her* protection.

She knew families in which the woman had to stand between husband and son, sometimes even physically, but she had never imagined that Luke and Sam would fall out. They had always been so close, so much in harmony with one another, so 'like father like son', as the old saying went. Now Luke had hurt Sam twice over: once by rejecting his advice and a second time with his absence.

'I expect we'll be hearing from Grace soon,' Jean told Sam as she poured his tea. She waited until she put the teapot down before adding as casually as she could, 'And Luke, of course. I was speaking with Mrs Gilchrist from five down today and she said that when they're doing their training the lads normally get to write home once a week on a Sunday.'

The wireless was on, and she and Sam normally enjoyed a good chat over their tea, listening to the news, exchanging news of their different days, talking about the children, as parents did, and it hurt her that Sam was shutting her out, even though they had been married long enough for her to understand that that was just his way.

Young Bella would soon learn that there was more to getting married than having a fancy wedding.

The house felt so empty without Luke and Grace, although hardly quiet. Not with the twins and that gramophone of theirs, she reflected as she waited for Sam to reply, trying not to show how anxious she was.

She had warned the twins about not playing their records too loudly when they had come home saying that they had bought a second-hand gramophone with the money they had earned from running errands, but to judge from the music she could hear from their bedroom they hadn't paid much attention.

Abruptly Sam pushed his chair back and then stood up, frowning as he looked towards the ceiling.

'I'm sick of that damned row.' His mouth compressed and he strode past her, opening the kitchen door and going up the stairs.

Jean could feel her heart suddenly contracting as though someone was squeezing it, filling her with a mixture of pain and concern.

The girls' bedroom door opened and then suddenly there was silence. Then Sam came back downstairs carrying a record in his hands.

'Sam, what are you doing?' Jean asked.

'What does it look like? If you've told them once about the noise, you've told them a dozen times. Well, you won't have to tell them again. I'm throwing this out.'

'Oh, Sam, no,' Jean protested. 'They don't mean to play their records so loudly.' She gave a small sigh. 'Remember how we used to love music ourselves when we were young.'

Sam slammed the record down on the table and opened the back door, striding down the garden. Jean could see him leaning over the fence at the bottom of the garden. Poor Sam.

The twins came downstairs, looking uncertainly round the door.

'Where's Dad?' Lou asked

'He's in the garden.'

'He took our record.'

'Well, you've both been told often enough not to play them so loudly. It's bin driving me and your dad mad, and half the street as well, I expect,' Jean scolded them.

'Mum, me and Lou have been thinking that we'd like to be singers and make records,' Sasha informed her.

'Yes. Like Auntie Francine. Well, like she'd be if she'd made any records. Is that why she's gone to America?' Lou asked.

'Your auntie Francine has gone to America because she's singing with Gracie Fields, and as to the two of you making records, well, I dare say your dad will have something to say about that,' Jean warned them firmly.

Sam was still leaning over the fence. Things couldn't go on like this. Jean wiped her hands on her apron and headed for the back door.

'Where are you going?' Lou asked her.

'Never you mind. You two stay here and no playing any loud music.'

'I bet she's gone to talk to Dad,' Lou told Sasha as soon as Jean had gone.

'I wish that Luke and Grace were here. It's horrid without them,' Sasha sighed.

Sam hadn't heard her coming, or he was ignoring her, Jean didn't know which but she did know that the sight of his unmoving back view wrenched at her heart.

The Michaelmas daisies they had planted the year after they had moved in were in full bloom, along with Sam's prized chrysanthemums, their cheerfulness at odds with the prevailing atmosphere at the Campions'.

As much as she missed Luke and feared for him, which she did, Jean could understand why he had done what he had, and yes, she was even proud of him, though at the same time so very, very frightened for him. But she wasn't Sam. Luke had not gone against her wishes and her advice; he had not turned his back on her as she knew Sam felt Luke had on him.

She took a deep breath and closed the distance between them. They weren't a couple who were physically affectionate with one another in public, but instinctively Jean put her arm round Sam and stood close to him. To her relief he didn't, as she had been half-afraid he might, pull away from her, and when he turned to look at her she saw that there were tears in his eyes.

Her heart trembled and ached for her husband. Oh, Luke! But how could she condemn her son for his father's pain? She loved them both.

'Our Reg was seventeen when he went off to war,' Sam announced without preamble. 'I can see him now, Jean. A good-looking lad, he was.'

Jean nodded. Sam and his family had lived close by when they were growing up and she could remember Sam's elder brother.

'He was always our mam's favourite.' Sam's breath shuddered in his throat. 'She were never the same after we got the news that he'd been killed. I allus thought that she'd rather it had been me if one of us had to go.'

'No, Sam, don't say that,' Jean begged him, her eyes filling with tears.

'It was only having that ruddy whooping cough that saved me from going, and I reckon if I had I would have been dead, an' all.'

Jean nodded again, but didn't say anything, sensing that now wasn't the time. She knew the story of how contracting whooping cough and being ill for so long had meant that Sam had been declared unfit for military service, and how although he never said so in so many words, that had left him with a feeling of guilt because his brother who had gone off to war had died whilst he who had not, had lived.

That had been before they had started courting, after the war was over. She had felt only relief when she had heard the story. It always made her heart clench with fear to think how easily she might have lost him before she had even loved him.

'War does terrible things to a man, Jean. Even them that did come back, they was never the same. You know that.'

'Yes,' she agreed. Both of them had seen within their own families, and amongst their neighbours, men who had returned from the trenches so changed, both physically and within themselves, by the horrors they had seen and experienced that they were condemned forever to live within the hell of their memories, isolated from those who loved them.

'*We* know that, Sam, but Luke's young. He doesn't know what we do.'

It was the wrong thing to say. Immediately

he tensed. 'Well, he should do,' he answered grimly. 'I've told him often enough what happens to men that go to war. But no, he thinks he knows better, he thinks it's all medals and glory and wearing a ruddy uniform. He doesn't know the half of it.'

'He's got your pride, Sam, you know that.'

'Aye, well, his pride won't do him much good when he's lying face down in the mud and dead, will it?' His voice was savage with pain.

Jean started to tremble. Sam's words were conjuring up an all too vivid picture for her. 'Don't say things like that,' she begged him. 'I can't bear the thought of it.'

'Do you think I can? Ruddy young fool. He could have been here, safe . . . and still have done summat for the war effort. Doing your bit isn't just about joining the ruddy army. There's many a chap worked for the Salvage Corps that's got more guts – aye, wot's done more for this city than any ruddy soldier.'

Jean reached out to touch him and Sam pulled away, rejecting her unspoken comfort. He felt things so deeply; Jean knew that, even if no one else did. As a young bride it had upset her dreadfully when his occasional dark moods of unhappiness came down over him, causing him to retreat from her into his own pain and silence, until she had learned to understand how affected he had been both by his elder brother's death and the fact that he had not been able to join up himself.

'I never thought it would come to this, Jean,

that me own son would look at me like he thought I was a coward.'

'Luke would never do that, Sam.'

'Looked at me just like me mam did, when Nellie Jefferies from number eleven give me them white feathers,' Sam told her, ignoring her protest. 'Walked off, Mam did, and left me there in the street, she was that ashamed of me, and no wonder. Lost three sons and her hubby Nellie had and there was me walking down the street, when every other lad that lived there had gone off to fight.'

There it was, the real unacknowledged source of Sam's pain, forced down and locked away and now brought back to festering life, moving Jean to an immediate defence of him.

'Sam, you were ill. The army wouldn't take you, and if Nellie Jefferies had had any sense she'd have known that.'

'It wasn't just her. Even me own mam thought . . .' He stopped and shook his head, his jaw set.

Jean had thought that Sam had got over believing that his mother blamed him in some way for living whilst Reg had died. It was such a long time ago. It worried her to hear him talking about it again now and in that kind of voice. She felt guilty for not recognising how he felt.

'It's only natural that this war should bring back memories of the last one, Sam. But . . .' she hesitated, groping for the words to say what she felt had to be said without making the situation even worse, and could only come up with a lame, 'well, that's all in the past now.'

'Is it?' Sam challenged her. 'How can it be, Jean, when me own son is acting just like me mam did and accusing me of being a coward?'

'Sam, that's not true at all,' Jean denied. 'Luke never said anything of the kind. And as for your mam . . .'

Jean had to pause then, remembering that Sam's mother had never really been as loving towards Sam as her own mother had been to her and her sisters. As the young girl Sam was courting she had simply accepted that Sam's widowed mother was different from her own much more openly affectionate mum without questioning it. In those days young girls were brought up to respect their elders and she would never have dreamed of criticising Sam's mother, or even of talking about her, to her own mother. However, she could remember now that her own mother had commented that the death of her elder son had turned Sam's mother 'a bit funny'.

Sam's mother had died shortly after Luke had been born, and Jean could remember how hurt she'd been at the way her mother-in-law had turned away from her new grandson the first time she saw him. Afterwards she'd put that down to her being poorly, but maybe there had been more to it than that, and Sam's mother *had* resented Sam for being alive whilst her elder son was dead.

'Well, like I just said,' she insisted to Sam, 'our Luke never said anything about you being a coward.'

'He may not have said it, but it's what he was

thinking. I could see that from the way he was looking at me. And besides, if he hadn't thought it then he'd have listened to my advice and stayed put.'

'Sam, that's nonsense. Luke thinks the world of you, and he always has done. It's just that he wants to do his bit and to be part of what his friends are doing. It must have been hard for him, listening to all the other lads talking about enlisting.'

She knew immediately that she had said the wrong thing, but it was too late. She could see the tips of Sam's ears burning dark red with anger.

'Hard for him? Don't you think it was hard for me when every lad in our street had gone off to war but for me, and me with me mam hating me for being there and not being our Reg? He was always her favourite.'

Jean searched her mind for something to say that would comfort him and realised that she could not think of anything, not for a pain that went so deep and which had been kept secret until now. Tears blurred her vision; not for Luke but for the young lad her Sam had been.

He'd always had a bit of a soft spot for Vi's Jack, and had blamed Vi for favouring the other two over him and now suddenly she thought she could understand why.

'Well, if he was then she was daft, if you ask me,' she said resolutely. 'There's no one who can hold a candle to you for being a good husband and father, Sam.'

When he shifted his weight from one foot to

the other in the familiar way that told her that he was taking in what she was saying even if he appeared not to be, she continued determinedly, 'And it's not only me that thinks so. It gets on me nerves at times, the number of women that tell me how lucky I am to be married to a chap like you.' She summoned up a frown and deliberately made herself look severe. 'Aye, and I've a pretty fair notion that more than one of them wouldn't mind stepping into me shoes if they thought they might get the chance, especially that Dolly Nesbitt wot works in the chippy. Always had a bit of an eye for you, she has.'

'What, her with the brassy-looking hair that wears all that lipstick? Do me a favour, Jean.'

Jean smiled to herself. She could see that he had begun to perk up a little bit. Not for anything was she going to tell him just how, over the years, she'd looked at her good-looking, tall, broad-shouldered husband and worried that some flighty piece might try to get her hands on him. Not these days, of course. She was too sensible for that now, what with them with a grown-up family, an' all.

'Come on in, love,' she urged Sam. 'It's beginning to feel really damp with the dew coming.' Jean rubbed her arms to take the evening chill out of her flesh, and then smiled when Sam reached for her, putting his arm around her and drawing her into his side.

He felt so warm and solid, so safe and strong, no one who didn't know him as well as she did could ever guess how vulnerable he could be, especially not Luke, who had always looked up to his father. Sam had never been one to talk about his own youth to his children – he just wasn't that sort. Jean leaned gratefully into his warmth.

'Our Luke is so young, Jean. All I wanted to do was to keep him safe.'

'I know, love.'

'Looked at me like he hated me, he did.'

'He'll be missing you, Sam. Allus thought the world of you, our Luke has, right from the start. Remember how it was always you that could stop him crying when he was teething and not me?'

She could feel his chest lift as he gave a reluctant laugh.

'Aye, I can see him now sitting there, watching for me coming in. It's a strange thing, you know, Jean, holding a little 'un and knowing that you've helped make it, knowing that you've helped give it life. It makes you feel that you can never stop worrying, never stop looking out for it, and at the same time it fills your heart with so much happiness that it could almost burst.' Sam shook his head.

Jean said nothing. As a mother she knew all too well the feelings Sam was struggling to explain.

EIGHT

She wasn't one little bit disappointed because Seb wasn't here at the wedding – of course she wasn't, Grace reassured herself. It was just that she would have liked to introduce him to her mother, in view of what that happened. But then again her mother had been preoccupied and on edge, looking worriedly at Luke, who had only arrived home this morning, after they had thought he wasn't going to get leave, and with barely enough time to change into the morning suit Bella had insisted the groomsmen were to wear.

Of course her mother was disappointed that she hadn't had time to talk to Luke properly; she was disappointed herself, Grace admitted. She had been looking forward to exchanging stories of what it felt like to live away from home for the first time with her brother.

She was finding her new life as a probationary nurse both exciting and nerve-racking and would have welcomed the opportunity to discuss with her family her apprehension about whether or not she was going to be good enough, but there just hadn't been time.

'That frock really doesn't suit you at all, Grace,' Lou told her as the twins came to sit down beside her.

It was true that the virulently bright pink sateen dresses with their puffed sleeves and gathered skirts were not at all flattering. Even the sweetheart necklines seem to have been cut in such a way that they gaped awkwardly.

'At least Grace looks better in it than the other bridesmaid,' Sasha defended their elder sister.

Poor Trixie, Grace thought sympathetically, their dresses might have been designed specifically to make the other girl look plain and gawky, and to make her hair look more gingery, in contrast with Bella's wedding dress, which was so stunningly beautiful that it was no wonder that the whole church had seemed to be filled with a sigh of appreciation when Bella had walked down the aisle on her father's arm.

Now the formalities of the marriage service were over, along with the wedding breakfast, and the guests were relaxing in the comfort of the Hotel Splendide's banqueting suite, which was on the first floor of the building and reached via an ornate sweeping staircase.

The hotel had originally been the home of a wealthy ship owner, and was very grand, with portraits of 'the family' still adorning the hallway and the stairs. The 'banqueting suite' had originally been the ballroom, along with the withdrawing room beyond it, according to the hotel's brochure.

It had been the withdrawing room in which the wedding guests had sat down at long trestle tables to a formal wedding breakfast of roast chicken with all the trimmings, followed by trifle and then cheese and biscuits, after which the guests had moved into the ballroom to dance to the music provided by the hotel's resident pianist. The collection of tables and chairs, which were set out around the edge of the floor, the tables covered in pale pink damask tableclothes, were dwarfed by the room's high ceiling and the gilded mirrors hanging on the walls.

'Look out, here comes Bella,' Lou warned her twin, the pair of them getting up as one to disappear, leaving Grace on her own with their cousin.

'There you are,' said Bella crossly. 'You are supposed to be here to be my bridesmaid, Grace. And where's Trixie? You'd think she'd be far more grateful that she's been included. All she's done is hide herself away in a corner. And as for Trixie's parents; all *they've* done is sit with Alan's parents. None of them has made any attempt to mingle. Daddy invited everyone from the council as well. But then, of course, Alan's father has rather shown himself up by refusing to buy the house I wanted. I don't know what we'd have done if Daddy hadn't stepped in and bought it for us.'

Grace said nothing as she listened to Bella's comments. It wasn't the first time today that her cousin had criticised Alan's parents to her and Grace wondered how she would feel if she was marrying someone whose mother she disliked as much as Bella disliked Alan's mother.

Bella opened the pretty little satin bag that matched her wedding dress and withdrew a packet of Sobranie cocktail cigarettes and a holder, her actions making Grace's eyes round. The only time she had ever seen anyone smoking the coloured cigarettes or using a holder had been in a film.

Bella extracted one of the five pastel-coloured cigarettes and inserted the gold filter tip into her smart cigarette holder and then lit the cigarette.

Bella had changed so much in the short time she had been engaged. Grace felt that she barely knew her any more.

'God, doesn't Trixie look dreadful? I can't imagine what on earth Alan ever saw in her. Poor thing, she's so dreadfully plain. Ugly really, almost.' There was satisfaction as well as malice in Bella's voice.

Alan might have chosen to marry Bella, but he was still spending rather a lot of time talking to Trixie and her parents, Grace noticed, but then they were seated at a table in the ballroom with Alan's own parents, who Bella had studiously ignored from the minute the formal wedding break-fast had finished.

The newly married couple were only having a short honeymoon, 'because of the war', as Bella had put it, pouting when she had informed Grace that she had wanted to honeymoon in Paris but was having to make do with a few days in Blackpool.

'You'll have to change into your going-away outfit soon,' Grace reminded Bella, mindful of her bridesmaid responsibilities and duties.

'In a minute. I want the photographer to take another photograph of me standing on the stairs in my wedding dress first. Go and find him, will you, Grace?'

Grace couldn't help thinking that in Bella's shoes she might have been feeling more eager to be alone with her new husband, but then Bella's dress was gorgeous and she did look beautiful in it, Grace acknowledged generously.

'Bloody army,' Charlie swore as he threw down his cigarette stub and then ground it out beneath his shoe. 'Christ, I haven't had a drink in two weeks.'

Charlie was certainly making up for that now, Luke recognised as he watched his cousin summoning a waiter to order yet another G and T.

'Want another yourself?' Charlie asked.

Luke shook his head. He had barely touched his shandy. He had been too busy studiously avoiding looking at his father.

Luke wasn't sure what he had been hoping for when he had arrived back home this morning, later than he had hoped because of the problems he had had making his way from his camp in Northern

Ireland back to Liverpool, but it had made his heart sink with misery when the first thing his dad had done when he had seen him had been to turn his back and ignore him.

When he had told Grace she had suggested that it might have been better if he had changed into his civvies before going home, because seeing him in his uniform was bound to make their father feel that Luke was deliberately making the point that he had joined up.

Luke grimaced now, thinking of Grace's sisterly advice. Changing into civvies had been the last thing on his mind as he had battled to leave the camp in time to catch the train for the ferry, standing up all the way and then having to stand again on the packed ferry. It had been touch and go whether or not he had made it at all, and the truth was that he had got home feeling more like going to bed and catching up on the sleep he had missed over the last forty-eight hours rather than going to a wedding.

Luke had missed his family, and especially his father, a very great deal, even if he still believed that he had had no option other than to join up and did not regret doing so for one minute. He was with a good bunch of lads, all very much from his own background and circumstances, and he was already making friends amongst his group, as they shared the rigours of their intensive training. But it hurt hearing the others joking about their proud fathers. All the more so because he and his father had always been so close. Normally, there was no one he'd sooner turn to for advice and to confide in than his father. As the two males in a household of four females they had naturally had a very special bond, and Luke really felt the loss of that.

Jean was right, though, in saying that Sam and Luke were alike and Luke had inherited his father's pride and his stubbornness. He was ready to forget their quarrel and his father's harsh words to him, but he was certainly not ready to abandon his belief that his decision to join up had been the right one.

'Mind you, I reckon the old man will bend a few ears and get me out,' Charlie was saying confidently, his tongue loosened by the amount he had had to drink. 'He's taking his time about it, though. He was in the devil of a temper with me when he found out I'd been called up. Not my fault, though, ishh it?' Charlie was slurring his words now as he knocked back another drink. 'Bloody stupid, thinking that. If I'd really wanted to volunteer I'd have gone for the RAF, not signed on in the ruddy TA.'

Charlie looked balefully at his father, who was standing with a group of his fellow councillors in front of the ballroom's imposing marble fireplace, his chest puffed out and his face red with heat and self-importance.

Edwin wasn't enjoying the wedding. For a start it had cost him an arm and a leg, and that was before he had been daft enough to let Vi persuade him into buying the newly married couple a house. Edwin still wasn't sure just how or why he had come to agree to part with so much money, but at least, as he had just told his fellow councillors in a voice deliberately loud enough to reach the ears of George Parker, Alan's father, he had had the sense to put the house in his own name.

Ruddy weddings. Edwin tugged at his collar, which felt too tight, constricting his neck. If he had cherished hopes of being envied and revered by his fellow councillors because of the extra business the war was going to put his way, and his daughter's marriage to Alan Parker, he had quickly come to realise that just the opposite seemed to have happened and that it was being made clear to him that he was still very much an outsider as far as Wallasey's long-time residents were concerned, even though they were more than happy to fill their glasses at his expense. And then there was that young idiot Charlie, who didn't have a brass farthing's worth of sense and who should have been here at home, working in the business, not playing at ruddy soldiers. Of course he'd have to find a way of getting him out of the TA and back where he belonged, but not yet. It would serve him right to have to wait, and teach him a well-needed lesson.

Jean looked across at the twins. They looked ever so nice in the matching dresses she had bought them at Lewis's, white cotton with an all-over pattern of blue and pink flowers, and nipped in a bit at the waist, making them suddenly look rather more grown up than Jean really liked. Even though Grace wasn't working there any more, she had had a word with the manageress of the Gown Salon and Jean had been given a bit of discount off the price because the dresses were really summer stock and would be going in the next sale.

Her own suit was new as well. Sam had insisted, and Jean had to admit that she felt proper smart in it. The tweed jacket had slightly padded shoulders and a bit of a military cut to it – a fashion that was now coming in because of the war, Grace had told her when they had gone to Lewis's together to choose it. It had given Jean a real thrill of pleasure to discover that her waist was still neat enough for her to wear something so tailored, even if she had worried that the suit's skirt was a little bit on the short side for a married woman with a grown-up family. Its brown heathery flecked tweed went perfectly with her best handbag and shoes, and she had trimmed up her brown hat with some new petersham ribbon and some feathers.

It had certainly been a posh do, but as she had said to Sam earlier, Bella and her new husband hadn't looked anywhere near as happy as she had remembered feeling when she and Sam had got wed. Vi was full of herself, though, over Bella's marriage, but then of course it was typical of Vi that she should be. She hadn't let Jean say so much as a word in praise of Grace and her nursing training.

'Come on, everyone, the bride and groom are about to leave.'

Dutifully everyone gathered in the hallway to watch Bella and Alan walk down the stairs together.

Her hand tucked through Alan's arm, Bella gave Trixie a triumphant look as the newly married couple ran the gauntlet of the confetti being thrown at them as they hurried from the hotel to Alan's waiting car.

She had done it, Bella congratulated herself smugly. She had got what she wanted, just as she always did.

NINE

Oh heavens, why had the bus stopped yet again, Grace fretted. They had all been later than they had planned leaving Wallasey, thanks to Bella making a fuss about wanting more photographs of herself in her wedding dress, and then the ferry had been full and they had to wait for the next one, and her precious pass out from the nurses' home expired at ten o'clock.

It was nearly that now and she had been holding her breath with every stop the bus had made on its way up from the Pier Head to the hospital, trying to make out – through the mesh covering the windows to protect passengers from the danger of flying glass should they be bombed – how far they had come, even though she knew that there would be nothing to see in the dark, thanks to the blackout.

The bus stopped yet again, passengers exchanging seats and standing space, some them getting off, others replacing them in their vacated seats.

They couldn't be far from the hospital now.

The bus picked up speed, allowing Grace's cramped stomach muscles to relax and then recramp even harder as abruptly it lurched to halt with a squeal of brakes and a suddenness that had standing passengers almost losing their balance. Raised voices started protesting.

'What the devil . . . ?'

'Ruddy driver.'

'Ruddy blackout, don't you mean?' one passenger joked, all of them silenced when the conductor called out.

'Driver says there's bin an accident up front and he can't go further until the road's been cleared.'

'It's this blasted blackout,' the man seated next to Grace grumbled. 'It ain't safe out there any more.'

Grace knew that it was true. There was lot of talk about the number of road accidents in the pitch-dark. It was even being suggested that the kerbs might be painted white as a preventative measure.

She really was going to be late now, Grace recognised worriedly as she joined the other passengers getting off the bus.

In the street a small crowd of bystanders had already gathered in front of the bus, which now had its lights full on to illuminate the scene. The driver of a lorry was half hanging out of the side of his cab, looking more like a rag doll than a human being, and to one side of the vehicle Grace could see a pretty high-heeled shoe. Just the one. Nothing else. Grace's stomach turned over and heaved.

A man in a smart suit stepped out of the crowd announcing, 'I'm a doctor. Has anyone sent for the emergency services?'

'Just sent for them now, sir,' another man responded.

The doctor had made his way to the cab and was feeling for the driver's pulse. Grace turned away, wondering how she was going to get past the accident and whether she should make a detour down another street.

'I need help – a nurse . . .' the doctor was saying tersely as he went to a car, which Grace now saw was stopped behind the bus, to remove a medical bag. 'Any nurses here?'

No one answered. Grace's stomach tightened again. She wasn't a nurse, not yet, but somehow her conscience was prodding her into stepping forward and saying uncertainly, 'I'm not a nurse, only a probationer, but . . .'

The doctor looked at her. 'Had first-aid training have you?'

'Yes,' she confirmed.

'Come with me.'

Gingerly Grace followed him, deliberately not looking at that one shoe.

The driver had gone through the windscreen of the truck before falling back against the side of the cab. Grace's stomach heaved when she saw his face, and the blood pumping out of his arm, which was hanging as an unnatural angle, but she reminded herself of all the things Sister Harris had taught them as she blocked out the image, concentrating instead on what the doctor was telling her to do, which was really just a matter of not panicking, she told herself stoutly, and ignoring the blood that was now all over her clothes. Determinedly she handed him the things he asked for, and helped him to put a tourniquet on the arm wound. It was, she knew, important that they did not move the driver any more than was necessary because of the injuries to his head.

She heard someone saying grimly, 'There's a couple gone under the ruddy truck but they're goners.'

Her hand trembled slightly.

Not one but two ambulances suddenly arrived, their crews rushing forward. Grace got up and stepped back to allow them to take her place, her face flushing when the doctor said briefly, 'Good work.'

She felt stiff and cold and very sick, and yet at the same time numb, as though she wasn't really able to take in what was happening.

'You all right, love?'

Grace looked up at the ambulance driver. The kindness in his voice made her eyes burn with tears.

'Yes. Thank you.'

'Not bin hurt, have you?' he pressed her. 'Only you're in a bit of a state.'

'I was helping the doctor. I'm a probationer nurse up at the hospital,' she explained haltingly.

'We've got to go past Mill Road on our way back to the depot. Jump in, love, and we'll give you a lift,' he offered.

'Oh. No. I don't think . . .' Grace began to protest, but his crew were already making their way back to the ambulance, saying that their assistance wasn't needed because the crew of the other ambulance were dealing with the emergency.

Suddenly Grace felt very weak and dizzy. She could hear concerned voices, and then two firm male arms were supporting her and that same kind male voice was telling her calmly, 'That's the spirit, just take a few deep breaths and you'll be fine . . .'

'I'm the one who's the nurse,' she managed to find the spirit to remind him as the ambulance driver helped her along the road and then up into the cab of the ambulance, refusing to listen to her shaky protests.

She wasn't too shaky, though, to notice in the lights of the bus that he was as tall as Luke and as broad-shouldered, with a cheeky grin and teasing blue eyes.

After he had helped her into the passenger seat, he closed the door and then went round to get in the driver's side of the vehicle.

'I reckon we'd better introduce ourselves,' he told Grace, once he had started the ambulance's engine, 'seeing as how we're going to be seeing a lot more of one another. I'm Teddy Williams.'

'Grace Campion,' Grace introduced herself. She was beginning to feel better now, and she looked round the interior of the cab with curious interest. The probationers had been shown around an ambulance station and one of its vehicles as part of their training. 'Are you stationed at Mill Road then?' she asked him innocently, then blushed when he laughed.

'As it happens, yes, but that wasn't what I meant. Mind you, I suppose a pretty girl like you has already got a chap in tow?'

'No. I mean . . .' Grace laughed and blushed even harder when she realised what he was getting at.

'Well, you could have now, if you play your cards right. I might even let you take me to see a film,' Teddy joked, giving her a wink.

She liked him, Grace acknowledged. She could sense that there was something kind and appealing about him that went deeper than his outward joking and teasing.

'Home Sister is very strict,' she told him. 'I've only been allowed out today because it was my cousin's wedding and I was her bridesmaid.'

'Well, in that case I'll just have to make sure that I'm on the duty roster for Mill Road,' he told her, 'if that's the only way I'm going to get to see you.'

They had reached the hospital now and he had pulled up discreetly out of sight of the night porter's small lodge.

'Thanks for . . . for everything,' Grace told him, suddenly feeling shy.

He had nice hands, she decided, big and clean and safe-looking, a bit like her dad's.

'I suppose you're wondering why I haven't joined up to fight.'

His comment surprised her. 'No, of course not,' Grace assured him.

'I had rheumatic fever when I was a kiddie – I'm OK now but the medics wouldn't pass me fit to fight. I'm only telling you 'cos I don't want you thinking that I'm avoiding doing me bit.'

'I wasn't thinking that at all,' Grace told him truthfully.

'Me dad has a small greengrocer's shop, and rightly speaking this is his van, but he's lent it out for the war effort.'

Grace nodded. She knew that the emergency ambulance service was based around transport offered by those who owned it, and that both the volunteers and the transport were then equipped as best they could be for medical emergencies.

'I'd better go in,' she told him, and then offered shyly, 'I'll look out for you being on duty.'

'Good,' he responded, 'because I shall certainly be looking out for you.'

He came round and helped her out of the van, then stood and watched her as she hurried past the porter's lodge and headed for the door to the probationary nurses' home.

She could hear him driving away as she knocked on the locked door.

It was Home Sister herself who unlocked it and stood confronting her with a very displeased look on her face.

'Campion. And what time do you call this? You were supposed to be back for ten o'clock.'

'I'm sorry, Sister,' Grace apologised. 'We were late leaving the reception and then the ferry was full, and then when I got on the bus there was an accident.'

Brought up as she had been, it never occurred to Grace to omit the fact that she had been late getting the bus and simply to use the accident as an excuse, so she didn't see Home Sister's mouth twitch into a small smile as she stepped back into the hall and beckoned her inside.

'An accident, you say—' Home Sister repeated, and then broke off, staring at Grace and frowning. 'Where are all these bloodstains from? Were you involved in this accident?'

For the first time Grace realised that the sleeve of her jacket was stained with blood and that there were more bloodstains on the skirt of the Viyella dress she had changed into, not wanting to wear her bridesmaid's frock any longer than necessary. The jacket and the dress had been new the previous winter, bought with her Lewis's discount in the New Year sale and her heart sank a little. This wasn't the time, though, to worry about how quickly she could remove them, not with Home Sister waiting for an answer to her questions.

'No, that is . . . not really . . . A transport lorry had crashed and the driver was hurt. There was a doctor there and he asked for nursing help. I wasn't going to say anything. I mean, I'm only a probationer,' she said hastily, seeing that Home Sister's frown was deepening. 'But then there was no one and the doctor said that as long as I knew some first aid I would do. It wasn't anything really, only holding things. The doctor had to apply a tourniquet and . . .'

'I see. Very well. Have you had any supper?'

Grace stared at her. 'No.'

'I'll arrange for the kitchen to make you a cup of cocoa. In the meantime you'd better go and have a bath.'

'Yes, Home Sister.'

Alan had hardly spoken to Bella since they had left their wedding reception and now that they were here in their hotel bedroom, he was still ignoring her, and drinking from the hip flask he had removed from his pocket.

His parents and that wretched Trixie and her mother and father had quite spoiled her day, sitting there with their long faces instead of making a fuss of her like they ought to have done, Bella thought crossly. It wasn't even as though Alan's father had had to put his hand in his pocket either, so he had had nothing to scowl about. Her father had paid for the wedding and bought them the house she'd wanted. Well, not bought *them* exactly, because he owned it, but he was letting them live in it rent free so it was as good as theirs.

They had been later arriving at the hotel than planned and the porter who had let them in had been scowling and unwelcoming. The room itself was nowhere near as elegant as it had appeared in the brochure, and smelled slightly stale and damp.

Bella eyed the double bed, with its slightly grubby-looking dark green sateen eiderdown, with distaste.

Their bedroom at their new home had been freshly wallpapered in a pretty pink and white floral paper and she had insisted of having the most expensive bed linen Lewis's could supply, and a lovely pale pink eiderdown and matching coverlet. Her trousseau contained a silk lace-trimmed night-dress with a matching peignoir in the same soft shade of pink, just like she had seen Vivien Leigh wearing in a photograph in *Picture Post*; only, of course, it would look better on her because she was blonde.

She didn't want to waste her new finery on a setting that so obviously did not deserve it, but since she had nothing else with her she would have to do so. She looked at her reflection in the room's single slightly tarnished mirror. Her tweed going-away suit, with its fur collar, was the new season's latest design, the last shipment they were likely to get from Paris, Lewis's À La Mode Gown Salon had told her. Her hat matched the blue flecks in the tweed exactly and high-lighted the colour of her eyes. She was wearing the single row of pearls her mother had removed from her own neck to fasten round Bella's before she had left the reception whilst looking point-edly at Alan. Bella's mouth compressed. She had not just hinted, but dragged him to the jeweller's to show him the double row of pearls she had expected him to give her as a wedding gift, and when he hadn't produced them she had been furious.

Angrily she removed the pin from her hat.

Alan was sprawling in the room's single armchair, watching her.

'You might at least have thanked Mummy and Daddy for everything they've done for us,' she told him as she took off her hat and shook her hair free.

'Thank them? For what? Forcing me into marrying you?'

He lifted the hip flask to his mouth and then when he realised it was empty, he threw it so hard into the empty fire grate that the grate dented it.

Two spots of angry colour started to burn on Bella's cheeks. Not once since the night at the Tennis Club had Alan mentioned the circumstances of their engagement and subsequent marriage, and Bella had assumed that he would never do so. He had wanted to marry her really, she had told herself, and it was only that Trixie who had put last-minute doubts into his mind.

'You'd as good as proposed to me. Everyone knew that.'

'Proposed?' He gave a coarse laugh. 'That's rich. Propositioned you, maybe, and only that because you'd been chasing after me so hard ever since we'd met.'

'Me chase you! I'll have you know there were plenty of other boys wanting to take me out.'

'Yes, for the same reason as me. Because they wanted to fuck you and they reckoned it would be easy to get into your knickers,' he told her crudely.

Bella was genuinely shocked. Spoiled and indulged all her life by her mother, and allowed to grow up believing that whatever kind of behaviour she indulged in in order to get her own way was acceptable, she had no awareness of the interpretation others might put on that behaviour, or the boundaries she ought to have put on it herself.

She would no more have genuinely allowed Alan or any other man the kind of sexual favours he was referring to before marriage than she would have contemplated marrying a poor man with no prospects. Physical desire, the intensity of emotional passion – these were not things she had ever experienced, nor did she have any wish to do so, nor any understanding of them. Desire, for Bella, was something she felt for a new frock or a piece of jewellery, for marriage and status.

In the world Bella had created inside her head, a wife permitted her husband the intimacies of marriage in exchange for her wedding ring; if she thought about those intimacies at all it was simply as a duty and nothing more. She neither feared them nor anticipated them. Marriage for her was about being envied by other young women because she was the first of a group to become a wife;

it was about having secured the best marriage prize available to her, having the best house, being an adored daughter and daughter-in-law, being the one that all the other women of her group envied and looked up to.

She took off her suit jacket. Their hotel room boasted its own bathroom, a shabby cold little room with a stained bath and a sour smell, and she had already made up her mind that she intended to use it as little as possible.

She had no idea what she could say to Alan and so she simply continued to get undressed, telling herself that he was being so vile because he had been drinking and that he would be his normal self in the morning. She had heard her mother complaining to her father when he had had a couple of G and Ts too many on a Sunday evening. Berating one's husband for bad behaviour was simply a part of being a wife.

She would have to use the horrid bathroom to finish getting undressed, she acknowledged.

Alan was now lying back in the chair with his eyes closed. Her mouth pinched into a sour look very similar to her mother's.

When she emerged from the bathroom ten minutes later, Alan had fallen asleep and was snoring.

Well, she certainly wasn't going to wake him. Let him stay there and be punished for his nastiness to her when he did wake up with an aching neck.

Of course, it was a pity that he wasn't seeing

her in her beautiful négligé, but he hadn't been at all appreciative of her lovely suit or the trouble she had gone to to look pretty for him.

Carefully skirting past him, Bella turned off the lights and climbed into the cold, slightly unaired bed.

It was the sound of Alan being sick that woke her. At first she didn't know where she was or what the disgusting noise was, but by the time she had focused on the thin light coming from beneath the bathroom door, she was fully awake.

She watched in angry silence as Alan staggered out of the bathroom still fully dressed, and came towards the bed, swaying slightly as he stared down at her.

'Bloody bitch,' he swore at her savagely. 'Bloody, bloody bitch. Well, I'll show what you're going to get for forcing me to marry you. There's only one way to treat a bitch like you.'

He had pulled away the bedclothes and was on top of her before she could move, his breath rank and sour, as he kneeled over her and unbuttoned his trousers.

Bella was too furious to be afraid as she pushed him away. He had left the bathroom light on and she could see his 'thing'. It was dark red and stiff. She looked at it dismissively.

Bella might not be interested in sex, but she wasn't ignorant – her mother had seen to that – and anyway, Charlie, being what he was, had thoroughly enjoyed tormenting her when they had been much younger by showing her what boys had that girls didn't, and showing her too what he could do with it with his hand.

Bella had thought the whole thing totally silly and unnecessary then, and she still did now.

Alan reached for her breast, squeezing it painfully. Irritably she pushed him away, her anger growing as he held on to her nightdress, causing the delicate lace to tear.

'Now see what you've done,' she demanded, trying to thrust him away from her.

In retaliation Alan pinned her down all the harder, pushing up her nightdress and dropping down on top of her. She could feel the 'thing' pressing against her body.

This was what happened when a couple got married, everyone knew that. It was what men expected and what women had to put up with.

Bella gave an impatient sigh and turned her mental attention towards the far more pleasurable activity of planning the furnishings of her new home, leaving Alan to thrust away, making odd grunts as he did so.

It was a pity her father had refused to buy them that new dining set she'd set her heart on, and insisted she had to make do with second-hand instead. And mahogany too. Her father had got it from some woman who was moving to the country because of the war.

What was taking Alan so long? As a boy Charlie had got it over and done with in seconds, and had looked disgustingly pleased with himself for having done so, as he showed her how far he could make the stream of fluid go.

She looked impatiently at Alan. His face was beaded with sweat and he had started to shake slightly. His 'thing' had gone soft.

Had he done it then? If so, she hadn't felt anything, and if he hadn't, well, that wasn't her fault, was it? She rolled out from under him whilst he was preoccupied with 'it', frowning as he looked at its flaccid paleness, and pulled down her night-dress. Let him sleep on the cold side of the bed, she certainly wasn't going to.

Jean couldn't so much as swallow a crumb of toast, her throat felt so raw with pain.

The two men she loved best, her husband and her son, sat at opposite sides of the breakfast table, ignoring one another.

There'd been more angry words between them last night after they'd got home from the wedding, with Sam telling Luke that he'd regret joining up and Luke retaliating that he'd regret even more being a coward. Of course his words to Sam had been like a red rag to a bull, and in the end they had ended up glowering at each other, neither prepared to back down.

Jean had longed to be able to persuade Sam to explain his true feelings to Luke but she knew that he was too proud to do so, and she knew too that Sam would never forgive her if she broke the confidence he had given her. And at the back of her mind she worried that Luke, being young and not understanding how things had been during that other war, might not truly understand how his dad felt and why. But, as everyone knew, you couldn't put an old head on young shoulders.

She'd been so proud of Luke at the wedding, but in some ways she had wished he had not been there so that the situation between father and son had not worsened.

'I've got to go, Mum, otherwise I'll miss the boat.'

'Don't forget this cake that I've made for you then, Luke,' Jean told him, fussing around busily to hide her tears. 'We'll walk with you to the bus.'

'No . . . no there's no need, Mum. I'm meeting up with another lad that had leave; we're travelling back together.'

She could at least go to the door with him, hoping as she did so that Sam would see sense and come with her to see him off.

At the front door she pulled Luke to her and hugged him tightly.

'I'm sorry about your dad, Luke. He—'

'It's all right, Mum,' Luke told her but they both knew that it wasn't.

She watched him until he had disappeared out of sight. He had told her that he would be given leave once his training was over.

'And then they'll be sending us off to join the BEF, so that we can help them push Hitler back into Germany, so they reckon,' he had added almost carelessly, whilst Jean's maternal heart had felt as though it was being squeezed dry of blood.

The BEF, the British Expeditionary Force, had left for France and Belgium almost as soon as war had been announced, and the thought of Luke fighting with them filled her with fear.

TEN

December

It was over, the most exhausting and testing three months of their lives, they all agreed, followed by the longest and most fear-inducing three days when they had sat their exams, and now, after lunch, they would be summoned individually to see Matron to get their results.

A pass meant going on to the wards to continue training; a fail meant handing in the uniform and going home.

'I had to do a many-tailed bandage for an abdomen wound,' Hannah groaned. 'I'm sure I got it wrong. Remember when Sister Tutor was showing us how she said my bandaging looked like a badly made birds' nest and yours showed a sense of balance and order, Grace.'

'I remember how I burned the consommé we had to make for sippy two diets,' Grace shuddered. 'I was dreading having to do one for my practical.'

'What did you have to do, Grace?'

Grace grimaced and said succinctly, 'Trays and Trolleys.'

During their three-month training they had had to learn by heart how to set up seventy-two different trays and trolleys in their individual specific order.

'First she asked me to make up a tray for passing the flatus tube, then a trolley for a patient's bath, then she asked me to bandage the left eye. I'm never going to pass.'

They only had fifteen minutes in which to do the practical side of their exams and every part was timed to ensure that they could complete the set tasks in the allotted time.

'I was so nervous by the time I did the bandaging that I nearly dropped the bandage, and I'm sure I took longer than I should have done,' Jennifer chimed in, her Yorkshire accent even stronger than normal with nerves.

They were all in the dining room, letting off steam and commiserating with one another after the ordeal. Of the girls who had started out at the same time as Grace, three had dropped out within the first week and another three at the end of the first month.

She just knew she wouldn't pass, Grace decided. She had done so many things wrong. The other girls were all saying the same thing as they exchanged stories and comforted one another.

'I know how a condemned man must feel now when he eats his last meal,' Iris announced theatrically, tucking into her lunch. Most of the girls, including Grace, were too on edge to want to eat, even though their set were all sitting down together at the table.

Jennifer shuddered as she looked down at Iris's plate of rissoles and cabbage.

'I don't know how you can eat anything, Iris, never mind Cook's rissoles. I swear she puts in the gristly bits on purpose.'

Grace felt slightly sick in a way that had nothing to do with their lunch menu. Her heart was thudding with nervous anxiety.

'How's that good-looking ambulance driver that's taken such a fancy to you, Grace?' Lillian asked teasingly.

Grace had learned how to stop herself from blushing whenever Teddy's name was mentioned. They weren't exactly an item, but Teddy did seem to manage to be 'around' rather a lot, teasing her and complimenting her and making it plain that he enjoyed her company.

'I'm sure I don't know now what you mean,' Grace responded with dignity, and then started to giggle as she admitted, 'He's asked me out to see a matinée tomorrow afternoon.'

'Well, you tell him there's to be no sitting in the back row and no trying to persuade you to give him the kiss of life neither,' Doreen joked.

This time Grace did blush. Whilst it was true that things hadn't got anywhere near as far as that between them, there was no denying that she had wondered what it would be like to be kissed by

211

Teddy and she had decided that she would rather like to find out, she admitted.

They had been told that with Christmas only a week away, and the phoney war, as it was now referred to in the papers, making it seem as though they weren't really at war at all – despite the sandbags, blackout, ARP wardens and other para-phernalia of civil defence – those who passed their exams would be allowed a week off to be with their families before their on-the-ward training began. But of course she wasn't going to pass, Grace reminded herself woefully, not with the mess she had made of that eye bandage.

'Home Sister's just come in,' Hannah hissed warningly.

They all looked towards the door where Home Sister was standing, her hands folded in front of her whilst she surveyed the dining room.

A sharp clap of her hands brought instant silence to the room, and then automatically the trainees pushed back their chairs and stood up facing the doorway. If there was one thing they had all learned, Grace reflected, it was that it was wise to accord immediate obedience to any of Sister's commands.

'I shall call out your names in alphabetical order and when you hear your name you will present yourself without delay to Matron MacDonald in my office.'

Grace felt as though her legs had turned to jelly and her stomach to liquid dread. At least she wasn't too far down the alphabet. She dreaded to think what state she could be in had she been a Wilson or a Wood.

'Campion, Matron.'

'Thank you, Sister.'

Grace was sure that Matron must be able to hear her knees knocking together as she stood nervously in front of her, whilst one of the sister tutors stood discreetly to one side of her.

Grace had only seen Matron once before, the day after the trainees had first arrived, when she had given them a warning speech about how hard they would have to work and how high the hospital's standards were. She had warned them then that many of them would not be able to meet those high standards, and now here she was, having failed them, Grace thought miserably, as she saw how Matron frowned as she looked down at the papers on her desk.

Abruptly she lifted her head and looked at Grace, subjecting her to gimlet-eyed scrutiny, before saying crisply, 'Passed.'

Passed? She had passed? Grace didn't know what to say or do. She heard Sister Tutor clearing her throat warningly and just about managed to gather her wits together sufficiently to stammer, 'Thank you, Matron,' before backing out of the door that Sister Tutor was now holding open for her.

She had passed. She was going to be a nurse; a proper nurse. Grace felt like turning cartwheels and whooping with joy, just like the twins did when they were excited. Giggles bubbled up inside her at the thought of Sister Tutor's reaction if she were actually to do so. She would probably be dismissed on the spot, or put in a strait-jacket.

All the girls, they discovered later, on being given their results, had been instructed either to return to their individual rooms to pack their things prior to leaving the hospital, or to go and be measured for their new uniforms. The dining room that evening positively hummed with the sound of young female voices forced down to the low tone they had been instructed to use as trainee nurses, as they exchanged results.

Grace's group were thrilled that all six of them had passed. They congratulated one another happily and exchanged horror stories of just what they had done wrong in their exams.

'Have you been told yet what ward you're going to be on?' Hannah asked Grace.

'Yes. Men's surgical. What about you?'

'Theatre,' Hannah told her, pulling a face. 'I'm pleased in a way, but I hope I don't disgrace myself by fainting the first time I have to help scrub up for an operation. I've heard that some of the housemen take bets on how quickly new nurses faint their first time in theatre.'

'You won't faint,' Grace told her firmly.

'I hope I don't. Did they tell you you had to be on the ward at seven thirty a.m?'

'Yes,' Grace confirmed, as the others chimed in with details of the wards they were to be in.

'I was told we'd have to move our things out

of our rooms and that we'd be given new rooms in the nurses' home when we report for duty on the Monday evening,' Iris offered. 'I've heard it's like a prison over there with all the rules they've got.'

'All I want to think about right now is having a week off,' said Lillian.

'Did you see the queue to use the telephone?' Jennifer groaned. 'I'm not bothering. I'm going to wait until I get home to tell everyone.'

Grace had come to the same decision. She still couldn't quite believe that she had actually passed, and she couldn't stop smiling either.

'What do you mean, there's no supper?'

Bella tossed her head and glared at Alan as he stormed into the kitchen. She was very proud of her kitchen. Everything in it was brand-new, including her Cannon gas cooker, in the very latest design. Its cream enamel was matched by the set of pans and oven dishes they had received as a wedding present. Not that she planned to use her cooker very much.

Her mother had had the white curtains, with the red cherry design on them, and the frill across the top of the window made for her. They had chosen the fabric together in Lewis's. A matching gathered skirt on elastic discreetly covered the space beneath the draining board and under the sink. A new gas water heater has been installed to one side of the kitchen window, and the smart linoleum on the floor made the rag rugs that Alan's mother had on her kitchen floor look very shabby indeed in comparison.

A decorator had been hired to distemper the walls pale yellow, and the oilcloth covering the kitchen table matched the pattern on the curtains.

The house had a good-sized walk-in pantry with stone shelves and plenty of storage space, but Bella had still insisted on having a kitchen dresser with shelves at the top and two cupboards underneath.

'I mean that there's no supper,' she told him, turning up the dial on the wireless and pretending to concentrate on the sound of Judy Garland singing 'Somewhere Over the Rainbow.'

'When a man comes in from work, he ruddy well expects his wife to have his supper ready for him,' Alan bellowed at her, red-faced, as he strode over to the wireless and turned down the volume.

'Work? You?' Bella scoffed. 'That will be the day, or has your father given you a job drinking G and Ts now? Mind you, he should because it's all you're fit for.' She turned the volume back up and started to hum along to the song.

She had spent the afternoon with her mother. They had gone to see a film together and then she had gone back to her parents where her mother had cooked her some supper.

With her father being so busy with all the extra work he was getting from the Ministry and no Charlie to help him, he was working all hours God sent, as Vi put it, and Bella knew that her mother welcomed her company.

It was certainly far more pleasant going back

home and being spoiled by her mother than staying here on her own or, even worse, having to put up with a husband who seemed to think a wife was some kind of skivvy on hand to wait on him hand and foot, instead of someone he should cherish and adore.

'Now listen, you,' Alan yelled, grabbing hold of Bella's arm and forcing her round to face him.

'Let go of me,' Bella yelled back.

'This is my house and I'll do what I ruddy well like in it,' Alan told her.

'Your house? That's a joke,' Bella taunted him. 'It's my father that bought it and you'd better just remember that. And if you want some supper you can go round to your parents and get your mother to make it for you,' she finished triumphantly.

She knew perfectly well that he wouldn't dare go to them in the state he was in, smelling of drink and hardly able to stand up properly.

'I should have married Trixie and not you. Things would have been different then.'

'Well, you didn't, did you? You're going to have to tell that father of yours he needs to pay you more, as well. I had to ask Mummy to help me out with the housekeeping again this week.'

'If you didn't waste so ruddy much, you'd have plenty.'

'Plenty? You spend more on petrol for that car of yours than you give me. Daddy was saying that he's surprised you can still get so much petrol.'

In fact what her father had actually said was that the Parkers must have access to someone who was prepared to let them have more fuel than the Government was allowing for private use – but at a price – and that he wouldn't mind knowing where they were getting it from as he could do with a bit more himself. Bella wasn't going to say that to Alan, of course. She didn't want him thinking that he was going to get her to ask him for something. He'd love that.

She had never imagined that marriage would be like this. She had expected Alan to spoil her and give in to her in exactly the same way as her parents had. But instead . . . her mouth tightened.

Her mother had tried to ask her if Alan was 'being a good husband' to her, as she had put it, and Bella had known from the look of embarrassment on her mother's face that she had been asking if Alan was fulfilling his marital duties in the bedroom. What a joke that was! They had been married going on for three months now and there'd only been one occasion in the whole of that time when he'd managed to get his 'thing' hard enough to be a proper husband to her. Not that she intended to tell her mother the truth – or anyone else. She had smiled sweetly instead and nodded her head, knowing that her mother wouldn't pursue the subject. No, as far as the rest of the world was concerned, Bella was determined that they must think of her marriage as perfect.

Not that she minded all that much about Alan's failure in the bedroom department. It wasn't her fault, after all. Alan could bluster and complain all he liked, but they both knew that his inability to do what a husband was supposed to do with his wife had given her the upper hand, Bella thought triumphantly. One word from her to anyone else about his failure and he'd be a laughing stock, and she'd told him so. His failure put her in a position of power, so far as she was concerned. She didn't need to do anything to try to please him if she didn't feel like it, and that included cooking his meals.

'I've ordered tickets for us for the Tennis Club New Year's Eve dance, and you'd better stay sober because I'm not having you showing me up,' she warned him.

She'd already got her eye on the new dress she wanted; the kind of dress, with its low neckline, that an unmarried girl like Trixie couldn't possibly wear even if she had the looks for it, but in which she, as a married woman, would easily outshine every other woman there. Alan was a very lucky man. Far luckier than he deserved to be. It was a pity Alan had had so much to drink, because she wished that he would go to his mother's for his supper. She wanted to try out that new nail polish she'd persuaded her mother to buy for her and listen to the wireless in peace. Thinking of her mother reminded her of the conversation they had had.

'Oh, and we're going to my parents for our Christmas dinner,' she told Alan.

'I told you last week that we were going to mine.'

'Did you? I must have forgotten,' Bella told him insincerely.

'Bitch.' Alan swore at her as he made another grab for her, lunging towards her and then staggering into the table when Bella sidestepped him neatly.

He was always aggressive and inclined to violence when he'd been drinking. She made to step past him, but he moved faster than she had anticipated, trapping her with the weight of his body, just like he did in bed, but now against the door.

She gave him a withering look and then gasped in shocked pain when he thumped her in the stomach. The pain sent her sick and too dizzy to move, fury filling her that he should dare to treat her like this. But then he hit her again and again and her fury became fear and that fear became a pain that overwhelmed and enveloped her to become a red haze of agony splintered by his continuing blows, until mercifully oblivion overtook her.

Bella came round to the savage thrust of Alan's body within her own. Slowly and painfully she opened her eyes. She knew she was still in the kitchen, because from where she was lying she could see the blurry outline of the legs of the kitchen table. She shifted her gaze to Alan, too weak to do anything other than focus helplessly on the blind fixed expression of hatred and triumph contorting his face, as he thrust violently into her, the friction of his movements within her unwelcoming body a fresh source of pain.

His lips were curled back against his teeth, his eyes narrowed and glittering.

'Bitch! Bitch!' He all but screamed the word at her when he saw that her eyes were open, his breath coming in short excited bursts until finally his frenzy overwhelmed him and it was over. The movement of his body blotted out the light as he leaned over her, his fingers fastening in her hair and then tightening, bringing fresh pain as he lifted her head and then banged it down hard on the linoleum, allowing her to escape back into nothingness.

ELEVEN

'You've passed! Oh, Grace love, I'm that proud of you.' Jean dabbed at her eyes with the corner of her apron. Grace had arrived just as Jean was finishing peeling the potatoes for dinner, and now her mother added, 'I knew it must be good news the minute I set eyes on you, you looked that happy.'

'I still can't believe it.' Grace shook her head.

Her mother was every bit as thrilled and pleased as Grace had known she would be, and it was lovely to be home. It was only now that she was here that she recognised just how much she had missed her family

'Your dad's gone down to the allotment and the twins with him. Him and a few of the others have decided to try keeping a couple of pigs. They'll be back soon. He'll be ever so pleased that you've passed, love.'

'I don't know how I ever got to pass. I keep thinking it's a mistake. I'm having to pinch meself to make sure it's real,' Grace laughed. 'I'm that happy that the Hospital is letting us all go home for Christmas, Mum. I was really upset thinking I wouldn't be able to be here. Do you think that Luke might get home?'

'I don't know, love.' Jean looked sad, her face crumpling slightly.

'I do so wish that Luke and Dad would make up,' Grace said. 'I had a letter from Luke on Wednesday. I think he must be in France, although of course he can't say.'

Jean tried to smile. Luke wrote regularly to them as well, but whilst she read his letters over and over again, Sam refused even to look at them.

'Seeing as you're back you can come down to St John's market with me this afternoon. I want to go and order a goose for Christmas Day. With your dad getting extra pay for doing his bit, I've managed to put a decent bit away for some Christmas treats. Might as well buy them now 'cos your dad reckons we'll have rationing before long. We can look round and perhaps order a nice tongue as well . . .'

'I'm sorry, Mum, but I can't go with you.'

'You can't? Why not?'

Grace looked self-conscious. 'I've promised to go to a matinée this afternoon.'

'With those girls you've made friends with?' Jean guessed.

Grace went pink. 'No, not them. It's a lad I've met. A decent sort, he is,' she told her mother hurriedly, seeing that she was beginning to look concerned. 'I told you about him. He's the one who gave me a lift back to the hospital after the wedding and that accident.'

Grace could see that her mother wasn't looking convinced.

'He lives in Wavertree,' she told her, 'with his mum and dad up on Oakhill Road. His dad's got a greengrocer's shop.'

Jean pursed her lips. 'Oakhill Road? It's all semi-detached's up there. Me and your dad looked at one. Nice big garden, it had, but only the three bedrooms, them not having any attic like we've got here.'

'We're closer to the shops as well,' Grace pointed out. 'Teddy says his mum is always complaining about how far she's got to walk.'

'Well . . .' Grace could see that her mother wasn't looking quite so concerned now that she had told her a bit about Teddy, but she still warned her with maternal concern, 'Just you be careful, Grace. There's a war on, after all, and some of these lads—'

'Teddy isn't like that,' Grace assured her. 'Bin just as he ought to be with me all along, he has. Anyway, it's only a matinée.'

'Well, I'm not sure what your dad will have to say.'

'I'm nineteen, Mum, and a nurse – well, I will be,' she amended before changing the subject. 'I've brought the twins some chocolate. I thought I'd get them one of those records they're so fond of for Christmas.'

'Your dad won't thank you for that. He threatens

to get rid of that gramophone at least once a week. Mad about their music, they are. I caught the pair of them doing this daft dancing the other day. Jitterbugging, they called it.' Jean shook her head. 'They've learned it from that Eileen Jarvis in their class at school, whose sister teaches dancing. In my day we knew how to dance properly, a nice waltz or a foxtrot, not this silly stuff.'

Grace hid a small smile. The other girls had been saying only the other day that they ought to be thinking of getting tickets for some dances over Christmas, and especially for New Year's Eve, and they had mentioned the new jitterbug craze, which was so popular in America.

Her head hurt so much she could hardly lift it off the pillow, and when Bella tried to move the pain in her stomach and her ribs took her breath.

The chair was still where she had put it last night under the door handle to keep Alan out of the bedroom, though. She could see it in the dim light coming in through the blackout blinds her mother had made for her, and which were press-studded to the window frame. She looked at the alarm clock. Eleven o'clock! She had vague memories of dragging herself upstairs and then being violently sick in the bathroom before shutting herself in the bedroom and propping the chair under the handle so that Alan wouldn't be able to get in.

Alan. He'd be at work now. He was always

moaning about the fact that his father insisted he work on Saturday mornings. She got out of bed cautiously, tensing in anticipation against the pain that movement would bring.

Bruises were already forming on her stomach and her ribs, her flesh too sore to bear the pressure of her own explorative touch. Bitterness calcified the angry contempt she already felt for Alan, overlaying last night's fear. He needn't think she was going to let him get away with what he had done, because she wasn't. She lifted her hand to the back of her head. She could feel a lump where he had banged her head on the floor, and her hair was sticky. She removed her had and looked in horror at the dried blood on her fingers.

Tears burned her eyes as she moved too quickly and pain savaged her back into immobility. Just let him wait until she told her parents what he had done. Mummy would have her back home with them before Alan could say a word.

Bella frowned, ignoring the thudding pain that struck right through her head. Was that what she wanted? Being a married woman was far better than being an unmarried daughter living at home. A married woman was to be envied by those girls not lucky enough to be looking forward to their own marriage. She could just imagine how some of those cats at the Tennis Club would gossip about her behind her back if it got out that she had let Alan treat her so badly that she had had to go running home to her mother.

No, she had a better idea. Another way of punishing him. A better way; a way that would scare him, and give her the upper hand, she decided triumphantly.

'Oh, it's you, Bella.'

Alan's mother certainly didn't look very pleased to see her, Bella acknowledged, but that didn't bother her. Mrs Parker wore her greying hair scraped back into a tight bun. She was a tall woman, taller than her husband and very well built, with an uncompromising no-nonsense manner.

'I hope you don't mind, Mother-in-law, but I feel ever so poorly, I really do.'

Bella might be having to fake her exaggerated politeness but she didn't have to fake the pain that had her lifting her hand to her head, or the dark shadows bruising the skin beneath her eyes. 'I would have gone home to Mummy, but, well, I wasn't sure I could . . .' She closed her eyes and leaned heavily against the open front door.

'You'd better come in,' Alan's mother told her, curtly taking hold of her arm, and urging her, 'Hurry up. I don't want the neighbours talking.'

Once she had closed the front door behind Bella, she released her, eyeing her with hostility.

'Now what exactly is it that's wrong with you?'

White-faced, her voice faltering, Bella told her truthfully, 'I've been ever so sick . . . and . . . and fainting. I wouldn't have come round bothering you but I just didn't know what to do. Alan will be back for his lunch any minute, but I've left him a note saying that I'm here. I thought that perhaps the fresh air . . .'

Bella could see that Alan's mother had looked more displeased and grim with every word she had uttered. Well, it would serve her right to be led up the garden path a little bit after the mean way she'd been with her, and think that she was pregnant, especially with her going on about goody-goody Trixie all the time, even if the truth was that Bella wanted herself to be pregnant with Alan's baby even less than she knew her mother-in-law did.

'Well, I still don't know what you've come round here for. It seems to me that it's a doctor you want to be seeing, not me,' she told Bella forthrightly.

'A doctor! Oh, no. I mean . . .' Bella allowed her eyes to fill with tears and her bottom lip to tremble. 'I know it was only an accident – Alan wasn't even there – but . . . well, it sounds so silly saying that I knocked myself out walking into a door, and then went and cut my head as well.'

Alan's mother's face was a picture as she struggled between immediate relief and the sudden horrified dawning that what she might be facing could be a lot worse than an unwanted grandchild.

'You've had an accident?' she demanded.

'Could I have a cup of tea?' Bella begged her. 'And p'haps sit down? Only I feel ever so weak.'

'You'd better come into the kitchen.'

Delighted that her plan was going so well, Bella followed her mother-in-law down the cold drab hallway. The Parkers' house was nowhere as nicely done out as her parents'. The skirtings and doors were painted dull dark brown, lincrusta wallpaper painted dark green stretched up from the skirting to dado rail height above, while the rest of the wall was papered in maroon and green striped wallpaper. The whole effect was overpowering and gloomy.

The kitchen was no better, its walls painted in shiny green paint, the oilcloth on the floor the same dark brown as the skirtings.

The smell of cooking tripe filled the kitchen. Bella's stomach heaved. She hated tripe and her own mother knew better than to cook it ever.

'So what exactly happened then?'

Bella sank down into the chair she was offered and tried to blot out the smell of the cooking tripe.

'It was just after Alan had come in from . . .' Bella bit down on her bottom lip and let her voice falter. She was enjoying this. 'Please don't say anything to Mr Parker, will you, only poor Alan is working so hard and if he does stop off on the way home for a bit of a drink, well, he doesn't mean any harm. Afterwards, he feels really bad about the way it makes him. He always says so.'

Alan's mother looked as though she was about to explode. Her face had gone a deep beetroot red and her eyes were bulging in their sockets. She didn't dress anything like as nicely as her own mother, Bella thought critically, and she certainly hoped she never got so stout.

'Alan was there with you then, was he?'

Bella opened her mouth and then closed it again, the picture of uncertainty and guilt, the picture of a young wife desperate to protect her husband.

'I . . .'

She was saved from having to reply by the sound of someone hammering on the back door, and she wasn't at all surprised when Alan's mother opened it to admit Alan himself, looking very different from the dapper full-of-himself young man who had first caught Bella's eye. Unshaven, his suit creased and his shirt cuffs grubby, he looked wildly from Bella to his mother.

'What's she been telling you?' he demanded.

'I was just explaining to your mother about my accident, Alan, and how I walked into the door, and then fell over and banged my head.' Bella gave him a reproachful limpid-eyed look, and had the pleasure of seeing the confusion darken his eyes.

'Your mother was saying that I ought to see a doctor.'

'No.'

Mother and son both spoke at once.

'No, you did right to come round here, dear,' Mrs Parker assured Bella, baring her teeth in what Bella assumed must be an attempt at a compassionate smile. 'A bit of arnica on your bruises and you'll be as good as new in a few days. And no going worrying your own parents, mind. I know how busy your mother is with all her charity work, and we wouldn't want her to get herself into an

230

upset state, would we, not now that she's my deputy?'

'Oh, no, I wouldn't want to worry Mummy,' Bella agreed.

She turned to Alan. 'I'm really sorry that I made you cross because I got all muddled up and told Mummy that we could go to her on Christmas Day, darling. Please say you'll forgive me.'

'Well, of course he does,' Mrs Parker told her firmly. 'Everyone has these silly little fall-outs when they first get married. And I dare say it was you being so upset about Alan being a little bit cross with you that caused you to be forgetful and have your accident in the first place, wasn't it, Bella?'

Bella got up and went to Alan's side, reaching for his hand and smiling up at him.

'Yes . . . that's exactly what happened,' she agreed.

Alan was looking at her as though he couldn't believe his luck, tears of gratitude sheening his eyes.

'Perhaps you could say something to Mr Parker about how hard Alan's having to work, Mother-in-law. He's coming home at all hours.'

Alan stiffened.

'I'm sure Alan won't want me to worry his father when he's got so much on his plate with all this extra war work that the council is needing to get done.'

The familiar frostiness was back in her mother-in-law's voice, but Bella didn't care. She had made her point and satisfied herself that neither Alan nor his mother wanted Alan's behaviour to get back to his father's, or her parents', ears.

When Teddy had asked Grace what film she would like to see she had told him *Wuthering Heights* with Merle Oberon and Laurence Olivier. She had seen it once already with her mother, but she knew she would enjoy seeing it again, because it was so deliciously spine-tingling and sad. A real girl's film, Luke had scoffed, which it was. Not that she was testing Teddy or anything by choosing it, of course. No, not for one minute. But she had been pleased by the way he had smiled at her and immediately agreed that he'd like to see it as well, even though she was pretty sure he had only said so to please her. And then soft-heartedly she had told him that really she'd just as soon see *Jamaica Inn*, and his eyes had lit up like a kiddie's at the thought of pirates and fighting, his relief making her laugh.

They'd arranged to meet outside the Odeon on London Road in the city centre, and although she was on time, Grace was pleased to see that Teddy was there ahead of her, smiling broadly at her when he saw her.

'I wasn't sure I'd recognise you out of uniform,' he teased her, giving her an openly appreciative look, which was nevertheless still respectful.

He was wearing a smart navy-blue suit and an equally smart shirt and tie. Beneath the hat he'd removed when he came over to her and was now replacing, his hair was flattened into obedience with Brylcreem. Grace felt proud to be with him as he guided her towards the Odeon.

She'd taken care with her own appearance, brushing the hair she had washed the previous night until her curls gleamed, her toilette critically overseen by the twins, who had shaken their heads over her first choice of last year's sensible heavy tweed skirt, insisting instead that she wore her 'best' woollen dress, also from last year, and giving their approval to her silk stockings and smart court shoes.

Grace had banished them before carefully applying the new dark pink Max Factor lipstick she'd been experimenting with in the privacy of her room all week, worrying that it might be just a bit too racy. But not even her mother had said anything when she had finally gone downstairs, the pretty scarf that had been a Christmas present from Luke last year tucked into the neck of the raincoat she had decided to wear 'just in case'.

Because they were early there wasn't a queue. Teddy headed straight for the shining chrome box office set between the two pairs of doors.

Grace's eyes widened when she heard him asking for front circle seats. She hadn't expected that!

'Seeing as we're a bit early we could go up and have a bit of something in the restaurant before the film starts, if you fancy it?' Teddy suggested once he had paid.

Grace shook her head. He'd spent enough already. But as though he guessed why she was holding back he told her, 'I wouldn't mind a bit o' summat meself.'

'Oh, well, yes, then that would be lovely,' Grace agreed.

'It's you who is that,' Teddy told her boldly as he guided her through the foyer and up the stairs to the lounge.

Grace could remember only one previous occasion when she'd sat in the front circle and that had been as a treat for her sixteenth birthday.

The carpet beneath her feet was so thick that she could feel herself sinking into it, and although she was trying hard not to look impressed, she couldn't help studying the elegant décor.

A smartly dressed waitress showed them to a table in the restaurant.

'Just tea for me, please,' Grace told her, not daring to think what the prices were here.

'Tea for two and cakes,' Teddy told the waitress firmly, winking at Grace.

As other smartly dressed cinemagoers filled the restaurant, Grace was glad that she had allowed the twins to persuade her into wearing her frock. Its soft mid-blue suited her and emphasised the colour of her hair and eyes, as well as emphasising her small waist.

She felt a bit self-conscious pouring the tea for them both, but Teddy was so relaxed and such fun to be with that she soon forgot her discomfort at being out on her first proper date, as she laughed at his jokes and enjoyed his company.

'I hope there isn't going to be too much soppy stuff in this film,' Teddy joked as they left the restaurant, his hand protectively under her elbow. 'Mind you, me mum gave me a clean hanky before I left, so you needn't worry.'

He was carrying his overcoat, and just in front of the doors to the circle he paused and rummaged in his pocket, producing a box of chocolates for her.

Grace blushed and smiled, and thought she had never been so happy.

They were back in their own kitchen, Alan looking at her as though he couldn't believe his luck in getting away with what he had.

'I'll have to go round and see Mummy now, Alan, seeing as we're supposed to be going shopping together this afternoon. It's a pity we haven't got a telephone. I'm surprised your father doesn't have one installed for us, seeing as you're working for him. Perhaps I should say something about it to your mother.'

'There's no need for that. I'll have a word with him. Look, Bella, what happened last night – well, it won't happen again.'

She liked his hangdog look and the humble note in his voice, Bella decided.

'No it won't,' she agreed coldly, ''cos if it does I *shall* tell your mother.'

'It wasn't all my fault.' Alan was getting angry again now. 'If you hadn't said what you did—'

'You'll have to drive me round to Mummy's, Alan,' Bella told him, ignoring his accusation. 'Oh, and if you want something to eat I'm sure your mother will have some tripe left.'

The film had kept Grace on the edge of her seat with fear for poor Maureen O'Hara, apart, that was, from those few brief occasions when Teddy had reached for her hand and held it comfortingly, drawing her closer to him.

Even her mother would have completely approved of the way he had behaved towards her, Grace acknowledged as they left the cinema.

'That Maureen O'Hara is so beautiful,' she said to Teddy as they emerged into the gloom of the late December afternoon.

'She's not a patch on you,' Teddy told her stoutly, before asking, 'What number bus do we want?'

'We?'

'Well, you don't think I'm going to let you make your own way home, do you? I should have brought the ambulance, then we wouldn't need a bus.'

'There's no need to see me home, Teddy.'

It was typical of him that he should offer, though, and Grace was pleased that he had done, even if by doing so he had inadvertently reminded her of another, very different, man, who had also wanted to see her home safely.

'I suppose you and the other girls will already have made plans for New Year's Eve?'

'We have talked about it,' Grace admitted.

'You'll be wanting to go dancing, I expect, somewhere like the Grafton,' he guessed.

'Lillian says it's got the best dance floor in Liverpool, properly sprung and everything, and she's going to get tickets for us all for New Year's Eve.'

'Happen I might get a ticket for meself, especially if a certain very special girl is going to agree to stand up and dance with me.'

'I'm sure any girl would be happy to dance with you, Teddy,' Grace told him, and meant it.

'I'm not talking about any girl, just one girl . . . Promise you'll save the last dance for me?'

Somehow or other he had taken hold of her hand without her realising it and now he was lacing his fingers between her own and she could feel a warm glow of happiness.

'I . . . yes, I will,' she told him breathlessly.

It had gone cold, and suddenly Teddy started to cough.

'That sounds nasty,' Grace sympathised when he had stopped.

Teddy shook his head. 'It's nothing, just got a bit of cold air on me lungs, that's all. Fancy going to the pictures again tomorrow?'

'I'd love to, Teddy, but Mum will be expecting me to help her at home,' Grace told him regretfully. 'Here's my bus,' she added. 'I'd better go . . .'

He caught her off guard when he suddenly put his arm around her and drew her to him, then kissed her on the cheek.

'It's all right, I'm not going to take liberties with

237

you,' he told her gruffly as he released her. 'Not that I'm saying that I wouldn't like to kiss you properly, mind, 'cos I would.'

There wasn't time for her to say anything; all she could do was let him walk her to join the queue already boarding her bus.

TWELVE

'Roller skates.'

'No, new gramophone records.'

The twins, giddy with the excitement of it being Christmas Eve, were giggling as they tried to outdo each other with what they hoped to find under the Christmas tree.

'I wouldn't mention gramophone records in front of Dad,' Grace warned them, 'not after him telling you off last night for all the noise you were making.'

'Dad doesn't understand, Grace. You've got to play them loudly,' Sasha explained patiently. 'Otherwise it doesn't work, does it, Lou?'

'Otherwise what doesn't work?' Grace asked them, putting her head on one side to study the effect of the candles she had just finished clipping onto the branches of the Christmas tree Dad had brought home from the market earlier in the week.

'That thing that happens inside your head when you're dancing that make you forget everything else. You need to have the music really loud.'

'When you were our age did you ever want to be a singer like Auntie Francine, Grace?' Lou asked her.

'No, never,' she said truthfully. 'And if I were you two, I'd put that idea right out of my head, 'cos Dad would never agree to you going on the stage.'

The twins exchanged looks whilst Grace sighed over her attempts to decorate the Christmas tree. No matter how careful she was, the weight of the candles in their clip-on holders kept making the branches bow and spoiling the symmetry of what she was trying to achieve.

'Proper fairy lights would be better,' Lou told her.

'Well, yes, but they aren't as pretty. Anyway, what are you two doing in here? I thought you were supposed to be making paper chains?'

'We were, but the taste of the gum was making us feel sick. Come on, Gracie, tell us what you've bought for us . . .' Sasha wheedled.

'It isn't slippers, is it?' Lou asked suspiciously, 'only it feels very light for such a big box.'

Grace hid a small smile. She had deliberately put the record she had bought them into a box she had packed carefully with paper so as to disguise it.

'What's wrong with slippers?' she teased them, keeping her face straight.

'Grace, have you got a minute, only I could do with you to give me a hand making the stuffing,' called her mother from the kitchen.

'Coming, Mum.' Grace got up.

The kitchen was full of steam and the familiar delicious smells of Christmas – only this Christmas wasn't going to be the same as the ones she remembered, Grace acknowledged. Luke wouldn't be with them, and they were at war, even though as yet nothing had really changed apart from the blackout, which everyone was grumbling had caused more accidents and been more of a nuisance than Hitler.

'I went and telephoned our Vi this morning from the corner shop,' Jean told Grace, having instructed her to grate the bread she had dried out in the oven for breadcrumbs for the stuffing. 'I thought she might have changed her mind about Jack being evacuated and had got him back home with it being Christmas, but she hasn't.' Jean gave a small sigh.

She had been worrying about Jack ever since Vi had announced that he was sending him off to the country, but she knew how stubborn her twin could be once her back was up, so she had held off from saying too much, knowing that Vi would tell her that the arrangements she and Edwin made for Jack weren't anyone else's business.

'What, she's not even having him home for Christmas?' Grace asked indignantly.

'She wants him to be safe, love, that's why she's sent him away.'

'There's lots of kiddies being brought back as their mothers don't see any sense in them being away when there's not been any bombs or anything. Is that enough breadcrumbs yet, Mum?'

Jean peered into the bowl. 'Better do some more, love. We've got old Mr Edwards coming in for a bit of Christmas dinner and I thought I'd ask Miss Higgins, that you used to run errands for, as well, seeing as she's all on her own. I know she likes to keep herself to herself but no one wants to be on their own at Christmas. I don't know if I'm going to be able to get this goose in the oven, Grace. I told him what has the poultry stall in the market that I didn't want it more than twelve pounds.'

'At least he let you have it for the same price as a twelve-pound one, Mum.'

'Yes, because he'd probably gone and sold mine to someone else. Next year I'm going to order from someone else.'

Grace smiled. Every year her mother grumbled about the goose and the poultry stall owner she always bought it from, threatening to buy from someone else.

'At least Dad and Luke won't be arguing over who's got the biggest drumstick this year,' Grace joked, and then bit her lip when she saw her mother's face. 'I'm sorry, Mum,' she whispered. 'I don't know what I was thinking of, saying a daft thing like that. Christmas just won't be the same without our Luke.'

'No it won't.'

'He said in his last letter that the officers have to serve the men their Christmas dinner and that that ENSA – you know, the singers and actors and them that go doing shows for the men – are putting on concerts for them and they've been told that Gracie Fields will be performing at them, and Billy Cotton and his band.'

'Well, I'd be surprised if she does, seeing as how it's bin in all the papers how poorly she's bin and how she's gone to that Capri place for a rest.'

The newspapers and the fan magazines had been full of veiled and not so veiled references to the cancer of the cervix the star had suffered, and her ongoing recovery from it.

'I thought you might have gone out dancing tonight, Grace, with them nurse friends of yours.'

'We can only afford to go out dancing the one night, so we've decided to get tickets for New Year's Eve,' Grace told her. 'For the Grafton.' Although she tried hard not to, Grace could feel herself colouring up slightly, as she remembered what Teddy had said to her when he had made her promise to keep the last dance for him. He probably wouldn't even be at the Grafton, never mind remembering what he'd said to her.

'I dare say that young lad will be there, hoping to get a dance with you, will he?' Jean asked her shrewdly.

'Teddy?' Grace tried to look nonchalant but she knew she was blushing again. 'He did say something about going, but I dare say I won't even see him, it will be so packed.'

Jean saw the blush and sighed inwardly. Grace might be trying to pretend that she wasn't interested in this Teddy lad, but Jean, with a mother's instinct, knew better.

'Here's your Dad back,' Jean told Grace unnecessarily as they both heard the squeak of the side gate into the garden from the passage. 'It will have to be a scratch supper tonight if I'm going to get everything finished here in time for the Midnight Carol Service.'

'By, it's cold out there,' Sam complained as he came in. 'I was talking to one of the old chaps from the allotments earlier and he reckons we're in for a bad winter.'

'Sam, them are hot. I've not long since taken them out of the oven,' Jean warned as he reached out for one of the mince pies cooling on a wire tray on the table. 'It will serve you right if you burn your tongue. They're for tomorrow, not for now.'

'That's if Father Christmas leaves us any,' Grace joked, straight-faced.

Bella looked towards the Tennis Club bar where Alan was standing drinking with some of the other men.

She was wearing the new dress he had bought her by way of a making-up present. It was red silk and very sophisticated, and a copy of one that Vivien Leigh had been photographed wearing, the owner of the dress shop had told her. Bella knew it showed off her pale skin and the nearly but not quite faded bruises on her arm where Alan had grabbed her. Those other bruises, on her ribs and her stomach, were of course hidden, like the tender spot on her head.

A group of young men and women on the other

side of the dance floor were laughing at something and jostling one another, as they played some sort of noisy game. Alan had stopped drinking to watch them. Trixie emerged from the middle of the mêlée, flushed and laughing, and triumphantly clutching a man's handkerchief.

'Oh, I say, well done, Trixie,' one of them congratulated her whilst the others all clapped.

Three older couples were occupying the table next to their own and Bella heard one of the women saying indulgently, 'Dear Trixie, such a good sort. She runs the local Cub pack, you know, and all the boys adore her.'

Bella gave Trixie with a sour look. She was the one everyone ought to have been fussing around and praising tonight, not Trixie. She was, after all, the only young bride here; Trixie was just Trixie, a dull boring maypole of a girl without looks or style. Trixie couldn't hold a candle to her and yet somehow and very unfairly she had managed to make herself the centre of attention, whilst she was left here alone as her husband stood at the bar and the other two couples they were seated with made excuses to go and get some supper. Bella could feel the sharp prickle of unwanted tears stinging the backs of her eyes.

This time Alan just better have bought her those pearls she had shown him in the jeweller's window, that was all. Otherwise . . .

She stood up and made her way to the bar, giving Alan a doe-eyed look of still newly married adoration as she put her hand on his arm and stood close to him, before pouting and then reaching up to fuss over him and straighten his tie, and whisper just loud enough for the others to hear, 'It's lonely at the table without you.'

'I always said you were a lucky chap, Alan,' one of the older men told him.

A couple of the other men laughed and warned him teasingly, 'Just you wait until you've been married for a few years; she'll be waiting for you with a hard rolling pin then, not soft words.'

They might be talking to Alan but it was her they were looking at. Bella revelled in being the focus of their attention, clinging to Alan as she laughed and pouted and flirted, and made sure that they saw her as an adoring young wife whilst Alan saw how much he was envied by his friends for being married to her.

This was what she had expected and wanted from her marriage: this attention and admiration; this knowledge that other men thought she was more attractive than their own dull wives, and her own husband's recognition of his extreme good fortune.

What had been merely a fiction when she had come to join Alan was now, as she basked in the attention, fact. She was what she had wanted to be. How all the still unmarried young women must envy her, especially poor Trixie.

Bella preened and posed, her eyes sparkling and her lips readily parting in a smile. She was the first of their set to become a wife. Others would follow her lead, but she had that lead and she intended to keep it.

Yes, she was feeling very pleased with herself, Bella decided half an hour later, standing in front of the mirror in the crowded powder room, re-applying her lipstick.

Two girls, whom she knew vaguely, were standing next to her, one of them admiring the other's engagement ring, whilst she spoke breathlessly of being in love with her fiancé.

Deliberately Bella looked at her own wedding ring and smiled at them, interrupting their conversation to say complacently, 'Personally I don't think it's possible to know what love truly is until one is married. Being a wife is so very different to being a fiancée.' She gave them a smile that said she was in on a secret from which they were excluded, showing off her married status.

Trixie was standing behind her, her plain face looking even plainer and her brown eyes stark with misery. Good, let her be miserable. Bella was sick of hearing Alan's mother and everyone else going on about how wonderful Trixie was, as though somehow she had something that she, Bella, did not, which was obviously ridiculous and impossible.

'Alan's sooo flattering about how happy our marriage has made him. He never stops telling me how much he loves me. He's always begging me to promise that I'll never stop loving him. He says that he couldn't bear it if that happened. But of course it won't. Nothing would ever make me stop loving him or make me leave him,' Bella smiled indulgently. 'Men can be such silly boys at times.'

* * *

They had been late leaving for the Christmas Eve midnight service because the twins had insisted on putting out mince pies and milk for Father Christmas, and when they had got there the church had been so full that they had only just managed to squeeze in.

Every pew contained families with someone in uniform, or so it seemed to Jean, tall broad-shouldered young men standing with their parents and their siblings. The fate of a nation rested on those shoulders and their bearing revealed their awareness of that responsibility.

Tears pricked at her eyes when the congregation sang the familiar Christmas hymns, words written to be sung with joy and awe at the coming of a Saviour. It was to these young men in their new uniforms that the role of saviours would fall, and Jean prayed that they would not have to bear the cross of pain and death that the child whose birth they were celebrating now had borne.

Luke was one of these young men. She turned towards Sam. He had lost some of his pride and stature these last weeks. He carried with him the shadow of his own pain even though he refused to admit that he felt any.

The vicar spoke of hardship and endurance, and the triumph of right over wrong, good over evil, love over hatred. There were special prayers for those who must fight, and prayers too for those men sailing convoys across the Atlantic, through its storms and the relentless pursuit of Hitler's U-boats to bring safely into port much-needed supplies.

There could, of course, be no joyous pealing of the church bells to ring out across the cold clear night air symbolically clamouring the news of the gift of a special birth, because church bells could be rung now only in emergencies.

After the service families and neighbours lingered outside the church, stamping their feet against the sharp cold, speaking in low voices of this, the first Christmas of a new war.

How many more would there be before it ended, Jean wondered starkly as they made their way home, and how many families would be changed for ever by it? It was bad enough that Luke wasn't here, but so very much worse because of the way he and Sam had parted. It would have made such a difference if she had been able to turn to Sam and share her fears for Luke with him, just as they had always shared their fears for their children.

This bitterness with Sam had put a barrier between them that separated them, now making it impossible for her to reach out to him for comfort as she so longed to be able to do, and to offer him comfort in return.

The kitchen welcomed them with the smell of cooking and warmth, and before Jean could stop the twins were reaching for the mince pies.

'It's too late to go eating pastry now,' Jean warned them, pushing the tray out of the way. 'You'll end up with indigestion. Besides, if you eat them now we won't have enough for tomorrow.'

'Aww, Mum, we're hungry,' Lou protested.

Jean sighed. 'Very well then, you can have those we put out for Father Christmas, but don't blame me if you do get indigestion.'

As the twins hurried into the parlour she said to Grace, 'I just hope this goose is going to cook properly. It only just fits in the oven. Now what is it?' she demanded when the twins came rushing back into the kitchen.

'The mince pies have gone,' said Lou.

'And the milk,' said Sasha.

Grace looked at her sisters, knowing how much they enjoyed playing tricks. 'You mean they have now that you two have had them,' she suggested wryly.

'No, Grace, they've really gone, honestly. Come and look.'

They all trooped into the front room where all that remained of the mince pies was a few crumbs.

Sasha and Lou had crept close to one another, their arms linked.

'Sam, do you think someone could have got in?' Jean asked uneasily, and then broke off as they all heard someone coming down the stairs.

For a moment no one moved, and then Sam strode to the door and wrenched it open, Jean and the girls clustering nervously behind him.

Looking back at them from the stairs was Luke, his hair tousled and his eyes blurred with sleep.

'Luke!'

It was Jean who spoke, hurrying into the hall to her son.

'Sorry I missed church, Mum,' he apologised

wearily. 'They didn't tell us we were getting leave until the last minute and then the ruddy train crawled all the way from Euston. I couldn't let you know I was on my way.'

'I'm sorry, Luke love, but your Christmas presents are on their way to France,' Jean apologised ruefully as they all trooped into the front parlour in their dressing gowns, following the family tradition of opening their presents around the tree, which she and Sam had begun when they were first married.

Sam had put a match to the fire he had laid for her yesterday and Grace, bless her, had been up before all of them, bringing her and Sam tea in bed.

'Well, nursing's certainly changed you,' Sam had teased Grace. 'Getting up before anyone else.'

Now they were all gathered in the front room, the sound of Christmas carols from the wireless adding to the festive morning atmosphere. Frost had iced patterns on the windows and Jean was glad of the warmth of her dressing gown as they all started to hand out presents to one another, Grace hiding her smile at the disappointment on Lou's face as she handed her her gramophone record disguised as a large box.

Luke's gifts stood out from everyone else's. They were all wrapped in fancy paper and tied with pretty ribbons. They also had gift tags on them saying 'A present from Paris'.

'We had to come back through Paris so one of

the lads suggested we did our Christmas shopping there,' he explained cheerfully.

'Paris?' Jean exclaimed with maternal anxiety. 'You mean that Paris, where all them French mademoiselles are?'

Over Jean's head, Luke and Sam exchanged exclusively male looks.

When Luke nodded his head, Jean protested, 'But how could you go shopping there? You can't speak French.'

'They have signs outside some of the shops saying "English spoken",' Luke soothed her, adding with a grin, 'Mind you, it weren't exactly "English" as we speak it here in Liverpool.'

'Come on, Mum, take a look. It isn't going to bite you,' Luke teased Jean as she looked at her own present, unwilling to open it because it was so prettily wrapped. For all his grown-up manner, Jean could still see in his eyes the eager anxiousness of the little boy who had carefully made her past Christmas presents at school.

Quickly she unwrapped her gift, her eyes widening when she saw the glass bottle of scent inside the elegant box.

'It's some of that Chanel No. 5,' Luke told her. 'I got some for Grace, an' all. Only a small bottle mind, 'cos it's pricey, but our sergeant was with us and it was him that told us to buy it.'

Chanel No. 5. Now Jean and Grace exchanged exclusively female looks, their eyes shining with thrilled awe.

'Luke, you shouldn't have gone spending your

money on summat so expensive,' Jean's voice trembled. Normally if she wore scent it was something like Yardley's – a bit of Lavender or White Violets, and she bought it herself, Sam not being the type to go buying things like scent. In fact, Sam preferred to give her the money to go out and buy her own present, which meant she normally ended up spending the money on everyone else, as mothers do.

'Look, Sam.' Her hand trembled slightly as she held out the bottle so that he could see it, whilst Grace flung her arms around Luke's neck and hugged him tightly.

'I'll wear it on New Year's Eve. It's ever such a lovely present, Luke.'

'What have you brought us?' Lou demanded eagerly.

'Open your presents and see,' Luke told her, then turned to Sam. 'This is for you, Dad.'

Jean held her breath as Sam unwrapped his gift. No mention had been made of the manner in which they had parted, and Luke was obviously doing everything he could to mend things between them, to Jean's relief.

The twins were unwrapping their presents, so Jean pretended to be watching them, although in reality her attention was on Sam, who was being maddeningly slow as he unwrapped his. Finally the paper fell away to reveal a leather wallet.

Sam had been using the same wallet for as long as Jean could remember. He had had it before they were married and over the years the stitching had had to be repaired many times.

'Have a look inside, Dad,' Luke was urging.

Sam opened the wallet. Inside it, in gold lettering were printed the words 'From your loving son, December 1939'.

Tears blurred Jean's eyes. Luke was trying to tell his dad how much he regretted their falling-out, she knew. She could see that he was waiting for Sam to say something to show that he knew it too, and she could see too the hurt in his eyes when, instead, Sam merely said curtly, 'You shouldn't have gone wasting your money. I've already got a wallet.'

Then he got up and walked out of the room and up the stairs. Torn between wanting to comfort Luke and go after Sam, Jean was obliged instead to admire the pretty silk scarf Sasha was holding up.

'Mum, look,' she demanded happily, and then flung her arms around Luke's neck to thank him.

Upstairs the bathroom door closed and Jean sighed. Sam would no doubt closet himself in there for hours.

Grace reached for her last present. She had been saving it for last deliberately since she had seen already that it had a card on it from her parents, and it looked tantalisingly different from anything she had been expecting, even if it was wrapped in paper she recognised her mother must have saved from last Christmas. They would be doing a lot more making do and mending from now on.

The twins were squabbling amicably over which of their records they wanted to play first, and her mother was saying something about needing to go and check on the goose, but Grace was oblivious to both conversations, her eyes widening and her hands trembling slightly as she smoothed the familiar silk of the green dress. Her mother had folded it in such way that Grace saw the insert of pretty cream lace immediately, and knew what it must mean even before she had shaken out the frock and held it up in front of herself.

'Oh, Mum!' she exclaimed emotionally.

'I took it to Mrs Noakes, who used to work for that posh dress shop on Bold Street before she retired, and it was her that suggested putting a piece in it. She said it's as good as new now.'

Grace hugged her fiercely, and was just folding the dress up again when Sam came back in.

Jean knew that what Grace had done was wrong, and that Sam would probably have disapproved of what she, Jean, had done to make the best of it, saying that Grace shouldn't be rewarded for her crime, but Jean was a loving mother and very practically natured. She just could not stand by and see such a lovely dress go to waste. Besides, Grace had learned her lesson, there was no doubt about that.

'I've brought some French stamps back with me for Jack,' said Luke as he helped Jean to clear up the wrapping paper. 'I know he likes collecting them. He'll be back home for Christmas, I expect?'

'No. He's staying with the family he was evacuated to. I wrote to Vi asking her where I should send the little bit of summat I'd got for Jack and she wrote back saying to send it to her and she'd put it in with what she was sending to him. She said there was no point in unsettling him by bringing him home just for a few days. Poor little lad, I feel so sorry for him.'

'He might be happier with his evacuation family,' said Sasha, pulling a face. 'Imagine having to live with Auntie Vi and Uncle Edwin and stupid Bella . . .'

'Sasha!' Jean rebuked her.

'Bella isn't living with them now. She's married, remember,' Lou corrected her twin.

'I'm never going to get married,' said Sasha.

'Yes you will,' Lou insisted. 'Everyone gets married. I bet Grace will be next.'

'No I won't,' Grace assured them. 'I'd have to give up nursing if I did, and I don't want to do that.'

'What about that Teddy you went to the pictures with, then?' Lou demanded.

'Teddy is just a friend,' Grace told her firmly, and to her own delight she didn't even blush.

Christmas dinner had been eaten, the table had been cleared and the washing up done, and thankfully the twins were for once not playing their gramophone records too loudly.

In the front room a small group of men – neighbours and friends who had somehow or other got to hear that Luke was home – were discussing the war and what was likely to happen next, and treating Luke with a new deference and respect now that he was a serving soldier just back from France. But it hurt Jean to see the way that Sam was holding back from the conversation, determined not to give an inch nor to show any pride in Luke's bravery in volunteering.

This wasn't Christmas as she would have wanted it to be, Jean thought sadly. She would have given anything this morning to see Sam giving Luke one of his old fierce fatherly hugs. Poor Luke, he had tried so hard, and he wasn't to know that just the sight of him now, surrounded by men who were praising him and showing their admiration for what he had done, could only drive even deeper Sam's bitterness over his memories of the Great War.

Despite the warmth of her kitchen Jean felt chilled by her fear of what the future could bring, and how it might affect the lives of those she loved.

THIRTEEN

'I'll tell you what, that brother of yours is a good-looking chap, Grace,' said Hannah.

Grace laughed. 'Our Luke good-looking? Give over.' But sisterly pride shone in her eyes as she watched Luke coming back from the bar.

He had been a bit dubious at first when she had suggested that since he hadn't made any arrangements for New Year's Eve he came to the Grafton with her, but he was certainly enjoying himself now, and no wonder, with all her friends making such a fuss of him. Even Lillian, who had said that she didn't think she'd be able to join them after all, but who had turned up at the last minute, just as they were queuing to get in, had demanded an introduction to him.

Grace had been a bit uncertain about wearing her green dress, partly because of her guilt about it and partly because she had thought it might be too dressy for the Grafton, but perhaps because it was New Year's Eve, or maybe because of the war, or perhaps a combination of both, all the women had really gone to town and were looking very elegant and glamorous indeed.

The Grafton was Liverpool's most famous ballroom. It had a properly sprung floor and special function rooms on the top floor that could be hired for private parties. The walls were painted a soft red, and the booths surrounding the dance floor were upholstered in matching red velvet.

The band had their own special alcove, and all the top bands played at the Grafton.

The booths round the dance floor were the province of courting couples, who liked the dimly lit privacy they afforded, whilst larger groups of young people opted for the tables and chairs so that they could see and be seen.

The girls had been lucky enough to bag a table right on the edge of the dance floor and within view of the band.

For the student nurses the expense of their tickets had not left any of them much money to spare for drinks and so they were making do with lemonade livened up to make very weak shandy.

Luke had offered to buy them each a drink but everyone apart from Lillian, who had immediately asked for a port and lemon, had shaken her head, out of what Grace guessed was a reluctance to put him to so much expense.

They were a nice crowd, and Grace was as proud of her friends as she was of her brother.

Grace tapped her foot in time to the music. Her mother claimed that her children's musical ear came from her side of the family, citing her younger sister as proof of this legacy. Grace had no idea if that was true, but they could all sing and dance and had a good ear for music.

Once they had learned that their elder siblings were going dancing on New Year's Eve the twins had insisted on putting them through their paces and teaching them the steps of the new dances from America; wild crazy jitterbug movements that had had Grace laughing and gasping for breath, and Luke complaining that he'd break something.

'I reckon that Grace has got a hot date as she keeps on looking at the door. Bet it's that ambulance driver that's so keen on you, Grace,' Iris teased, making everyone laugh, although Grace could see that Luke was wearing a questioning older-brother look.

'Teddy did say he might be here, and I've promised him the last dance,' she revealed.

'Ooohh, I told you he was sweet on you,' said Jennifer.

'We're just friends, that's all,' Grace insisted truthfully.

'Well,' said Hannah, 'perhaps you'd better tell him that because he's coming this way now.'

Grace turned round to see Teddy coming towards her, smiling. She smiled back happily, and then saw him check as he realised that another man was seated next to her.

'Move up, Luke,' Grace urged her brother.

The two men eyed one another appraisingly.

'Grace has brought her brother along with her,

seeing as he's on leave,' said Hannah, breaking the male deadlock and taking pity on Teddy.

Immediately Teddy was all smiles, extending his hand to shake Luke's, and sitting down next to him. Within seconds the two men were engrossed in a discussion about the war.

'It's New Year's Eve and I want to dance and forget about the war,' Lillian pouted.

Taking the hint, Luke excused himself to Teddy to get up and go over to her. Within seconds of Luke and Lillian taking to the floor, or so it seemed to Grace, the other girls had all been asked to dance, leaving her and Teddy on their own.

'The floor looks a bit crowded now – do you mind if we sit this one out?' he asked her.

Good-naturedly Grace assured him that she didn't, even though in reality she was a bit disappointed. He offered her a cigarette and took one for himself, lighting them both.

'You're a smashing girl, Grace, one of the best. The kind of girl any chap would be proud to call his own.'

Grace shook her head at him, still trying to pretend she didn't mind about not dancing, but as though he had guessed what she was feeling, Teddy put out his cigarette, reached for hers and put it out as well.

'Come on, let's dance,' he told her gruffly.

'I thought you didn't want to dance,' Grace protested.

'You want to dance, don't you?' he told her, smiling. 'And that's good enough for me.'

Grace was touched that he had changed his mind on her account. He was a good dancer, holding her firmly but not too close, nicely light on his feet and with a sense of rhythm.

The band played on without stopping; none of the dancers left the floor, as though everyone was determined to take what pleasure they could from the evening to store up against the bleakness of what might lie ahead.

Whilst they danced Teddy talked, asking Grace about her Christmas and she asked him in turn about his. She knew that he lived with his parents, and from what he had told her about them Grace sensed that they were a family very similarly circumstanced to her own. Teddy's father owned the small greengrocer's shop, where Teddy also worked when he was not driving his ambulance.

'Phew, you're dancing me off me feet,' Teddy joked, putting his hand over his heart. 'I could do with a bit of a sit-down to get me puff back. Serves me right for nattering too much.'

He did sound a bit breathless, and although she could have danced all night, and indeed would have loved to have done so, Grace immediately agreed that they return to their table.

'So you reckon you're going to continue with this nursing lark, do you?' Teddy asked her.

'Yes. I want to complete my training more than anything.'

Teddy smiled at her as though she had said something that pleased him and then reached for her hand, holding it in his own beneath the table.

They sat out a few dances after that, gradually joined by the others as they returned to the table.

'Oh, no, just listen to that.' Hannah pulled a face when the band broke into a fast jitterbug number. 'I can't dance to that.'

'We can, can't we, Gracie?' Luke laughed, reaching for Grace's hand and pulling her to her feet despite her objections, to join the reduced number of couples brave enough to try the new dance.

'Luke, we'll make total fools of ourselves,' Grace warned him, but she admitted to herself that it was fun to see the look of astonished admiration on the faces of her friends as she and Luke showed off the moves the twins had taught them.

She was laughing and out of breath when they returned to their seats at the end of the dance.

'I hope you realise that you're going to have to teach all of us to do that,' said Doreen as Grace sat down. 'We were all so envious watching you, weren't we, Teddy?'

'Very envious,' he agreed.

There was a note in his voice that Grace neither recognised nor understood. She looked at him and was reassured when he smiled back at her with his familiar happy jokey Teddy smile.

It just wasn't fair. This wasn't how she'd expected to spend New Year's Eve at all, in her in-laws' front room surrounded by her parents and the dullest and most boring people she had ever met, Bella thought crossly.

And what made it worse was that Charlie had

come home two days earlier on unexpected leave, and was going to the Tennis Club dance using *her* tickets because Alan had put his foot down and insisted that they had to accept his parents' invitation.

Even her mother had taken his side, whilst her father had gone on and on about how important it was that councillors supported one another, especially now that some idiots had started making all sorts of ridiculous accusations about councillors getting benefits that other people couldn't have.

Bella supposed that her father was in a temper because of the criticism he was receiving over the petrol allowance he had managed to get for himself through his connection with the Ministry, but why that meant that she had to sit here listening to her mother-in-law's dull bridge-playing friends going on about the need for everyone to do their bit, and asking her stupid questions about what kind of voluntary work she was doing, Bella had no idea. She certainly didn't intend to waste her time making bandages or knitting. If she had to play a role in this silly war then it would have to be doing something much more glamorous than that. She started to drift off into a very pleasant daydream in which her mother-in-law's jaw was dropping at the news that she, Bella, had been invited to Buckingham Palace to have tea with the Queen as a thank you for the wonderful effect the Women's Enlistment poster photograph of her wearing a Norman

Hartnell-designed uniform had had on recruit-ment numbers.

Bella was just enjoying listening to the Queen saying admiringly, 'And it's all down to you, my dear,' when her daydream was rudely interrupted by Alan's father's raised voice.

Bella did not like her father-in-law. Of course, she didn't like either of Alan's parents but she particularly disliked his father, who according to Alan had said that the only reason she wanted to marry him had been because she had thought she was 'on to a good thing'. That was why, according to Alan, his father had refused to buy them a house or give Alan a salary raise.

He was saying something about the local papers taking a dim view of those who were using the war as an excuse to line their own pockets, and Bella guessed from her father's angry red face that the comment had been directed at him. He looked as though he was about to explode and, knowing her father's temper, Bella wasn't entirely surprised when he burst out, 'If you're referring to the work I'm doing for the Ministry, then at least my son's in the army and doing his bit for the country, instead of staying at home and pretending to work for me, unlike some I could name.'

Alan's mother's face went dark red, whilst Bella saw that her own mother was looking equally flushed but triumphant. Alan himself was scowling, whilst his father looked furious.

And then suddenly Trixie spoke up, her voice polite but very clear and cool as she pointed out to Bella's father, 'But your son didn't really plan to volunteer, did he? I remember him telling us that he'd only joined the TA to escape conscription.'

The three Parkers were looking gratefully at Trixie whilst Bella's father was glaring at her as though he couldn't believe his ears.

'That's right, Trixie, I remember Charlie saying that as well. In fact, Father-in-law, I seem to remember him also saying something about being sure you could get him out of the TA,' said Alan smugly.

'Rubbish, I don't know where you've got that idea from. Charlie wanted to do his bit, and I'll not have anyone say any different.'

Her father was blustering now, Bella recognised, and it was plain from the looks on the faces of her husband and her in-laws that they knew they had won the encounter.

Thanks to Trixie.

Bella gave her a baleful look. She was so plain that it was no wonder she had to suck up to their parents' generation, and that consequently Alan's parents thought the sun shone out of her backside, Bella thought angrily. You'd never catch her doing anything like that.

'It might not be a bad idea to warn your brother that Lillian wants to marry a doctor,' Hannah told Grace meaningfully, as they sat out a dance together whilst Luke danced yet again with Lillian. 'You wouldn't want to have him falling for her and getting hurt.'

'Don't be daft, Hannah. Luke is just having a good time because he's home on leave, that's all.' Grace laughed.

'Have it your own way,' said Hannah good-naturedly, adding, 'I'd have thought you'd have bin dancing a bit more yourself, seeing as you are so good at it and don't have two left feet like me.'

'Hannah, you haven't got two left feet at all.'

'Well, I feel like I have, especially when I watched you doing that jitterbugging with your brother.'

Grace laughed again. 'It's our sisters, the twins, that got us doing that. It fair takes your puff, though.'

'What's that then?' Teddy asked, coming back to the table just in time to catch the end of their conversation.

'Dancing,' Grace told him.

'It does that,' he agreed. 'I'm saving meself now for the last dance.' He gave them both a wink and grinned, and Grace couldn't help but be amused. He was such fun to be with and she could tell that the other girls and Luke all liked him. She was glad that he'd said what he had to her about them just being friends, but at the same time she also felt a bit disappointed. She knew that she wanted – and needed – to concentrate on her nursing training and that the last thing she needed was to fall head over heels in love with someone, and yet a little daringly a part of her still wondered what it would be like if Teddy wanted to go further than just holding her hand and telling her how much he liked her, whilst the more sensible part of her was glad that he was content to keep things as they were.

The last dance of the evening was announced and within seconds the floor was packed with couples determined to take the opportunity to be close to one another. The dimly lit dance floor permitted the kind of intimacy that was normally frowned upon, the war adding to the sense of urgency and poignancy that everyone was feeling, but whilst Teddy got her up to dance, he certainly wasn't holding her as close as he could have done, not even as close as Luke was holding Lillian, Grace noticed as they danced past them. She was glad, of course, that Teddy respected her and that he was behaving so decently, she told herself firmly. But it was New Year's Eve, and if he had attempted to hold her closer she would have understood.

'Penny for them?' Teddy asked her.

Unwilling to tell him the truth, Grace fibbed. 'I was just wondering where we'd all be this time next year.'

'Why waste time thinking about tomorrow? It's today we should be thinking about and enjoying.'

That was true, but it was hard not to think of what might lie ahead, especially now, Grace thought, as the dance came to an end and the band broke into the familiar and emotive strains of 'Auld Lang Syne'.

*　　*　　*

'Luke's got to leave from Lime Street Station today to rejoin his unit,' Jean reminded Sam as she poured him a second cup of tea.

'Yes, I know,' Sam agreed tersely.

'He's upstairs packing now, and I've told him that we'll go to Lime Street to see him off.'

Sam's mouth tightened with hostility, as Jean had known it would, but her heart still sank.

She had hoped so much that this unexpected period of leave that had brought Luke home to them to share Christmas and the New Year would have softened Sam's heart and turned him back into the loving father he had been.

'You can do what you like, I've got better things to do than waste me time hanging around Lime Street making a lot of fuss about nothing.'

Jean went paler. 'Sam Campion, how can you call seeing your only son off to fight "nothing"?'

'Fight?' Sam snorted with derision. 'From what I've heard all he's done so far is go sightseeing in ruddy Paris.'

'You know better than that, Sam. They might have had a bit of leave in Paris, but it's obvious from what Luke's not said that they've been doing a fair bit more than that. Please come to the station with me, Sam,' she begged.

'I've got some work to do down at the allotment. We'll be needing everything I can grow there now when this rationing comes in.'

Jean didn't argue with him. She knew there wasn't any point.

For Luke's sake she tried to put on a brave face

when they left the house together an hour later, telling him brightly, 'Your dad would have come with us but—'

Luke's quiet, 'It's all right, Mum, you don't have to explain,' cut her to the heart.

The twins had wanted to go with them but Jean had visions of the pair getting into all kinds of mischief in the busily packed station, and had refused to let them, and Grace, whose company she would have welcomed, was now living in at the hospital and had started the second part of her nurse's training.

Lime Street Station was seething with young men in uniform and their families, some of them returning to their units, some leaving for their first tour of duty, having completed their basic training, and others just starting out on that training.

Groups of WVS in their uniforms were manning information points and providing welcome canteen facilities, and Jean felt proud of Luke's calm soldierly manner as he found out which platform his train would be going from and where he needed to report.

'Two family members only are allowed onto the platform,' the tired WVS lady in charge of one of the desks informed them, adding, 'That's if you can get a platform ticket, otherwise family are allowed only as far as the barrier.'

Jean was relieved when Luke took hold of her arm and told her, 'This way, Mum.'

She had been to Lime Street before but she had never ever seen it as packed as this, not even during summer holiday weeks. You couldn't move for other people, but somehow Luke managed to carve a way between the packed crowd jostling for space, until they finally reached the barrier to the platform guarded by a large sergeant with a long list in his hand.

'Private Campion, Number 813320,' Luke told him, putting down his kitbag and handing over his papers.

He had grown so much broader since he had been in the army, Jean recognised, with muscles now that rivalled his dad's.

'And this is your sister, come to see you off, is it?' the sergeant joked, smiling at Jean, before letting them through without even asking her if she had a platform ticket.

'Better not tell Dad about that,' Luke warned her.

Down on the platform where the train was waiting, its doors open, the air was thick with smoke and bitterly cold.

'Hang on here a minute, Mum,' Luke told her, 'whilst I go and nab meself a seat, otherwise I reckon I could end up standing all the way to the coast.'

His movements now were those of an army-trained man, careful and economical, and so very different from the boyishness he had had before he left.

Jean watched as he secured himself a seat and then let down the window, and leaned out so that he could talk to her.

The train was filling up fast, and already the

271

carriage Luke was in was nearly full; mothers clustering by its windows, all, like Jean, anxious to spend as much time as they could with their sons, fathers shaking their sons' hands, their faces set.

Luke hadn't said one single word against his dad, but he must be feeling, as she was, that Sam should have been here, Jean acknowledged.

Three young men hurried down the platform and jumped into Luke's carriage, one of them exclaiming, 'Ruddy well thought we weren't going to make it and that would have put the fat in the fire!'

'Fat in the fire? Got you on a charge, more like,' one of his companions told him, as he took out his cigarettes.

The smell of khaki, cigarettes and young male virility was filling the air. Young women, – girls still, really – shiny new wedding rings very much in evidence, were clinging to equally young men. Older women with young families clung tightly to their children's hands or the handles of perambulators whilst husbands bent to kiss each child in turn, and still older women, like Jean herself, watched, remembering when the sons they were saying goodbye to had been small enough to keep safe in such prams.

The train was getting up steam. Jean could see the guard making his way down the platform, slamming the carriage doors as he did so. Jean's stomach muscles tightened. She must not cry and disgrace Luke, upsetting him when he had to be strong, but she couldn't stop the anxious maternal love flooding her, and with it her fear for him.

The guard blew his whistle. Luke leaned down out of the window to kiss her cheek. The train was starting to move. Jean's eyes blurred with tears, and she had to turn her head away so that Luke wouldn't see them. And then unbelievably as she did so, she saw Sam, pushing his way through the crowd.

'*Sam!* Over here.' She jumped up and waved her hand, telling Luke, 'Look, Luke, it's your dad. Sam, quick, over here . . .'

The train was moving now, families moving with it, desperate for every precious last second of time with those they loved. Jean had lost sight of Sam.

The train was gathering speed.

'Dad.'

She could hear the joy in Luke's voice as Sam broke through the crowd and reached up to take Luke's hand in his own.

'You see you take care of yourself, you ruddy young fool.'

Sam's voice might be gruff but it was filled with love, and Jean could see from Luke's expression that he could hear it too.

Sam released Luke's hand and reached for hers. Together and in silence they watched the train until they couldn't see it any more.

Only then did Jean turn to Sam and say emotionally, 'Oh, Sam.'

There was no need for any other words. And for the first time in the whole of their married lives, to Jean's astonishment, Sam took hold of her in a public place in front of other people and held her so tightly she could hardly breathe. She could feel the betraying dampness of his tears against her own skin as they stood locked together, sharing their love and their fear for their son.

FOURTEEN

'I'm so tired, I nearly fell asleep when I was feeding a patient this morning. I would have done, I reckon, if she hadn't given me a nudge in the ribs to warn me that Staff Nurse Rodgers was watching me,' Jennifer moaned.

Those members of Grace's set who were on 'days' rather than 'nights' were sitting huddled over the fire in the junior nurses' sitting room, snatching a much-needed few minutes of relaxation after their evening meal.

'That's nothing. Three patients on my ward were sick after breakfast this morning, and Sister had me scrubbing their sheets and nightgowns. I thought I was going to throw up myself, I did,' said Doreen.

'I've heard that at least four girls from other sets have left, saying that they thought they were supposed to be training as nurses, not working as skivvies,' Iris told them.

Grace was so exhausted that she would quite happily have let the complaints of the others wash over her unregarded if Hannah hadn't nudged her and demanded, 'What about you, Grace? How are you doing on Men's Surgical?'

Grace stifled a yawn and told them ruefully, 'Staff Nurse had me and the other junior doing five bed baths this morning, and they all went and got you-know-whats.'

The others all laughed.

They might have been on the wards for just over a month but it seemed a lifetime ago since they had been in PTS, with its male torso minus any sexual organs. Grace might be able to laugh now at the shock it had given her on her first week on the ward the first time she had been instructed to give a patient a bed bath. Both her face and the poor patient's had been bright red when the unfamiliar male arrangement of 'bits' had suddenly stiffened into an erection.

Staff Nurse, who must have been watching, had called her over to the large desk in the middle of the ward afterwards and calmly explained the workings of the male anatomy to her, advising her that the male patients, much to their own embarrassment, tended to get erections when pretty nurses bed bathed them, and that it was a fact of nursing life that Grace would have to get used to. On the other hand, Staff Nurse had added firmly, if any male patient suggested that she do anything with that erection, she was to walk away and report him to a more senior nurse immediately.

The routine of the hospital wards, with its temperature, pulse and breathing rate charts, its timed-to-the-second visits from stern-faced doctors and consultants, who never ever acknowledged the existence of the most junior nurses, plus the fearsomeness of staff nurses and sisters, might now be familiar to them, but they all agreed that the exhaustion caused by the amount of physically hard and often dirty work they were required to do had proved far harder to adjust to.

'Me hands are red raw from cleaning floors and scrubbing sheets,' Doreen complained. 'And me feet feel like they're on fire after walking up and down that ruddy ward. They were that swollen last night I thought I'd have to sleep in me stockings and shoes.'

'On fire?' Iris chivvied her. 'You're lucky. Mine are half frozen, and covered in chilblains.'

It was the coldest winter that anyone could remember, although you wouldn't have known it, since the Government had given orders that there was to be no weather reporting in the papers or by the BBC because, so rumour had it, it might be bad for morale.

All manner of things were 'not being reported', or so Teddy had told Grace when he had taken her to the pictures earlier in the week on her half-day off. And yet on the other hand there were constant 'Chinese whispers' about Hitler's imminent invasion, and there had definitely been sightings of enemy reconnaissance planes over Liverpool, as well as an attempt to destroy the Forth Bridge, with bombs dropped in Scotland.

But worst of all for a city like Liverpool to bear

was the increasingly bad news about the number of British vessels being torpedoed and sunk. Everyone in the city knew how much the whole country relied on safe passage of the convoys crisscrossing the Atlantic and bringing home much-needed supplies for the war effort; and virtually everyone in the city also had or knew of someone who had a family member on board those ships.

The bombing raids they had been warned to expect might not have materialised, the stored cardboard coffins may not have been needed as yet, but death had still come to the streets of Liverpool and mourners were still weeping for those they had lost.

The cinema newsreels, of course, focused on those things that would boost the country's morale rather than damage it; scenes of the routing of the *Graf Spee*; of British troops abroad enjoying ENSA-sponsored shows; cheery WVS workers manning tea urns, and happy evacuated children frolicking in a sunny countryside.

Just seeing that sunshine had made Grace long for its warmth. Everyone was saying that they couldn't remember there being such a bitterly cold winter. Even in the cinema it was so cold that Grace had half hoped that Teddy might put his arm around her once they were inside, but he hadn't.

They had several patients on the ward who had been injured in accidents caused by the icy roads, and when Grace had gone home on her full day off to visit her family her mother had told her that her father was complaining about the weather stopping him from working on his allotment.

Although officially, as trainee nurses, they were supposed to have one half-day and one full day off a week, as Grace had discovered, with all the studying they still had to do, more often than not that time off was spent in their rooms poring over notes and books.

She was reminded of what Teddy had told her about news being held back when she went on duty one the morning in early February.

As soon as daily prayers were over, Staff Nurse Reid informed them that they had received eight new patients overnight, four of them in beds on the ward itself and four more in the much smaller side wards, normally reserved for paying patients or special cases needing individual nursing.

The hospital had been built on the Florence Nightingale principle, the so-called Nightingale wards having high ceilings and tall windows to facilitate the flow of the fresh air, which Florence Nightingale had considered important in defeating the spread of infection and aiding patients' recovery. The beds had to be a certain distance apart, with the wheels turned inwards to allow for proper cleaning and to prevent the spread of cross infection. Heavy screens were pulled around a bed should the patient need privacy. Ward Sister sat at a table in the middle of the ward, keeping a steely eye on her domain.

The nurses' home at the hospital was attached to the main hospital via an underground tunnel, the entrance to which was guarded by an extremely fierce porter.

'It's going to be like living in a convent,' Lillian had complained when they had first arrived earlier in the month.

'Ah ha, now we know why you're so keen to date a doctor,' Hannah had joked with a grin. 'It's because you think they're the only men that will get anywhere near the place.'

They might have finished their initial three-month training but in hospital hierarchy terms they were still the lowest of the low as had been made clear to them from the first moment they set foot on the wards.

Grace's first duty of the morning was to help serve the patients their breakfasts.

'We had some Merchant Navy lads brought in last night off one of the convoy ships,' the junior nurse going off duty managed to whisper confidentially to her as they changed shifts. 'In a real bad way they are, an'all. Got torpedoed by the Germans.'

There wasn't time for her to say any more. Screens were drawn around four of the beds on the ward and the doors closed to the side wards, and Sister told Grace that she was not to take breakfast to those patients.

After breakfast came the inevitable 'bottle' round, and then the collection and removal of the bottles to the sluice room ready for the urine to be tested for 'sugar', albumin or blood, depending on what was written on the patient's chart.

Then after that came the first of the many 'locker' rounds of the day, for which Grace had to set a trolley with a basin of carbolic, a cloth, a small pail for rubbish and a large jug of fresh water. Each locker top had to be wiped with carbolic. Any rubbish such as papers had to be removed, ashtrays had to be emptied and wiped, and finally the patient's drinking glass had to be filled with water.

All the patients' lockers were supposed to be finished by the time of the first nurses' coffee break. During her first week it had taken Grace nearly half as long again as it should have done to complete this task but now she could work quickly and smoothly and still find time to chat to the patients as she did so, taking the letters she was given for posting and exchanging banter with those men who were well enough to want to indulge in it.

Several patients were recovering from serious operations and Grace always tried to spend a little more time with them. Today, though, even those patients who had seemed the most poorly were now making an effort to be more chipper and were asking anxiously after the new arrivals.

'Heard as how one poor lad has lost both his legs,' said old Mr Whitehead, in a wheezy whisper.

Grace's hand shook slightly as she filled his water glass.

There had been several occasions since she had come on the ward, when the things she had seen – and smelled – had made her stomach heave, but the thought of some poor young man losing his limbs still shocked her.

It was a relief in many ways to be told not to go near the small side wards, although Grace couldn't help but notice the number of white-coated doctors and surgeons coming on to the ward to see the new patients.

By dinnertime Grace was more than ready for a break. It was her half-day off, and she'd promised to meet Teddy after she'd had her dinner, but since she was starting 'nights' from seven o'clock, she had decided against doing anything other than snatching a bit of fresh air and some much-needed 'extra' sleep.

Nurses weren't allowed to leave the hospital grounds wearing their uniform, but since she would be seeing Teddy in the hospital grounds Grace had not bothered to get changed. Huddling into her cloak, she made her way carefully across the icy yard to where Teddy had parked his ambulance, her breath coming in white puffs on the frosty air.

Teddy had obviously been on the look-out for her because he opened the door and climbed out of the cab, coming to meet her, rubbing his hands and then blowing on them to ward off the cold.

'It's soooo cold,' Grace complained, her smile turning to a concerned frown when Teddy started to cough.

'It's all right, it's just the cold air getting on me chest,' he reassured her.

'I can't stay long,' Grace told him. 'I start nights tonight.'

'You'll have them poor sods that came off that convoy on your ward. One of the lads was telling us about them this morning. In a bad way, they are, by all accounts. Makes my blood boil when daft folk complain about a bit of rationing. They'd sing a different song if it were their kin wot was sailing with the convoys.'

'I don't think people always understand – about the rationing, I mean.'

Teddy smiled at her. 'That's typical of you, Grace; you never want to think badly of anyone. Well, one day you're going to have to if ruddy Hitler gets his way.' He gave a frustrated sigh. 'It really narks me, not being allowed to join up and do me bit.'

'But you are doing your bit, Teddy,' Grace protested. 'My dad says that one of the biggest mistakes they made in the last war was making all the young men enlist and that's why this time they've said that there's got to be reserved occupations.'

She could see that Teddy wasn't looking convinced. Grace shivered. Although she tried not to worry, sometimes it was hard not to feel afraid when other people were talking about how things would be if Hitler invaded and took over the country.

'Is your Luke still writing to that flighty piece from your set?' Teddy asked her abruptly.

Grace had been surprised when Luke had told her in one of his letters that he was writing regularly to Lillian, especially when Lillian herself hadn't said anything to Grace about it.

'Told you so,' had been Hannah's comment when Grace had confided in her. 'It won't last, mind, at least not on her part, not once she gets that doctor she's wanting in her sights. She'll drop your brother like a hot potato then, just you wait and see.'

'Yes, I think so,' Grace told Teddy. 'Why?'

'I saw her going into Lyons with a chap the other day when I was driving past, that's all.'

'He was probably just a friend,' Grace felt bound to defend the other girl. 'And anyway, she and Luke are only writing to one another, nothing more.'

'Some chaps place a lot of store on that kind of thing.'

What was Teddy trying to say? Grace looked at him uncertainly.

'She can't be serious about anyone, not with us all only just starting out on our training. None of us can,' she reminded Teddy.

'You'd better get back if you want a couple of hours' sleep before you start on nights,' he warned her, looking significantly at his watch.

'Oh heavens, you're right.' Grace reached up to hug him. His chin and nose were turning blue with the cold and she supposed her own must be doing the same.

The other girls teased her about her relationship with Teddy, wanting to know if they were going steady and then shaking their heads when she told them that it wasn't something they had discussed.

'It's not natural, that isn't. Stands to reason that

if a lad is asking you out all the time he must have summat in mind,' Iris had told her forthrightly.

'Teddy knows how important my training is to me, and we know that we have to stay single if we want to be nurses. We're just friends, that's all,' Grace had responded firmly.

She knew, though, that they weren't entirely convinced and the truth was that she wasn't entirely convinced herself either. It wasn't that she wanted Teddy to ask her to be his girl or say that he loved her, but it did seem funny that he never made any attempt to, well, do the kind of things she had heard other girls saying their dates did. Of course, it was a good thing that Teddy respected her and treated her properly, but surely there was nothing wrong in him putting his arm around her in the pictures, or perhaps kissing her good night?

Teddy was a decent sort and she ought to be grateful for that, Grace told herself sternly after they had said their goodbyes and she was on her way back to the nurses' home.

Because she was now on nights and would be changing shifts with the girls on days, Grace was already eating when Hannah joined her at the table. Whilst the sisters had their own dining room, the junior nurses ate in the same room as the seniors and the staff nurses, although each rank had its own separate area of the room.

'We've had one of the merchant seamen from your ward in theatre today,' she told Grace as she tucked into her shepherd's pie. 'He'd got frostbite in his toes on account of being in the water when his ship went down, and Mr Stewart had to amputate them in case he got blood poisoning. Poor chap, he's in a very bad way – and not the only one, by all accounts.'

Hannah loved working in the operating theatre, and Grace suspected that she would ultimately choose to specialise in theatre work. Her comments, though, coupled with Grace's own tiredness, had made Grace feel slightly nauseous.

The rest of their set were filling up the table, all of them, except Lillian, who was also now on nights, chattering about their day.

'Shepherd's pie again,' said Lillian, shuddering as she sat down.

'Well, with any luck you'll soon have that new doctor you've bin making eyes at all week taking you out for dinner,' Doreen ribbed her good-naturedly.

'What do you mean, making eyes at him? I've been doing no such thing,' Lillian denied sharply.

'Well, from what I've heard, you'll be wasting your time if you have because he's already spoken for, and engaged to a girl down in London,' Jennifer announced, sliding into the last empty seat in time to join the conversation. 'And I collected your letters for you seeing as I was coming past anyway. Looks like Grace's brother is still pretty keen on you: there's three letters here from him.'

'I don't know why he keeps writing to me, because I've told him I haven't got time to keep writing back. Some people just can't seem to take a hint, though,' said Lillian.

Grace could feel her face burning with a mixture of anger on Luke's behalf and embarrassment on her own, at the open contempt in Lillian's voice. She pushed away her unfinished meal and stood up, too angry and upset to trust herself to say anything.

Hannah caught up with her halfway down the corridor, catching hold of her arm and saying comfortingly, 'That was a rotten thing of Lillian to say, but take no notice. My guess is that she's made a bit of a fool of herself over this new doctor, and he's told her that he isn't interested, so now she's taking it out on everyone else.'

'I just wish that Luke had never met her and it's my fault that he did. I never thought that he'd be silly enough—' Grace broke off and shook her head. 'You did warn me, I know, but I thought he'd see through her like we have.'

'Men aren't like us,' Hannah told her wisely, 'All it takes to pull the wool over their eyes sometimes is a pretty girl letting them think she's in love with them. And, of course, it's so much worse during wartime. It might be a good idea, though, if you were to write to him and drop him a hint, for his own sake.'

'I've tried that already,' Grace admitted, 'but so far as he's concerned, she's the sweetest kindest girl ever and he can't believe I could think they may not be suited.' Grace gave a small sigh. 'I suppose I could have a word with my mother, but I don't want to worry her . . .'

What she didn't want to say even to Hannah, who was probably her closest friend out of the whole group, was that from what he had said in his letters to her Luke genuinely believed that Lillian was far more committed to him than Grace knew her to be. So much so, in fact, that he had even talked of them becoming engaged just as soon as the war was over.

'Lillian should have been straight with him from the start instead of leading him on. Now, of course, she'll be worried about how it's going to look if she sends him a Dear John letter whilst he's away. If you ask me that's why she's acting the way she is, and hinting that she never encouraged him in the first place,' said Hannah.

Grace sighed. She knew that what Hannah was saying was probably true.

She was still thinking about Luke and all the other young men like him for whom letters from their loved ones were so important when she went on to the ward. Even here in hospital, letters from their families were important to the men. Grace had seen the expectant look on their faces when the post was brought in and the disappointment when there was nothing for them.

The blackout coverings had already been put in place over the windows, which were now latticed with sticky tape to protect the patients from flying glass if the hospital were to be bombed, and the ward was shadowed and quiet. But that did not mean that there wasn't plenty of work for her to do, Grace recognised, as Sister raised her head.

'Lockers I think first, Campion, and then Staff Nurse Willetts will show you how to change Mr Simmonds' dressing.'

'Yes, Sister.'

Alfred Simmonds had been on the ward longer than anyone else. He had a nasty ulcerous sore on his leg that needed twice-daily dressing and which Grace had heard was ultimately unlikely ever really to heal.

'He should be in a chronic infirmary ward really,' Staff Nurse Willetts had told her, 'but Sister reckons it would be the end of him if he was to leave here.'

Twice daily he was given M and B tablets, as the only medication available against blood poisoning was known, and the smell of the bandages that were removed from his leg and which it was Grace's job to take away to the sluice room were enough to make her stomach heave.

There were screens around one of the beds, and Sister herself had disappeared behind them, a sure sign that the patient in the bed was poorly.

Seeing Grace looking toward it, Staff Nurse Willetts told her grimly, 'We've got one of the merchant seamen in there. He had his operation earlier, and he's not too well, poor chap. Now let's go and see how you manage with Mr Simmonds' ulcer, shall we?'

Cleaning Mr Simmonds' leg was every bit as unpleasant as Grace had expected, but he was a kind man and he didn't wince at all, despite the fact that Grace knew she must be hurting him. Her hands were trembling dreadfully by the time she had finished and his leg was finally rebandaged to Staff Nurse Willetts' satisfaction. It was all very well practising bandaging and getting good marks; actually having to do it in reality was a very different matter, and Grace shuddered to think of what Staff might write in the plain cardboard-covered book all the junior nurses had to present to their seniors for their report every time they undertook a new procedure.

'Now I want you to give Mr Simmonds his M and B. Can you remember the dosage?'

'Two,' Grace started to say and then changed it quickly to a three when she saw Mr Simmonds raising three fingers behind Staff's back.

'Good.' Staff gave an approving nod of her head. 'I'm glad to see you're paying attention, Campion. Dr Lewis only increased the dosage yesterday.' She looked at her watch. 'Once Mr Simmonds has had his medication, and you've given out the urine bottles, you can go off for your break.'

'Yes, Sister,' Grace responded meekly.

The M and B tablets were huge and she wouldn't have wanted to swallow one herself, but Mr Simmonds, bless him, was as good as gold, winking at her when she thanked him for helping her earlier and telling her that he wouldn't mind a glass of whisky to help the pills go down.

Grace shook her head reprovingly. He knew as well as she did that alcohol was forbidden on the wards, although the patients were always trying to get some smuggled in by their visitors.

'Always check the parcels that visitors bring in, Nurse,' Staff Nurse Reid had told Grace on her first day on the ward. 'Remove them from the visitors and take them straight to the sluice room for proper inspection.'

'You'd be surprised the tricks the patients get up to,' one of the other junior nurses had told Grace. 'I had one a while ago that tried to sneak in some beer in a hot-water bottle.'

Grace had carefully loaded all the urine bottles onto the trolley and was just wheeling it past the curtained off bed when she thought she heard a sound from behind the curtains. She stopped the trolley and listened and heard it again, a sort of dripping noise. She looked towards the table in the centre of the room where the night sister and the staff nurse were working.

Staff Nurse looked up and, although Grace hadn't said anything, she got up and came over to her demanding quietly, 'What is it, Nurse? Why aren't you giving out the bottles? The visitors will be here soon.'

'I thought I heard something,' Grace told her, feeling more foolish and uncomfortable by the second as she looked towards the screens.

Staff Nurse looked too. 'Continue with your duties,' she instructed Grace, before disappearing behind the screens, only to reappear again very quickly, so quickly in fact that Grace hadn't had time to move.

It was an absolute rule that no nurse ever ran in sight of the patients, no matter what the emergency, so as not to panic or upset them, but Grace had never seen anyone move as swiftly as Staff Nurse did now as she went to the desk and then returned to the patient, accompanied by Sister, both of them gliding at such a speed that it was as though their feet didn't even touch the floor.

Within seconds a doctor had been summoned and within minutes after that, the patient was being wheeled out of the ward.

'Wonder what's up wi' him,' one of the other men mused as Grace handed him his bottle.

Grace had to wait until she had come back from her break to find out. Staff was waiting for her as she walked into the ward and told her to follow her into the sluice room.

Once they were behind the closed door she told Grace approvingly, 'That was very quick of you to spot that something was wrong, Campion. The patient had started to haemorrhage. He's had to go back down to theatre, but with any luck he should be all right. However, next time you spot something don't just stand there looking green, waiting for someone to notice. The patients get upset if they think that something's wrong with someone. The correct procedure would have been for you to walk over to the desk and inform either myself or Sister of your concern.'

'Yes, Staff,' Grace agreed woodenly.

Bella glowered bad temperedly, as she stared round the shabby-looking school hall, with its smell of cold and damp and its hard wooden benches. She hadn't wanted to come here in the first place, and she wouldn't have been here if it hadn't been for Alan's mother sticking her nose in where it wasn't wanted and volunteering *her* spare rooms as billets for refugees. *Her* spare rooms, mind, not Alan's mother's own spare rooms. It was because of that that she, Bella, was here in this freezing cold school hall along with all the other householders who had been asked to come along and be matched up with the Polish refugees who had arrived in the area, and for whom the local council needed to find accommodation.

Alan's mother had only volunteered her because Mr Parker was on the council and Alan's parents wanted to be seen to be doing the right thing, thought Bella crossly.

The refugees were a sorry-looking bunch, mostly family groups of shabbily dressed men and women clutching grubby bundles with even grubbier-looking children clinging to their side. Some of the men looked positively disreputable, and Bella wasn't surprised to see her mother-in-law's friends making a beeline for the few refugees who seemed to be on their own – older women, in the main, who looked too exhausted and beaten down by what they had endured to be much trouble.

Bella had already told both her own mother and Alan, in no uncertain terms, what she felt about what she was being forced to do. Her mother naturally had been sympathetic and had agreed with her that Alan's mother had a nerve volunteering her, but she had also reminded Bella that the Government could force her to provide billets for the refugees, if she didn't volunteer, and that at least by volunteering she could have some say in who she had.

'What you want to do is look for a strong sturdy woman who could do the rough work for you, darling,' her mother had told her. 'But make sure that she hasn't got any children.'

Alan, typically, had sided completely with his mother, and had added fuel to the fire of Bella's irritation by going on about all the voluntary work Trixie was doing, as well as working full time in the Parker family's office.

Bella scowled now, remembering how furious she had been when she had learned that her father-in-law had given Trixie a job answering the telephone and typing letters in his office.

'What's he asked her for?' she had demanded, when Alan had told her. 'I could have done that, and I'm sure the customers would much rather look at me than at Trixie.'

'You?' Alan had retaliated nastily. 'You can't even type. Trixie's a proper shorthand typist. She's got her head screwed on firmly, *and* she's a lot pleasanter to be with than you are.'

Bella had been too furious to say anything, but she had poured out her fury to her mother later.

'It's Alan's mother that's gone and got her working there. I just know she has. She's never liked me. Well, she can wish that Alan had married her precious Trixie as much as she likes, but it won't do her any good because it's me that's his wife.'

A young woman with four small children all clinging to her looked pleadingly at Bella. Determinedly, Bella looked away, ignoring the desperate anxiety in her gaze.

She could see an older woman standing on her own. One of Alan's mother's friends was also studying her. Bella made up her mind. Determinedly she pushed her way to the desk, ignoring the fact that the three WVS women manning it were all already occupied with other householders, and announced firmly, to the one closest to her, 'I'll take that woman over there.'

The woman who had already been speaking to the WVS volunteer behind the desk looked crossly at Bella but Bella ignored her. The WVS volunteer sighed and reached for a fresh form.

'Very well. And you are . . . ?'

Bella gave her details, imperiously beckoning over the refugee she had chosen.

'She'd better be able to speak English,' she told the WVS worker, who had now turned to the refugee and was speaking to her slowly and politely, for all the world as though she was a proper person and not someone who was only here because of the war, Bella thought contemptuously. It seemed that the Polish woman could speak English, although not very well.

It was horribly unpleasant in the hall, and Bella couldn't wait to get home. She would have to tell the woman to have a bath and make sure she washed all her clothes. She had been horrified when her mother had warned her that she must check to make sure that she didn't need delousing.

'Please sign this,' the WVS woman told Bella, handing her a form.

Impatiently Bella signed it. 'Do I have to take her with me now?' she asked.

'Yes, please.' The WVS volunteer turned back to the waiting woman, and told her, 'You and your daughter will both be billeted with Mrs Parker. She will take you home with her now.'

Her daughter? Bella stared at the WVS worker in furious outrage. 'I never said anything about taking two of them.'

Was that triumphant dislike she could see in the volunteer's eyes as she told her calmly, 'Well, you've signed for them both, my dear, so I'm afraid you have no alternative. Next,' she called out determinedly, ignoring Bella's fury.

Two of them! Just what she hadn't wanted, and she had been tricked into having them, she knew she had, Bella fumed as she glared at the two women who were now standing huddled together watching her.

The daughter was as plain and unprepossessing as the mother, both of them sallow-faced, with brown eyes and limp brown hair. They were as thin as sticks, and their clothes looked like rags. Bella was ashamed to be seen with them, even if they were only refugees and nothing really to do with her at all. How dreadful it was that these wretched refugees should have come over here like this, expecting to be taken into decent people's homes, and how wrong of the British Government to force people to accept them.

By rights Alan should have been here to help her with them instead of expecting her to manage on her own. It was his mother's fault, after all, that she had been landed with them, Bella decided crossly, ignoring the two women following her as she walked quickly home, hugging the warmth of her fur coat around her, her feet snug inside the thick fleecy boots her mother had bought for her.

Luckily, because of his business, her father was able to get a regular supply of coal and had had the good sense to stock up with it down at his business premises so that Bella was able to keep two good fires burning in the house, which was more than Alan's mother was able to do, she thought smugly as she turned her key in the front door.

'You two are to go down there,' she told the two refugees, indicating the pathway that led to the back door of the house. She wasn't going to allow them to use the front door.

When she had let them into the back kitchen, Bella made them stand there whilst she went to telephone her mother.

'But, Mummy, you'll have to come round,' she insisted. 'Daddy can drive you. I can't let them go upstairs until I'm sure they haven't got you-know-what.'

Having persuaded her mother to come round, Bella went into the kitchen and lit a cigarette, sitting down at the table so that she could watch her unwanted lodgers through the open door.

Half an hour passed, by which time Bella had smoked another cigarette and made herself a cup of tea, without bothering to offer her lodgers one.

The daughter looked angrily at her and said fiercely, 'My mother is very tired. Where is her bedroom, please? She needs to have some rest.'

Bella stubbed out her cigarette. The cheek of it – making demands as though she had every right to do so.

'I don't care how tired she is. She's not going anywhere until I've made sure that she's fit to sleep in one of my beds.'

'Fit?' The girl looked puzzled. 'But I have just said that she is not fit. She is tired.'

'Look, I've just told you, she isn't going anywhere—' Bella broke off when she heard the doorbell.

'They're in the back kitchen,' she told her mother after she had let her parents in.

'Where's Alan?' her father asked sharply. 'This is his responsibility, not ours.'

'He's still at work,' Bella told them. 'He's always at work. Just wait until you see them, Mummy. They're virtually dressed in rags. No wonder Hitler doesn't want them.'

Bella could see from the expression on the daughter's face that she had heard her. Good! She needed to know how lucky she was instead of looking at Bella with that proud angry look on her face.

'Do they speak any English?' Vi looked uncertainly at Bella.

'We do speak English but my mother speaks less than me.'

Vi and Bella exchanged looks.

'What are their names, Bella?' Vi asked, still ignoring the refugees.

Bella began to shrug but the daughter spoke up again, saying proudly, 'I am Bettina Polanski and my mother is Mrs Maria Polanski.'

'I didn't realise there were two of them,' Bella told her mother. 'And by the looks of her the older one isn't going to be much good at doing my cleaning.'

'Well, let's get them bathed first, darling. It's a pity there isn't one of those old-fashioned tin baths, like the poor have.' Raising her voice, she looked at the refugees.

'You will both have to have baths and wash your hair, and your clothes will have to be washed before you can wear them again. I've brought them some things to wear in the meantime. Luckily Mrs Forrest had left some things with me for the Red Cross.'

'Come along, the bathroom is this way.'

'My mother is hungry. She needs food before anything else. We were told we would be given a meal and a comfortable bed. Your government has told us this and said that it will pay for us to have these things; they did not say that we would be treated like this.'

Bella looked at her mother.

'You can't expect my daughter to make you a meal at this time of night.'

The older woman turned to her daughter and said something in Polish. Her voice was quiet and as tired as her expression. The daughter looked bitterly at Bella before very gently taking her mother's arm and guiding her through the kitchen and into the hallway as they followed Bella's mother.

'But are you sure that they didn't have any . . . anything?' Bella asked her mother anxiously for the umpteenth time. 'It's all very well saying that they've both had a bath and that you'll get their clothes laundered, but . . .' Bella shuddered theatrically. 'I can't bear to think of having to have them here in my lovely house. It just isn't fair.'

'At least it's only two women, Bella,' Vi tried to comfort her. 'No children, thank heavens.'

Bella certainly wasn't prepared to give up two bedrooms to them, and had told them that they would have to share. Heavens, for all she knew they probably slept in a cowshed or something wherever it was they had come from, she thought.

'I do hope they aren't going to make a nuisance of themselves, Mummy,' she told her mother now. 'The cheek of it, actually asking for food.'

'Well, yes, darling, but the Government has said that they must be given their meals, but that doesn't mean that you should have to put yourself out for them. The girl looks healthy and strong. I dare say between them she and her mother can do all

300

the cleaning and the cooking. It's the least they can do for you, after all the trouble they're putting you to. I should suggest it to them in the morning, if I were you.'

Bella's face brightened a little. She hated cooking, and the thought of having someone to take over her domestic responsibilities was certainly appealing.

FIFTEEN

'Seeing that ambulance driver of yours tomorrow, are you, Campion, seeing as it's your day off? Mind you, I have to say that it's a bit of a rum do, you and him, with you saying that he's not said anything to you about you being his steady. You'd never catch me allowing a lad to monopolise me like that if I didn't have a bit of a promise from him that he was serious. You don't want to let him go messing you around, you know.'

Grace knew that Doreen meant well but that didn't stop her from feeling self-conscious and uncomfortable. Not that she was going to show it. Instead she smiled brightly and said firmly, 'Oh, me and Teddy are happy as we are, just as friends.'

'Has he really not said anything to you about you and him being an item, Grace, or are you just keeping quiet about it because we've got to stay single?' Hannah asked her later on, when they were on their own. 'Only with you being such a good-looking girl I'd have thought he'd at least have tried a bit of something on, if you know what I mean.'

Grace did, but she wasn't going to say so. She was beginning to feel increasingly uncomfortable when the other girls asked her about her relationship with Teddy.

Should she say something to him or should she just leave things as they were? She was happy enough when she was with him, after all, and it was only sometimes, like when she saw other couples whispering together and snatching kisses, that she felt that funny ache in the region of her heart that made her feel that she was missing out on something very special.

Did that feeling mean that she was in love with Teddy? Grace admitted that she didn't know. And there wasn't anyone really that she could ask. None of the other girls was going steady, not even Lillian, who seemed to have given up on the doctor she was supposed to have been chasing. According to Luke, he and Lillian were still writing to one another and it was obvious from her brother's letters how he felt about her. Grace wished she was a bit closer to Lillian so that she could have talked to her properly about Luke and how she really felt about him, but Lillian seemed to have taken a bit against her and was making comments she knew Grace could overhear about 'people who went around interfering in other people's lives' without ever coming out and saying exactly what was on her mind.

'Take no notice of her,' was always Hannah's

advice whenever Grace worried about what she should do. 'Now that she's acting like she's keen on your Luke, she's probably afraid that you might go saying something to him about the way she was.'

'I wouldn't do that,' Grace had protested. 'I wouldn't do anything that might hurt him.'

'People like her don't understand things like that because they don't mind who gets hurt so long as it isn't them,' had been Hannah's pithy response.

Tonight was Grace's last stint on night duty, and she was looking forward to her day off tomorrow.

All but two of the young merchant seamen who had been admitted to the ward in February had been discharged now. Only Davie, who had had his toes amputated, and Harry, who had lost both his legs, were still with them.

Davie had had his nineteenth birthday the previous week and Sister had arranged for the kitchen to bake him a cake. His face had been a picture when he had seen it. Sister had turned a blind eye as well when both his parents and his sisters had come to see him at visiting time.

Grace had told her parents about both young men – the youngest on the ward, as Harry was even younger than Davie and only seventeen. Her mother had been moved to tears for them, like Grace herself worrying about what kind of future they would have.

Sister had said that since Davie was good with his hands he might be able to manage a factory job if he could work from a wheelchair.

Staff was just coming out of Harry's room when Grace walked on to the ward.

'He's had a bad day today,' she explained quietly. 'Sister's asked Dr Lewis about increasing his medicine and he's said yes.'

Grace said nothing. Harry was on morphine, and sometimes he got the shakes so badly when the effect of it was wearing off that it was pitiful to see and hear him, but Grace acknowledged those things didn't fill her with the fear and panic she would have felt at the beginning of her ward training, because now she not only knew the cause of them she also had the nursing experience to know how to deal with and alleviate them.

She may have learned a lot but there was a great deal more that she still had to learn, she knew. In another week or so the next lot of trainees would be coming on to the wards, and Grace and her set would be moving up a step, provided they were given good reports. She hoped desperately that she would be. She loved nursing even more than she had thought she would.

Jean had just finished drying up and putting everything away when she heard the knock on the front door. Since she wasn't expecting anyone, and Sam and the twins were out, she wiped her hands carefully on her apron and then removed it before going to see who it was.

They weren't back on daylight saving yet and because of the blackout she switched off the hall light before opening the door, but even though she couldn't see her visitor's face clearly, she knew she would have recognised her voice anywhere as she heard her younger sister, Francine, exclaiming, 'Jean, it's me!'

'Francine! My goodness!'

It was such a shock seeing her younger sister so unexpectedly that Jean didn't know what to say, or do.

It was Francine who, with a sound somewhere between a sob and laughter, moved first, hugging Jean tightly, stepping past the large trunk on the pavement next to her, as she burst into a small torrent of explanations, of which Jean could barely comprehend more than a few words.

Somehow they were inside the hallway, although Jean had no notion of how they had come to be there. She looked anxiously at her sister, almost afraid of what she might see in her face. Nine years was a long time. They might have exchanged regular letters and photographs, but they couldn't tell what was really in a person's eyes – or their hearts.

At sixteen Francine had been a stunningly beautiful girl with the kind of looks that turned heads in the street, and a happy-to-lucky attitude towards life, a trust and joy that had shone out of her like her own special sunshine. The beauty was still there, and if anything had grown, but the trust and joy were not, Jean recognised sadly.

When she looked at Francine now what she saw was a woman, not a girl, and yet she still stroked her heavy curls off her face, just as she had done when Fran had been a little girl and she her 'big sister' lovingly taking on the duties of a 'second mother' to her as instructed by their mother.

'Oh, Jean.' Francine was crying now as she gave Jean another fierce hug. 'I've missed you so much.'

'I've missed you, an' all,' said Jean. She'd missed her, worried guiltily about her, wished so desperately that things might have been different for her.

'What are you doing here anyway? Why didn't you write and let us know you were coming back? It gave me ever such a turn, opening the door and seeing you standing there.'

'Like a bad penny turning up when you thought you'd got rid of me for good?'

Francine's words were light enough but Jean could see the pain in her eyes. Now it was her turn to hug her and reassure her.

'I've never thought that about you, Fran. I just thought that you were settled in America, especially when you wrote that you were doing so well with your singing, an' all.'

'I was, but I couldn't stay there, with all that's happening. I had to come back, Jean, especially now with this war, and . . . and everything.'

A look passed between them that both understood, and it was Jean who looked away first, her heart suddenly heavy with foreboding.

'This is still my real home, after all,' Francine reminded her. 'I was making plans to come back, and then what should happen but Gracie Fields decided she wanted to do her bit and she asked me if I wanted to go along with her, so we both ended up in France entertaining the boys. Poor Gracie, you'll have heard perhaps that she's had to have an operation, and now there's all this fuss with the Government not approving of her having married an Italian. Ever so upset, she is. They're in Capri now, her and her new husband, waiting to see what's going to happen.'

'I remember reading summat about it in *Picture Post*,' Jean agreed, 'Mind you, there are them that's bin saying they don't know why she should want to go and marry a foreigner in the first place.'

'He's good for her and he's kind to her, and sometimes . . .' Francine shook her head. 'Never mind about Gracie, I want to hear all about the family and what's been going on.'

'In a minute. I want to hear what you're doing first,' Jean told her, taking up her old familiar elder-sister role now that she was over her initial shock.

Francine pulled a face and then laughed. 'Very well. I volunteered for ENSA whilst I was in France with Gracie, but since they've gone and made such a mess of sorting out things – poor Billy Cotton was supposed to be playing for Gracie at her Christmas concert and he never even made it on account of them not getting the transport they'd been promised – anyway, I thought I might as well come home and see how you all are whilst I'd got the chance. The BBC has said that they might have some work for me, singing with Vera Lynn. Luckily I've brought my stage clothes with me.'

Whilst Francine was speaking Jean studied her

younger sister. Jean might have kept her own trim figure but Francine looked, if anything, slightly thinner than she had done when she had gone to America. Mind you, Jean acknowledged to herself, she'd need a good figure, wearing a frock so snugly fitting on the waist before its full panelled skirt curved out softly over her hips. Not that it wasn't smart, it was, and in a lovely shade of soft blue as well. The collar of the little fitted jacket that went with it was trimmed with fur, and Jean could just imagine how Vi's eyes would almost pop out on stalks when she saw how glamorously Francine was dressed. Her shoes and bag were the same colour as her suit, and her hat was trimmed with the same fur as her jacket collar. When you weren't with her it was easy to overlook the mesmerising effect Francine could have on a person, Jean admitted. It wasn't just that she was beautiful, which she was, it was more than that somehow. There was something about her that had you looking at her and not wanting to look away – warmth, somehow, and an excitement. It was hard to explain but it was impossible not to be aware of it, even though Francine herself never acted as though she cared two hoots about it. Singing, that was all that had mattered to her when she had been growing up. Mad on it, she had been, singing morning noon and night, determined right from being a little thing that she was going to be a singer. Mind you, she did have a lovely voice. Francine had a voice that was as different from other people's as plain old walking was from dancing. You caught yourself listening for it and straining to hear more of it even when she was just talking.

'How is everyone?' she was asking Jean, her voice suddenly strained with a tension that sent Jean's heart plummeting.

'Let me put the kettle on. You just be dying for a cuppa.'

As she bustled busily about her kitchen, Jean was glad of an excuse not to have to look directly at Francine.

'Well, Luke and Charlie are both with the BEF in France. I dare say you might even have sung for them without knowing it. Bella's married, of course, and our Grace is training to be a nurse. The twins will be leaving school this summer.'

'And Jack?'

'Vi's had him evacuated into the country for safety.'

'She never said anything about that when she wrote to me last.'

'Let's have that cup of tea, and then we can sit down and talk properly.'

'I've got a favour to ask you,' Francine warned her as she took the proffered cup. 'I hate to put on you but I haven't made any arrangements about where I'm going to stay and I wondered—'

'You're welcome to have Grace's room,' Jean told her immediately. 'I know she won't mind. She's living in at the hospital. Mind you, I dare say it won't be what you're used to.'

'No it won't,' Francine agreed quietly. 'It's a long time since I've lived in a proper home.

Everyone thinks that being a singer is glamorous. Well, it might look like that when I'm up on the stage, but it's not much fun going back to a single room in a boarding house every night.'

Jean frowned as she heard the weariness and sadness in her sister's voice. Francine's voice betrayed her feelings in the way that other people's expressions would betray theirs.

'I thought you was doing really well in America, making records and that.'

'I was, but then there was a problem.' Francine gave a dismissive shrug.

'A man?' Jean guessed.

Francine gave her a small smile. 'That was quick of you, but then I suppose . . .' Her voice trailed away. 'I suppose I was naïve. I thought I wasn't, of course. But Hollywood is a different world, where they live by different rules. "Casting-Couch Rules", they call them.' She gave a bitter laugh. 'Only I didn't want to play the casting-couch game, and because I didn't all that talk of records and big deals remained just talk. Luckily for me Gracie took pity on me, otherwise I'd have ended up working in a car wash – or worse.'

'Well, you won't find the luxury here that you'll have got used to, love. Especially not now with this rationing.'

'It isn't luxury I want, Jean. That's not what I've come home for at all.'

There was look on her face that made Jean's heart sink a little.

*　　*　　*

'Come along, Campion, don't dawdle.' They were doing 'beds and backs', a process in which each patient had to have his sacrum, heels and elbows washed with soap and water and then rubbed with methylated spirits to harden the skin, which was then dusted with talcum powder. This was to help prevent bed sores, and it was Grace's job to apply the methylated spirits.

Once that had been done, Staff Nurse Reid asked her, 'Have you given morphia to a patient yet?'

Grace shook her head.

'Come with me and listen carefully. Harry is due to have his next injection.'

First, Staff Nurse went to the Dangerous Drugs cabinet and removed one quarter of a gram of morphine, which Grace then had to dissolve over a spirit lamp in 5.5 cc of water in a teaspoon, and then place the liquid into a hypodermic syringe.

After Staff Nurse Reid had relocked the Dangerous Drugs cabinet she beckoned Grace to follow her into the private room where Harry was.

The young man was in a great deal of pain, his face lacking colour and his skin sweaty. Grace felt for him as she injected the morphine into his upper arm, holding her own breath a little as she waited for the drug to take effect. She could see a telling sadness in Staff Nurse's expression as she leaned over him and spoke to him before straightening his bedclothes.

Once they were both back outside the room Staff Nurse turned to Grace and said quietly, 'As you know, morphine is addictive and we have to be careful about how much we give, but thank heavens Sister believes that if someone is dying then it doesn't matter if they become addicted, and that it's far more important that they remain free of pain.'

She didn't say any more; she didn't need to. Grace understood what she was being told and it both shocked and upset her. Harry was, after all, only seventeen – not much older than her own twin sisters and younger than she was herself.

Harry was very much on Grace's mind the next day when she met Teddy.

They might be in March now but she had noticed that increasingly Teddy was having to slow down when they were walking together, complaining that the cold winter had got on his chest and left him struggling sometimes with his breathing. Grace had felt like a bit of fresh air and so they had gone to Wavertree Park or 'the Mizzy', as the park was fondly known by locals. Its nickname had come about because the land itself had been given to the people of Wavertree by a 'mystery' donor who had specified that it was to be used to create a large open playground for children, and for recreation rather than a formally landscaped park. The original lake had been filled in but there was still a pretty circular structure, which was used as a bandstand on fête days, and before the Great War the park had even hosted the Royal Agricultural Show.

It was, Grace knew, because he was sensitive

about having had rheumatic fever as a child, which had prevented him from joining up, that he didn't like talking about it, but she still couldn't stop herself from frowning as she watched him having to stop walking, his hand on his chest.

'You should see someone about that, you know,' she told him gently.

'Oh, give over, will you? I've already told you it's nothing serious.'

'You mean, like you and me are nothing serious?' Grace replied impulsively. What on earth had possessed her to say that? She felt mortified by her own silliness.

'And what's that supposed to mean?' Teddy sounded angry.

Neither of them was making any attempt to walk now. Instead they stood in the park, confronting one another, oblivious to the curious glances they were attracting.

'You know what I mean,' Grace told him miserably. 'I know you do. All the girls keep on asking me if you and me are going steady, and if you've asked me to be your girl. They want to know if . . . I need to know where I stand with you, Teddy, I really do 'cos the way things are is making me feel ever such a fool. What with me not knowing . . . and you never so much as . . .' Her face was burning with self-conscious embarrassment now, but despite that a part of her was glad that her concern about their relationship was finally out in the open.

'I'm not staying here to listen to silly stuff like

this,' Teddy told her angrily. 'I thought you and me was friends, Grace. I thought you were a sensible sort of girl, not the sort who'd go acting daft and listening to what others have got to say . . .' He shook his head, his mouth compressing, and then to Grace's shock he turned on his heel and walked off, leaving her standing on her own.

At first she was too shocked to do anything and then she started to hurry after him, but he was already halfway across the road, and jumping onto a bus. Tears blurred her eyes. Well, let him go then. He was right about one thing. She was a sensible sort of girl, the sort of girl who would never ever go running after a lad who didn't want her.

Too unhappy to bear the thought of spending the rest of her day off on her own, she decided to go home.

If her mother was surprised to see her so early when she had told her that it would be teatime before she came round, she didn't say so, simply looking searchingly at her pale face and then saying placidly, 'Sit down, love; I was just about to put the kettle on.'

'Jean, I still haven't heard back from Vi. I've got half a mind to go round and see her . . . Oh, Grace, hello, love.' Francine gave Grace a warm hug as she came into the kitchen.

Grace had been surprised and just a little bit wary when she had learned that her mother's younger sister was back in Liverpool and sleeping in her own old room, but then when she had come home and Francine had been so warm and loving and such fun, Grace had immediately stopped feeling stiff and just that little bit jealous that someone else might be taking her place in the family.

Of course, the twins adored Francine and were forever plaguing her to listen to them singing, but she was very firm with them, telling them that a career as a singer was more hard work and disappointments than glamour, whilst at the same time assuring them that they did indeed have very pretty singing voices.

'I hope you're eating properly at that hospital Grace, only you're looking thin,' Jean fussed maternally.

'I dare say she's run off her feet,' Francine defended Grace.

'We are busy,' Grace agreed, giving her aunt a grateful look. The truth was that her growing anxiety over her feeling that something about her relationship just wasn't right had led to her losing her normal appetite.

She could see that despite Francine's reassurance her mother wasn't looking convinced, and with her recent upset still very much on her mind she acknowledged that she couldn't keep what she was feeling to herself and that she desperately wanted to unburden herself. There was something she just had to know, even though she couldn't quite bring herself to look at her mother as she asked the question that had been burning so painfully inside her.

'Mum, how do you know when you're in love?'

Over her downbent head Jean and Francine exchanged helpless looks.

'Well, love, it's hard to explain but you just do. But why are you—'

'What your mum's trying to say, Grace,' Francine intervened firmly, 'is that if you were in love you wouldn't need to ask, because you would know you were. It's because you aren't in love that you need to ask.'

'So you can't be in love with someone and not know?'

'No.'

'Not even the first time?'

'Especially not the first time,' Francine assured her.

Grace looked from her aunt to her mother.

'Francine is right, love. If you were you would know,' Jean assured her. 'I suppose you're thinking about this Teddy you've bin seeing? If he's bin pressing you about, well, anything, just you remember that you're training to be a nurse.'

'It isn't that, Mum. Teddy isn't asking me do anything I shouldn't be doing.' Grace got up and paced the room, her colour high, but having come this far she might as well come out with what was really bothering her. Normally she'd have felt really uncomfortable talking like this with her mother, but having Francine here, who was closer to her in age and who had travelled all over, and must know so much as well as being her mother's sister, somehow made it all so much easier.

'It's just that . . . well, even when we go to the pictures he never puts his arm round me or . . . or anything else . . . and the other girls . . . well, they keep asking me . . .'

'Never mind the other girls. It sounds to me as though he's a decent well-brought-up young man who knows what's proper,' Jean told her with relief, deliberately choosing not to remember the passionate kisses she and Sam had shared in the dark privacy of the cinema in their own courting days.

Francine, on the other hand, was frowning slightly and Grace found that it was to her aunt she was looking for an explanation of Teddy's unfathomable behaviour and not her mother.

However, before she could say anything the twins came bursting in in their normal noisy fashion, hugging Grace, and chattering nineteen to the dozen and making the kind of discussion Grace had wanted to have impossible.

Instead they wanted to talk about the ENSA variety show Francine was rehearsing for, which meant she would be staying in Liverpool for the duration whilst the show toured local Armed Forces bases and some of the factories where women were working long shifts making parachutes and munitions.

They were going through one of their periods of wanting to look as alike as possible and so were wearing matching plaid skirts and green jumpers, with red ribbons in their plaits.

'Fancy singing here in Liverpool.' Lou pulled a

face. 'If it was me I'd much rather be going overseas, wouldn't you, Sasha?'

Before her twin could reply Francine was saying calmly, 'After the mess that was made of getting us to our venues when we were in France, the last thing I feel like doing at the moment is being sent overseas. Billy Cotton was fit to spit feathers, I can tell you when a bridge went and collapsed when him and his band were on their way to a show. You should have seen his face when he ended up with a coachload of players on one side of the river and their instruments on the other. We might not have been crossing the blue Danube, but the air was pretty blue, I can tell you. It's all right for Basil Dean running ruddy ENSA from Drury Lane and never putting a foot outside the Theatre Royal. Billy Cotton completely missed his Christmas Day concert with Gracie.'

'Was that the one you were singing in as well, Francine?' Lou asked eagerly.

'That's right. Three numbers, I had.'

'And you wore that blue dress with the silver embroidery, didn't you?'

The twins were entranced with everything about their young aunt. They had only been five when she had left for America, but they were approaching the same age Francine had been when she had first started to sing on stage.

'Yes. I bought it in Bloomies just before we left New York. That's Bloomingdale's,' Francine explained for Grace's benefit. 'It's a big famous store in New York.'

'I wish we could go to New York,' Lou breathed enviously. 'We'd volunteer for ENSA if we were old enough, wouldn't we, Sasha?'

When her twin nodded, Jean told them both firmly, 'Well, it's just as well you aren't because your dad would never agree to you going.'

'Why not? Auntie Francine does it,' was Sasha's wide-eyed response.

'Ah, but there's only one of me,' Francine told them quick-wittedly, earning a grateful look from Jean.

'It's not that me or their dad have anything against singing,' Jean told Francine later when the twins were upstairs and Grace had gone back to the hospital, 'but they haven't got a sensible thought between them and that's the truth. They egg each other on and, never mind double trouble, it's more like four times the trouble of having one.'

Francine laughed dutifully. 'I don't blame you and Sam for not wanting them to follow in my footsteps, Jean.'

'Oh, it isn't that,' Jean assured her quickly – too quickly, she realised, when she saw Francine's expression.

'I thought I might go over and see Vi this week, seeing as she hasn't written back to me,' Francine announced, changing the subject.

Now it was Jean's turn to look wary. She could feel the heavy anxious thud of her heart, and that same feeling of foreboding she had already experienced returned.

So much had happened since Francine had left; she and Sam had moved so that they could put the past and their loss behind them, and have a fresh start; Edwin and Vi had left Liverpool for Wallasey. As much as she loved her younger sister she was afraid of the problems her return could bring – for all of them, but most of all for Francine herself.

There were some things – some sadnesses, some secrets – that were surely best left undisturbed.

'Why don't you give it a few more days?' she urged Francine. 'Vi might not have had your letter yet, and you know what she's like, she's never been one you can get round easily, unless you're her Bella, of course. Spoils her rotten, she does, and talk about not being able to see the wood for the trees and not seeing how she's winding her round her little finger . . .'

'She should never have had Jack.'

Francine's statement was so abrupt that it left Jean floundering for a response.

'Well, he's so much younger than the other two.'

'She doesn't love him, I'm sure of that.'

'Of course she does,' Jean automatically defended her twin. 'But she's had a lot on her mind this last year, what with Edwin's business and them moving house again, and then Bella getting married.'

'She'd never have sent him away like she has if she did,' Francine continued, completely ignoring Jean's attempt to defend Vi.

'She's only done what she thought was best for

him, Fran. Me and Sam were in two minds about evacuating the twins,' said Jean. 'We only decided against it because I couldn't have gone with them, not knowing that Sam would then be fending for himself.'

'You see,' Francine pounced triumphantly, 'you would have gone with them. You've just said so yourself. You wouldn't have sent them off on their own. Can you imagine what Mum would have said, Jean? She'd never have done anything like that to one of us.' Tears had filled her eyes and Jean's heart ached with a pity that overwhelmed her anxiety.

She couldn't deny Francine's claim, but encouraging her wasn't going to do any good and wouldn't help anyone, least of all poor little Jack.

Francine and Vi had never really got on. They had always been complete opposites, and Francine's decision to become a singer, and Vi's marriage to Edwin, had not just widened the gap between them, it had also armed it with hostility.

Jean knew there was some truth in Francine's accusations but she also knew that getting Vi's back up with hostile remarks about her role as a mother wasn't going to improve things and could end up making them even worse. On top of that she had her own burden of guilt to carry.

'Me and Sam would have had Jack . . .' she began, 'but . . .'

Immediately Francine hugged her contritely. 'I wasn't getting at you, Jean.'

'Vi's got Edwin to deal with, remember? I don't

like speaking ill of folk behind their backs, but well, he wouldn't be my choice of a husband.'

'He never wanted her to have Jack, not really.'

Jean said nothing. She knew after all that it was the truth. Much as she loved her younger sister and had been delighted to have her back home and living with them, there was no getting away from the fact that there were old sores in their shared past that it wouldn't be wise to go disturbing.

'I'd better look sharp otherwise you're going to be late for your rehearsal,' Jean told her, deliberately changing the subject.

'Yes,' Francine agreed. 'We've got our first show coming up soon at Seacombe barracks. I reckon they're testing out the shows here to see which work best, ready to send the cast overseas, so with a bit of luck you won't have me hanging around making a nuisance of meself for too long, Jean.'

'There's no need to go saying that. You aren't a nuisance. Me and Sam are glad to have you here, Fran,' Jean told her stoutly.

She *was* glad to have Francine here, Jean insisted to herself after her sister had left, of course she was, but at the same time a part of her couldn't help worrying, about what was going to happen when Vi and Francine met.

'And where do you think you're going, with my kitchen floor not washed and the rations not collected yet?' Bella accosted Bettina angrily, folding her arms and standing in front of the back door.

'I have to go to my work,' Bettina answered her equally furiously, her dark eyes flashing with pride and temper.

Bella's expression hardened. It was bad enough having the two of them here, what with the mother spending nearly all her time in bed claiming not to be very well, without having to put up with the daughter somehow having managed to persuade the Government into giving her some trumped-up job working as a translator, when she could have been earning her keep here doing Bella's cleaning.

'Well, you'd better be back in time to feed that mother of yours,' Bella told her spitefully, 'because I'm certainly not going to do it. Making out she's too poorly to get out of bed.'

Once again fury flashed in Bettina's eyes. 'Mama is very poorly with her chest. The doctor has said so.'

'A bit of a cough, that's all she's got. If she was that poorly she'd be in hospital instead of here, keeping me awake all night with her coughing.'

That much was true, and Alan was already complaining about it.

They were over six months into the war now and Hitler hadn't invaded. Optimists were beginning to say that the BEF would soon rout the Germans if they dared try marching into France, and some were even saying that it would all be over by summer and the men would be home. Grace didn't feel like being optimistic, though, as she got off the bus outside the hospital, not when she was still upset about what had happened with Teddy earlier in the day.

She had almost reached the entrance when she heard him calling her name, and was half minded to pretend that she hadn't, but she wasn't really the sort that could ignore a person just because they had caused her to be upset, so she stopped walking, turned round, and was rewarded with a relieved smile from Teddy as he caught up with her.

'I've been looking out for you all afternoon, and then I nearly went and missed you.'

Grace said nothing. After all, it wasn't her fault that they had spent the day apart.

As though he knew what she was thinking, Teddy said quietly, 'I'm sorry, Grace, about . . . about what happened earlier. That's why I've bin waiting for you, so that I could explain.'

'I'll have to be in the nurses' home in half an hour otherwise I'll miss supper.'

He needn't think she was going to go and act all soft as if he could treat her any way he liked, because he couldn't. He might not be in love with her, but she wasn't in love with him if what Francine had said to her was true. He had hurt her, though.

'I'll buy you a bag of chips to make up for it.'

He was teasing her, trying to lighten the mood between them, Grace knew. It wasn't in her nature to sulk or be difficult and so she exhaled shakily and said, 'I was upset by what you did, Teddy, and I can't pretend that I wasn't, but since you've said you want to explain—'

'I do.' He reached for her hand. 'Come on, we can go and sit in the ambulance so that we can talk properly.'

'What if you're called out?'

'I'm not on duty, but if we was to be, then the lucky so-and-sos will have a nurse to look after them, as well as an ambulance, won't they? Come on . . .'

That was typical of Teddy. He always had an answer to everything, Grace acknowledged, as they walked towards the ambulance.

'So what was it you want to say?' Grace demanded once they were inside.

Instead of answering her immediately, Teddy offered her a cigarette, lighting one for himself when she shook her head.

'You know you was asking me earlier about you and me, and how I hadn't said anything about us going steady or you being my girl?'

Grace nodded.

'Well, the thing is, Grace . . .' he took a deep drag on his cigarette, and then exhaled, 'it wouldn't be fair to you if I was to do that, and . . . and it's for your own sake that I've not said anything.'

'You mean that you don't want to go steady with me?' said Grace. She could feel tears pricking the backs of her eyes. Everyone knew that when a lad didn't really want you he made out that he was holding himself back for your sake.

She heard Teddy curse suddenly and then he

put out his cigarette and reached for her hands, holding them tightly.

'No! Of course I want to go steady with you, but I can't, Grace. Like I just said, it wouldn't be fair or right. You see the thing is . . .' he took a deep breath, 'well, you know that thing I told you about when we first met, about how I wasn't medically fit for the services, on account of me having had rheumatic fever when I was a kiddie?'

'Yes . . .'

'Well, after I'd had me medical they sent for me, and seemingly, this rheumatic fever wot I'd had has left me heart a bit dicky.'

Grace felt her own heart give a sudden flurry of anxious thuds.

Teddy was still holding her hands but he wasn't looking at her, and Grace remembered how badly the cold weather had affected him and how he'd struggled to walk and breathe in the cold. She'd thought nothing of it at the time, but now . . .

'The medics wanted me to wrap meself up in cotton wool and lie in bed for the rest of me life 'cos they've said that me heart won't stand me doing too much. But I can't do that, Grace. That's no kind of life for a grown man. In fact it's not living at all and I might as well be dead. It's like I've told them, I'd rather have a few months of proper life than years of lying in me bed watching others get on with their lives around me.'

'A few months of life?'

Grace wasn't aware that she had spoken the shocked words aloud until she realised that Teddy was now looking at her. In his eyes she could see confirmation of what he had said, along with his fear and his pride.

She wanted to reach out to him and hold him as tenderly as she might have done a child. She wanted to comfort him and tell him that everything would be all right and he would be well, but she knew that she could not do those things.

'That's why I haven't said anything to you about you and me. No matter what I might feel about you, Grace, it would be wrong of me to let you fall in love with me, knowing that I'm not likely to be around for very long. When I do go I don't want you getting yourself upset and grieving, and thinking that you've got to mourn me on account of us being an item when you should be out enjoying yourself and falling in love with a chap who's got his health and strength, and who can give you the future that I can't.'

She must not cry. She must not, not when Teddy was being so brave and so decent. Why hadn't she thought of something like this for herself? She had seen how he sometimes struggled to walk and breathe. She knew from her lectures that there was a connection between childhood rheumatic fever and heart weakness.

'I wasn't going to tell you any of this because . . . well, I just wanted to live like any other chap would and . . . and I didn't want to go burdening you with all of this or have you pitying me. But when you said what you did today, I knew that I wasn't being fair to you, not being straight with you, and that I'd have to say summat. I couldn't have you thinking that I don't care about you, Grace, or that I wouldn't ask you to be my girl like a shot if I could and I thought it would be right. You're all the girl I could ever want, and if things were different . . .'

He was making it all sound so cut and dried. So final and unavoidable.

'You shouldn't be doing what you're doing, Teddy, not with a bad heart. You should be resting.'

'No! I'm sorry,' he apologised when he saw how upset she was. 'It's just . . . well, I can do all the resting I want when I'm dead, can't I? I want to *live* my life, Grace, even if that means I won't have as much time to live it in. I don't want to look at life through me bedroom window, I want to feel it. I want to be part of it. That's why I volunteered for this lot. I want to feel I'm part of what's happening and at least wi' me doing the driving I'm not overdoing things. They weren't going to take me on at first – the doctor who examined me was dead against it – but in the end I managed to talk him round.'

Grace just did not know what to say. His revelations were so very different from anything she might have expected, and so much more painful. She'd been acting like a silly girl fretting over a lad not wanting to kiss her, when all the time poor Teddy was facing what he was. A huge wave of emotion rolled over her and sucked her down into its undertow. She looked at Teddy, wanting to tell him how much she wished things were different.

She tried imagining how she would feel if she was in his shoes, but couldn't. It frightened her to think what it must be like and how much he must want to live as she would herself. Love for him filled her. Not so much a woman's love for a man, as a human love for another human that was truly caring and giving.

He was still holding her hands. She lifted one of his to her face and placed her cheek against it. It felt so cold.

'I am your girl, Teddy, whether you want me to be or not.'

Suddenly he was holding her and kissing her, not as she had imagined but just like they did in the films, his mouth hard against her own, his heart thudding into her chest. Too hard? That fear came between her and his kiss, her anxiety for him making her ache to be able to protect him and keep him safe.

It was hard to go on the ward and act as though everything was normal after what Teddy had told her, but Grace knew that she must. He had made up his mind, Teddy had said, that he intended to live as though there was nothing wrong with him, and Grace knew that he had meant that.

It made her heart ache to know that he had wanted them only to be friends because he had wanted to protect her, and it had made it ache even more when he had admitted to her that he could very easily fall in love with her, and that she was not to fall in love with him.

'I mean what I said,' he had insisted. 'If it does happen and I go, then I don't want you spoiling the rest of your life thinking that you owe it to me not to fall in love with anyone else. And don't try telling me that you aren't that sort, 'cos I know you too well.'

'But if they could do something for your heart . . .' Grace had protested.

'They can't,' he had answered her. 'The doc has already told me that. He can't say either how long I've got, only that it will be longer if I rest up all the time and, like I said, I'm not doing that.'

She had desperately wanted to beg him to be careful but she had known that she mustn't and that that was not what he wanted. What he wanted was to be treated like a man and not an invalid, and Grace wasn't sure if she had the womanly strength to do that.

Since it was her first night back on nights, she knew from past experience that she would be struggling to stay awake by the time it got to three and four in the morning. It got easier after the first few nights, of course.

The now familiar routine of the ward absorbed her, demanding her physical and mental attention. Visiting time came and went; lockers had to be cleaned and water glasses refilled, bottles had to be taken round, charts had to be written up and Night Sister herself had to be accompanied on her ward round, and then finally at last it was time for Grace to take her tea break.

The dining room was always quieter on nights,

even though the same number of nurses were there as were on days. No one wanted to say much and when they did, voices were lower. Somehow nights were like that.

Back on the ward it was time for the patients' medication.

Her first patient was Harry, and Grace frowned as she checked his chart.

'It says half a gram of morphia, Staff.'

'Yes, that's right,' Staff Nurse Reid confirmed. 'Dr Lewis has increased his dosage. He's in a lot of pain, poor boy, and it doesn't look as though his amputation wounds are healing as well as they might.'

Grace knew what that meant, even if the putrid smell of his wounds whenever they changed his bandages had not told her. Slowly, inch by inch, Harry was dying, killed by his own flesh as it rotted away, and there was nothing any of them could do to stop that, no matter how devotedly they nursed him.

He was only semiconscious when she gave him his morphine injection, his flesh burning hot to the touch and his temperature up over 103.

Another bottle round, the last one before lights out. Sister didn't look up from her dimly lit desk where she was writing up reports as Grace went past on her way to the sluice room, to do the necessary urine tests. By the time she came out again all the patients were asleep and several were snoring.

She had to take Harry's temperature again.

When she went in he was rambling feverishly and still only semiconscious. His temperature was now nearly 104.

As though somehow he had sensed her presence suddenly, he opened his eyes and cried out quite clearly, in a boy's voice, 'Mam, Mam. Please make the pain go away. I can't bear it, Mam, it hurts so much,' before lapsing back into unconsciousness.

Tears stung Grace's eyes. Hurriedly she wiped them away and went in search of Staff Nurse Reid, who was down at the end of the ward.

'It's Harry, Staff,' said Grace. 'His temperature's up at 104.' She hesitated and then added, 'He thought I was his mother.'

Staff Nurse Reid, who had been writing up a chart whilst she listened, suddenly stopped writing and looked at her.

'What did he say?' she asked.

'He said, "Mam, Mam. Please make the pain go away."'

Staff had the chart replaced and was on her way towards Sister.

'Campion, go down to the desk and ask one of the porters to send up the chaplain. Tell them we need him quickly.' When Grace's eyes rounded, she explained quietly, 'Most patients, but especially the men, call out for their mothers when they are near the end. Quickly now, but remember, no running.'

The porter was sympathetic and understanding. 'Yer first death, is it, love? Well, never mind, you'll get used to it. You get back to yer ward. I'll tell the chaplain and make sure he gets there.'

It was all over so quickly Grace could hardly take it in. She had only been back on the ward a matter of seconds when the chaplain arrived and was ushered into Harry's room by Sister.

Staff had instructed Grace to refill all the water glasses even though most of them didn't need it, and Grace suspected she was just trying to keep her occupied and her mind off what was happening in the side ward.

She hadn't even reached the end of the ward when the chaplain emerged, accompanied by Sister.

'Gone has he, then, young Harry?'

Grace nearly dropped the water jug. She hadn't even realised the patient who had just addressed her was awake, never mind aware of what was happening.

'You should be asleep, Mr Whitehead,' she told him, imitating Staff's firm voice. 'And if Sister catches you talking we'll both be for it.'

'Poor lad, but I reckon he'll be better off where he's gone now. Had a bad time, he has, and we all reckoned he wasn't going to pull through.'

'When you've finished filling those glasses, Campion, Sister wants a word with you.'

Grace nodded, dutifully going over to the table.

'Staff is going to lay out the patient's body now, Campion,' Sister told her. 'You will assist her with this.'

Grace felt sick. And afraid. She had never seen a dead body, never mind touched one, but Staff was waiting for her and she knew she couldn't disgrace herself by giving way to her feelings.

'You've already been taught how important it is to respect a patient's dignity, Nurse. Well, that respect is just as important now.'

As she spoke Staff was carefully folding back part of the sheet, preparatory to washing Harry's body, taking the same care not to expose more of him than needed to be exposed as she would have done were he still alive.

The smell from his flesh was appalling, especially once they had removed the bandages, but Staff worked as calmly as though it wasn't there. Grace's hands trembled as she helped her to re-bandage his poor stumps with their blackened flesh, but for the most part, Staff Nurse Reid simply instructed her to watch whilst she worked busily but carefully.

All Grace could think of was that one day soon this might be Teddy . . . that one day soon Teddy might be dead and his body the one that received this final service. Teddy, who had told her she must not love him but who she knew now did love her. How would she be feeling now if she had fallen in love with him? Guilt filled her because she wasn't; because what she felt for him was the love of a friend and not a woman's love of a lifetime.

She must concentrate on what was happening here in this room and not think about Teddy.

Already Harry's face was relaxing out of pain and into peace, his features softening and becoming slightly waxen and not quite real somehow. She mustn't think about death; she must watch Staff carefully instead, and remember everything she was showing her.

Harry's fingernails had to be pared and his hands washed, his hair combed and then those things done for him that were part of the laying-out process: the packing of mouth, nostrils and rectum, and the tying up the jaw with a chin strap.

Only when it was time to cover Harry's body with its shroud did Staff summon Grace to assist her.

Grace was trembling so much she felt sure she would be sent off duty in disgrace, but all Staff said to her was a quiet, 'Brace up, Campion. You're doing very well. Don't let the side down now.'

Harry's body was covered with a sheet and then it was time to summon a porter to wheel him down to the mortuary, his journey there accompanied by a nurse. Grace had feared that she might be sent but as though she sensed what she was feeling, Staff summoned one of the other junior nurses instead.

Death. Grace had never really thought about it in any great detail, not really. Nursing was about helping people to get better, after all, but today she had been confronted with the reality of death and its harshness, not once but twice.

It was four o' clock in the morning. Nearly two hours since Harry had passed away. Grace remembered that she had heard other nurses calling two a.m. the death hour. She started to tremble so violently that her teeth were chattering together.

All she could do was take refuge in the sluice, but once there Grace found that she couldn't cry. What she was feeling was too raw and went too deep for the release of tears.

SIXTEEN

Alan hadn't left her any housekeeping, and not for the first time either. Well, it just wasn't good enough, Bella fumed, and she was going to go to his father's office now and tell him so. That would show him.

She was sick of this wretched rationing already. How was anyone supposed to manage without a decent amount of butter? Alan put more on his breakfast toast every day than they were supposed to manage on for a full week. Everyone knew that there was a black market where you could buy as much butter as you wanted provided you were prepared to pay for it, and if Alan wanted butter on his toast then he was the one who was going to have to find the money.

Alan's father's business premises were in the centre of the town. The bus stop was at the bottom of the street, but the bus had lumbered to a halt right outside the office because of some commotion in the street. From where she was seated on the top deck – where she had had to go because it was full – Bella could see right in through the window of the Parkers' office. She could see that stupid Trixie seated at her desk, in front of a typewriter. She could see too Alan coming into the office, closing the door behind him.

He was smiling at Trixie and she was smiling back at him. As she watched, Bella saw Alan go over to her, put his arm around her and then bend his head to kiss her.

Bella started to stand up, her face red with fury. Neither of them had seen her. They were oblivious to everything but what they were doing. And it was disgusting. Alan was fondling Trixie's breast. Well, they wouldn't be feeling so pleased with themselves when they found out that she'd seen what they were up to.

The bus started to move, throwing Bella back into her seat. Alan, *her* husband, was messing around with Trixie. Well, she'd soon put a stop to that. Just wait until he got home.

Until he got home? Why didn't she go to the office now and confront them, and then let everyone know what a sly cat that Trixie really was? Kissing another woman's husband and letting him do what he shouldn't with her.

Bella was beside herself with rage, but eager as she was to confront Alan, something was holding her back. Perhaps she ought to tell her mother first. Yes, she decided, that was what she would do.

*　　*　　*

'Oh, it's you, Bella.'

Bella wasn't used to her mother greeting her with such a lack of enthusiasm.

'Mummy, something dreadful's happened.'

'If it's those refugees getting on your nerves again, then all I can say is that it's a pity that you aren't expecting. No one would expect you to house the likes of them then. You'll never guess what your aunt Francine's had the cheek to do,' she continued without pausing for breath or to allow Bella to say anything. 'She's only written to say that she wants to know where Jack's been evacuated to. I'll have to go over to Jean's now, otherwise I'll have Francine coming over here and your father won't like that.'

Bella wasn't interested in her mother's anger with her younger sister. She had far more important things to think about, after all, and her mother's comment about the benefits of her being pregnant had given her a wonderful idea.

If she were to get pregnant then that would really put that cat Trixie in her place.

Bella mentally visualised herself making the announcement in front of Trixie and watching the look on her face. There was a name for girls who carried on with married men the way Trixie was doing, and it wasn't a name that came with the respectability of the title 'Mrs' in front of it. There'd be no more talk about Alan and Trixie having been an item before Alan had married her either, not once she, Bella, was having a baby. And when she showed Trixie up for what she really was it would be her that everyone sympathised with.

Not even Alan's parents would be able to dote so much on Trixie then. Alan would have to change his tune as well, Bella decided with satisfaction.

She was glad now that she hadn't tackled Alan. Far better to wait, Bella decided, as she made plans. Alan had probably only kissed Trixie because she'd encouraged him. Men were like that, after all. Her mother was still going on about Jack and Francine. Bella gave her an irritated look. She needed to get home. She'd got plans to make, plans that would put that plain-faced Trixie in her place for once and for all.

'Hey, Frankie . . .'

Francine stiffened, ignoring the looks she was attracting from the people forced to avoid her, as she stood immobile in the middle of the lunchtime-busy pavement, wanting to turn round and walk away without acknowledging the greeting, but knowing that she must. If her time in Hollywood had taught her nothing else it had certainly taught her how to fake a smile. She pinned it to her face now as she confronted the man coming towards her, skilfully dodging his attempt to embrace her by sidestepping him slightly and putting her hand on his arm – to hold him off, not draw him close.

It might have been ten years since she had last seen him but he hadn't changed. He might be well into his thirties now, but a man like Con could carry an extra ten years and not look any the less handsome. Clark Gable and the others wouldn't stand a chance against him as a swoon-inducing leading man if they were in competition. That mingling of Italian, Irish and heaven knew what other blood had given him the gift of outstandingly good looks, and of course he knew it and had always known it. Known it and used that knowledge without compassion or compunction to get what he wanted.

She should, she supposed, hate him, but here again Hollywood had taught her a lot. She had seen how far good looks and the ability to trade on them could take a person, and she knew how much Con would have relished the opportunity to cash in on his physical assets if he could have brokered it. But unfortunately for him Connor Bryant had tied himself into a deal with a contract without any break-out clause, the day he had sold himself in marriage to Emily Friar.

Even if he hadn't been standing outside a theatre, most people would look at him and know that he was connected with the stage, Francine acknowledged. His clothes, his manner, and yes, his good looks as well were all somehow larger than life. He had been calling himself 'West End show producer' when she had first met him. She had been as green as grass, anxious to impress and please, anxious to be something more than a girl from the chorus who could sing, but vulnerable about her ability to make it big. Of course, Con had sensed that vulnerability. That was what men like him specialised in, attracting the vulnerable to them like moths to a flame. She had been totally taken in by him and by his talk of making her a success on the London stage. She had been such a fool, but she knew better now, Hollywood hadn't just provided her with somewhere to escape to, it had taken her naïvety and beaten it into awareness. Con was, as the saying went, flash and foolish, all show and no substance, handsome on the outside, but with nothing behind that façade except hollow emptiness. It amused her to see the telltale way in which his eyes widened slightly as he took in her polished appearance. Hollywood had 'made over' the girl who had known nothing whatsoever about how to dress or present herself. But not even Hollywood had been able to remould her completely into its preferred image of a Hollywood star in the making. Francine preferred cool elegance to lush sexuality, which was why she was wearing a smart coat and a matching hat, the coat open over a toning cashmere sweater and a slim-fitting brown tweed skirt. New clothes she had bought in New York before sailing home. In Hollywood you never knew who you might bump into, which was why you learned quickly to dress your best.

No city on earth could rival New York for the variety of its affordable and stylish women's clothing, least of all perhaps a war-ready city like Liverpool, and Francine's oatmeal tweed coat with its dark mink collar had already caused a lot of envious female looks to be directed her way.

She could see Con assessing her, his gaze, he being the man he was, lingering on the curve of her breasts beneath the cashmere. No doubt he was comparing her appearance now – her hair sleekly styled, and her clothes a perfect fit – with the teenager he had known in her ill-fitting clothes and with her untidy tangle of wild curls.

Being Con, though, he wasn't likely to acknowledge that change, and she wasn't surprised when he didn't, attempting instead a casual, 'I thought you were in America.'

'I was,' she agreed. 'I was working with Gracie Fields and she wanted to come home.' No harm in letting him know she was working with one of the world's top names.

'Aye? Well, I'm putting on a new review if you're looking for work.'

Francine was hard put not to laugh. Did he really think she was fool enough to fall for that a second time?

'I've already signed on with ENSA,' she told him calmly, 'and in fact I'd better go otherwise I'm going to be late for rehearsal.'

'ENSA? You wouldn't catch me wasting time on that. You're a fool to come back. It's America where the money is, not entertaining the troops.'

A girl plastered in makeup, beneath which Francine suspected she couldn't be a day over fourteen, came tottering out of the theatre behind Con to put her hand possessively on his arm and glower at Francine.

Francine felt sorry for her and smiled at her, despite her hostility.

'Another of Mrs Friar's nieces?' she asked Con

drily whilst the girl pouted and scowled and Con's handsome face turned an unhandsome shade of dark red. Not that he would be angered by her comment; Con didn't have the backbone to be angry about anything.

'Leave it out, Frankie,' he muttered, trying to step closer to her, only to be yanked back by his companion. 'She's just one of the girls out of the show.'

Like she had been, and probably just as smitten and stupid as she had been too, Francine thought wryly. What hurt her more now was not that Con had lied to her and led her on with promises of love and happiness and marriage, but that she had actually been daft enough to believe him.

The other girls had tried to tell her but she hadn't listened because she hadn't wanted to hear what they were saying. It had taken a visit from his wife and her contemptuous and mocking information about how far down the long line of girls just like her, who Con had picked up and then put down, she actually was, to make her see the brutal reality of their relationship.

That poor kid with him, she really did feel sorry for her, but as Francine knew from experience, she'd have to learn the hard way that he was a liar and a cheat. Funny how now she could look at him and simply feel nothing at all for him apart from irritated contempt.

She wouldn't tell Jean that she had seen him, though. Her sister would only worry and there really was no need for her to do so. It seemed laughable to Francine now that she could ever have been taken in by such a cardboard cut-out of a man. What a little fool she had been. No man would ever be able to deceive her and hurt her now. Sometimes Francine wondered if there were in fact any decent men in the world – or at least in her world – and the honest truth was that she wasn't prepared to risk trying to find out.

SEVENTEEN

Well, it had just better work, that was all, Bella thought fiercely. Six times now she had had to put up with 'doing it', Alan panting and grunting on top of her. The first night, after he'd said he wanted to listen to the wireless and then fallen fast asleep the minute he'd got into bed with her, had been the worst.

First she'd had to wake him up. Then when she had, he pushed 'it' into her hand and made her touch it, his breath stinking of beer as he moaned and groaned. And then as if that hadn't been bad enough, when he'd finally 'done it' inside her, he'd made a funny sort of noise and shouted out Trixie's name at the top of his voice before rolling off her and then falling back asleep before she could say anything.

The horrible unwanted Polish refugees she was forced to have living with her were bound to have heard him. In fact, she knew they must have done because the daughter had given her such a smug look in the morning.

Bella didn't know which she hated the most, Alan or what she was having to do. One thing she was determined on, though: Trixie was going to be put in her place and her nose very firmly rubbed in the dirt. Alan was her husband, and she intended to make sure that Trixie was forced to accept the public shame of what she had made herself.

Once Bella had set her mind to something she didn't give up easily and so every night since she'd seen Alan kissing Trixie, she'd waited for him to get into bed and then she'd made sure that he did 'it'.

Men were supposed to do anything you wanted them to do once you'd let them do it, but instead of being grateful to her, Alan had been even worse-tempered and horrible than normal. It was all right for Trixie, sitting there in that office, thinking she was something special because Alan was kissing her. Bella was ready to bet that she wouldn't be making up to him the way she was if she knew how rough and horrible he could be. Bella had bruises all over her body from him grabbing and pinching her.

When he was doing it he looked at her as though he hated her, and wanted to hurt her, his face hard and angry. Well he'd be sorry for the way he'd behaved when he found out she was going to have a baby. They all would. She could see herself now, pushing her smart new pram, and getting admiring and envious looks from everyone who saw her. She'd insist on Alan's father getting rid of Trixie, of course. At first she'd just drop a few hints to

Alan's mother about it not being right that Trixie was there, and then she'd come right out and tell her why – and in front of Trixie and her parents. Oh, she was looking forward to that, and to the humiliation that Trixie would suffer.

Then she'd tell those wretched refugees that they had to go. She couldn't be expected to have strangers living with her when she was having a baby. Where was Alan? If he was letting that Trixie make up to him . . . Bella didn't like the feeling that thinking about seeing Alan kissing Trixie gave her, so she decided to ignore it. Alan would have to start giving her more housekeeping, of course. She would have to buy lots of things for the baby – and for herself.

Francine looked anxiously at her watch.

'Vi said she'd be here at two and it's half-past now.'

'She's probably been delayed,' said Jean. She was every bit as anxious as Francine, although she was trying very hard not to show it.

'If she doesn't come I'm going to go over there and see her.'

Jean's anxiety grew as she heard the desperation in Fran's voice. 'She will come, Fran, I'm sure of it,' she tried to sooth her.

'It certainly put the wind up her when I telephoned her and told her that if she didn't I'd be over there. Edwin's probably told her not to let me into the house. He never liked me, and he certainly doesn't approve of me.'

'Sam reckons Edwin looks down on all of us,' Jean told her, and then paused, wanting to warn Francine not to expect too much from Vi or to get her hopes up too high, but worried that if she did she might only make matters worse. 'Vi's changed, Fran. You'll see that for yourself, you not having seen her for so long. I suppose it's only natural, what with Edwin's doing so well for himself.'

'You always did defend her, Jean.'

'She means well, but she likes having her own way. She always has, and she doesn't take kindly to being criticised.'

Francine pounced immediately, demanding sharply, 'You don't think I should be doing this, do you?'

Her voice might sound sharp but Jean could hear the telltale emotional break in it. Her heart ached for Fran, but she knew what Vi could be like. The truth was that it was little Jack himself she was most worried about – and about whom she felt so much guilt. She struggled to find the right words to calm Francine down and yet at the same time acknowledge her own sympathy for her.

'I didn't think it was right them sending Jack away myself,' she told her truthfully, 'but you know what Vi's like once someone gets her back up. She wouldn't even give me his address so I could send him his Christmas presents. Said I had to give them to her and she'd send them. That did shock me, her not having him back home for Christmas,' Jean admitted, 'but—'

'I know what you're going to say,' Francine stopped her. 'You're going to remind me that Vi is the one who has the right to say where he should go and what he should do.'

Jean looked at her, her heart filled with pain for her. 'Vi and Edwin are his parents, love.'

'Yes, I know that. And I've no room to talk, I know. It's just—' she broke off as they heard the front doorbell.

'That will be Vi now,' said Jean. 'I'll go and let her in.'

'About time, Jean. I've been standing here for ages,' said Vi sharply.

'You've only just rung the bell,' Jean told her twin mildly.

'I really haven't got time for this, what with all I've got to do. I'm the second in charge at our WVS now, you know, and I have responsibilities.'

Jean thought privately that no responsibility could be greater than the one a woman owed her child but she knew better than to say so.

Vi was on the attack the minute she walked into the kitchen, refusing to be parted from her expensive coat. She might be smartly dressed in her plum-coloured Jaegar skirt and toning twinset, but she had thickened out over the years, much more than Jean had herself, and in Jean's eyes Vi looked nowhere near as elegant as Fran. Say what you liked, their younger sister stood out a mile as someone who had lived a different life, in her black woollen dress with its white collar and cuffs. Fran looked so bandbox smart she could have stepped right out of the pages of one of those expensive magazines that Vi boasted about reading.

Both Vi and Francine looked out of place in her kitchen, Jean thought. You'd never have imagined looking at the three of them now that they'd all grown up in the same shabby little terraced house with no proper bathroom. Not that she envied either of her sisters their material success, not one little bit. Jean reckoned that of the three of them she was the one who was the happiest.

'It really is most inconvenient, me having to come here,' Vi was saying crossly, 'and it's very selfish of you to carry on like this, Francine.'

'All I want is the address of where Jack is staying. You could have saved yourself a journey if you'd given it to me straight off when I asked.'

For a moment Vi looked taken aback, and Jean guessed that her twin had still been thinking of Fran as the cowed sixteen-year-old she had last seen nearly ten years ago.

'I don't know why you should be making all this fuss anyway, Francine. What business is it of yours where Jack is? You haven't seen him since he was born,' Vi reminded her, then rounded on her twin. 'This is all down to you, Jean, making trouble, because you haven't had the good sense to evacuate your two.'

'Don't go blaming Jean, Vi,' Fran answered. 'It's me that has asked after Jack and wants to know where he is.'

'Well, you can ask all you like. I'm not telling

you. I'm not having him upset when he's settled. I'll thank you to remember that me and Edwin are his parents.'

'You aren't acting much like parents, are you, sending him away and not even having him home for Christmas? And as for your Edwin, I reckon he never wanted him in the first place.'

Vi's face was blotched with angry colour. 'You've got no right to say that.'

Jean went cold and her heart missed a beat. She had been hoping against hope that Vi would not say that. But now it was too late, she had said it, and Francine had drawn herself up to her full height, which was a good two inches taller than Vi, closer to four with those high-heeled shoes she was wearing.

'Oh yes I have.'

Francine's voice was as soft as butter but as clear as the noonday sun. It shattered the careful ten-year-old fiction they had all spun between them with all the force of one of Hitler's bombs being dropped on a glasshouse, and to just as devastating an effect.

'After all,' Francine pointed out fiercely, 'Jack is my son.'

Jean bit her lip. This was what she had been dreading from the minute she had opened her front door and seen Fran standing there. There had been something she had seen in Fran's eyes that had warned her that it wasn't just the war that had brought her sister back. Even so, she truly believed that if Francine had seen that Jack was happy and loved by Vi and Edwin, she wouldn't have said anything. After all, it was plain that she loved her son and wanted the best for him.

Francine had been so young when she had had Jack, and unmarried. Jean would have taken Jack herself if she hadn't been so ill, and then afterwards, when she had lost her own baby, she had wished desperately that she had had Jack, but it had been too late then. Vi and Edwin had stepped in and offered to take Jack and bring him up as theirs.

'He's been nothing but hard work since we took him in,' Vi was raging now. She had never liked being put on the spot or criticised, and of course she was taking it out on Francine. 'There's bad blood in him and no mistake.'

'He's a little boy,' Francine protested furiously. 'All you had to do was love him; that was all. But you don't love him. If you did he'd be here with you, not sent away to live with strangers.'

'Me and Edwin have done our duty by him and by you. I don't know how you dare speak to me as you are doing after the shame you brought on yourself. The shame you could have brought on all of us if it had got out what you'd done. There's many a man would have said that kind of child should be sent to an orphanage and not brought up in a decent family. I've done my best with him but when there's bad blood there it always comes out. If you ask me it will do him good to find out how lucky he was when me and Edwin had him. Teach him a bit of a lesson.'

'I want to know where he is.'

'Well, I'm not telling you.'

'It's only natural that Fran should want to see Jack, Vi,' Jean intervened to try to calm things down. 'I'd like to go and visit him meself, the poor little lad. I know how busy you are with your war work an' all.' She paused and looked at Francine, whose eyes were shining with tears. 'After all, Fran does have the right, and I can't see that it would do any harm.'

'That's the trouble with you, Jean: you're far too ready to see more good in people than there is. Edwin was right. He warned me that no good would come of us having Jack. And as for you, Francine, I've never heard of such ingratitude. In your shoes I'd certainly not want to be talking about what I'd done, but then of course I'd never have done something so shameful.'

'You're right you wouldn't – not with your Edwin.'

Francine's temper was up now, Jean recognised and her anxiety grew.

Vi's mouth had gone thin and vengeful. 'You're a disgrace to our family and you should have stayed in America. That way I wouldn't have to be reminded that my sister was an unmarried mother and wouldn't even tell anyone who the father was – if she knew.'

Francine went white and for a moment Jean feared for her self-control, but Francine simply drew in her breath and then let it out again unsteadily.

'I wanted to take Jack to America with me where we could have a new start, but you begged me to let you have him. You said that he would have a better life with you, that I wouldn't be able to give him the time or the love that you could because I'd be on my own and working. You said that if I really loved him then I'd let you have him because you and Edwin could give him so much more than I could. You said that you would be the best mother in the world to him and that Edwin would be his father. You said all those things to me, Vi, but none of them were true were they, because if they were then Jack would be at home with you.'

Tears filled Jean's eyes. She really felt for Fran and always had done; right from the moment Fran had come to her and told her about her trouble and the man who had caused it. Not that Jean would ever have dreamed of telling Vi the name of Jack's real father, knowing how her twin felt about actors and the stage.

'This is ridiculous. There's a war on in this country, I'll have you know, and it was the Government that said that children should be evacuated, not me and Edwin.' Vi was blustering now. 'We've done our best for him and no one could have done any more, but he's not been an easy child. I've never known a baby cry so much, or be so sickly. Drove Edwin mad, it did; kept us all awake and upset poor Bella dreadfully. She couldn't bring her school friends home because of him. He was that slow at walking we thought there must be something wrong with him. Edwin reckons that Jack hasn't got a brain in his head.'

'Give over do, Vi,' Jean stopped her firmly. 'Sam says he's proper bright and you've said yourself that he's always got his nose in a book.' She turned to her younger sister. 'He's a lovely lad, Fran, a son anyone could be proud of.'

'Well, you and me have got very different opinions of what makes a mother proud, then, Jean. That's all I can say,' said Vi.

Nothing that either of them could say to her could persuade Vi to change her mind and tell them where Jack was, and as Jean confided to Sam that night when they were in bed, she reckoned that Vi knew she had done wrong but was refusing to admit it.

'I never thought I'd say this about me own twin, Sam, but what she's done is downright wicked. Poor Francine went up to Grace's room after she'd gone and cried her eyes out. I felt for her, I really did.'

'I said all along that no good would come of your Vi having Jack,' Sam reminded her.

'I should have teken him meself and I blame meself for not doing, Sam. Poor Fran's that upset.'

'There was nothing you could have done, not with you being so poorly.'

In Grace's bedroom Francine lay awake and dry-eyed, looking up through the darkness. *Jack.* The pain that tore at her was as real and as sharp as the birth pangs she had felt bringing him into the world. She could remember his birth as clearly as though it had only been yesterday. She had been so frightened when she had first realised that she was pregnant. She hadn't even known what was happening to her at first, and then when she had she had been terrified. Con had already deserted her and she had known there was no point in turning to him for help.

Vi had been wrong about one thing. Con had been both her first and her only lover. Frightened though she had been to discover she was pregnant, she wasn't going to pretend that she hadn't enjoyed what had led to that pregnancy. Con had known all the right moves and all the right touches all right, and besotted with him as she was, she had been swept away on a tide of physical longing that had been at full flood. That, though, had been before she had learned that he was married and that she was just one in a long line of girls he had seduced and then abandoned. She had made a promise to herself when it was all over and she was on her way to America that she would never make a fool of herself in the same way again, and she had stuck to that promise, not risking dating any of the many men who had asked her out just in case the body she didn't feel she could trust any more betrayed her a second time.

She had hated giving Jack up but she had wanted to do the best for him. Despite the disgrace and shame she had brought on herself she had loved Jack from the first minute she had held him in her arms; loved him with a helpless aching love that she hadn't expected and didn't understand. She had been sixteen when he had been born, and when Vi had told her that the best thing she could do for him would be to allow her and Edwin to bring him up as their own son she had let her elder sister convince her that giving him up was what was best for him. Jean had been too ill to help her, too ill for her even to talk to her after the tragic death of her own baby. Poor Jean. Francine could only imagine what she must have suffered, knowing how badly she had ached physically as well as emotionally for her own baby in those first months without him, waking up wanting him and going to sleep crying for him. The only thing that kept her going had been her belief that she had done the right thing for him.

'Come on, Grace, it will be fun going dancing. You might even get that chap of yours on the floor for a smoochy number if you're lucky.'

'Me and Teddy don't want to go dancing, all right?' All Grace had done since Teddy had told her about his heart had been worry about him. When she was with him she was constantly begging him not to overdo things, constantly trying to make sure that when they were together they didn't walk too far or do too much, and the anxiety was wearing her down. It wasn't like worrying about Luke being in France or worrying about Hitler invading England. Those were worries that she shared with other people, and that somehow made them easier to bear. And as well as feeling anxious she also felt guilty. Guilty because she was well and Teddy was not.

'All right,' Lillian answered her snappily. 'Keep your hair on. I was only asking. Don't come with us then.'

'No I won't,' Grace agreed, equally snappy, picking up the notes she had been studying.

She might as well go to her room as stay here and fall out with Lillian. If Teddy had been properly well she'd have loved to go dancing, and she knew that if she were to tell him what the rest of her set were planning and that they were included, he'd have been eager to join in. But how could she let him? What if something were to happen to him?

She pushed her textbooks to one side and looked towards the window. They were back to double summer time now and the last of the day's sun was warming her room.

There was a brief knock on her door.

'It's only me,' Hannah called out.

Grace opened the door to let her in.

'Are you OK, Grace?' she asked, 'only you haven't seemed yourself just lately, and you were a bit sharp with Lillian. Is it because of your brother? I know he's still writing to her.'

Grace shook her head. 'No. It's nothing,' she lied. Tears brimmed in her eyes. Cross with herself, she wiped them away. 'I'm sorry, Hannah. I don't want to cause any upset.'

It was true that she wasn't particularly fond of Lillian, but the other girl was a member of their set, and that meant that traditionally they owed one another a certain loyalty.

Hannah came in and closed the door behind her. 'Look, if it's the work, Grace, or if something's happened on the ward, well, there's nothing to be ashamed of in saying so. There's been several girls drop out since we started out training, although . . . well, I'd got you down as the sort who would see things through.'

'It isn't the work . . . or anyone on the ward. It's . . . it's Teddy,' Grace admitted.

'You've had a fall-out?' Hannah guessed. 'And that's why you don't want to go dancing.'

It was no use, she would have to tell Hannah, Grace recognised, otherwise she would be imagining all sorts of things that just weren't true.

'We haven't had a fall-out,' she told her carefully. 'But Teddy can't go dancing, Hannah. In fact, he can't do very much at all. He's very poorly, you see.'

Hannah listened in silence whilst Grace explained, waiting until she had finished to say shakily, 'Oh, Grace, how awful.'

'Yes, it is, isn't it?' agreed Grace bleakly. 'But you mustn't say anything to anyone, Hannah. Please promise me you won't. Teddy doesn't want anyone fussing. That's what's making me so on edge, knowing that he won't be careful. I'm so afraid for him. It's on my mind all the time. I can't understand why he's doing what he is. He didn't need to volunteer to drive an ambulance. He could be living quietly at home resting, but he says . . . he says . . . he says . . .' Grace couldn't go on. Her emotions had overwhelmed her. She could tell, though, from Hannah's expression that she under-stood what she was trying to say.

'I'll have a word with Lillian, if you like, and tell her that you've not been feeling too good.'

Grace gave her a weak smile. 'Well, you won't be able to tell her that I'm having me monthlies.'

Hannah laughed. They had all been bemused at first when their periods had altered so that they all had them at virtually the same time but then Doreen had discovered from one of the more senior nurses that this was something that tended to happen when young women lived and worked together closely.

It just had to have happened, that was all, because if it hadn't . . . Bella felt sick with fury at just the thought of what had occurred yesterday when she had called round at Alan's parents. She, *Trixie*, had been there, sitting in the garden with Alan's mother, whilst Trixie's own mother and Alan's fussed round her. None of them had seen her at first. Trixie was crying, her plain face looking even plainer. Alan's mother had been holding her hand, comforting her, telling her quite openly that Alan had made a terrible mistake in marrying Bella.

That was when Trixie had seen her and had pretended to be embarrassed, but of course Bella had known she wasn't.

Bella had been so furious that she had confronted the three of them there and then.

'Well, Alan is married to me whether you like it or not,' she had said, 'and there's nothing you can do about it.' And then she had left and gone round to her mother's, but her mother hadn't been there so she had had to come home.

Just let them wait, all of them. She'd make them sorry and she'd give their precious Trixie something to really cry about when she dropped a few hints to other people about keeping their husbands away from her because she was the kind that went after married men.

The back door opened and the refugees, as Bella insisted on mentally referring to Bettina and her mother, came in.

'What do you two want?' Bella demanded, taking her bad temper out on them.

'It is time for my mother to eat and have a rest,' Bettina told her.

'If she wants to eat you can take her to a café. And as for her resting, it's high time she did a bit of work. This kitchen floor needs a good scrub—' Bella broke off as the door opened a second time and a man followed them in and went to join them.

Bettina immediately linked arms with him, all over him like a rash. Bella could see why. He was extraordinarily handsome, tall, with very dark hair cut short. But no matter how handsome he was he had no right to be here.

'I don't know what you think you're doing,' Bella told Bettina nastily, 'but I'll tell you what you're not doing and that's bringing your fancy man here to this house.'

Bella looked at him as she spoke. He was looking

back at her with angry contempt. He turned to Bettina and said something to her in Polish.

'Jan is my brother,' Bettina told Bella proudly. 'He is here in England with the Polish Air Force and he has come to see our mother, who is not well. He will be staying here with us for two days whilst he is on leave.'

'Staying here? In this house? My house? He most certainly will not.'

'You have the spare room – why should he not stay? Your Government is paying you for the use of two of your bedrooms already, although you have forced Mama and I to share one.'

Bella could feel her temper rising. How dare this . . . this nobody, who did not even have a country any more, start acting as though she had the right to make demands?

The mother had started to cough, just like she did at night. Bella glared at her whilst Bettina and her brother fussed over her.

'There's nothing wrong with her, you know. She just puts it on for sympathy.'

They were speaking in Polish again, and ignoring her, whilst Jan guided his mother to a chair, and Bettina filled the kettle and put it on the stove.

'I'm not putting up with this,' Bella began, but Bettina overruled her, telling her fiercely, 'It is you who is making my mother ill. Do you really think that we want to be here, living like this, in this? At home in Poland we had—' She stopped, bright red spots of colour burning in her face, and then continued passionately. 'My father was a well-known and respected medical specialist. We lived in a beautiful and very old house. Our home was filled with music and laughter and friends. It was a life that someone like you could never understand. My parents loved one another very dearly and you could not understand that either. You, who has a husband who never wants to come home and who when he does needs to get himself drunk before he can bear to be with you. You see, it is as I told you, Jan,' she continued, turning to her brother. 'We must find somewhere else to live. I have complained already to the organisation that put us here and they have promised to find us somewhere else as soon as they can.'

Bella couldn't believe her ears. Bettina had complained about her?

'You come over here to our country,' she raged at her, 'where you don't belong, expecting to be housed and fed by our government. You take jobs from our men and you can't even speak English properly, and then you dare to complain? Why don't you go back where you came from?'

Bettina burst into a torrent of Polish, stopping only when her brother put his hand on her arm and shook his head slightly before turning towards Bella, and telling her coldly, 'You are the most despicable person I have ever met.'

Then, without waiting for Bella to respond, he went to his mother and said gently, 'Come, Mama, lean on me. Yes, that's it. Now we will go upstairs and you will rest, and then tonight I shall take you both out for a meal.'

Now the three of them were behaving as though she didn't exist, Bella saw wrathfully. If anyone needed helping upstairs for a rest it was her, not their mother, because she really did feel very odd all of a sudden. Very odd indeed.

'Look.' Gently but very firmly Teddy put his hands on Grace's shoulders and gave her a small shake. 'Stop worrying about me, please. Everything's fine. I'm fine. The thing you should be worrying about is this war, not me, Grace.'

'It's easy for you to say that. How can I stop worrying when I know . . . ?' Too late Grace realised what she had said. Of course it wasn't easy for him. How could it be?

'I shouldn't have told you.' Teddy sounded weary and his smile had gone.

They'd taken the ferry across to New Brighton because Teddy had said that it was a shame not to enjoy the spring sunshine even if they couldn't walk on the beach because of its fortifications against enemy landings, and now Grace felt guilty because she'd spoiled what should have been a happy day out.

'You mustn't say that,' she told him, fishing in her pocket for her handkerchief in case she disgraced herself by starting to cry. The beaches looked so ugly and frightening with the defences in place. She wished passionately that things were different, that there was no war and that Teddy could be well.

'I'm glad you told me, I really am.' It was the

truth. 'I would have hated it if . . . if I hadn't known,' she finished lamely.

'I told you because I wanted there to be honesty between us, Grace, and because, selfishly, I wanted you to be the one I could turn to and talk to.'

'You can talk to me, Teddy,' insisted Grace.

Teddy shook his head, the soft floppiness of his hair already tangled slightly by the sea breeze. 'No I can't. Not as I want to. Just then you were going to say you'd have hated it afterwards if you hadn't known, but you didn't say it. That isn't being straight about things, Grace. That is not what I want. I know it's hard for you, and I know I'm asking a lot of you, things that I don't have any right to ask. I don't want you fussing like me mum, or thinking the worst every time you don't see me for a few days. What I want more than anything else is to live whilst I can. I want to share that living with you, Grace, but what I don't want when I'm gone is . . . One day, Gracie, you'll meet someone and fall in love.'

Grace made a small murmur of distress but Teddy shook his head again.

'Of course you will, and it's only right that you should. You and me aren't sweethearts, Grace. We're friends. I'm not saying that if things had been different we couldn't have been different, but they aren't. When you do fall in love, I hope you'll tell him about me and when you do I don't want him feeling or thinking that I did badly by you. By that I mean that I don't want to feel I'm leaving you with a burden of guilt – for anything.

'When you look back at this time I want you to look back with happiness, not pain. What I want more than anything else, Gracie, is for you to remember that we laughed and had fun. I want the time we spent together to be as if nothing was going to happen. Even when we die, a part of us lives on in the hearts and the minds of those who've known us. I know I'm asking a lot of you, asking you to carry me with you into the future, but I know you can do it. I don't want you clinging to the past, and when you and this chap you're going to fall in love talk about me, I want him to think what a decent sort I was, and I want you to know that your happiness is the future I want for both of us. I won't be here for that future, Gracie, so you have to be happy and live it a little bit for me.'

I can't do that. The words would be so easy to say but Grace knew she mustn't. She felt older and more grown up than she had ever imagined she could feel.

'I want you to promise me that you will do that, Gracie.'

'I promise.'

As though by magic, just as she spoke, the wind dropped so that instead of being carried away out to sea her words hung softly on the air between.

Teddy didn't kiss her and Grace was glad in a way that he had not done so, because that made the moment and her promise somehow more sacred.

He did kiss her later, though, after they had competed with one another to see who could skim the flat pebbles they had picked up from what was accessible of the beach over the flat sea as it waited for the tide to turn.

It was a bittersweet kiss. Both tender and fierce. A kiss that she knew instinctively was both a taste of what could have been and a reminder of what must not be.

Bella could hear the laughter coming from the kitchen the minute she opened the front door, and for a moment it held her immobile in the hallway, her face warmed by the shaft of sunlight coming in through the window and catching motes of dust in the air, gripped by an unfamiliar piercing sense of loss and pain and a feeling of being excluded and unwanted, an outsider.

Just as she had been at school; just as she was now at the Tennis Club.

That was ridiculous. She had been the most popular girl at school and the prettiest, just as she was at the Tennis Club. And as for being an outsider, this was her home.

She walked down the hall and pushed open the kitchen door. *They* were sitting round the kitchen table, with the back door open to let in the sunshine and the fresh air. There was a bottle of wine on the table and three now almost empty glasses, and the air was rich with the smell of something cooking that was alien and spicy.

The mother looked apprehensive when she saw her, but the other two simply looked at her. Both of them were smoking, and Bettina's expression was both mocking and defiant, whilst Jan's somehow made her feel . . . Bella didn't know really what she actually felt but she knew that she hated it just as much as she hated him.

She was still furious that despite her refusal to allow him to stay he had done so. When she had complained to Alan about it when he had eventually come in he had simply shrugged and ignored her.

Bella wasn't used to having her wishes ignored and nor was she used to feeling helpless.

'Cigarette?'

The drawled offer caught her off guard. She looked down at the packet Jan was extending towards her. His fingers were long and lean, and something about them quickened her heartbeat although she had no idea why.

Without answering him, Bella turned on her heel and left the kitchen.

Halfway up the stairs she heard the sound of his laughter following her and mocking her.

Alone in her bedroom she lay down on the bed. Her head was swimming and she felt dreadfully tired. For the first time in her life as she lay on her bed, listening to the sound of voices and laughter drifting upstairs, Bella knew what it was to feel completely alone and isolated from other people. A feeling, a mixture of panic and fear and sickness, curdled in her stomach. What was the matter with her? She was a married woman with a husband, parents, an extended family of aunt, uncle, and cousins, whilst those three downstairs were refugees with nothing. How could they laugh? How could they possibly be happier than she was? They certainly had no right to be. If she wasn't feeling so dreadfully and uncharacteristically tired she would have gone downstairs to the kitchen and told them so.

'We had two amputations in the theatre this morning, but we aren't getting anything like as many road accidents now that we're back to double summer time,' said Hannah tiredly as she sank into a chair opposite Grace, who had been making the most of having their sitting room to herself to write up her notes on the new patients admitted to the ward. She would be on nights herself again soon and Night Sister expected the junior nurse to accompany her on her ward round and to know off by heart each patient's condition, symptoms and treatment.

'Did you hear about those girls from the barrage balloon site?' asked Hannah. When Grace shook her head, Hannah explained, 'It seems they decided to have a bit of a night out, seeing as things seemed quiet, only when they got back the balloon had broken loose. Now, as punishment, the whole lot of them have been sent up to some remote island off Scotland.'

'Oh, poor things,' Grace sympathised.

'Never mind poor things. If you ask me it serves then right,' Hannah contradicted her robustly. 'That's the trouble with you, Grace, you're far too sympathetic. It won't do in a nurse, you know,' she joked, adding, 'Mind you, I suppose you're still worrying about Teddy.'

'Yes. I am,' Grace agreed, 'and not just about him.' She closed her exercise book and leaned forward, interlinking her fingers and looking down at them as she rested her forearms on her crossed knees. 'I keep thinking about what's going to happen to him and I can't help wondering if I ought . . . well, that is to say . . .'

'You mean he's asked you to go all the way with him?' guessed Hannah immediately.

'No, no, he hasn't, but I think that if I offered . . .' Grace coloured up. Normally speaking this wasn't the sort of conversation she'd have dreamed of having with anyone, but the situation she was in now was so different from anything she had ever thought she might experience that somehow it made normal conventions seem less important. Even so, she couldn't quite bring herself to tell Hannah that she suspected from the occasional passionate kisses Teddy gave her when he couldn't help himself that even though he wanted to protect her, he did want to go further.

'There's plenty of men that are asking their girls to do it, scaring them half to death by saying that they might not come back, and there's plenty of girls too that wish they hadn't let them,' Hannah told her warningly.

'Yes I know.'

'Are you in love with him after all, then?' Hannah asked.

'I don't think so. Anyway, it's not like that. It's

just that I keep thinking that if I don't then he'll never know what it feels like, will he? And that makes me feel guilty.'

'How do you know that he hasn't already with someone else?' asked Hannah practically.

She didn't, of course, Grace admitted.

'And what would happen if you were to get caught and fall for a baby?' Hannah pressed on ruthlessly. 'That would be a fine thing, wouldn't, it? Him dead; you carrying and not wed.'

Grace felt sick at the thought of the shame of such a situation.

'And then even if you weren't, what would happen if you were to meet someone else who you did fall in love with? What would you tell him? There's not many chaps who'd take kindly to their girl saying that she'd done it with someone else.'

'I suppose you're right,' she agreed, 'but I just can't help thinking—'

'Well, don't go thinking, and yes, I am right. If you want to know what's really what, then you should go down to the women's ward where they have the woman that have been brought in because they've tried to get rid of a baby they don't want. We had one in theatre last week. Mr Anslow did his best to save her but she was in that much of a mess inside with septicaemia from what she'd had done that he couldn't. Nurse Perry that's a full year ahead of me went in to a dead faint just with the stink from her.'

Grace's own stomach heaved, not so much with sickness as fear and horror. Everyone had heard the stories of the horrible deaths suffered by those women who had broken the law and gone to a backstreet abortionist in a desperate attempt to avoid having an unwanted child.

'Mind you, if she'd survived she'd have ended up in prison,' said Hannah matter-of-factly. 'Not that there aren't those with the money and the connections who can get themselves sorted out properly with no questions asked, of course, but it's different for the likes of us.'

'I thought it was supposed to be all right if a man used . . . something,' said Grace self-consciously.

'Aye, supposed to be,' Hannah agreed, 'but there's many a couple thought themselves safe and then found out that they were no such thing. If you want my advice, Grace, you'll leave things as they are. And if Teddy does start hinting about you doing it with him, then make sure you say no.' Her expression softened slightly and she reached out and touched Grace's arm. 'Look, I'm not saying that I don't understand. I dare say I'd feel just the same meself in your shoes.'

'I just keep thinking how I'd feel if I was Teddy and I knew I was going to die without ever having known what it's like. I know we're supposed to wait until we fall in love and get married, but what if you don't have time for that? What if all the time you've got is now, Hannah? What would we do then?'

'I don't know,' Hannah admitted quietly.

*　　*　　*

It wasn't fair. It just wasn't fair. After all she'd done, putting up with Alan and 'it', there wasn't going to be a baby after all. Her monthlies had started two days ago and even though they'd been mercifully short-lived this time, they'd been really bad and had left her feeling pulled down and tired. So tired, in fact, that her mother had insisted that she ought to see the doctor, and had made her an appointment there and then for this afternoon.

'You probably need a bit of a tonic,' she'd told her.

Bella hadn't said anything. The only tonic she needed was getting those refugees out of her house and getting Alan to behave towards her as a husband should, and that Trixie put in her place.

She was on her way to see Alan now. He hadn't left her any housekeeping this week – again – and when she'd told her mother, she'd said that it was disgraceful and that her father would have something to say to Alan's father if things went on like this.

The refugees had gone out this morning and when they'd come back Jan had been in uniform. The first time she had seen him he had been wearing a tweed jacket, a pair of cavalry twill trousers with a tattersall checked shirt, and a V-necked pullover all in soft shades of brown; the kind of clothes she was used to seeing men in, but somehow Jan's had looked different, softer and older, and in some indefinable way they had seemed to fit him better than her father and Alan's new clothes ever seemed to fit them.

Jan was one of those Polish Air Force pilots who, when Poland had been forced to surrender, had managed to fly his plane to Britain, along with many other Polish pilots, his mother had told Bella proudly. Those men were now forming a squadron under the auspices of the RAF.

In that case, the sooner he got posted the better, Bella had told her sharply and the further away the better, because she certainly wasn't going to put up with having him thinking he could sleep in her spare room whenever he felt like it.

Mr James, her father-in-law's fussy elderly clerk, opened the office door to her and told her that both Alan and his father were out. The offices were decorated in the same drab brown as Alan's parents' house; the furniture was equally old-fashioned, and the atmosphere equally formal. An oil painting of Alan's father hung on one wall. Beneath it, in a locked cabinet, were several silver-gilt trophies won by both Alan and his father. The whole place had an air of self-satisfied prosperity and smugness.

'Miss Trixie is in, if you want to leave a message with her,' he informed Bella.

Oh, yes, she'd certainly leave a message with her, Bella decided angrily. A message that told her that she shouldn't go around kissing other women's husbands.

Trixie was busy typing when Bella pushed open the office door, her fingers fairly flying over the keys, short practical fingers with short unpolished nails. Not manicured like her own.

The fact that Alan could actually want to kiss

someone so plain and dull when he was married to her, further enflamed Bella's temper.

Trixie had seen her now and had stopped typing.

'Alan isn't here, I'm afraid,' she told Bella quietly.

'No, I dare say he's trying to do the decent thing and stay away from you, after the way you've been throwing yourself at him.'

Trixie's face turned bright red.

'I suppose you thought he wouldn't tell me about you making up to him and kissing him,' Bella continued. 'Well, of course he did, seeing as I'm his wife and he's my husband. And let me warn you that if you don't leave my husband alone I'm going to make sure that people know just what kind of woman you are. Poor Alan, he said he didn't know which way to turn when you started chasing him. He's been that worried that I'd be upset about it, but it's like I told him, no one would ever think that he'd look at someone like you when he's married to me. So you just stay away from him in future, otherwise it won't just be me who knows what you've been up to.'

Trixie was crying now. 'I love Alan and—'

'Well, he certainly doesn't love you,' Bella cut her off ruthlessly, 'because the other night when he was in bed with me doing what married people can do, he told me that he loved me.'

Trixie had gone a really funny colour now, and her stupid face was convulsing into an even plainer expression than usual. It was clear that what she had told her had shocked her, Bella recognised triumphantly.

'Just you remember,' Bella told her as she opened the door ready to leave, 'in future, keep away from my husband.'

Once Bella was back out on the street, the giddy sense of power and triumph she had felt in the office receded, leaving her feeling very odd and weak. So weak that she almost felt as though she might faint. Perhaps her mother was right and she did need a tonic.

EIGHTEEN

Wednesday 15 May

'It's bad news, isn't it, now that the Dutch have surrendered?' Jean asked Sam worriedly.

They were alone in the house, the twins having gone to the cinema and Francine being at a rehearsal.

'Ay, love, it is,' Sam agreed. He saw her expression and knew what she was thinking.

There had been so much bad news these recent weeks. The Germans had already overrun Norway and now this. The Bank Holiday had been cancelled because of the crisis and the papers had been full of the shocking fact that the German Wehrmacht had invaded France and Belgium.

'Don't worry about Luke,' he tried to reassure her. 'I reckon that now Chamberlain has gone and Churchill's taken his place he'll have our lads back safe and sound.'

Jean knew that Sam was trying to comfort her but she knew him too well for him to be able to deceive her. He was as worried as she was, and not just for Luke. Everyone was talking about how easy it would be for Hitler to bomb England now that he would be able to set up bases in Holland. Jean still couldn't believe the awful finality of what had happened.

'Everyone said that it would never happen, that Hitler wouldn't be able to overcome Holland's defences.' Her voice shook.

'I know, love,' Sam agreed. There was no real comfort he could offer her. He was as shocked as she was. The Germans had moved with such speed and such force. It seemed that nothing and no one could stand in their way.

'Well, Mrs Parker, I have some good news for you.'

The doctor was smiling encouragingly at her. He probably wasn't going to give her a tonic because it was on ration or something, Bella thought crossly. Well, she wasn't going to leave until he gave her one.

'I'm just exhausted, Doctor,' she told him, 'what with having to look after these refugees I've been landed with and everything.'

'Well, yes, of course you will be feeling tired. That's quite normal in the early months, especially with a first pregnancy. You mustn't overdo things, you know, my dear. You must put Baby first now.'

Baby? Bella stared at him. 'But I can't be having a baby,' she told him flatly.

He had stopped smiling now and was looking at her rather sternly. 'Indeed you are, my dear, and

I'm sure you'll be very pleased about it once you've got used to the idea.'

'But I've just had my monthlies and—'

'I see,' said the doctor. 'Well then, in that case it may well be that you were carrying twins. Sometimes it happens that one of them is lost in the early weeks. I can assure you, though, that you are most definitely pregnant.'

She was pregnant after all, and now Trixie would have to keep away from Alan. She had done it. She had got what she wanted, so why was she feeling all sick and shaky, and as though she wanted to sit down and cry?

Bella could hear the wireless as she opened her front door. They were clustered around it, listening to it in silence. She was tired and still in shock but instead of jumping up to make a fuss of her as her mother would have done, her unwanted house guests simply ignored her. She should be feeling angry, Bella knew, but somehow she felt more as though she wanted to cry. She went into the kitchen and filled the kettle, making a lot of noise as she banged it down on the stove to show her disapproval and relieve her mood.

If they had to have the wireless on without asking her permission first, then why on earth couldn't they have some music on instead of some dry, dusty news-reader, boring on again about the war and Hitler?

The telephone rang and when she went to answer it, it was her mother, asking how she had gone on at the doctor's.

'He says that I'm having a baby,' Bella told her. There was a sound from behind her and as she turned round she saw Jan standing in the hallway.

'The kettle was boiling,' he told her. 'So I have switched the gas off.'

Had he heard her telling her mother about the baby? What did it matter if he had? After all, she hadn't done anything wrong, had she? Not like Trixie. Bella nodded her head and then turned her back on him, as he walked back to join his family.

'Yes, of course I'll make sure I get plenty of rest, Mummy,' Bella told her mother. 'No, I haven't told Alan yet, but I will tell him when he comes in . . . When? Oh, not for ages yet, not until January.'

Bella was upstairs lying down when Alan came home – early for once – and her stomach muscles tightened as she heard him coming up the stairs. Outwardly she might be blaming Trixie for that kiss she had witnessed, but inwardly no matter how hard she fought against it, there was a small hard impossible-to-destroy kernel of knowledge that said otherwise.

If Trixie was to blame and she had told Alan that Bella had confronted her, then surely Alan would be returning home feeling both guilty and anxious to reassure her. She was the one who had the upper hand after all, because she was his wife.

Alan thrust open the bedroom door carelessly, letting it bang against the wall before slamming it closed again.

'What the hell do you think you're doing, going into the office like that and upsetting poor Trixie?'

This was not what Bella had been expecting. Guilt, defensiveness and, hopefully, remorse, yes, but not this savage anger.

'All I did was warn her to keep away from my husband,' Bella defended herself.

'Your husband? I've never been your husband. All I've ever been is the fool you managed to trick into marriage. Well, it's over now, Bella. I've spoken to my father and he reckons that I can get the marriage annulled; after all, it was never properly consummated, not really. And once I'm free of you I'm going to marry Trixie. She's the one I love. She's the one I've always loved, and I'd be married to her now if it hadn't been for you.'

Annulled? A thrill of horror electrified Bella into sitting up in bed. The thought that Alan might actually be planning to leave her hadn't crossed her mind, at least not properly. All she'd feared had been looking a fool because he spent more time at work with Trixie than he did at home with her. And he wasn't just planning to leave her, he wanted to have their marriage annulled, making it look as though she hadn't been a proper wife to him; as though there was something wrong with her. Well, they'd soon see about that!

'Is that what you've told Trixie?' Bella accused him furiously. 'Because if it is you'd better go back and tell her that it isn't the truth, hadn't you? Our marriage is a proper marriage.'

'A proper marriage, when I had to be so drunk

that I could hardly perform, just to go anywhere near you.' Alan's face was red and he had raised his voice to such a pitch that he was almost screaming at her.

'But you did do it, didn't you, every night for a week? Have you told your precious Trixie about that?'

'Yes I have,' Alan shot back. 'She's not like you, Bella; she's the most darling brave girl. I'm not worthy of her and I never will be. She actually blames herself because she said that we had to wait until I could leave you officially. She knows that it was only my frustration with wanting her so much that made me turn to you. I should have paid a whore instead. It would have been cheaper and I'd certainly have enjoyed it more. God, but you're cold. It's like having it with a dummy.'

'Keep your voice down,' Bella hissed at him. 'The refugees will hear you.'

'I don't care if they do,' Alan yelled at her. 'In fact I hope they do. The more people who know what you're really like, the better. It doesn't matter anyway if I can't get an annulment; I'll get a divorce instead. Trixie will wait for me.'

'You can't divorce me, Alan. I'm pregnant. I'm having your baby.'

'What?'

This was the moment, her moment, when she should have been feeling triumphant and smugly self-righteous, knowing she was in an unassailable position. Whatever Alan's father might choose to say to his son in private, Bella knew her in-laws well enough to realise that neither of them, but especially Alan's mother, was going to want the stigma of having a son who walked out on his pregnant wife. There'd already been one or two comments from people about the fact that Alan hadn't joined up, and Bella knew that her own father, despite the fact that he had been so angry with Charlie for having done so, had taken full advantage of the fact that his son was doing his bit, whilst his co-councillor's son was dodging doing his by claiming that he was needed in his father's business.

Yes, this should have been her moment of moral superiority over Alan but instead, when she saw the way he was looking at her, what Bella did actually feel was a sharp stab of very real fear.

'*What?*' Alan's face had lost its colour. He looked shocked and trapped and absolutely furious.

He was coming towards her, panicking Bella into scrambling off the bed, ignoring the weakness that dizzied her. In order to reach the door she'd have to get past him. He had already bunched his fists. Bella felt sick. It was too late now to remember that other time that she had pushed so determinedly to the back of her mind as though it had never happened.

There was a knock on the bedroom door. Before Alan could stop her, Bella ran past him and opened it.

Jan was standing outside, his expression unreadable in the shadows of the landing.

Bella couldn't bring herself to look directly at

him. A feeling she didn't recognise was spilling painfully through her. It burned her face and hurt her pride. It made her want to run and hide herself away from everyone.

'I would like permission to use your telephone. I have to call my commanding officer.'

It was just coincidence that he should choose now to ask to use the telephone, paid for by Bella's father when Alan's father had refused to do so; there was no reason for her to feel she had to be grateful to him, Bella reassured herself. After all, he'd hardly bother to come to her rescue, would he? Jan had made it plain enough with those cold dismissive looks of his what he thought about her, and Bella was pretty sure that his sympathies would lie with Alan, not her.

But he had given her the opportunity to escape.

'Yes, of course you can use it.'

She couldn't stay here now; not when she felt so afraid of Alan. She would go to her parents and tell her mother what had happened. Her mother would know what to do.

'Oh, Teddy, I'm so frightened. It said in the *Daily Mail* this morning that the Allied line had been pierced in three places.'

Teddy hugged Grace tightly, even though she was in uniform and they were standing by his ambulance.

'Don't worry, the RAF Advanced Air Strike Force will stop them.'

'Do you really think so?'

'I wouldn't say it if I didn't,' Teddy assured her, but Grace wasn't convinced.

The Germans' advance, smashing into the Low Countries and forcing them to surrender, had been such a shock to everyone, and Luke and Charlie were both in France with the BEF. Grace prayed that they were safe, especially Luke. No one could talk of anything else but the war and their growing concern, both for the men in the BEF in France and for themselves.

'If you ask me we've just got to get on with things as best we can,' Hannah said stoutly when they were having their lunch.

'You should try telling that to Lillian,' said Jennifer. 'She was in tears on the ward this morning, crying that she couldn't cope with all the worry. You should have seen Sister's face. She wasn't at all pleased, I can tell you. Mind you, Lillian got away with it in the end. One of the young housemen just happened to be there and she managed to faint right into his arms. She's been sent to the san to rest her nerves, but I reckon if there wasn't a war on and so many nurses needed, she'd have been told to pack her bags and leave.'

'I should think so too,' said Hannah firmly.

'I had a letter from home this morning,' Doreen told them. 'Mum says that they've had two Dutch refugees billeted on them.'

'One of them wasn't wearing a crown, was she?' Iris joked, referring to the fact that it had been in all the papers that Queen Wilhelmina, and the rest of the Dutch royal family had been brought to safety in England ahead of many other refugees.

Grace was touched when, despite everyone's growing concern about what was happening, Hannah still managed to find time to catch up with her as she left the dining room to ask how Teddy was.

'It still upsets him that he can't do more,' Grace answered her.

Alan was sleeping in the spare bedroom, thankfully empty again now that Jan had left to rejoin his fellow Polish pilots at Northolt in Middlesex, where the Polish squadron was based.

Bella was at her mother's, sitting in the garden and enjoying being fussed over. Her mother had already assured her that it had now been agreed that there was to be no divorce.

'Daddy has told Mr Parker how shocked we are by Alan's behaviour, but that we understand that in times of war young men do things they would not normally do, especially when unscrupulous young women encourage them to do them,' she informed Bella, blithely disregarding the fact that Alan wasn't involved in any way with the war.

'But what about Trixie, Mummy?' Bella pressed her mother. 'She means to have him, I know she does, and now with me having the baby to worry about . . .' Theatrically Bella placed her hand on her still flat stomach.

'Well, naturally that young hussy won't be able

to work for the Parkers any more, and I said as much to Mrs Parker at the WVS meeting yesterday. One or two of the other ladies who happened to overhear me came up to me afterwards to say how dreadful it was that she had behaved so disgracefully. It was very noticeable that that mother of hers wasn't there lording it over everyone like she normally does. Alan's mother didn't have much to say for herself either, especially when I said how the doctor had said that he wouldn't be surprised if it wasn't the shock of finding out what was going on that caused you to lose one of your babies.'

Mother and daughter exchanged a complicit look. Of course, Bella's doctor had said no such thing, but Bella certainly wasn't going to object to her mother rubbing Mrs Parker's nose in it a bit, after the way the woman had favoured and fawned over Trixie.

'I think those parents of hers should be ashamed of themselves, and it's no wonder they've sent her away to stay with relatives in Scotland,' Bella told her mother virtuously.

'I agree. Someone like that shouldn't be allowed to mix with respectable folk. Like I said to Mrs Parker, I feel sorry for *her*, really I do, for having been so taken in by her. It's shameful the way that Trixie behaved.

'I shouldn't be surprised if your father's right when he says that the Parkers being so friendly with her parents could mean that Mr Parker won't be re-elected to the council. People don't like women who go round breaking up marriages. It's like I said to the other ladies at the WVS meeting, you've nothing to blame yourself for. You've been a perfect wife, and with Daddy being generous enough to buy that house for you, and Alan not even having to worry about being called up or pay a mortgage, he should be grateful he's in such a fortunate position. Mind you, as Mrs Nicholls said, sometimes it's a matter of having too much of a good thing and some young men need a taste of army discipline and doing their duty to make them appreciate how lucky they are.'

Bella nodded as she listened to her mother. It was just as she had hoped it would be. When she had arrived on her parents' doorstep in tears after Alan's demand for a divorce, she had told her mother everything, apart from the fact that Alan had already been violent towards her once and she had been afraid he might be again. Men who hit their wives and the women who were married to such men did not live in Wallasey. They lived down by the docks and off Scotland Road in the slum areas of the city. There was something too shameful about that kind of violence to discuss with anyone, and now that she was safe, and Alan was being forced to behave as he should, Bella wanted to forget that horrible moment when she had thought he was going to hurt her.

'Your father's told Mr Parker that in his shoes he'd think again about Alan staying at home whilst other young men are fighting. Everyone knows that some unscrupulous families are getting their sons jobs in reserved occupations, and Daddy told him outright that he didn't think that kind of thing would go down very well with the rest of the council, or in the newspapers if they were to get wind of it. People talk, and it certainly doesn't create the right impression, not now that so many young men arc volunteering.

'No, I know. Alan's joined the Local Defence Volunteers this week, so when he isn't working, he's out doing things with them.'

'Daddy's had a word about those refugees you've got billeted on you, and said how worried we are that running round after them all the time might be too much for you in your condition. I'm afraid, though, that nothing can be done at the moment, darling, not with all these new refugees coming over from Holland and Belgium.'

Bella nodded again. In some ways now that Jan had gone to join the other Polish pilots at Northolt, she didn't mind quite as much as she had done about having the two women there. At least their presence meant that she didn't have to be on her own with Alan, who thankfully had started going home to his mother's for his tea, and not coming home until Bella was safely in bed.

Monday 27 May

'They've said in the papers that Hitler's given the order to the Panzers to halt so that the Luftwaffe can finish off the BEF, and then bomb England.' Jean's face was white and set, her voice shaking.

'Do they know, do you think? Luke and all those other boys?'

'Oh, Mum, don't,' begged Grace. It was her half-day and she had come home to spend it with her family, knowing that they, like her, would be filled with anxiety and despair over the increasingly bad news that had been coming in ever since Amiens and Arras had fallen to the Germans on 20 May, and the German Forces had then broken through to reach the English Channel, whilst the British Expeditionary Force retreated. But what would happen when they reached the Channel and were at Hitler's mercy?

Even the twins were affected by the mood of fear and despair that was gripping everyone, their gramophone silent and their faces drawn with apprehension.

Francine listened to her elder sister, her own heart feeling as though it was being wrenched apart. She should not have come back. She knew that now. Better perhaps to have stayed in America and not known how Vi had betrayed her and she in turn had betrayed Jack. Nothing she could say could persuade Vi to change her mind and tell her where Jack was. She had even tried to find out from his school, but the school had told Vi, who had been furious with her – and anyway, as she had discovered, Vi had arranged a private evacuation for Jack, sending him away before his school had gone.

Now with Jean so obviously sick with fear for her own son, Francine couldn't bring herself to ask her yet again to try to persuade Vi to relent. At least Jack was safe. But was he happy? Vi did not love him – Francine had known that immediately. That was the hardest thing of all for her to bear. How could she not have known before? Why had she not had a mother's instinct to warn her that Vi had not kept her promise to her and loved Jack as though he truly had been her own?

'What will happen to them, Sam? If the Germans take them prisoner.' Jean's voice cracked with fear.

'General Lord Gort will have them all evacuated before that happens,' Sam told her, but Jean could see that he wasn't any more convinced than she was herself that it would be possible to bring so many men home safely so very quickly.

According to the papers, Hitler's Panzers had now taken Calais and were surrounding the BEF at a place called Dunkirk, where they were now trapped. The inconveniences of war the month had brought, like the increase in the cost of petrol and the butter ration being cut, meant very little when compared with what was happening on the other side of the Channel.

Jean went to put the kettle on whilst they all sat close to the wireless, waiting for the BBC news, just like virtually every other household in the land.

British and French Forces held a thirty-mile stretch of coastline running from Gravelines through Dunkirk to Nieuport. Inland the front reached almost to Lille, where the French Divisions were surrounded by seven German ones.

Lord Gort's BEF was determined to get home

come hell or high water, according to the papers, and despite everything the Germans could throw at them on land, by sea and in the air, and Lord Gort was equally determined to have them home. But the country waiting desperately for news of its men knew the enormity of that task and the slenderness of it being accomplished.

The news came on. Jean's hand trembled so much she couldn't even pour the boiling water onto the tea leaves and had to let Grace do it for her.

When the newsreader announced that eight thousand men had been evacuated from Dunkirk's beaches Jean sobbed out aloud.

'Eight thousand? But there are three hundred and fifty thousand of them to bring home.'

Sam got up and went over to her, putting his arms around her. Sharp tears stung Grace's eyes. She had never seen her mother like this, and her stomach churned sickeningly at the thought of the fate of all those brave men who were still there.

NINETEEN

Saturday 1 June

Every man on the ward was listening to the wireless that Sister had unexpectedly allowed to be brought in, as the BBC reported the latest numbers of soldiers evacuated from Dunkirk.

The nurses were listening as keenly as the patients as they went about their duties of setting up trolleys and trays for bed baths, temperature taking, and the giving out of medicine.

'Another sixty-eight thousand brought off yesterday,' old Mr Whitehead announced with evident satisfaction. 'That's just under two hundred thousand brought back safe, by my reckoning.'

Grace paused to smile at this good news before checking that the wheels of his bed were all turned inwards just as they should be.

The whole country had been holding its collective breath and saying its heartfelt prayers, following the speedy evacuation of the BEF, elated with relief when they heard a new report of more men brought off, and then plunged down into anxiety again when there were reports of the ships bringing them home being hit by the Luftwaffe despite the RAF's stalwart attempts to keep them at bay. At least three Allied destroyers had been sunk and seven more damaged in one of the worst air attacks, on 29 May.

'Aye, but what about them that are still there?' Bill Johnson, another patient, asked grimly. 'By my reckoning there are still a hundred and fifty thousand of them left.'

'Time to take your temperature, please, Mr Johnson,' Grace warned him firmly, but she was smiling at him as he dutifully obliged and stopped speaking so that she could carry out her task and then mark his temperature down on his chart before moving on to the next bed.

'Gort won't stop until he's got them all back safe, and neither will Admiral Ramsay,' Mr Whitehead insisted loyally.

'Gort's back in England now and what's left of the BEF will have to look to Major General Harold Alexander, poor sods. They haven't got a cat in hell's chance,' said Bill Johnson.

'We can't give up on them,' Grace burst out, looking up from the empty bed she and Nurse Ellis, the other junior, were about to start making up, forgetting herself for a moment as her emotions overwhelmed her, her face burning when Staff Nurse Reid frowned in her direction.

'The lass is right,' one of the other men said. 'We've got to keep hoping and praying for them, even if it's a miracle we'll be praying for.'

No explanation had been given to the junior nurses as to why they had had to make up extra beds and prepare those patients who were considered almost well enough to go home to leave earlier than originally planned, but they had all guessed that the empty beds could be needed for returning injured soldiers.

Teddy confirmed this when he and Grace managed to snatch five minutes together at lunchtime.

'We're all on standby in case we're needed to bring back the wounded from Lime Street when they're brought off the trains.'

He wasn't looking very well, and it seemed to Grace that he was finding it harder than normal to breathe but she knew that telling him to rest was all too likely to have the opposite effect to what she wanted.

There'd been no word as yet from Luke, and although her father kept on saying that no news was good news in an attempt to cheer up her mother, Grace could see in her eyes what she feared. For the first time since she had started her nurse's training, Grace wished she was still in the St John Ambulance Brigade, since their volunteers were all being sent to the stations to be ready for the troop trains coming up from the south coast bringing the BEF men back to their bases.

The military hospitals down south had taken those most in need of emergency treatment, of course, but as Teddy had warned her, their own hospital was on an alert ready to take injured men for whom there were no hospital beds else-where.

Seb closed his eyes, but it was no use, the images were still there. Marie, her brown eyes fierce with determination as she told him that even if she could leave for safety with him, she would not do so.

'France is my country. And if I must die for her then I will do so. I cannot do the work you have trained me for in your country, Sebastion, you know that. My place is here.'

Had he been naïve or just stupid in not under-standing how the pressure of the secret and urgent work he had been sent to France to do might affect him? When he had been recruited in England, trained and then sent to France to help set up and, in turn, train cells of Frenchmen and women to use special codes and wireless equip-ment to report back to England, if, as now looked likely, France should fall, it had never occurred to him that he might feel like this. He had argued fiercely with Command in England to be allowed to stay on and work with those he had trained, but he had been told that his role was now over and he must return to England. Like a coward, leaving those braver than he to face the enemy and, in all probability, to die. None of them was under any illusions. The life of a member of an underground cell was more likely to be short than long. Short and extremely unpleasant, if they were captured and tortured. He could feel the sweat breaking out on his forehead.

The train travelling north had been full of BEF men returning home and he had only just managed to squeeze on to it. He'd been later leaving France than originally planned and had got caught up in the retreat. When the Luftwaffe had machine-gunned the line of men he was standing in, waiting to get on board one of boats at Dunkirk, he'd ended up with a shoulder wound – nothing serious, he'd been told. He had a day in London being debriefed, with his shoulder hurting like hell, unable to get Marie's face out of his mind, and now he was on his way to Liverpool to take up his new post at Derby House, as a member of an offshoot of what was known as the 'Y' Section. Their 'secret' job was to listen in to enemy Morse code and other messages, translate them, and then pass them on to their headquarters at Bletchley Park.

Sebastion had not wanted to recruit Marie in the first place. She had been too young, in his opinion, and too pretty, the kind of girl that men would always look at. They had been taught to look for recruits who could fade into the background and pass unnoticed. Marie, though, had been determined. She had been good as well, quick to learn, cool and controlled, where some of the recruits were too hot-headed and reckless.

Her circumstances had been perfect for their purpose as well. Her parents owned a small bar where she worked, the kind of place where comings and goings were a normal part of its daily routine. Even better had been that beneath the tabac was a series of interconnecting cellars, two of which they had hidden behind a false wall.

From that cellar Marie would report back to England. He should have been there with her. He had recruited her and he felt responsible for her. But orders were orders, and his were to return to England. He'd still felt like shit climbing into that boat, hearing a young sailor telling him cheerfully, 'Soon have you back in Blighty, old chum.'

No, he shouldn't have recruited her. He should have turned her away, left her safe to grow up and get married and have children of her own, instead of risking her life. And she would risk that. He had read that in her face. She was fiercely and proudly partisan about her country and her desire for its freedom, for its liberty, and equality.

He had left her knowing that the German Army was advancing, knowing that it was his duty to obey his own orders, and knowing too that he despised and hated himself for leaving her behind to face what she would have to.

'I would not have it any other way,' she had told him when he had said this to her, and begged her to let him take her to safety. 'My choice is to fight for my country. My safety counts as nothing compared with that.'

Jean had been working down at Lime Street as a volunteer, her heart shredded with shocked anguish by what she saw in the expressions of the returning men. Some were still wearing their battledress, sea-stained and in some cases bloodstained as well, the smell of damp khaki sharp on the nostrils, especially when allied to unwashed flesh.

Some of the men were so exhausted that she'd had to hold the cup for them so that they could drink the tea she was handing out. Great big tall, broad-shouldered men, trembling and crying like babies in their disbelieving relief at being spared the fate they had thought would be theirs, and shame for their public defeat.

And all the time she was offering kind words and a drink of tea, Jean was scanning the sea of male faces, looking for Luke's.

Some families had already had word via one of the postcards provide by the WVS, which the men had filled in as they passed through the English ports; others had received telephone calls. But the Campions had heard nothing. And now, six days after the final evacuation had taken place, Jean could hardly bear to think of where Luke might be.

Over forty thousand men had been left behind to be taken prisoner by the Germans – if they were lucky. Others had been killed by the Luftwaffe in those ships that had been sunk. The needs of the living must, of course, always come before those of the dead and, as Sam kept saying, they shouldn't give up hope.

'I'll take over here now, Mrs Campion,' one of the other members of the WVS group offered.

Tiredly, Jean nodded. She had been at Lime Street since early this morning and she needed to get home. Sam would be wanting his tea.

* * *

'I thought they said we'd be taking a few of the overspill that they couldn't find beds for,' Hannah complained wearily to Grace as they each grabbed a quick bite of supper. 'We've been operating non-stop since nine o'clock this morning.'

'Our ward's full,' Grace agreed between mouthfuls of shepherd's pie, 'and as I came down for supper Sister was saying that we'd have to fit in another four beds. Some of those poor men, though, Hannah. What they must have been through.'

'I know,' she agreed quietly. 'We've had some really nasty injuries in, arms and legs gone – and worse – caused by shrapnel.'

They looked at one another.

'Mr Leonard operated on two men who he reckons won't last the night. And then there was a lad, only seventeen, half his face gone.'

Grace put down her fork, her food suddenly tasting like sawdust.

The first thing Jean saw when she walked into her kitchen through the back door was the army greatcoat thrown over the back of a chair, salt-stained and encrusted in places with dark splodges that her brain hoped were mud, but which the sickening twisting pain in her heart told her were blood.

Then she looked up from the coat and saw Luke standing in the doorway to the hall, his gruff, 'Mum,' having her running to him, tears spilling from her eyes, a choke of something she couldn't truthfully articulate clogging in her throat as his arms closed round her and she hugged him tightly.

'You're back.'

'Got home half an hour ago. Wasn't sure whether or not there'd be anyone in so I went round to the Salvage Corps' HQ in Hatton Gardens to see if Dad was around, and luckily he was.'

Now Jean could see that Sam was standing in the hallway behind Luke, a look of fierce fatherly love and pride in his eyes. Fresh tears filled her own as she mentally said a thankful prayer for her son's safe return home, and added another for the renewal of the father-and-son bond she had feared at one time had been destroyed for ever.

From upstairs the sound of one of the twins' favourite records suddenly broke the silence.

Releasing Luke, Jean shook her head and exclaimed, 'Oh, for goodness' sake. I'll go up and tell them to turn that off.'

'No don't, Mum,' Luke urged her. There were shadows in his eyes and in the sharper lines of his face Jean could see the man he had now become. 'There's bin many a time these last few days when I've have given anything to know I'd hear them playing that gramophone of theirs again. Aye, and plenty of times when I thought I wouldn't, an' all.' His voice broke, his hand shaking as he reached into his pocket for his cigarettes, turning away from her to light one. Because he did not want her to see what he was feeling?

Sam's calm, 'Get the kettle on, love; we're both gasping,' and the quick jerk of his head in Luke's direction behind Luke's back helped to steady her. This was a time when Luke needed his dad, perhaps even more than he needed her. There were things they could say to one another man to man, perhaps, that Luke would not want to say to her.

'He's had a bad time, hasn't he?' she asked Sam later when, after a bath and a change of clothes, Luke had insisted on going up to the hospital to try to see Grace and tell her that he was back safely.

'I've got a couple of injured mates who might be up there, so I can see them as well,' he had told them before he left.

'Yes,' Sam told her. 'He's told me a bit about it but not all of it, I reckon. That's how it is for a man; there are some things that he can only talk about freely with them that was there with him. It's a bit like that in the Corps sometimes, when we've had a bad 'un to deal with. According to what he's told me they were given the order to retreat to Dunkirk and then told it was every man for himself. The Royal Engineers had built a bridge, which they held for them. Seemingly they only just got across it before the RAF blew it up to stop the Germans from making use of it. When they got close to Dunkirk, Luke said that all they could see was smoke from the fires because of the Germans bombing the oil depots. They were sent to a place called La Panne. Luke said if you've ever imagined hell then La Panne was it.'

Jean bit her lip. She knew how it would have

affected Sam to think of his son exposed to such horror and danger, and him not being there with him to protect him.

'There were men queuing everywhere: across the sand and right out into the water waiting to be taken off the beach, and all the time the queues were getting longer. Luke said he saw one captain threatening to shoot his own men when they broke ranks and tried to make for the sea instead of joining one of the lines. There was a beach master in charge of it all, but he didn't have any control over the Germans, who were dive-bombing the men as they stood there.'

Jean had started to tremble. Even though Luke was safe, the pictures Sam was creating inside her head were sharply shocking and painful.

'Three days it took them to reach Dunkirk, and then another two waiting to be taken off, all that time with no food and only the water they'd brought with them.'

Sam sighed. 'Our Luke was only a lad when he left us, Jean, but he's come back a man. They were dive-bombed by the Germans over and over again, and Luke said that you never knew when it was going to happen but when it did you didn't dare leave the line in case you lost your place so you just had to throw yourself down in the sand where you were and hope for the best.

'He said that the captain, the same one that had threatened to shoot his own men, had to put a bullet through a poor lad who'd been that badly wounded he couldn't have survived. Then, when they finally got their turn to get onto one of the boats taking the men out to the ships, it almost capsized and the three men last on had to get off again. Luke said he saw a ship bombed and set ablaze from stem to stern, men jumping off it in all directions.'

'Oh, Sam, it just doesn't bear thinking about.'

'Maybe not, love, but it has to be thought about, because if we don't think about it then we won't fight ruddy Hitler and he won't be stopped. We need to stop him, Jean. We need to stop him, and we ruddy well will.'

Grace had never seen the area inside the main entrance to the hospital as busy and crowded as it was today. Everywhere she looked there seemed to be men in uniform – mainly the walking wounded, who had been told to report to their nearest hospital once they reached home, and also, of course, the close relatives of those who had received far more serious injuries and who had been brought to the hospital by ambulance.

She just had time to dash outside and have a quick word with Teddy before she was due back on her ward, to reassure herself that he was not overdoing things, and she was squeezing past the crowd in the doorway when she heard Luke calling her name.

By the time she had turned round to look for him Luke had reached her and her relief at seeing him uninjured made her hug him tightly and blink back her tears.

'Come and say hello to Teddy,' she begged him. 'He'll want to hear everything. We've read such dreadful stories in the papers.'

A quick look at Luke's face told her that the reality had been even more terrible than the stories.

'I'll catch up with Teddy another time,' Luke told her. 'I was hoping that Lillian might be on duty. I wanted to tell her myself that I'd made it back. She's the loveliest girl and very special to me, Grace.'

Grace's heart sank.

'She is, and she's on Women's Surgical, but I doubt that you'll be able to see her. The sister on that ward is a real dragon. Luke . . .' She wanted to warn him not to expect too much. She had no idea what Lillian might have said privately to him, of course, in the letters they had been exchanging, but she did know that Lillian had been going out with other men, and that she did not in any way consider herself committed to him.

'At least Charlie's safe. He sent us a telegram to tell us.'

'Did he say when he was coming home?' Bella asked her mother. Every returning BEF man who did not require hospital treatment had been given an extended period of home leave.

'He says that he isn't. He feels it's his duty to help one of his friends who had a bit of a bad time so he's going to be staying with him in London.'

Bella yawned in the afternoon sunshine of her

parents' garden. Being pregnant was so dreadfully tiring. All she seemed to want to do was sleep.

Teddy had been as pleased about Luke's safe return as Grace had known he would be, and Grace's heart was light with relief as she made her way back to the ward. The four empty beds were now occupied, along with the small private side wards. An army officer, his own arm bandaged, was touring the beds, accompanied by Sister.

'We've got six new patients down from surgery, Campion,' Staff Nurse Reid informed Grace crisply, 'two who are very poorly and in the side wards; two with amputations and two with shrapnel wounds. Go and collect the necessary bowls and start with these two in beds twelve and fourteen.'

The bowls were for the patients to be sick in after they recovered from the anaesthetic, and beds twelve and fourteen held the less seriously injured shrapnel-wounded patients who would come round properly first.

The young soldier in bed twelve retched gratefully into the bowl, looking embarrassed when he had finished, and Grace wiped his face and then allowed him a small sip of water.

'Eee, Nurse, I feel that helpless, just like a baby,' he told her.

'Well, you aren't a baby; you're a very brave man,' Grace comforted him, 'but you must try to lie still. We don't want all Mr Leonard's nice stitches coming out, do we?'

The grin he gave her told her that she had hit

the right note. And Grace smiled at him as she took his temperature and then noted it down on the chart at the bottom of his bed.

It was normal, which was good, because hopefully that meant that his wound was infection free.

He was already closing his eyes and relaxing into sleep as she moved from his bed to the next one.

Its dark-haired occupant was lying with his face turned away from her, his shoulder bandaged.

'I dare say you'll be feeling a bit poorly,' she began as she walked round the other side of the bed, but the automatic words she had now learned by heart remained unspoken when she recognised him.

'Seb . . . Sebastion.'

His eyes had been closed but now they opened and he focused on her. When he had told her how important it was that she went ahead with her nurse's training, Grace knew that neither of them had really imagined that those words would have such a real and personal meaning.

'You . . .' He was frowning now and Grace suspected he was having difficulty remembering her name. Any chagrin she might have felt was quickly set aside by her training and professionalism as she recognised that he was in pain and still very much under the influence of the anaesthetic.

'Yes, it's me, Grace Campion,' she told him calmly. 'You've had an operation to have some shrapnel removed from your shoulder, and I dare say you're

feeling a bit poorly right now. You may want . . .'
Just in time Grace thrust the bowl under his chin.

Unlike her first patient, Seb had a temperature
a bit higher than it should have been. She made
the appropriate note on his chart.

It had given her quite a turn at first to see him
lying there. She'd certainly make sure she gave him
the best nursing she could to thank him for what
he had done for her.

She told Teddy about the coincidence of having
Seb on her ward as they shared a cigarette together
after she had come off duty.

'I'm so glad that Luke is all right. Mum will
be over the moon. He's her favourite, although
she'd never admit it. He told me that two of the
men in front of him in the queue for the boats
were killed when they were dive-bombed. Those
poor boys, Teddy – from what I've heard they've
been through so much. It's a miracle we've got as
many of them back as we did, but Luke said he
reckoned there were a lot that didn't make it.'

'Aye,' Teddy agreed, 'and a lot that did make
it that are in a bad way. We brought some back
from Lime Street with injuries that bad you wonder
if they'd have been better off if someone had
finished them off,' Teddy told her bluntly.

'We've got two boys on our ward in a terrible
state,' Grace agreed. 'Mr Leonard's done his best
but one poor boy has half his face missing and the
other's lost his mind. He still thinks he's on the beach.
It's pitiful, Teddy.'

He put his arm around her shoulders and gave her a brief hug. 'You've got to be strong for them, Grace, otherwise you won't be able to do your job. They've done their bit for us, now we owe it to them to do ours.'

'Luke said that the worst thing to bear was feeling ashamed because they'd had to retreat. He said they couldn't believe it when they were on the train and they saw so many people at every station they passed through waving to them and cheering them on.'

'That's because it weren't their fault . . . I've been down to the Odeon today and booked us tickets for that *Gone With the Wind* you said you wanted to see. I thought it might cheer you up a bit.'

Grace had almost forgotten about the film that had taken America by storm and which had now premiered in London.

'Oh, Teddy, you are kind,' she told him gratefully.

'We could have a bit of summat to eat first, if you like, p'haps at Joe Lyons?' Teddy suggested.

'I'd like that,' Grace agreed, stifling a small yawn.

It had been a long and very tiring day, and the relief of having Luke safely home on top of so much hard work had left her feeling drained.

'You look half asleep on your feet,' said Teddy. 'You'd better go in and get some kip.'

'Yes, I must,' Grace agreed. 'Sister warned us before we came off duty that we're going to have to make up more beds in the morning because more troop trains are due. We may even need to put beds in the corridors.' She stifled another yawn.

Britain might be on daylight saving time and it was still light outside, but Sister was a stickler for routine and rules, so that on her ward, the blackout curtains were put in place at ten p.m. promptly, and her patients expected to go immediately to sleep.

Seb, though, could not sleep. He had refused the morphine he had been offered by the very efficient-looking senior nurse who had come round after Grace had gone off duty, and now his shoulder hurt like hell, far more so than it had done before he had had the shrapnel removed. Quite a coincidence, being nursed by Grace . . .

Lying here surrounded by injured men from Dunkirk reinforced the enormity of what had happened, and the battle that now lay ahead of them if they were to have any hope of winning this war. So many thought that they could not win it.

The man in the side ward who had lost his mind was reliving the hours he had spent on the beach, sobbing and screaming as he pleaded to be saved.

The solder in the next bed to his own muttered, 'Poor sod. Every time I close me eyes all I can see is me mate lying there next to me with his legs blown off, and saying he was worried about getting in one of the boats because he couldn't swim. We had to leave him there on the beach. Best not to think about it, though, otherwise you'd go as mad as him over there. Then ruddy Hitler would have won, wouldn't he, 'cos he won't be doing no more fighting. I will, though, and when I do, and when I aim that gun, it will be me mate I'll be thinking about. I can't bring him back but I can sure as hell make them pay for what they did to him.'

The screaming had stopped now but the sobbing continued. Seb thought of Marie. There didn't seem much chance of the French and those British who had been left to fight alongside them holding back the Germans for very long.

The Germans would deal ruthlessly with anyone who opposed them, and Marie was so bloody patriotic and proud of it that she would stand up to them and put herself in danger. He had never known anyone like her. Being French had been more important to her than anything else, including being a woman. She put many men he knew to shame, including himself. He could quite easily have imagined her in a different age, storming the Bastille and demanding liberty for the people and death for those who oppressed them. But knowing that could not take away the guilt he felt at leaving and being safe, whilst she and her family were not.

'They have their work and you have yours,' his commanding officer had told him. 'That is the nature of this work. You have done your bit with them in the field, now you are needed here to work on something else.'

'Have you heard the latest?' Hannah asked Grace as they walked to their rooms together. 'Lillian's found herself that medic she was wanting; one of the new housemen, that one who caught her when she fainted. Doreen says he's besotted with her and she's like a cat with a full bowl of cream.

What's wrong?' she asked when she saw Grace's expression.

'Luke, my brother, came to see me this afternoon. He was at Dunkirk and lucky enough not get be injured. I did try to warn him not to get too keen on Lillian, but she's obviously still been writing to him and he seems to think that they're an item.'

'Oh, what rotten luck for him,' Hannah sympathised. 'She'll have to tell him, of course. Let's just hope that she lets him down lightly.'

'Yes,' Grace agreed hollowly.

Seb watched as Grace approached his bed. He hadn't slept very well and the wound in his shoulder was throbbing painfully.

The men who had been on the ward for the greatest length of time had been quick to fill in the new arrivals on the ward's routine and its nurses. Grace, he had learned, was well liked by the patients, who considered her to be kind and compassionate as well as a good nurse.

'A lovely-looking lass, 'an all,' one of the men had said. 'Walking out with one of the ambulance drivers, she is, so I've heard.'

Seb wasn't surprised, of course, that a pretty girl like Grace was walking out with someone.

He remembered very well how tempted to kiss her he had been himself. The Tennis Club dance seemed to belong to another life now, one he could hardly relate to any more. He tried to move and stopped as pain shot through his shoulder.

Immediately Grace was at his bedside, smiling calmly as she fluffed up his pillow and poured him a fresh glass of water.

To his embarrassment his body was responding to the thought of kissing her in a way it had no right to at all. To stop it he said to her, 'It's not just a nurse's uniform you've got now, from what I hear. You're going steady with an ambulance driver as well.'

Grace looked over her shoulder to make sure that Sister wasn't watching them. They weren't supposed to talk about their private lives to the patients.

'If you're meaning Teddy, then him and me aren't going steady, we're just friends,' she told him with great dignity.

Seb was surprised at how much that pleased him.

'I've just got to take your temperature now,' said Grace, determined to be professional, 'and if you could use this . . .'

She didn't look at him as she handed him the urine bottle, and Seb was surprised at how self-conscious he suddenly felt in view of the way he'd been prodded and checked over by so many nurses these last few days. War, after all, had a way of causing a man to lose his embarrassment about any bodily functions – or at least some of them, he corrected himself, remembering his discomfort over his 'short arm' reaction to the thought of kissing Grace.

Seb's temperature was higher than it had been

last night. Grace frowned. His colour was high as well.

'I'd better just check your pulse.'

'Give over, Nurse,' the man in the next bed joked. 'We all know you only do that 'cos you want to hold our hands.'

Grace laughed and managed to fight back her unwanted blush. Seb's pulse was faster than it should be and his skin felt hot and dry. He was manifesting all the classic signs that his wound could be infected. There wasn't anything on his chart about changing his dressings but Mr Leonard would be doing his round later, she knew, and would naturally check up on those patients on whom he had recently operated. Even so, it wouldn't do any harm just to mention her suspicions to Staff, would it?

She waited until the staff nurse was on her own and then hurried over to her, quickly explaining what concerned her. Staff Nurse Reid gave her a searching look before going over to Seb's bed, where she checked both his chart and redid his temperature.

As discreetly as she could Grace watched her whilst she collected the bottles to take to the sluice for urine tests. Staff was now speaking with Sister. They both went over to Seb's bed, and then Sister demanded, 'Screens, please, Nurse.'

Leaving the bottles, Grace hurried over to help the ward's second-year nurse wheel the heavy screens into place around Seb's bed.

As soon as they were in place Sister told her, 'Dressings trolley, Campion.'

It was Staff Nurse Reid herself who removed the dressing on Seb's shoulder wound. Grace had plenty of experience of unpleasant sights now but for some reason the hole left in Seb's flesh where Mr Leonard had removed the shrapnel so shocked her that she thought for a moment she might actually faint. Or was it the smell of the infected wound that was affecting her? It shouldn't be. She had seen and smelled far worse on gangrenous wounds and amputations.

Grace tried to focus professionally on Seb's shoulder. The skin had been torn by the shrapnel, one piece having been removed originally and the wound stitched without the surgeon realising there was a smaller piece left inside. Mr Leonard had had to dig deeper to remove it, and the area around the wound was very inflamed and infected, probably because of the shrapnel left inside, Grace recognised.

'Mitchell, go down and ask Dr Greenlow if he can spare a minute, will you?' Sister was saying to the second-year nurse.

'This looks a bit sore,' she said to Seb. 'I'm going to ask the houseman to let you have some morphine to ease the pain a bit.'

Within ten minutes Mitchell was injecting the morphine into Seb's arm whilst the houseman frowned over his wound and instructed Sister to place a temporary dressing on it until Mr Leonard did his round.

'Well spotted, Campion,' Staff Nurse Reid complimented Grace as she followed her into the sluice.

Grace desperately wanted to ask her if Seb would be all right but she knew that she couldn't. Septicaemia from an infected wound was something they all dreaded. All they could do was keep the wound as clean as possible and give the patient M and B tablets. If with a wound like Seb's the infection did spread, then that meant that the infected limb had to be amputated to save the patient's life. Grace's hands shook.

TWENTY

'Aw, come on, old girl, you can spare a tenner for your hero brother, surely?' Charlie wheedled.

'Charlie, please stop asking me. I've already told you that I can't. Besides, you're making my head ache,' Bella complained.

It was hot, and she felt so uncomfortable, what with being sick in the mornings.

She had been pleased at first when Charlie had come back from London to spend the remainder of his leave at home and had then taken to calling round to see her. She had persuaded him to take her to the Tennis Club, where they had sat in the bar and she had basked in the glory of having a hero brother, whilst the men who were not themselves in uniform clustered round Charlie, wanting to hear the story of how he had saved the life of a fellow soldier when he would have drowned and had dragged him on board the ship that had brought them home.

'Well, I just hope they give you a medal for it, risking your own life like that,' had been their mother's reaction.

Bella was bored now, though, with hearing the tale of Charlie's heroism, and cross about his constant requests for money.

'I should have thought you'd have wanted to help me out, seeing how I helped you out when you wanted to marry Alan,' Charlie told her pointedly.

'Well, I have helped you out. I gave you ten pounds on Saturday and another five yesterday.' Her head really was aching and her ankles were dreadfully puffy and swollen, although her tummy was still flat, probably because she was being sick so much.

She looked fretfully towards the back door, half wishing that Charlie would leave so that she could go upstairs and lie down.

'Speaking of Alan, he doesn't seem to be around much,' said Charlie.

'He's very busy at work.'

'Good-looking piece, that girl that's billeted on you. In Alan's shoes I reckon I'd have taken to coming home for my lunch just to get an eyeful of her,' Charlie grinned.

'Well, you aren't in Alan's shoes,' Bella snapped, not wanting to be reminded of the fact that Alan had already had far more than an eyeful of another woman.

'Where did you say she worked?'

'I didn't,' Bella told him, wondering suspiciously if her brother really thought she was going to lend him money that he might spend on taking out a refugee.

No matter how much she had initially resented their presence in her home, the truth that she hardly dared to admit to herself was that she still felt safer having them there, especially with the temper Alan always seemed to be in. Not that she would ever admit as much to anyone, much less to them. Instead she had told herself that everything would be all right once she had had the baby and Alan had calmed down. He just needed a bit of time to get used to the fact that she was his wife, and that he was a husband and a father, that was all. With Trixie now out of reach with those relatives of hers up north, he would soon forget all about her and realise where his best interests lay.

'You want to watch that temper of yours, Bella,' Charlie warned her. He got up, putting his hands in his pockets and jingling his change. 'I'm off to the Tennis Club. I won't ask you to come with me, seeing as you're in such a sour mood.'

Bella went into the kitchen half-heartedly splashing cold water on her face and wrists in an attempt to cool herself down. The post had brought yet another letter for Bettina and her mother from Jan. Bella recognised his handwriting. How could she not do when he seemed to write to them virtually every other day?

Grace knew the minute she walked into the kitchen at home on her day off and saw Luke, that whilst Lillian had obviously 'let him down' it had not been lightly.

'Where is everyone?' she asked him.

'Mum's gone down to the allotment to see Dad, Aunt Francine's at a rehearsal and the twins are at school. I suppose you know about me and Lillian, do you?'

Grace nodded. 'Don't look like that,' she begged him. 'She isn't worth it, Luke, honestly she isn't.'

'She looked at me like I was the last person in the world she wanted to see,' Luke told her miserably. 'Said she was seeing someone else and that it was serious. *Serious*. When she'd been writing to me like she was my sweetheart! She said she wanted to tell me that but that you'd begged her not to.'

'That's not true,' Grace gasped. 'It was me that wanted her to tell you.'

Now wasn't the time to tell him that she had tried to warn him, not when he was so very upset.

'So who is he, then, this someone else she's so serious about?'

Grace shook her head.

'Come on, tell me. I suppose it's someone in a reserved occupation, is it?'

Grace recoiled from his bitterness even whilst she could understand it. Lillian's rejection of him was bound to be so much worse for coming so closely on top of Dunkirk and what he'd been through.

'He's a doctor,' she told him quietly. 'She told us right from the start that that was why she was going into nursing; because she wanted to marry a doctor.'

'A doctor. No wonder she was turning her nose up at me then.'

'Luke, don't.'

'Don't what? Make the same mistake again? You can bet your boots I won't. From now on I'm going to make sure that no woman gets the chance to make a fool of me a second time.'

Their parents' return from the allotment brought an end to their conversation, Luke giving Grace a warning look that told her that he didn't want her saying anything about what had happened.

'Do you think that Hitler really will invade us like everyone's saying he will?' Sasha asked her parents anxiously later when they were all having tea.

'I don't know, love,' Jean admitted, whilst Luke and Grace exchanged silent looks.

Grace knew that Luke was pretty sure that the Germans would invade now that they had broken through to the Channel.

'We've all got to be prepared for the worst,' said Sam sombrely. 'France has surrendered and the Germans have got the Channel Islands now.'

'They'll never take Liverpool, though, Dad,' said Lou stoutly, tucking into her fish pie, her words making them all smile.

'Aye, well, we'll certainly put up a good fight, love,' Sam agreed, nodding his head when Jean offered him a second helping of pie.

'Have you had any news about where you'll be posted to yet, Luke?'

'I met up this morning with one of the other

lads who came back on the same troop train. He reckons that since we've both been told to report for duty to Seacombe barracks, we'll be based there on Home Duties, because Churchill won't want to risk not having the men to defend the country if Hitler does try to invade. You know, Mum, you might want to think again about you and the twins evacuating. They reckon that Liverpool is bound to be one of the Luftwaffe's targets, on account of the docks,' Luke warned.

Jean shook her head. She'd eaten her own pie and was about to get up to fetch the Eve's pudding, which she knew was Sam and Luke's favourite. 'Me and the girls are staying here. My place is here with your dad, and we're a family. If Hitler's going to go for us then we're better off sticking together.'

'Well, I certainly don't want to be evacuated, like poor Jack,' Sasha told them. 'We were talking about him when we came home from school, weren't we, Auntie Francine, and me and Lou think it would be really nice if we could all go and see him. It's very mean of Auntie Vi not to tell us where he is.'

Jean put down the pudding she had been about to serve up and looked at Francine. She knew how her younger sister felt and she sympathised with her, but she didn't want her involving the twins in matters that were far more complicated than they could realise.

'I heard today that the BBC do want me to go to Bangor to try out for that show with Vera Lynn.

They've evacuated the Variety Entertainment Department out there, and Tommy Handley and that lot are there, according to one of the girls in the show with me.'

'It's a long way to go on the off chance, when you're already rehearsing for a show here, isn't it?' Jean asked her doubtfully. 'I mean, even if they want you it's not as though you can rely on the trains.'

'They've said that they'll send a car for me, and if they think I'm suitable then they'll put me up at an hotel in Bangor whilst I'm doing the shows.'

'They must think that you'll be good, otherwise they wouldn't ask you to go all that way,' said Grace.

'She is good, and we think she's better than Vera Lynn and Gracie Fields, don't we, Sasha?' Lou demanded of her twin.

Sasha nodded, and Jean's heart sank. The twins were rapidly growing to hero-worship Francine, and to her dismay they were constantly talking about wanting to go on the stage themselves, something she knew that Sam would never allow and something she wouldn't really want for them herself, not after what had happened to Francine.

Francine laughed and shook her head. 'I'm nowhere near as good as either of them. If I was I'd be the one who is a big star, wouldn't I?' said Francine.

'Me and Sasha think you should be. I bet the BBC will think so as well.'

'I doubt it, and even if they want me they don't pay very much.'

Francine was uncomfortably aware that Jean wasn't happy about the twins' admiration of her. She hadn't deliberately attempted to get them on her side, but they were evermore enthusiastic about their singing and dancing, and it was only natural that they should turn to her as someone who would understand how they felt.

They were excellent little dancers, and with them being identical twins Francine didn't think they would have much difficulty in polishing up a nice little act for a theatre show. She didn't want to do anything to alienate Jean, though. Not only was she genuinely fond of her elder sister, she also felt very grateful to her for letting her stay with them and for her attempts to persuade Vi to tell them where Jack was.

'I'd better go and get ready. We've got a show tonight,' she told them all.

After tea Grace helped her mother to do the washing up and told her about Seb.

'You say he's a bit poorly, then?' Jean asked her.

'Yes,' Grace confirmed. 'I went in to see how he was this morning before I came off duty. His temperature hasn't risen any higher, but it hasn't gone down either.'

Jean tried not to feel worried. She knew that Grace had a tender heart, but she had suspected all along with a mother's instinct that her daughter had been far more taken with Alan Parker's cousin than she had wanted to let on, and now she felt that her suspicions were being confirmed.

'So what's he doing in hospital up here, then? I thought you said he was from down south somewhere.'

'His parents live near London, but Seb said that he'd been posted up here after coming back from France. He didn't realise that he'd still got some shrapnel in his shoulder until he told the MO at Derby House when he reported for duty that he was having a lot of pain in his arm, and he sent him to us.'

'Have Bella and Alan been told that he's in hospital here?' Jean asked.

'I don't know,' Grace admitted.

'Well, dare say they will want to visit him, and Alan's parents as well, seeing as he's their nephew.'

'I don't think he cares very much for the Parkers,' Grace felt obliged to reveal. 'At least that's what he told me. He's only related to them by marriage really.'

There was no sign of Teddy or his ambulance when Grace arrived back at the hospital that evening, not that she expected to see him. He had told her that he planned to go to see his family, who Grace hadn't met but who she felt as though she knew from listening to Teddy talk about them.

They had agreed that it would only complicate things if they were to meet one another's families, mothers being the way they were. Her own mother had asked after Teddy as Grace was leaving, and she had told her truthfully that they were still just very good friends and that was the way they intended to stay.

When she walked into the hospital the only thought in her head had been to go to her room to catch up on some studying and then go to bed, but somehow or other she found herself making her way to the ward.

Staff Nurse Reid raised her eyebrows at the sight of her out of uniform and on her day off.

'I just thought I'd look in and see how Seb is,' Grace told her self-consciously, feeling obliged to explain when Staff started to frown, 'I know him, you see. Well, that is to say, his cousin is married to mine.'

Staff Nurse Reid studied her thoughtfully but her frown had gone.

'Sister normally expects nurses to tell us of any connection they have with patients on her ward when they're first admitted.'

'Yes, I'm sorry,' said Grace penitently, 'only with us only being related through marriage, and me having met him only the once, I wasn't sure.'

'Well, try to remember another time, Campion.' Staff was already turning away and Grace still hadn't found out how Seb actually was.

'Is he any better?' she asked.

'His temperature hasn't risen any higher, but when Mr Leonard came to look at his wound this afternoon he felt that it was looking a little bit worse.'

Her frown was back and Grace guessed that Staff

Nurse Reid shared the surgeon's concern. Grace had already noticed how the best kind of nurses seemed to develop with experience a sixth sense about their patients that went beyond the material evidence of temperature charts and the like.

TWENTY-ONE

Staff had been right: Seb was worse. So much worse, in fact, that Mr Leonard had ordered that he was to be moved into one of the private side wards. The same one in which the young sailor had died.

Remembering that now, Grace felt her heart contract as she looked down at him. His morphine had been increased to give him some relief from his pain, and although he was asleep, his body twitched violently on the bed with the onset of the withdrawal symptoms that came when the drug needed readministering.

He was talking in his drugged sleep, but not in English, Grace recognised, and not only in one language either, but the only word she could understand was the name he kept on saying.

'Marie.'

Whoever this Marie was, she was obviously on his mind, Grace acknowledged as she straightened his bed.

Sister came in, her uniform rustling with starch.

It was almost unheard of for her to do something as mundane as take a patient's temperature but that was exactly what she did now, informing Grace, 'I want you to check this patient's temperature every half an hour, Nurse, and report any changes to me.'

She then folded back the bedclothes and looked briefly at Seb's shoulder. Grace knew that she was looking for any telltale signs that he was suffering from blood poisoning from his wound. She had just looked herself, her heart thudding with relief when she had not seen the red line that would have meant the infection had entered his bloodstream.

'In addition you are to prepare and apply a fresh kaolin poultice to his wound every hour starting from now.'

Grace nodded. She knew that the kaolin clay, which had to be heated in a container placed in a pan of boiling water and then smeared on a sterile bandage before being placed as hot as possible against the infected wound, should draw any infected matter to the surface of the wound.

Mr Leonard had prescribed regular doses of M and B 693 for his patient, sulphanilamide being the only drug that had any effect against septicaemia.

Of course, Grace still had her normal ward duties to perform as well as the extra work Sister had given her, but she still made sure that she followed Sister's instructions to the letter, even foregoing her morning break rather than hurry the application of the kaolin poultices.

The edges of his wound, which had had to be reopened to remove the second piece of shrapnel, were very badly swollen and inflamed.

Mr Leonard did his round escorted by Sister and Staff, and stopped for a long time in the small side ward, but of course Grace, as a lowly first-year nurse, wasn't able to hang around in the hope of learning how Seb was.

Instead she had to do a locker round, and then go for her lunch, where she was dismayed to have to listen to Lillian going on about how wonderful her doctor boyfriend thought she was.

Poor Luke was better off without her, even though he himself couldn't recognise that as yet, Grace thought as she ignored both Lillian and her own sisterly desire to remind her of how much she had hurt her brother.

It was late in the afternoon before Grace was finally and almost disbelievingly able to look at the thermometer and see that Seb's temperature was finally dropping. She was so worried that she might be wrong that she took it again, ignoring Seb's irritated protests.

Her hand shook slightly as she wrote down the new temperature and then went to inform Sister.

They had given their first show at one of the munitions factories in Liverpool, and Francine was suffering from the normal tiredness that always hit her after a first public appearance in a new show as she opened the gate to the small front garden to Jean and Sam's house, and then stopped when she saw that the back gate was open.

Only the family used the back gate so she assumed that someone must already be in, and headed automatically for the back door instead, coming to a halt as she rounded the corner of the house and saw a small shabbily dressed boy curled up asleep on the back step.

She recognised him instantly and her heart turned over.

Going to him, she kneeled down beside him and put her arm around him, saying gently, 'Jack?'

He was awake immediately, fear tensing his body. His face was grubby and he had obviously been crying.

'It's all right,' Francine reassured him. 'You're Jack, aren't you? I'm your . . . I'm your Auntie Francine . . .'

He still looked apprehensive.

'Have you been here long?' Francine asked him. 'Only I expect you're feeling a bit hungry, aren't you? I know I am. Why don't we go inside and have something to eat whilst we wait for your Auntie Jean to come home.'

The sound of Jean's name had an immediate and relaxing effect on him, and although he didn't say anything he stood up readily enough whilst Francine unlocked the back door, keeping one arm around him whilst she did so. He was so thin, it tore at her heart. She could feel his bones through his shabby blazer and shirt – too thin, surely, for a boy his age.

* * *

Half an hour later, she'd made him a ham sandwich, which he'd eaten as though he was starving.

He'd run away, he'd admitted after she had patiently coaxed him into telling her what had happened. He'd run away because the couple he was living with had told him that the Government had stopped sending them money to pay for his keep and that his parents didn't want him any more.

The couple, who ran a smallholding of some sort, from what Francine could gather, had had three boys living with them, and all of them had been expected to work on the smallholding after school and at the weekends, but two of them had been taken home by their mother, and Jack had been forced to do their work as well as his own. He'd been kept short of food and threatened with beatings if he complained to anyone. The final straw had been when he had accidentally broken a plate and the woman had locked him in the cellar all night as punishment and then sent him off to school without any breakfast.

Instead of going back to the smallholding after school he had decided to run away and come home. He had walked to the local station and managed to get on to a train to Liverpool without anyone seeing him.

His quiet, 'I thought I'd come and see Auntie Jean instead of going home, and ask her to speak to Mum,' had torn at Francine's heart and she had only just managed to hold back her tears.

Now bathed and fed and wrapped in a towel

– she couldn't let him put his own filthy and shabby clothes back on again – and his story told, he was leaning against her so exhausted that he was falling asleep.

Very carefully Francine lifted her arm and put it round him, pulling him close to her. It seemed like a small but very special miracle that he was here, this thin ungainly boy who was all arms and legs but whose body curved as sweetly and rightly into her hold as he had done the day he had been born. Her arms tightened around him.

She was still holding him half an hour later when Jean and Sam came home.

Jean's face lost its colour when she saw him.

'Oh, Francine, what have you done?'

Francine shook her head and said quietly, 'It isn't what you think,' as Jack woke up and looked uncertainly at Jean.

'Well, Vi will have to be told.'

'But not yet, Jean,' Francine pleaded. 'At least let him have a decent night's sleep.'

Sam had carried Jack upstairs and laid him on Francine's bed when he had fallen asleep again halfway through retelling his story to Jean.

'Fran's right, love,' he said. 'Let the poor lad at least have his sleep.'

'But Vi will be so worried.'

'Mebbe, if she knows what's happened, but my guess is that this couple that had the lad and were supposed to be looking after him won't be in any rush to report him missing. Not after the way they've been treating him. They probably think he's around somewhere and that he'll have to come back to them. It will probably be the morning before they let anyone in authority know that he's gone, and even then I doubt anyone will be in a rush to let your Vi know. It was a real bit of luck for the lad, him getting on a train for Liverpool. He could have ended up anywhere.'

'He was so desperate to get away from those dreadful people that he probably would have risked doing that,' said Francine.

'Well, I suppose you're right, Sam, but if I were our Vi and it was my son—'

'But that's the whole point, isn't it, Jean?' Francine pointed out emotionally. 'If he had been your son, this wouldn't have happened.' Francine's voice broke. She got up and ran into the hall and up the stairs.

'Oh, Sam, I feel so awful. Fran's right. If we'd had him—'

'I'm not having you blaming yourself for any of this, Jean. Like I've said before, you were in no fit state to do anything for anyone when Jack was born. If anyone's to blame then it's the so-and-so who went and got your Fran into the trouble in the first place, and then your Vi for not doing right by Jack when she and Edwin took him on. I'm not saying that I don't feel it's a damn shame that the poor little tyke's bin treated the way he was, and I'm not saying neither that I don't feel like going and finding the chap who's bin treating him so badly and letting him know what I think of men like him, because I do. But we both know that it's ruddy Edwin who should be doing that. Not that he will. Let Francine have her bit of time with Jack, love. It's little enough, and even if your Vi does know that Jack's gone missing, which I doubt, it won't do her any harm to worry about him for once.'

Jean looked at her husband. 'Well, if that's what you think, Sam . . .'

'It is,' he told her firmly.

'Hello, there.'

Seb's voice might sound weak but there was no mistaking the fact that he was a lot better than he had been twenty-four hours ago, Grace acknowledged, hoping that her smile wasn't quite as wobbly as it felt and that it looked properly professional.

'Nurse Reid told me that it is thanks to your kaolin poulticing that I'm not going to lose my arm.'

Grace knew that she was blushing now.

'It's Staff Nurse Reid,' Grace reproved him firmly, 'and I dare say she said no such thing.'

She was doing a locker round and Sister encouraged her nurses to chat to the patients whilst doing this chore because she believed that giving the men a chance to talk about themselves could sometimes highlight problems they weren't willing to mention during a formal consultant's round.

'I admit I never really thought I'd be here and that you'd be nursing me when I made you promise to do your training.'

'I owe you such a lot over what you did for me,' said Grace.

'It all seems such a long time ago now, and in another life.'

'Yes,' Grace agreed. For no reason at all she was remembering how she had felt when he had kissed her and she suppressed another blush.

'Sister said I was rambling away in French. I just hope I didn't say anything too ripe that I shouldn't have said in a woman's presence.'

Grace shook her head. 'The only word I could make out properly was "Marie". You kept saying it over and over again, and I thought that maybe she was a girl you'd fallen in love with.' She had said far too much but it was too late now to wish that she hadn't.

'She's a French girl. We were billeted in the village where she lived, and . . . and working together. I wasn't in love with her, but I felt guilty about leaving her behind, knowing what she and her family were likely to be facing, but she wouldn't have had it any other way. She's a patriot, you see, and France means everything to her.'

It surprised Sebastion to discover how easy it was to talk openly and honestly to Grace about Marie and his feelings.

'I think I can understand that. I know I'd hate to think of this country having to surrender to Hitler.'

'We've got to win this war otherwise there is no hope for any of us,' said Sebastion.

'Everyone's afraid that Hitler will invade us like he has done those other countries.'

'Everyone? Does that include you, Grace?' Sebastion asked her.

'Yes,' she told him honestly, 'but I try not to think about it and to get on with my work. My family have been so lucky. My brother, Luke, came back from Dunkirk uninjured, and so apparently did Charlie. Luke's been posted to Home Duties now at Seacombe barracks.'

'Churchill will want to concentrate all his manpower at home to defend the country if Hitler does invade,' said Seb, thinking privately about the role he would be playing in that defence as soon as he was fit enough to leave hospital. His gift for languages made him an important part of the team being assembled at Derby House, the Headquarters for Joint Strategic Planning, involving both the navy and the RAF coast defence units, as well liaising with Fighter Command Group 12. His job as a special operator and a member of the 'Y' Section would be to spend his days incarcerated in a silent set room, listening for designated enemy coded messages, mainly in German.

It would be someone else, sitting in a similar room in a different part of the country, who would listen in for Marie's coded messages. Perhaps it was just as well that it would not be him, Seb admitted, but he knew too that she had made a lasting impression on him and that he could never forget her even if, as he had truthfully told Grace, he was not in love with her.

Being at war acted like a pressure cooker on the emotions when people worked closely together, forcing them into something they might otherwise not have been.

There had been nights when his own desire to give in to temptation and take the physical pleasure Marie had suggested they should share had come perilously close to overwhelming him. The only thing that had stopped him had been knowing that if he did he would have been breaking the rules he had been warned explicitly against breaking. A soldier away from home might with moral impunity visit a brothel, but he should not and must not become sexually involved with another member of a close-knit team. Marie's attitude towards sex had been very different from his own, and he suspected that he would not have been her first lover, and certainly not her last. It was, though, France that held her heart, no matter what she chose to do with her body. Grace was very different, softer and warmer, a gentler, sweeter-natured girl, and far more dangerously easy to fall in love with.

Jean couldn't believe it. She had only left the house half an hour ago, and only to go up to the shop and use the telephone to alert Vi to what had happened. That alone hadn't been very pleasant, what with Vi getting so cross and refusing to believe at first that Jack had been as badly treated as he had said, and even threatening to send him straight back again. But now to come back home and find out that Francine and Jack had disappeared and that Francine hadn't left so much as a note behind saying where they had gone had been enough to have Jean sitting down at her kitchen table with her hand pressed against her heart in an attempt to still its anxious racing beat.

Now what was she going to say to Vi when she arrived to collect Jack? She had known the moment she had seen the way Francine had been holding Jack so tightly and so possessively last night that there was going to be trouble. Jean felt desperately sorry for her nephew and for Fran herself, but she was still shocked that Fran could do something so thoughtless and silly.

Francine watched with a hungry loving maternal gaze as Jack tucked into the fish paste sandwiches she had ordered for him. They were in Joe Lyons, and Jack's eyes were constantly rounding with curiosity and excitement as he stared about and took everything in.

All she could manage herself was a cup of tea, she was that strung up inside. More than one of Joe Lyons' famous nippy waitresses had paused long enough to give Jack a brief smile as she had hurried past, causing Francine's heart to swell with motherly pride. Vi had taught him nice manners, she had to say that for her, even if Francine suspected they had been taught through fear rather than kindness. He spoke well too, not posh, but well, and she thought she could detect a hint of the rhythm of her own voice in his.

She hadn't had any plans in mind when she had given into the impulse that had brought them here.

All she had known was that she was desperate to have him to herself for a while, to pretend that they were what they could have been and should have been if only things had been different.

She had taken him to Lewis's first to buy him some new clothes, not that there had been much choice, thanks to the war, but at least now he was wearing clothes that fitted him and were new. She had felt so proud and at the same time so humbled when he put his hand in hers of his own accord and before she had reached to take it.

He had lost that reserve and hesitation with her now that he had had at first, and she had felt a dangerous thrill of delight this morning over breakfast when it had been her he had turned to to speak to first and not Jean.

When he wasn't afraid or intimidated, his smile was mischievous and his eyes so clear of any guile and so lovingly innocent that she felt as though she could eat him up. All she wanted to do was to sweep him up into her arms and keep him safe there for ever. She couldn't bear to think about what he had been through and she couldn't bear to think either that he would have to be handed back to Vi.

He was quick and bright, and interested in everything: one minute a little boy, the next a heart-breakingly protective man-child, who obviously saw it as his duty to watch out for her.

Francine had soon learned that Sam and Luke were his idols and that he adored them. Edwin and Charlie he seldom mentioned, and it seemed to Francine that it was fear, not love, that filled him whenever Vi was mentioned.

They had walked from Lewis's to the church where her mother was buried and Francine had shown him her stone.

'She was my grandma, wasn't she?' he had asked knowledgeably.

'Yes,' Francine had agreed with a small choke in her voice. After all, it was true.

There had been one shocking moment when they had walked past the theatre just as Con was coming out with his girl. Francine's first instinct had been to hide Jack from him, as though there was a risk of Con recognising him and immediately demanding that she hand his son over to him. Which, of course, was ridiculous. The last thing Con would be likely to do was to acknowledge an illegitimate son. He and his wife did not have any children and the rumour had always been that she was unable to have any.

As bad as that was, it surely couldn't get any more painful than having the child you had had wrenched from your arms and given to someone else.

Jack's touch on her arm brought a lump to Francine's throat.

'What's going to happen to me?' he asked her, his appetite for his sandwiches suddenly vanishing. 'I don't want to go back to Mr and Mrs Davies. Will Mum make me, do you think?'

Hearing that word 'Mum' and knowing it did not refer to her hurt so very much. And Vi wasn't his mum at all, not really. What if she didn't take him back to Jean's? He was her child, after all. She could go back to America and take him with her. Her heart had started to thump far too heavily. She knew that what she was thinking was impossible. Legally, she was not his mother, and apart from anything else what would she tell Jack himself: 'I'm really your mother but I gave you away'?

The bond she was building with him was too new and too fragile for that. Reluctantly she let the impulse pass and concentrated instead on being practical.

'Me and your auntie Jean are going to talk to . . . to Vi and explain to her what happened.'

'But what if she still wants me to go back?'

This was so heartbreaking.

'We won't let her,' she told him firmly.

'Promise?'

Francine thought of the way that Vi had so stubbornly refused to tell them where he was and how she had been so determined that she did not see him, and her heart quailed at the thought of giving him a promise she knew that Vi would do her utmost to make sure she could not keep. But he was only a little boy and she could not explain any of the complex adult emotions that underlay Vi's actions, and so instead she had to say and pray she could mean it, 'Promise.'

She saw the Wolseley car parked outside Jean and Sam's as soon as they got off the bus. Immediately Jack tensed and pulled back.

'That's Dad's car.'

Francine had guessed that it must belong to Edwin and her own heart had sunk but she forced herself to sound cheerful and unconcerned.

'Is it? I expect they've come to take you home.'

Home! His home should be with her; she was his home.

Jean let them in, her face set and anxious as she guided Jack into the front room. As soon as he saw his parents he cowered back against Jean, causing her heart to ache with sadness for him and anger against her twin. It wasn't his fault that he had been born the way he had, and Vi had been the one to say she wanted him. He hadn't been forced on her although to have heard what she had been saying whilst they waited for Francine to bring him back you'd have thought that she'd had no say in the matter whatsoever, and that Francine had simply left her baby with Vi and Edwin and taken off.

'At last,' Vi greeted Francine, giving her an acid look before turning to Jack and saying sharply, 'Well, I hope you're pleased with yourself, Jack, causing me and your dad all this worry and upset.'

'Give over, Vi.' That was Sam, who had slipped home to support Jean, knowing that Vi would try to bully her. 'The poor kid's had a pretty rotten time of it, by all accounts.'

'By his account, don't you mean?' Vi snapped. 'According to Mr and Mrs Davies when they telephoned us this morning from the village post office, they've been off their heads with worry about him.

And if he's been that unhappy why on earth didn't he write and tell us instead of causing all this trouble.'

'They told me that you didn't want me, and that was why you didn't write to me,' said Jack.

The adults looked at Jack with varying emotions in their hearts.

Jean could see that Vi wasn't looking at all pleased that he had spoken up, and although she said crossly, 'That's nonsense. Of course I wrote to you,' Jean suspected that she had not written as regularly as she would want them to think.

It had been ever such a relief when Francine had finally returned. Jean had really thought at one stage that she wasn't going to.

'Well, obviously the lad can't go back to these people,' said Sam firmly. 'And if I was you, Edwin, I'd be writing to whoever is in charge of this private evacuation lot you used and reporting them. I reckon the woman who took her kids away got it right, and that Jack here deserves a pat on the back for having the good sense to do what he did. It seems to me that these Davies people were just using their evacuees as unpaid labour, aye and getting paid for it by their families and the Government as well, seeing as the Government gives them as take the kids a bit of an allowance. I dare say you and Vi paid a fair bit more to make sure that Jack was looked after properly as well, and I shouldn't like to think that someone was cheating me out of my money like that.'

Jean listened to Sam in admiration. He had got

exactly the right way of dealing with Edwin and appealing to what mattered most to him – his bank account. She could almost see Edwin puffing out his chest and mentally preparing the letter he would send to the Davieses, demanding his money back. She gave Sam a grateful look.

Vi had started to frown.

'And what's that Jack's wearing, might I ask, because those certainly aren't his clothes?'

'No, I bought him some new things when we were out,' Francine told her. 'What he was wearing were little better than rags, weren't they, Jean?'

'He'd certainly outgrown them,' Jean agreed diplomatically.

Vi pounced triumphantly. 'Well, if he's grown then he certainly can't have been as badly treated as he's told you. If you've been lying to your aunt Jean, Jack—'

'I haven't. It's true, all of it.'

Francine could hear the panic in his voice and moved closer to him whilst Jean's heart sank. Didn't Vi have any tact? Couldn't she see what she was doing? And poor little Jack – he was the one who was going to suffer the most because of all this upset.

'Well, you'd better come home with us now until we sort out somewhere else for you to go.'

'You're not thinking of sending him back?' Jean protested.

'It's not safe for him here. You know that. Wallasey's already been bombed once, and four killed. There's hardly two nights together now when we don't have the air-raid sirens going on.'

None of them could dispute the truth of Vi's words.

'Come along, Jack,' she insisted sharply. 'Your father's been put to enough trouble already having to leave his work and then wait around for your aunt Francine to bring you back, after she'd taken you out without a by-your-leave, or telling anyone where she was going.'

Jack was leaning back into her, and now, as Francine put her hand on his shoulder, he looked up at her.

Jean looked helplessly at Sam.

Francine's eyes were swimming with tears, and Jack looked so helpless and afraid, whilst Vi was clearly furious. Any minute now something would be said or done that would cause the kind of family trouble that could never be put right, thought Jean worriedly.

'Why don't you leave him here with us for a few days, Vi, whilst you sort out what you're going to do?' Sam suggested.

'No. He's coming back with us now, and as for sorting something out, we've done that already. First thing tomorrow Edwin is taking him back to Wales. We've found another family that's willing to take him. Very highly recommended, they are as well, by a fellow member of my WVS committee. Come along, Jack.'

Francine dropped on her haunches and wrapped her arms around him, hugging him fiercely and giving him a kiss.

She hoped he'd remember about the little card

she'd given him with the address of the theatre on it, and that he'd be able to keep it hidden from Vi. She told him he could write to her any time he wanted to, and that he must if he wasn't happy. It wasn't what she wanted but what else could she do?

It was Jean's turn to hug him now, and then Sam was leading him over to Vi, who frowned and grumbled over a mark on his shirt and said that his hair was untidy and needed cutting.

'I can't bear it,' said Francine to Jean after they had gone. 'I really can't.'

'You must,' Jean responded. 'Because there's nothing else you can do.'

Grace had just come off duty and was halfway across the yard on her way to see Teddy when it happened. Teddy was standing outside his ambulance, watching the crew of another ambulance help an elderly man to walk towards the hospital, and smoking a cigarette. He saw Grace and waved to her. Then out of nowhere a young boy came running past, whilst from the hospital entrance one of the porters was calling out, 'Stop him. He's just nicked my watch.'

Immediately Teddy dropped his cigarette and set off in pursuit of the thief, but he had only run a few yards when he stopped, and doubled over, clutching his chest and then collapsed onto the ground.

Grace couldn't remember moving but somehow she was there, alongside his colleagues, who had also seen what had happened, kneeling down beside him whilst over her head anxious voices issued curt instructions.

His face was deathly pale, his lips almost blue, and beneath her searching fingers his pulse was so frail and thready it might almost not have been there.

The other ambulance men were attempting to lift him onto a stretcher. Grace reached for his hand. His eyes opened and he looked at her. Grace's heart did a slow sickening dive that dizzied her.

'Don't move him,' someone was instructing. 'Doc's on his way.'

'It's too late for that,' another responded in a shocked voice. 'It looks like the poor lad's a goner.'

'Teddy. Teddy . . .' But Grace knew it was no use. She could see it in his face, and in his eyes was a look that told her that he knew it too.

She lifted his hand to her lips and pressed them against it. *Don't die, Teddy, please don't die.*

As though he had heard the words beating inside her head he gave her a crooked smile. He was trying to say something and she had to lean even closer to him to hear it.

'Don't you go forgetting what I said to you about you having to do the living for both of us.' His voice was like the dry rustle of dead leaves swept aside by the wind. 'And think on what you do 'cos I'll be watching you from up there.'

'Teddy. *Teddy* . . . No.'

But Grace knew even as she said his name that it was too late and he had gone.

* * *

They let her go with his body into the hospital but later she was glad that they had refused to allow her to help lay him out. Somehow it wouldn't have been proper really, her seeing him in such a personal way when they hadn't been like that with one another.

Matron was very kind to her, telling her she was sending her home in the care of a senior nurse Grace didn't know but whose family apparently lived a couple of streets away from her own.

It was a beautiful evening with a clear sky and a perfect sunset, the air balmy with summer, and the evidence of living things at their fullest flowering was all around her in gardens and on allotments. Teddy should have lived to experience that fullness of life instead of being denied it.

Elspeth, the other nurse, let her walk down her own street on her own, and to Grace's relief she managed to control herself until she was inside, but the moment she saw her mother she threw herself into her arms and cried her eyes out.

TWENTY-TWO

'The bloody Luftwaffe were at it again last night. They got the dockers' umbrella this time and the docks,' Mr Whitehead told Grace gloomily as she did the morning locker round.

The dockers' umbrella was the local name for the overhead railway that ran the length of the docks and under which dockers often sheltered when it came on to rain.

'Yes, I know,' Grace agreed calmly. 'My dad's with the Salvage Corps and they were called out, but seemingly the damage wasn't too bad.'

'They've bin bombing the south-east coast and Dover, an' all,' Mr Whitehead continued, determined to look on the black side. 'Hitler wants to destroy our RAF so that he can invade us unchallenged.'

'Hellfire Corner, the papers are calling Dover now, but the RAF will soon see them off,' the cheerful young sergeant in the next bed, who was now recovering from his injuries, told him.

'Them German Stukas are no match for our Spitfires.'

Grace dutifully tried to concentrate on the newspaper report they were both discussing, which explained how the German Stukas protected by Messerschmitt fighters had roared in over the Channel coast in bomber formation to attack harbours, naval bases and airfields, whilst the Spitfires protected by the Hurricanes of Bomber Command had carefully fed into the battle to take a terrible toll of the Germans who had lost 31 planes to the RAF's 17.

'It says here,' the young sergeant read, having got out of bed against regulations and picked up Mr Whitehead's paper: '"Among the most successful of the RAF pilots are the Poles, who have fought the Germans in their own skies, over France and now over Britain. They burn with hatred for the Nazis and roar into battle with reckless courage."'

The other men in the ward all burst spontaneously into applause when the sergeant had finished reading.

As pleased as Grace was by the news, poor Teddy's death was still very raw with her.

They had buried him yesterday, and for the first time she had met his family. Grace's mother hadn't really wanted her to attend the funeral, worrying that she might not be up to it, but Grace had insisted that she must pay her last respects, so Jean had gone with her.

Grace had been surprised to learn from Teddy's mother just how much he had talked about her at home and even more surprised when it had turned out that her own mother and Teddy's had gone to the same school.

There had been a good deal of talk from Teddy's family about how he would never listen to reason about not overdoing things and Grace had thought of the rueful 'I told you so' smile he would have given her had he been there to hear them.

The other girls in her set had all been sympathetic, even Lillian, although Grace had suspected that her outward show of sympathy was just that – a show put on because it was what she thought she should do.

Grace still couldn't quite believe that it had actually happened somehow, and, this morning, once she got into the sluice room she discovered to her dismay that she was crying.

This wouldn't do, it would not do at all, and it was the last thing that Teddy would want, but still she leaned her head against the wall and gave way to her tears.

The sluice-room door opened and Grace tensed with shock when Seb walked in.

'You can't come in here,' she told him. 'Sister will have a fit.'

'I heard about your friend. And I just wanted to say how sorry I was.'

Grace could feel fresh tears filling her eyes. 'He knew it was going to happen. He'd told me. But I never thought . . . I'd warned him that he was doing too much. He must have known when he ran after that lad.'

Seb pushed a clean handkerchief into her hand.

'He'd be that cross if he could see me now. He told me that he didn't want me crying over him, and that was why we could only be friends and not anything else. He said he didn't want me feeling guilty like I would do if we'd been a proper couple. But I do feel guilty,' Grace said wretchedly. 'Teddy wanted so much to live and I can't stop meself from thinking that if I had been his girl, you know, properly, then he'd have known what that was like instead of dying without knowing.'

The words were tumbling out on top of one another, things she would never normally have dreamed of saying, but instinctively Grace sensed that Seb would understand what she was feeling and what she was trying to say.

He did. And he understood too that his own feelings for Grace had become far more personal than he had realised until now.

'You've nothing to feel guilty about, Grace,' he reassured her, 'except that you're upsetting yourself when Teddy didn't want you to, and over something he wouldn't have wanted you to be upset over.'

'How do you know that? You didn't even know him.'

'No. But just from what you've said about him now I can tell that he was a man of honour and decency,' Seb insisted truthfully. 'Maybe he did want what you've just said, but I reckon that what he wanted more was what he'd already said he wanted for you. You should respect that and respect him for it, because I certainly do. He sounds a fine man and I wish I'd had the opportunity to meet him.'

'He *was* a fine man,' said Grace, her tears subsiding, and then starting up again as she wept, 'It's so unfair, Seb.'

He crossed the small distance separating them and took her in his arms, holding her comfortingly.

'It is,' he agreed. 'Bloody unfair. But that's life, Grace. You know that. It *is* unfair. And if you want to be fair to him, then the best thing you can do is to remember him as he wanted you to.'

Grace raised her head to look at him, her eyes widening slightly as her body registered the fact that she was in his arms.

'Grace.'

He hadn't intended to kiss her. He hadn't even thought of doing so, not for one minute, Sebastion assured himself. He had seen her rush into the sluice room, had guessed she was upset and had simply followed her to offer his sympathy.

But now that he was kissing her, Seb realised, he didn't ever want to stop.

A sound outside the door brought them both back to reality. Seb released her and Grace stepped back from him. They were both breathing unsteadily and Grace knew that her heart was racing – not with shock but with excitement.

'We shouldn't have done that,' she told Seb weakly.

'No,' he agreed, 'but I'm glad that we did.'

Her mother had been in such a bad mood since Jack had run away and they had to collect him from Aunt Jean's and then take him back to Wales, that Bella just didn't feel like going round to see her.

Bettina and her mother were carrying on as if the Poles were the saviours of the nation, ever since it had been in the papers about them being such daring fighter pilots, and Bella was sick of listening to them.

Now just because the post hadn't brought a letter from Jan this morning they were acting like the world had ended and had rushed off to see what they could find out, fearing the worst and that Jan might have been shot down in one of the now almost daily air battles between the Luftwaffe and the RAF. Well, good riddance if he had, Bella thought nastily.

She wished they weren't having such a hot August. It was really draining her, what with the heat and the air-raid sirens going off night after night, and her having to get out of bed and go down to the shelter until the all clear came. At least today, though, she didn't have to worry about having to put up with Alan's temper, seeing as he was playing golf with his father. And yet even though she resented Bettina and her mother, the house felt empty without them there to complain to about how miserable she felt.

It was definitely too hot outside. She might as well go upstairs and lie down comfortably on her bed, as stay out here in the garden, thought Bella.

Less than an hour later Alan woke her up when he came storming upstairs, obviously drunk and in a furious temper.

'What are you doing back?' she asked him irritably. 'I thought you were playing golf.'

'Trixie's father was at the golf club, and do you know what?'

Bella gave an exaggerated sigh and got up off the bed. 'No, and I don't want to know either,' she told him as she walked past him.

He caught up with her on the landing, grabbing hold of her arm and pushing her back against the banister rail so hard that it hurt her back.

'Well, you're going to know. He said that Trixie's getting engaged,' said Alan bitterly. 'That's thanks to you, you bitch,' he raged. 'It's because of you that I've lost the girl I love. The only girl I'll ever love.' He was sobbing now, drunken tears streaming down his face. 'It's all your fault. Everything. You've ruined my life.'

She'd ruined his life! Her back really hurt and so did her arm where he was still holding it in a painful grip. Bella gave him a baleful look and demanded crossly, 'Let go of me, Alan. You're hurting me.'

'Am I? So what? It's what you deserve. In fact . . .' He was looking at her now in a way that sent an atavistic prickle of warning up under Bella's skin, lifting the hairs at the back of her neck.

As though in the very second that it flashed through her mind that being trapped between Alan and the banister rail meant she was in a perilous position, the same thought seemed to occur to him, so that when she tried to twist her body round to escape from any danger he slammed her back against the banister. The force he used sent the breath gasping from her lungs. Instinctively Bella reached out with her free hand to try to drag Alan's fingers from round her wrist. She was panting now, her ears filled with the sound of Alan's drunken jeering laughter. He was gripping her wrist so hard she thought it might actually break.

Panic filled her. She clawed wildly at his face, but he still didn't let her go. Instead he grabbed hold of her by the hair with his free hand, banging her head against the wall.

Her ears ringing with pain and nausea, Bella sobbed in panic, begging him, 'Stop it, Alan, please stop it.' She was crying and too frightened to conceal her terror as Alan dragged her towards the top of the stairs.

'One push and that would be it,' he told her. 'You and that brat you're carrying would be dead and I'd be free. Trixie wants me really, I know she does. She's always loved me and she always will. She said so. She's only got engaged to this other chap because of you.'

He had pushed her back against the banister and was leaning in to her. Bella could hear the wood creaking and moving beneath their combined weight.

Abruptly he swung her round, and away from the banister, so that she had her back to the stairs.

Bella hiccuped in sick relief. Thank God he had

come to his senses. He was still holding on to her wrists, manacling both of them now.

She tried to pull them free and then screamed in sick terror as Alan jerked her backwards, causing her to fall off the top step, suspended for a nauseating heartbeat of time in nothing other than the air before he yanked her back to the safety of the stair.

'That's it, you go ahead and make me let you go, and then it will be your own fault. I'll tell them that I tried to calm you down and stop you, but you just went ahead and fell all by yourself.'

He was grinning at her now, a maniacal drunken grin, his eyes savage with his hatred of her.

He was going to do it. He was going to let go of her wrists and push her down the stairs. Bella could see it in his eyes. Sobbing in terror, she was trembling violently. She was going to die. Alan was going to kill her. She felt him release her right wrist. She reached out frantically towards the banister.

Suddenly there were feet on the stairs; an RAF uniform; Jan, his body supporting hers as he punched Alan once and so hard that he collapsed onto the landing like a deflated puppet.

Bella sagged against Jan, too shocked and weak to do anything other than let him take charge. She was trembling so much she could hardly stand, never mind walk, and she had to lean heavily on him. She could smell the scent of his skin and his hair.

He took her into the kitchen and sat her down on a chair.

'I'll call your doctor.'

'No,' Bella protested. 'There's no need.'

'He would have killed you if I hadn't come in.'

'No,' Bella denied, but she knew that it was true and that in his drunken fury Alan had intended to do just that. Bella, though, had been brought up by a mother who had taught her that appearances were everything, and Bella couldn't endure the shame of other people knowing what Alan had tried to do.

Now that she was out of danger, all she wanted to do was to pretend that it had never happened. The last thing she wanted was everyone knowing what kind of husband Alan was, and even worse, that he loved someone else and had wanted to leave her.

Alan! She could hear him lurching down the stairs and she looked anxiously towards the door but to her relief he didn't come into the kitchen, and within a few seconds she heard the front door being slammed behind him as he left.

'You need to see the doctor and tell him what's happened,' insisted Jan.

Bella shook her head and then stopped, wincing. Just moving her head hurt because of the way Alan had banged it against the wall.

'What are you doing here anyway?' she challenged Jan. Now that she was safe, her normal desire to make sure that the refugees knew their place reasserted itself. Far easier to do that than let herself think about those moments when she had feared for her life. 'I thought you were busy being a hero. Not that it managed to stop Hitler invading your own country, of course.'

There was a small pause but he didn't respond to her gibe, simply saying instead, 'I had a twenty-four-hour pass. I knew my mother would be worrying with everything that's been in the papers about the fighting over the Channel, so I decided to come home to tell her myself that there was no need to worry about me.'

Bella wished he would go away. She wasn't feeling very well at all, but she wasn't going to let him see that. She hated him, she really did, and she would rather anyone but him had seen what Alan was doing to her. He must have hit Alan very hard.

Her head was swimming and a cramping pain was invading her stomach.

'You'll find your mother and sister down at the WVS Refugee Centre. And I don't know who gave you a key to my house but they had no right to do so.'

The pain was becoming so intense now that she could hardly speak. It was seizing her in red-hot waves like wires being dragged through her insides.

Jan was saying something but the pain was too intense for her to listen.

She heard him curse and saw him get up and go into the hall.

The pain invaded her, possessing her, growing ever stronger as it surged and seethed in a relent-less tide of agony. She tried to stand up and collapsed on the kitchen floor. She could hear doors opening and closing and then voices – her mother's, the doctor's, Jan's, his mother's. She could see anxious faces bending over her, but all that really mattered was the pain. She wanted to tear it from her as it was tearing the child from her womb but it was too strong for her.

On and on it went, relentless and unending, until finally it was over, and her body expelled the life the pain had destroyed.

Grace and Seb had both agreed that they would take things slowly and that they would not allow themselves to be swept away by a kiss exchanged in a very emotional moment, especially now, with the air-raid sirens going off almost every other night and the whole country on edge, knowing that the raids by the Luftwaffe were just the first stage in Hitler's battle to break the spirit of the British people and invade the country.

This was a time to give their hearts and their minds to the war effort and not to themselves and their own feelings for one another.

Seb had told her that now he was going to be based in Liverpool at Derby House, they would have plenty of time to get to know one another properly and that there was no need for them to rush into anything, quite the opposite. They would start off as they meant to go on. Seb wanted to introduce himself properly to Grace's parents before they became a couple, and there must be respect for Teddy, even though he and Grace had not been romantically involved.

For her part Grace had said that she had no intention of allowing anything or anyone to stop her from completing her training. Qualified nurses were going to be needed if Hitler went ahead and invaded and there was fighting in the streets.

And then despite all that, and the practical decision they had made, the very first thing they had done afterwards had been to seal their agreement with a kiss of such sweet and intense passion that it had left Grace trembling and Seb wondering how one earth he was going to keep the promise he had just made.

Bella lay motionless in the bed, staring up at the ceiling, watching the patterns made by the sunlight coming in through the curtains. Sunlight that her baby would never see.

The pain started again. A different kind of pain from the one that had ripped through her yesterday. This pain filled all of her, not just her body, which now felt so drained and empty, as, of course, it was.

It bewildered her that she could feel like this. She hadn't really wanted the baby, except as a means of bringing Alan to heel and yet just acknowledging that brought a searing emotional agony so intense that she could hardly endure it.

How was it possible for her to feel this overwhelming loss and devastation?

When she had woken up this morning and known that the baby was gone, her own reactions had made her feel as though somehow she was different from the person she knew. Her emotions confused and frightened her. She wasn't used to feeling things so deeply and painfully. She didn't want to think about the baby and how she had not protected it as she should have done, and yet she couldn't not do.

The fact that now there was nothing to tie Alan to her and he could walk away from her meant nothing. All the things that had seemed so important before meant nothing. All that mattered was her baby, and that was gone.

Her grief filled her completely, totally absorbing her. At some deep level she knew, even if she didn't want to recognise it, that nothing could ever be the same as it had been now. Her life was changed for ever and she with it.

She put her hand on her flat stomach and the urge to howl like a wild animal in mortal agony filled her.

TWENTY-THREE

'Well, thanks for letting me stay here with you, Jean.'

'You know you're always welcome, Francine.'

They were avoiding looking directly at one another, both of them knowing there were questions that must not be asked and answers that could not be given.

'I bet this B & B the BBC are putting me up at in Bangor won't be anywhere near as comfortable.'

'What do you think you'll do when you've finished doing these BBC programmes?'

Safer to talk about Francine's singing than about the fact that she had broken her contract with the theatre to take on this nowhere near so well paid work where she wouldn't even be the main act but would merely be supporting Vera Lynn, just because it was in Bangor, and because Wales was where Jack was. Safer too, Jean felt, not to mention either the letter that had come for Francine in Jack's schoolboy handwriting. That way, if Vi should find out and object, she would be able to deny that she had been involved.

Outside the car the BBC had sent was waiting, its driver standing on the pavement smoking a cigarette.

'You've got everything?'

Francine nodded. 'I'll write and let you know when I'm settled in.'

She hadn't wanted to say anything but Jean discovered that she had to.

'You . . . you won't do anything silly, Fran, will you?'

Francine looked at her, and shook her head, bending down to pick up her case. She was only taking a few of her clothes with her, leaving the rest behind in her trunk.

The twins came rushing in just in time to see her off, hugging her and saying how much they were going to miss her.

'You know why she's doing it, don't you?' Jean said to Sam later as she poured him a cup of tea. 'She's doing it so that she can see Jack.' She put down the teapot. 'If Vi finds out . . .'

Sam reached for her free hand and held it tightly within his own. 'You've got to let them sort out their own lives, love.'

The B & B in Bangor was every bit as dreary as Francine had known it would be, but the other entertainers billeted in the town were a cheerful lot, including in their number some of Liverpool's most famous comedians such as Tommy Handley from the programme *ITMA*, but Francine's mind was on other things.

Jack had written to her to tell her that the new couple he was living with were much kinder than the Davieses but that he wished he was still in Liverpool. He missed her, he had written, and Francine certainly missed him.

The first thing she had done – even before unpacking her case and introducing herself to the other entertainers billeted in the boarding house – had been to find out how far it was to the small Welsh village where Jack was staying and how easily she could get there.

She would be best driving there, she had been told, since it was too far to cycle and there was no direct route by train.

It hadn't been easy finding someone prepared to lend her a car, but eventually Francine had managed to persuade a local garage owner into doing so, with the aid of an enormous sum of money.

Now, following the carefully written down directions that had accompanied his even more detailed instructions on the proper care of his precious car, she was driving along virtually empty roads that climbed upwards into Welsh mountains so high that their tops were lost amongst the clouds. Great barren sweeps of granite mountainside rose starkly either side of her, as she drove through valleys so narrow that the towering mountains cast shadows that Francine felt must never be penetrated by the sun. This was a dark and ancient land that wore its scars and its survival proudly.

She had brought sandwiches and a flask with her, but she didn't bother to stop to enjoy them. She would share them instead with Jack.

She exhaled with relief when she found the small village with the long and unpronounceable name, which was close to the farm where Jack was living. She stopped the car outside the post office and got out. It would be a good place to enquire which direction she should take out of the village to reach the farm.

As she walked out of the sunshine into the gloom of the low-ceilinged room, the half a dozen or so people waiting in a queue all turned to look at her, as people do when strangers arrive in close-knit communities.

'I'm looking for the Thomases' farm,' Francine told them, feeling that some explanation of her presence was called for.

The people in the queue looked at one another and there was a groundswell of muted conversation in Welsh.

It was the woman behind the counter who answered her. 'It's down the road on the left as you go past the chapel, but you won't find much of it left, not after what the Luftwaffe did to it last night. Dropped one of their ruddy bombs right on top of it, they did, see, and flattened the whole place.'

The singsong words danced inside Francine's head, impossible surely to believe, for what reason could the Luftwaffe have for dropping bombs out here where there was nothing but sheep and a handful of scattered farms, and Jack.

Francine started to walk and then run from the post office towards her borrowed car.

The road up to the farm was potholed and narrow, and at the end of it lay what must have once been a building but was now a heap of rubble, over which hung a pall of dust and smoke from the still smouldering rafters.

A group of rescue workers, their faces smeared with smoke and their expressions bleak, stood silently beside a couple of battered trucks.

Francine got out of the car.

'You can't go over there, *bach*,' a short burly-looking man told her, barring her way. 'Too dangerous it is, see, with the building half collapsed already.'

'Please let me past. My son was staying here. I have to know what's happened to him.'

Something – pity, perhaps – came and went in the man's eyes before he explained, 'There was no one survived – took a direct hit, the place did, see. They reckon the pilot was after Liverpool but lost his way and had to turn back so he dumped his bombs in Wales. Half a dozen or more gone off last night, there was, so they say, but this was the only one that hit anything.'

'He wouldn't have known nothing, *bach*,' another man told her gently.

'Killed old Thomas's prize dog, it did, an' all. Promised me one of her pups, he had,' a third mournful voice joined in.

Francine wished they would go away and leave her here on her own.

Jack. She couldn't take it in that he was gone. Dead. Killed. Here in this burned-out wreckage of what had once been a home. She couldn't visualise him here; not at all. When she created a picture of him inside her head she saw him in Liverpool, smiling up at her . . . and alive.

But he wasn't alive. How could he be? Francine looked at the still smouldering wreckage and knew that the men were right and that no one, nothing could have survived. Jack. What she had previously thought of as emotional pain had been nothing. This now was real pain, and it had only just begun.

As she drove past the small stone-built chapel on her way back to Bangor she looked at the message written outside. It read, 'God is with you.'

She started to laugh hysterically.

The now-familiar wail of the air-raid sirens brought Bella out of her sleep. She lay in bed listening to it without making any attempt to obey its summons. She could hear Bettina and her mother getting up, and making ready to take refuge in the communal air-raid shelter at the end of the road. Still she didn't move.

There was a sharp rap on her bedroom door and then it opened and Bettina warned her, 'The air-raid siren's gone.'

'I'm not going.'

She could almost feel Bettina's angry frustration as she wondered what to do and then, after hesitating, she closed the door and Bella heard her hurrying down the stairs to join her mother.

The front door opened and closed. The wail of the sirens stopped. Bella counted the seconds that ticked by. She had reached forty-five when she heard the first undulating hum of approaching desynchronised aircraft engines, the noise swiftly growing louder. Soon the scream of falling bombs and explosions would fill the air, along with the thump of the anti-aircraft guns. Familiar noises now, that had fallen into a familiar pattern. In the morning, newspapers would carry reports of where the bombs had fallen and how much damage they had done.

Bella tensed as she heard the first whining whistle of descending bombs, followed by the dull crump of explosions.

It had started. Well, she didn't care. She didn't really care about anything any more.

A bomb screamed earthwards so close at hand the noise hurt her eardrums. Silence. Then an almighty explosion that shook the whole house to its foundations and brought the toiletries on her dressing table crashing to the floor, filling the air with the scent of her Ma Griffe perfume.

At the hospital, as soon as they had heard the air-raid siren, the nurses and porters had rushed to get the patients to safety, following a now well-organised procedure after a month of constant alerts. Seb, who had been told he would be discharged in the morning, made sure he kept a protective eye on Grace, as he and the other mobile patients helped the nurses with those who were bedridden.

'I dare say it will be the docks that will be getting the worse of it,' Seb shouted to Grace above the noise of the sirens.

Grace nodded, feeling more anxious about her father and her brother, who were both bound to be more closely involved in the raid, than she was about herself.

The night was filled with the sound of exploding bombs and destruction, whilst the ack-ack guns of the batteries spat out rounds of gunfire that lit up the sky. Shattered glass covered the ground, crunching underfoot.

'They've got the Customs House,' one of the porters yelled, 'and a couple of warehouses.'

Just as they reached the shelter a dozen or more incendiary bombs hit the ground, bursting into flames. One of them came so close that Grace felt the heat of it singeing her uniform before Seb dragged her out of the way.

Another landed on the entrance to a corporation bus that had just stopped outside the hospital. Whilst Grace watched, the conductress kicked it off so that it exploded harmlessly in the street.

Dodging the broken glass from windows blown out by the bombs, and the incendiary bombs themselves, Grace finally got her patients into the shelter.

In answer to Seb's, 'You OK?' she gave a brief nod and acknowledged, 'Yes, thanks to you.'

There was no time to say any more. She had her patients to attend to, and Sister was doing a roll call to make sure that no one had been left behind by accident.

By the time that had been done the German bombers had turned for home and the all clear was already sounding.

Luckily the hospital itself hadn't been hit, but there'd been a lot of damage down by the docks and Wallasey Town Hall had been hit, as well as several houses, Seb reported to Grace before she went off duty.

'You won't be here when I come back on duty tonight. The ward won't be the same without you.' Despite her best intentions Grace knew that her voice was betraying how she felt.

Seb squeezed her hand. 'I'll be waiting for you here at the hospital when you come off duty on your day off, just like we've arranged.'

Grace looked at him. 'Do you think it's too soon, after Teddy?'

'No, I don't, and I don't think that Teddy would think so either,' said Seb seriously, still holding her hand. 'We already know how we feel about one another, and my guess is that your Teddy's up there somewhere watching over you and that what he wants more than anything is for you to be happy, Grace.'

'Oh, Seb . . .' Grace's voice was muffled. 'I think you and Teddy would have got on really well together.'

'I think so too,' Seb agreed.

The public air-raid shelter at the bottom of the street was crammed with people. One household had been having a party when the siren had gone off, and the men had grabbed their beer and the women the sandwiches, and now the party was continuing inside the shelter in a very jolly way indeed, with one of the guests playing his harmonica and several of the men singing at the tops of their voices.

Jean gave the twins a warning look when she saw them exchanging looks and giggling. Of course the old-fashioned songs weren't to their taste, but at least they drowned out some of the noise of the bombs going off.

Sam was on standby down at the Salvage Corps headquarters in Hatton Gardens, and Luke was on duty at his barracks.

The harmonica player had stopped to have a sandwich, allowing them all to hear the fierce retaliatory fire from the ack-ack guns defending the city.

'It's been the early hours of every other night damn near all month now that we've had this going on,' one of the women complained. 'I'm sick of having to get up out of me bed and come down here.'

'Well, you'd be a hell of a lot sicker if one of them bombs landed on the house whilst you was in the ruddy bed,' her husband pointed out.

A couple of women had young children with them and were hugging them protectively, making Jean think of Vi and Jack – and Francine, of course.

There was no doubt in Jean's mind that Francine had taken the BBC work so that she could be close to Jack.

Of course, Vi was bound to be feeling smug about sending Jack away now that Wallasey had been bombed a couple of times – not that Jean had seen anything of her twin since the day she and Edwin had come round to collect Jack.

Vi had told her then that Charlie, like Luke, had been posted to Home Duties in case of an invasion, and of course she had been full of Charlie's bravery at Dunkirk, saying how she thought he deserved to get a medal.

Up at the hospital Grace would be on duty, and Jean said a special prayer for her eldest daughter. It had been terrible what had happened to that young lad she had been friendly with, but Jean had noticed a certain sparkle in Grace's eyes on her last visit home, and there'd been a lot of references to 'Seb' to accompany that sparkle.

The all clear sounded, breaking into Jean's thoughts and bringing with it a wave of relief that had everyone in the shelter gathering up their possessions and getting ready to go home.

Outside the sky was already lightening, revealing the familiar and blessedly undamaged outline of the street and their homes.

The air, though, tasted of smoke and dust, and there were fires burning down by the docks.

*　　*　　*

'They got the Customs House and a couple of warehouses, and by all accounts there was a fair few bombs dropped on Wallasey again,' Sam told Jean as he demolished the breakfast she had made him when he had arrived home just after six in the morning.

'I can't stay. We've got some salvage work to do on some warehouses that got hit,' had been his first words to her after he had given her a reassuring hug and a kiss on the cheek, 'but I wanted to make sure you were OK. Oh, and there was a bomb went off up near the hospital but no one was hurt.' He was pushing his chair back and standing up as he finished his cup of tea, kissing her again and telling her cheerfully, 'Better get back, love.'

Vi was still in shock, still unable to do anything other than stare in disbelief at the scattered still smoking rubble that had once been a house. She hadn't been able to bring herself to look at the shrouded stretcher she had seen carried away.

'Well, I never thought that Hitler would bomb a nice road like this one,' said a woman wearing a dressing gown to no one in particular. 'All three of them were killed, so I've heard. He was a councillor, you know.'

'Yes,' Vi agreed, for once unwilling to boast of Edwin's position and their connection to the Parkers.

She hadn't been able to believe it when Edwin

had told her that the Parkers' house had been hit by a bomb and that the Parkers had been inside it at the time. No one would ever know why they hadn't been in their Anderson shelter now, of course.

Bella had behaved very oddly when they'd told her, laughing so wildly that Edwin had said she was hysterical. It was the shock, of course. But like Edwin had said, there'd be things to do, seeing as Alan's parents had been killed as well, and Bella was bound to come into a tidy sum of money, Alan being their only son and Bella his wife, or rather his widow.

'Fran!' Jean exclaimed in surprise when she opened the door to her younger sister later in the morning.

'Jack's dead,' Francine said bleakly. 'Killed by a bomb dropped on the farmhouse where Vi had sent him because it was safer than being here.'

'Oh, Fran, no! Oh, my poor girl.'

Jean could hear the twins coming clattering down the stairs, exclaiming, 'Auntie Fran, you're back!' their voices changing when they saw that she was crying.

'What is it? What's wrong?' Sasha asked uncertainly.

'Go back up to your bedroom, you two,' Jean instructed them. There'd be time enough to tell them what had happened later.

'I never even got to say goodbye to him properly, or hold him or anything They couldn't find anything, you see. Not anything at all. The bomb was a direct hit and . . .'

Very gently Jean guided her sister into the kitchen and then closed the door.

TWENTY-FOUR

'I can't go, Jean. I'm sorry but I just can't.'

Francine's face was thin and pale from the amount of weight she had lost in the three weeks since Jack had been killed, but her expression was resolute and Jean knew that she was not going to change her mind.

In a way Jean wasn't surprised that Francine was refusing to go to the memorial service that was being held at Vi's parish church after the normal Sunday morning service for those who had been killed in the recent bomb attacks on Wallasey, and which was to include Jack's name. Francine had already told her that she would never be able to forgive herself for not insisting to Vi that Jack should stay in Liverpool, and even though Jean had told her that she should not feel like that, she could understand why she did.

'There's something else I've come to tell you as well,' Francine added. 'I don't want to stay here now. I don't think I can, so I've asked ENSA to see if they can find me a place in an overseas tour.

If they can't then I'll go back to America. In the meantime I'm going to London to see if ENSA can come up with anything, and I'm leaving tonight. It's for the best. I just couldn't stay here.'

There was nothing that Jean could say, no comfort she could offer her, other than a swift hug and a mental prayer that somehow her troubled younger sister might find peace.

'I still can't believe that Alan's father could have kept something like that hidden. It must have been a terrible shock to Bella to discover that, as well as losing her husband and his parents, Alan's father's business was so much in debt, and that Alan himself had borrowed so much money,' said Grace.

'It was a shock all round,' Seb agreed. 'I must admit that I never really took to the Parkers, but it didn't occur to me that Alan's father might actually be cheating the Government by submitting false invoices to them for work his company had been doing for the war effort.'

They were standing together outside the nurses' home where Seb had met up with Grace a few minutes earlier, and they were waiting for the bus that would take them to Grace's parents. From there the whole family, including Seb, were to go to Wallasey for the memorial service for those who had lost their lives in the recent bombing of Wallasey, including, of course, the Parkers.

'Mum says that Auntie Vi was beside herself when she found out what had been going on. It's just as well that Uncle Edwin owns Bella's house because if he didn't, according to Mum, Bella would have been left penniless. As it is, Uncle Edwin has felt obliged to pay off Alan's debts.'

Grace paused for a minute before continuing sadly, 'They're going to mention Jack in the service as well, even though he was killed in Wales. I still can't believe that he's gone, poor little boy.'

Seb squeezed Grace's hand comfortingly.

Grace knew that her mother had been a bit hesitant about the fact that Seb was going to accompany them to the service, but Grace had stuck to her guns, reminding her mother that Seb was technically at least connected to the Parkers, and that therefore in one sense it was only right that he should be there for formality's sake, if nothing else.

'That's all very well,' Jean had told her, 'but I'm not sure about him coming along with us, Grace, especially in view of what's come out about Alan and his parents. Vi's in a bad enough state as it is.'

Grace had understood what her mother was saying but she had grown up a lot in the year and a bit since war had first been declared.

'Me and Seb aren't going to rush into anything, but that doesn't mean that we don't know how we feel about one another, and so it's plain daft for us not to go together, especially with him living on this side of the water and everything. I don't want to cause any upset to Auntie Vi, but I'm not having Seb being upset either and made to feel that he isn't wanted, just because of the Parkers. After all, one day when this war's over he's going to be a part of this family, and I'm not having him hidden away like him and me don't exist because of Auntie Vi.'

Grace remembered that conversation now, and the way her father, who had been listening to it, had given a brief nod of his head and said, 'The lass is right, Jean, and besides, I think it's time we had a look at this lad for ourselves, seeing as our Grace seems to have made up her mind he's the one for her.' Grace smiled to herself. She knew that her dad and Seb would get on.

Now, as they watched the bus trundling towards them, Grace asked Seb lovingly, 'How's your shoulder?'

'A bit stiff still but apart from that it's fine, even though I've had to work a couple of double shifts on account of the number of messages that are coming through.'

The bus had arrived but before they got on Grace noticed that Seb's tie wasn't quite straight and needed her attention.

'Stop looking at me like that,' Seb warned her, 'otherwise I'm going to have to kiss you right here in front of everyone.'

They were both flirting with danger as well as with one another Grace knew, but the feeling was so deliciously heady and exciting that it was too wonderful to resist. Now she knew why Teddy had wanted her to wait, and every night when she said her prayers, she said a special one just for him, thanking him for the strength of his love for her and the protection it had given her.

* * *

The church was packed, not just with those who had come to mourn but also with those who had come to pay their respects to those mourning.

Today there were no white flowers decorating the inside of the church as there had been on the day of Bella's marriage to Alan. Instead there were wreaths. Where there had been bunches of flowers and white ribbons to decorate the ends of the pews, today the pews of the mourners and their families were marked by black ribbons.

Hushed voices and sombre music were the order of the day, the hush broken now and again by the sound of grief-stricken sobs, bearing witness to emotions that could not be denied.

But along with those who had come to mourn, there were also those who had come to give thanks for the miracle that was the RAF's victory over the Luftwaffe in what was being termed the Battle of Britain, so whilst the mood was one of grief and loss, for many there was also a sense of reaching out for the hope that ultimately there would be victory, and that mood spread gently amongst the congregation like a benison.

As they all knew, with heroic bravery and endurance the men of the RAF had gone up again and again into the September skies above the south of England to engage the Luftwaffe in a fight to the death that would decide the fate of the whole country.

Even those who mourned the loss of loved ones were still thankful for the RAF's victory, and Bella, standing silently outside the church, dressed in black, before the service, saw how people turned eagerly to speak to Jan, in his RAF uniform, and shake his hand as he waited to escort his mother and sister into the church.

At her side Bella could hear her own mother still complaining to anyone who would listen about the Parker's dishonesty and Bella's own 'poverty', but she couldn't summon any interest in what her mother was saying. She felt nothing for Alan or his parents, no sense of loss, no sense of grievance, nothing, her grieving and her pain was all for the baby she had miscarried and the intensity of those feelings was still as strong now, a month later, as it had been when it had happened, and still as bewildering to her. Why, after all, should she mourn so fiercely a life she had never wanted for its own sake, only for what it could be used for?

It frightened her – on those occasions when awareness pierced the comforting numbing cotton wool nothingness that occupied most of her waking hours – to realise how hard it was for her to recognise herself in this grieving woman whose pain would not go away, because she was so very different from how she remembered herself. But then the nothingness would come back to claim and comfort her and she would sink back into its welcome embrace.

She didn't even really feel anything for Jack, her brother, other than a mild sense of disbelief that he had actually been killed.

One day she knew that she would have to leave

the safety of her numbness and return to real life. But definitely not yet.

'Auntie Jean's here,' she told her mother as she caught sight of her mother's twin and her family.

The last time they had been here had been for Bella's wedding, Grace reflected as she and Seb waited to file into the church behind the rest of her family, having paused whilst Seb introduced himself to Jan as a fellow member of the RAF.

The service was simple but poignant, and it was obvious that many tears were being discreetly shed by the congregation as the vicar spoke of the great bravery and sacrifice of the pilots of the RAF during their recent dogfights with the Luftwaffe, and then went on to speak of the equal bravery and sacrifice of those families who had lost loved ones in the recent bombings of Wallasey itself, with a very special mention of Jack right at the end of his address.

Prayers were said for all those who had died, and for their families, and Grace was grateful for the clean handkerchief that Seb passed to her.

'At least Bella won't lose the house, seeing as it was Edwin who bought it,' Sam commented afterwards when they were on their way home.

'Vi wants her to move back in with them,' Jean told him, 'but Edwin says there's no point in trying to sell the house at the moment because no one wants to buy property when it could be bombed and destroyed, and besides, Bella's got those refugees billeted on her. Vi thinks they should leave after what's happened, but I'd have thought that

Bella would be glad of the company. They seemed decent sorts. What did you think, Seb?'

Grace expelled a small sigh of relief. Although her parents hadn't exactly been unwelcoming to Seb, they hadn't actually welcomed him into the family either, and Grace had known that they were reserving judgement on him. Now by inviting his opinion she knew that her mother was signalling her approval of him.

'Like you, I thought they seemed very decent,' said Seb.

'So did I,' said Luke, 'although I got the impression that Charlie isn't very keen on Jan. He was making some pretty near-the-bone remarks about foreigners getting into the RAF when British lads can't, at one point. Not that he could get anyone to agree with him. But you know what Charlie's like,' he added frankly, before turning to Seb and asking him what he thought the chances were of Hitler actually invading now that the RAF had beaten off the Luftwaffe.

'Well, none of us is privy to everything that's known, of course,' Seb answered, 'but the Government has said that Hitler has cancelled "Operation Sealion", which was the codename for his planned invasion of Britain.'

'The German Navy is still a very real threat to our shipping, though, and we mustn't forget that,' Sam put in.

They all looked grave, knowing that only that week 12 ships in one convoy had been lost, and a U-boat torpedo had sunk the SS *City of Benares*, which had been on its way to Canada, killing 77 children and 248 crew.

'How much longer can it go on for?' Jean asked. 'We're having air raids every other night, and London's taking a real pounding from the bombers; even Buckingham Palace has been hit.'

By the time the Mersey had been crossed, and they had all disembarked from the ferry, Grace had the satisfaction of knowing just from listening to her parents and her siblings talking to Seb and without there being any need to say so, that they liked him and were prepared to accept him into the family.

Not of course that she had imagined for one minute that they would not.

Even so, as Seb himself remarked later as he walked her back to the nurses' home, he felt relieved that he had 'passed muster' and that they were now an official couple.

Grace sent up a small prayer for an early end to the war so that they could all get on with their lives in peace and safety.

TWENTY-FIVE

'In less than a month it will be Christmas.'

Seb grinned and hugged Grace closer to him as they sat together on the tram. They'd spent the evening with Grace's parents and now Seb was seeing Grace back to the nurses' home before returning to his own billet.

'Ernest Brown Junior Technical School, Durning Road,' the conductor sang out as they approached a tram stop.

Ignoring him since it wasn't their stop, Seb teased, 'If that's a hint about Father Christmas . . . ?' but then fell silent as the familiar sound of the air-raid siren began.

'There's a public shelter at the Technical School, just past the tram stop,' the conductor yelled as the tram came to a halt, and dutifully everyone stood up and filed off.

Because they had politely held back to allow the older passengers to go first, Grace and Seb were amongst the last to reach the shelter, which was so packed with people that they only just managed to find a small patch of standing space right by the door. It was too late to look for somewhere else, though, as they could already hear the planes quite clearly approaching.

Those in charge were grumbling about the extra intake of people as the doors were closed.

In the distance they could hear bombs exploding.

'We wouldn't normally be out so late but we'd bin visiting the wife's parents,' a man standing next to them, his wife and two young children with him, explained to Grace and Seb.

Deeper into the shelter people had started to sing Christmas carols, and the children, one held tightly by each parent, immediately started to join in.

Some typical Liverpudlian wag started up singing 'Silent Night' and after a laughing cheer, others joined in. They had just reached the end of the first verse when there was the loudest explosion Grace had ever heard, followed by the thunderous sound of falling masonry and breaking glass, thick brick dust filling the air as the lights went out.

'We've bin hit,' someone announced unnecessarily.

In the darkness Seb reached for Grace, pulling her close. She could feel the heavy thud of his heart and she knew that her own was racing with fear. All around them people were crying and calling out to one another. There were other sounds too, moans and worse, familiar to Grace, who started to turn towards those sounds, driven by her training to want to go and give what aid she could, but it was impossible for anyone to move.

People were demanding that the doors were opened, but they wouldn't move.

Torches were being switched on so that people could see their way to the emergency doors, and then several voices shouted out that the emergency exits themselves were all blocked as well.

'Don't worry,' Seb told Grace robustly. 'I reckon your dad and his mates will be here any minute now and they'll soon have everyone out of here.'

'I've got to go and see if I can help the injured, Seb,' Grace told him.

'Grace, no, it's too dangerous,' Seb protested. Grace could hear his love for her in his voice and along with it his fear. She felt afraid herself but she knew what she must do.

'I've got to, Seb.'

She had turned away from him when someone called out frantically, 'The bloody roof's fallen in back here, and there's hundreds trapped underneath it.'

Seb had grabbed hold of her hand and was holding it tightly.

'The ruddy place is on fire,' another voice called out, and Grace stiffened in horror as she looked back into the shelter and saw that a fire had started at the furthermost end.

'There's water coming through, an' all,' another voice chimed in. 'Looks like the flaming water main's bin hit.'

Thick choking smoke was pouring into the part

of the shelter where they were trapped. Helplessly Grace buried her face in Seb's shoulder and clung to him. She had never felt so afraid.

The sounds of pain from the injured and dying trapped behind the fallen masonry, and echoing on the dusty air were hellish and harrowing. All the more so because the victims could not be seen.

Duty and fear struggled within Grace, but she knew what she had to do. She lifted her head and whispered to Seb, 'I've got to try to help, please understand and let me go.'

She could feel the unsteady breath he exhaled as he held her tighter, and then released her, his muffled, 'I love you,' echoing in her ears as she called out, 'I'm a nurse. Please let me though to see if I can help.'

'It's no use, love,' one of the men in charge told her gruffly, blocking her way. 'You can't get through to them poor sods that have bin trapped.'

'But I must try,' she protested.

'It's no use, lass,' the ARP warden told her thickly.

The water from the burst main was rising swiftly. It was almost up to her knees now, Grace noticed with a new shock of fear, as its fierce movement forced her back to cling to Seb or risk losing her balance. Men were lifting small children onto their shoulders, whilst women sobbed and prayed for their little ones.

'We're going to die. We're all going to die,' one woman screamed before starting to sob hysterically.

Seb wrapped his arms around her and Grace moved as close into his embrace as she could. She was shivering, trembling with the horror and cruelty of it all. But at least if they were going to die here she would be with Seb, she tried to comfort herself.

'You're cold,' Seb told her. 'Here, take my jacket.'

She tried to protest that he needed it himself but he was insistent and the smell of him on it as she slipped it on was sweetly comforting.

She could feel the water lapping above her knees. In the darkness someone stumbled against her. Without Seb's strong arms around her the weight of them falling against her could easily have over-balanced her. A person wouldn't have much chance if they lost their footing.

'We're going to die anyway,' a woman sobbed. 'Why don't we just lie down in the water and get it over with quickly?'

'Here, we don't want none of that talk,' another woman called up sharply.

The water was still rising. The smoke from the fire burned her throat and she could hear people coughing, and children crying.

Grace felt Seb bending his head down towards her. His skin felt warm, alive. Surely it wasn't for this that he had been spared septicaemia? A sob tore at her throat but she suppressed it.

'If it gets any deeper I'm going to kneel down so that you can climb on my shoulders,' Seb told her.

Grace shook her head. 'No, Seb. If we have to die then I want us to die together.' She had to stop speaking to cough against the acrid smoke filling air. When she had stopped, Seb kissed her.

It was dark enough for them not to be seen, even if their kiss had to be brief. Brief, but oh, so tender. Now the tears stinging Grace's eyes weren't only from the smoke.

They were just drawing apart when a woman's voice called out excitedly, 'I've found a window and I can see a light outside. Quick, someone flash a torch to let those outside know we're here.'

Several men rushed to do as she said, and in the torchlight Grace could see that the woman was wearing an ARP uniform.

'They've seen us,' one of the men shouted. 'They're flashing a light back.'

'They know we're alive now,' the ARP warden told them. 'It won't get long before they get us out.'

Not long in terms of real time, Grace acknowledged, but to those trapped it felt like a lifetime before the rescuers finally managed to break through to them, bringing with them clean night air to breathe, and relief and joy to fill their hearts.

A heartfelt cheer went up and fresh tears were shed, Grace's into the warmth of Seb's shirt. It was the children who were helped out first, handed over the heads of the men and women who stoically held back their own longing for freedom and safety to give them theirs, to be carried to safety, one by one.

Then it was the turn of the women, starting with the oldest and the frailest although one doughty old lady insisted that it should be the young mothers who went first, saying courageously, 'I've had my life; it's them kiddies we should be thinking about. They need their mothers.'

'Brave words, Missus,' one of their rescuers praised her, adding reassuringly, 'Don't you worry, though. We're going to get you all out safely.'

'Your turn next,' Seb told Grace. 'And don't worry, I won't be far behind you.'

She had just smiled at him and turned to follow the woman ahead of her, when one of the men called out, 'There's a kiddie trapped here and she's bleeding.'

Immediately Grace turned back. 'Where . . . ?'

The man shone his torch and Grace's heart turned over. Right up against the worst of the debris that had caved in was a little girl, obviously unable to move, her arm bleeding. She was alive though, Grace could see.

'Grace, no,' Seb protested, but Grace shook her head, calmly asking for first aid supplies.

She didn't dare to look back at Seb after she had left him and started to make her way through the wreckage, and water towards the child she could see more clearly now in the light of the ARP and rescue workers' torches. What she could also see in the debris around the little girl were the still mounds of clothing, which she realised with horror were the bodies of two adults.

There was barely enough room for her to squat

495

down by the child, who miraculously was trapped just high enough for her head and upper torso to be above the water, which had now thankfully stopped rising.

She spoke gently and reassuringly to the little girl, who told Grace that her name was Mary.

Something – a broken piece of wood, Grace guessed – had gouged a jagged tear in her flesh, which had bled profusely though thankfully the injury was not to an artery. It was not so much the wound in her arm, which she could see, that was dangerous Grace acknowledged as she cleaned it as best she could, but the fact that Mary's legs were trapped beneath some of the debris – and the bodies.

'It's your turn now, mate,' the burly man standing next to Seb told him but Seb shook his head, without taking his gaze off Grace.

'I'm staying with my girl.'

'You'd better make yourself useful then,' the man in charge of the auxiliary fire service workers told him bluntly.

Seb ignored the pain in his shoulder as he worked under the instructions of the other men, helping to pass out to those waiting the pieces of debris as they were removed.

An hour passed whilst the men worked tirelessly. Grace tried not to think of their danger but to focus instead on keeping little Mary's spirits up and assuring her that they would soon be safe.

They were removing one of the bodies now, and the little girl was asking about her mother.

Through the dirt caking the body Grace could just about make out the blue of a skirt. Was the body that of little Mary's mother? If so it was better that she did not know that until she was safely out of here.

'Won't be long now, love,' the rescue worker closest to them said comfortingly.

He was as good as his word. The second body was being lifted away. Quickly Grace checked to make sure that Mary hadn't broken anything before she too was lifted to safety.

'Your turn now, love,' a burly auxiliary fireman told her.

At last it was over and they were both safe.

As he took Grace in his arms in the cold smoke-tasting night air, Seb knew that no matter what happened in his life from now on, no moment could possibly be sweeter than this one.

He was still hugging her tight when Sam walked up, his face, as Grace told her mother later, a real picture when he realised that the stubborn young woman who had risked her life for a little girl and the chap who loved her too much to leave her, were Grace and Seb.

It was mid-afternoon the following day before Jean finally stopped fussing over her eldest daughter and allowed her to get dressed and come downstairs. Everyone knew now about the terrible tragedy of the previous night: how a landmine had drifted inland and hit the Technical College, sending all three floors of it smashing down into the basement on top of those who were sheltering there from the air raid.

In Jean's eyes Grace was a heroine and Seb was a man in the same mould as her own Sam for insisting on staying with her. She welcomed him with very real affection when he arrived to see how Grace was when he had come off duty.

'I kept her in bed all day, she looked that washed out, and we've heard that the little girl is all right, and that her mother was rescued as well, so that's a mercy,' said Jean.

As a mark of her feelings, Jean allowed the young couple the privacy of the front room and with a closed door.

The first thing Seb did when he saw Grace was take her in his arms and then kiss her with all the passion she'd been longing for but which they'd denied themselves, saying that it wouldn't be 'sensible'.

'I know we said we wouldn't rush into anything, and I know there are a hundred reasons why I shouldn't be saying what I'm going to say to you, Grace,' said Seb huskily when he was finally able to bring himself to stop kissing her, 'but so far as I'm concerned there's only one thing that matters to me right now and that is telling you how much I love you. Whatever lies ahead of us, whatever this damn war bring us, I want you to know that.'

'We said we wouldn't do this,' Grace reminded him shakily.

'I know,' Seb agreed, 'but I love you so much.'

'I love you too,' Grace told him.

He was kissing her again and Grace was kissing him back, holding him as tightly as she could and kissing him with all the love and passion she felt for him. She just couldn't stop thinking about how close they had come to death. All she wanted right now was to hold him and be held by him, and to feel his heart beating against hers, telling her that they were both safe and alive.

'If I'd lost you, I couldn't have gone on,' Seb told her gruffly when he had stopped kissing her.

'I wouldn't want to live without you, Seb.'

They kissed again, unable to stop themselves from holding one another; both of them needing the sweetness of knowing they were alive and in love.

There were so many words they could have used to share the fear they had known and the joy they now knew but their kisses said it so much better.

'When this is finally over, if we both live to see it through, will you marry me, Grace?' asked Seb. His voice was unsteady, his gaze full of love.

'Yes. Yes, I will,' Grace answered him, exhaling on a deliriously happy breath of anticipation when Seb took her in his arms again.

The twins couldn't wait any longer. Despite their mother's stern warning that they were not to interrupt, Sasha pushed open the door and looked expectantly at them.

'Are you and Grace going to be married?' Lou demanded excitedly.

Seb looked at Grace.

'Yes,' he told them softly. 'Yes, we are.'

*   *   *

The country had already lived through well over a year of war. No one knew what might lie ahead, or how much longer the war would last, but for now, for a precious handful of minutes, the war could be forgotten and their love celebrated.

Of course, Seb had to wait for Sam to return home in order to ask him that all-important question that every young man had to ask the father of the girl he loved, and of course, Sam, as a loving father, had to point out to him that Grace was young, that there was a war on, but as Jean had already said to him, how could they stand in the way of their happiness, when that happiness was all the more precious *because* there was war on? And so it was agreed that they could be engaged at Christmas.

The most special Christmas of her life, as Grace whispered to Seb in the jeweller's shop not far away from Lewis's when the salesman had discreetly disappeared to let them both admire the shiny sparkling diamond engagement ring they had chosen together.

A Chat with Annie

In *Across the Mersey we are once again transported back to WWII Liverpool. What continues to inspire you about Liverpool?*

"The very nature of the people of Liverpool and the way in which they face life's hardships will always inspire me. The people of Liverpool have a special brand of humour and a tough gutsiness that I admire and respect."

What drew you to write about twin sisters and their very different lives, in Across the Mersey?

"I love writing about twins. I longed to be a twin, and I am fascinated by the closeness twins share and the happiness and problems that closeness can bring. I think the moment when young twins begin to realise that for the sake of their own emotional health they need to become two separate individuals is especially poignant, and that is something I shall be writing about in the Campion books."

Which of your characters do you most identify with?

"I think I identify most with Jean. I love my younger characters and feel both excited and worried for them as they start out on the journeys of their adult lives, but it is Jean with her love for her husband and her children, her memories of her own childhood, and her hopes and fears for those she loves, with whom I 'talk' most of all about the progress of my characters and their lives."

How would you describe your typical day writing?

"Most days I am at my desk for 8.30 am although I don't normally start writing until around 10.00am. When I'm starting out on a completely new book I do my main research beforehand, to get a feel for the era and the area in which I shall be writing, and then once I start writing I research and check the facts I need as I work. I aim to write a minimum of 3,000 words per day, which then need to be read through and checked ready for the next day, so it is normally around 10.00 p.m. at night before I finish working."

Is there another profession you have secretly wanted to try out?

"I love writing and I consider myself to be very fortunate to be able to do something I love so much. I also like interior decorating and that would be my second choice of career, although it could never replace my love of writing."

What was the first novel you read that made you cry?

"Black Beauty. I'm a sucker for anything with animals, and still have to run out of the room if I'm watching a nature programme on TV and there's an animal in danger."

Thanks Annie.

Looking forward to

Daughters of Liverpool!

If you've enjoyed *Across the Mersey*, why not
try Annie's other novels?

Ellie Pride
978-0-00-714955-1
£5.99

Connie's Courage
978-0-00-714957-5
£5.99

Hettie of Hope Street
978-0-00-714959-9
£5.99

Goodnight Sweetheart
978-0-00-720963-7
£5.99

Some Sunny Day
978-0-00-720965-1
£5.99

The Grafton Girls
978-0-00-720967-5
£6.99

As Time Goes By
978-0-00-720969-9
£6.99

**Save 10% when you buy direct from HarperCollins.
Call 08707 871724.**

Free postage and packing in the UK only.